DEVIL'S GATE

Also by F. J. Lennon

Soul Trapper

DEVIL'S GATE

A KANE PRYCE NOVEL

F. J. Lennon

EMILY BESTLER BOOKS
—
ATRIA PAPERBACK

New York   London   Toronto   Sydney   New Delhi

ATRIA PAPERBACK
A Division of Simon & Schuster, Inc.
1230 Avenue of the Americas
New York, NY 10020

First Atria Paperback/Emily Bestler Books edition August 2012

EMILY BESTLER BOOKS / ATRIA PAPERBACK and colophon are trademarks of Simon & Schuster, Inc.

"Under the Bridge" © 1991 Moebetoblame Music. Lyrics used by permission.

For information about special discounts for bulk purchases,
please contact Simon & Schuster Special Sales at
1-866-506-1949 or business@simonandschuster.com.

The Simon & Schuster Speakers Bureau can bring authors to your
live event. For more information or to book an event, contact the
Simon & Schuster Speakers Bureau at 1-866-248-3049 or visit our
website at www.simonspeakers.com.

Manufactured in the United States of America

10 9 8 7 6 5 4 3 2 1

Library of Congress Cataloging-in-Publication Data

Lennon, F. J., date.
  Devil's gate : a Kane Pryce novel / by F. J. Lennon.—1st Atria pbk. ed.
     p.   cm.
  1. Paranormal fiction. 2. Musicians—Fiction. 3. Psychic ability—Fiction.
4. Haunted places—Fiction. I. Title.
PS3612.E5426D48 2012
813'.6—dc22   2011027764

ISBN 978-1-4391-8660-2
ISBN 978-1-4391-8666-4 (ebook)

For Laura, Olivia, and Clara

Life is neither a good nor an evil:
it is a field for good and evil.

— SENECA THE YOUNGER

Under the bridge downtown
Is where I drew some blood.
Under the bridge downtown
I could not get enough.
Under the bridge downtown
Forgot about my love.
Under the bridge downtown
I gave my life away.
Oh, no
Here I stay.

—RED HOT CHILI PEPPERS

DEVIL'S GATE

One

It's dark. I'm scared shitless. My heart pounds out of my chest, and I can't seem to steady my breath.

The corridor is narrow. Walls are closing in on me. I breathe deep—in and out. Stomach does cartwheels.

I'm not alone. I hear them out there—voices crashing together, forming a roar that steadily builds. How did this happen? Most of it's a blur. But here I stand and there they wait.

Then, thundering like God commanding Moses: "Hollywood! Would you please welcome Astral Fountain!"

Troy counts off eight on his drumsticks and—*Boom*—I lay down the first three power chords in the opening riff of our first song. The crowd erupts and surges forward. We're out the gate. Troy's laying down a solid beat. Drexel—in his black leather pants, Ray-Bans, and tee depicting Colonel Sanders' head sticking out of a bucket of chicken—tears into the vocals and flies the length of the stage in three giant leaps. Jay blisters the bass line. It's a wonder his fingers aren't bleeding.

Sounds loud and mighty.

I'm shaky. Too stiff. Not looking at anyone yet. Imagining I'm alone in my shitty apartment playing to my mirror instead of a nearly packed house of 500 plus. I hit the solo hard, but I'm tight. All brain, no balls.

I can't fuck this up.

A&R execs are in the house. The night is dubbed *The Best Unsigned Bands in L.A.* Four groups—Sunset Nation, Year Long

Disaster, the Pontius Pilots, and us—each play an hourlong set with one encore. After the coin toss, we ended up the closers. Our job is to send the crowd off with—as our flier promises—an unforgettable dose of straightforward rock with a modern edge.

I stare up at the massive crystal chandelier that hangs over the floor of the El Rey Theatre. Try my damnedest to turn my brain off. Zone in on a cluster of crystals blinking like a beacon and let their flickering crayon box of colors envelop me. And then a wave of peace hits me square. My hands begin to move on their own. My Blackie Strat starts talking and I'm not pulling the strings. I'm out of my own way. Finally. I start to surprise myself, get lost in the music, and feel possessed.

Hands reach up to me from the mosh pit. I see faces out of the corner of my eye, but I won't acknowledge them. Not yet.

A blast of euphoria as I start my solo. Goddamn—I love this. This is why I was put on this earth.

Solo nailed. Drexel spins across the stage like the Tasmanian Devil and finishes the song on his knees. The crowd explodes. "Fuck yeah!" Drexel screams. "We are Astral Fountain and we are here to ring your ears."

By our third song—an anthem Drexel and Jay wrote called "Creed"—I'm in the zone, standing taller. The band is right in the pocket. The crowd sways in unison. The chandelier is a wicked kaleidoscope. Finally, I'm at ease and make eye contact with the crowd. The first pair of eyes I lock with are bloodshot. Dude in the pit with a yin-yang tattoo on the top of his head is drenched in sweat. Crusty lips. Looks like he could drain a water cooler dry. Ecstasy. Too much of it. Probably won't remember he was here tomorrow. I scan the first two rows. A blonde—silicone jugs like basketballs—mirrors my solo on her air guitar. She's spilling out of her Kings of Leon tee. I nod and wink. She smiles back. Target acquired. I play my balls off for Blondie and her twins. I do some harmonizing with Drexel and Jay.

I soak up the ambience of the theater. The chandelier dominates the room, but so does the sea of red. Everything's seriously red—the walls, carpets, ceiling, and booths that line the side walls. It feels like I'm trapped in an artery. The place used to be a movie theater back in the thirties. Hit the skids and wound up as a concert venue in the early nineties. It's a building with a lot of shadows. Definitely haunted. I feel restless spirits in the air, but I don't care. They can do their thing. I'm doing mine. I'm not in that business anymore.

Next up is our ballad—"Shelter." Journey through Hollywood's underbelly. Drexel introduces the song with the story of how he and Jay wrote it in rehab in 2007. Then he makes his little public-service announcement about the scourge of drugs. Speak for yourself. I hate this part of the show. Wish he'd just shut up and sing.

Drexel's vocal range on this one runs the gamut of the vocal scale. Starts down in Barry White territory and ends up somewhere in Robert Plant-land. Amazing range this kid has. And charisma to boot.

We close the set with the song that got me hired—"Layla." And I'm the star on this one. When I end with the bird chirp, the crowd goes apeshit.

We pulled it off.

The house lights come on. Barbie waves and flashes me from the pit. Yes!

We take our bows.

That's when I see him—three-quarters of the way back. Can't be. Jay pulls me off stage before I can pinpoint if it's really him.

We stand in the wings soaking up the cheers. "Dude, you were a mad man out there," Drexel says to me. He takes a huge swig of Tazo tea. A twenty-one-year-old kid who doesn't drink. A pity.

I nod and grin. "You, too."

Jay types on his phone. "What the fuck?" I say to him.

"Tweeting," he says.

The house lights dim. We march back on stage for our encore. Zone in on the location where I thought I saw him. He's not there. Move toward center stage for my solo when I spot him again. It is him. He's made his way to the center of the pit.

Ned.

Excuse me—Dr. Ned Ross. Standing there in the same lame khakis and brown sweatshirt he was wearing the last time I saw him a year ago. Hasn't lost a pound. I lock eyes with him for an instant before redirecting my gaze to the chandelier. No way. Not tonight. But a mini-glance back toward him confirms that he knows I've seen him. He's grinning, reaching up with the rest of the hands tomahawking me during my solo. The yin-yang *X*-tripper runs amok in the pit. He's bulldozing like a sumo champ when he plows into Blondie, knocking her flat on her ass. Then he barrels the other way and Ned extends a leg all nonchalantly, trips him, and gets a dozen high fives for the effort. A brawl breaks out as we take our final bows. The house lights go up and we watch six guys stomp the shit out of the yin-yang wrecking ball. Ned has moved aside to watch the carnage, laughing his ass off. He waves and yells my name but I ignore him as we leave the stage.

Our manager, Bo Flanigan, herds us into the closet-sized dressing room and slams the door shut. It flies opens a second later, but Bo slams it shut again and orders Syd, our stage manager, to stand guard and tell any would-be trespassers that the band is locked down for fifteen minutes of mandatory decompression. "No one gets in until I open the fucking door," Bo shouts. "Understood?"

Syd nods and ducks outside.

Bo's always edgy. Talks fast. Always looks like he just rolled out of bed. Midthirties, but looks fifty. Stringy red hair. Drinks like a champ, but not even the hint of a beer gut. Sweats like a contestant on *The Biggest Loser*. You don't need to slap a cuff on his arm to know his blood pressure is up there. Just standing next to him, you can taste his stress. He owns two pairs of jeans, a dozen concert shirts from the nineties, an official Rolling Stones tour jacket from the *Bridges to Babylon* tour, and a Rolex—a parting gift from The Killers. Bo led them to the promised land and they dumped him after they signed their record contract.

Bo knows music.

Bo's smart. He's aggressive, but not pushy.

"You slayed 'em, boys," Bo says. "I smell a record deal. Ira Bowersock was in the crowd. I spotted him."

"Me, too," Jay says. "He was into us."

Bo reaches in a cooler and hands Red Bulls to Drexel and Jay. He cracks open a Stella for himself, but glances at Drexel and then Jay before taking a swig. "This gonna bother you?" he asks them for at least the hundredth time. "I'll dump it if it does."

"Fuck no," Drexel says.

"Drink up. Celebrate," Jay adds.

Bo hands Stellas to me and Troy. Beer has never tasted better. Troy downs his in two gulps and throws his head back. He's the elder of the group—thirty-one. A decent drummer—nothing special. But he's a presence—big, thick, blond, always bloated and puffy. Only wears head-to-toe red. I call him the fire truck. I'm standing next to him, all in black. We look like Crips vs. Bloods. He's a serious binge drinker, mostly beer. The way he just downed that first one . . . we're in for a long night. Troy cracks open a second one. "I'm getting righteously fucked up tonight," he says. Hollywood, be warned.

Now that drinking has commenced, Drexel and Jay put a few feet of distance between me and Troy. They play for the clean team. Drexel's demon was heroin; Jay's, booze and pills. They met at Promises Treatment Center in Malibu. I assume they were born with golden spoons. Twelve steps with an ocean view doesn't come cheap. Neither does their gear or their clothes.

Jay McCollum—stage name JayMac—is the best musician among us. He's a gifted guitarist, keyboardist, and harmonica player, but on bass, he's truly brilliant. Plays with such speed and power that the instrument transforms into a six-string rhythm guitar. A twenty-five-year-old African-American god of thunder and a solid, even-keeled guy. Always looks cool on stage with his Kangol and expensive silk shirts. Dead serious when it comes to music. Never flies off the handle . . . unlike Drexel.

Word on the street is that Drexel (no last name) is the bastard son of a famous rocker. Rumors run the gamut from Axl Rose to David Lee Roth to Flea. He won't confirm or deny it. It's one of those juicy rumors that gets us some mileage on the local music websites. He's twenty-one going on twelve. Bitches about everything. Doesn't believe in paying dues. But he possesses an authentic stage presence. Impossible not to look at. A triple-E front man: entitled, egotistical, and exceptional. Those are the guys who usually make it. A giant pain in the ass, but he's going to be a rock star. I know it. And I'm along for the ride.

Bo knocks on a table, demands attention. "When Ira comes back to chat, I do all the talking. Understand?"

We all nod. This'll be our third meeting with the legendary Ira Bowersock. The man who discovered and signed Garbage, Green Day, Marilyn Manson, Kid Rock, and Nickelback—to name a few. Been at Warner Music twenty-three years. Started out as a radio-promo scrub; worked his way up to executive VP of strategy and business development. Fucking big shot. Just got run out in a reorg when the new CEO came in.

Ira spotted us before EMI or any of the other major labels. He took us all to dinner at Bouchon. Sized us up. Spent time chatting with each one of us. Asked a lot of questions about our musical influences. He struck me as smart and driven the first time we met.

"So does he have a label or not?" Drexel asks. "I don't care about his past. What's he doing now?"

"Still counting his severance package and cashing in his stock options," Bo says. "Word on the street is he's flush, he's pissed off, and his new label will be launched within sixty days." Bo raises a hand of caution. "What we have to find out is if Ira's little venture is a midlife crisis or if he seriously wants to get back in the ring and make music."

"A start-up?" Drexel gripes.

"If this guy is serious and we can get in on the ground floor . . ." Bo lets it hang. Can't speak for the others, but I understand. Big fishes in a small pond wouldn't be a bad place to start.

Drexel pouts. "I don't know," he whines.

Drexel's still licking his wounds, still pissed off that we got turned down by EMI. It was fun the few weeks it lasted. A metrosexual A&R exec with a cheesy smile and a wimp-ass handshake wined and dined us for a couple of weeks. Steak dinner at Cut. Praised us up the ass. Kept using the word *solid*. Told us he'd help us find our sound. Take us global. Make us rock gods. Three minutes in and I pegged him as a hollow chocolate Easter Bunny. Didn't know dick about music.

Did I mention I pretty much hate everyone? That includes trust fund pups with uncles high up on the EMI food chain. Fuck them. They're a big bloated megacorp. And while Drexel and Jay were drooling over his every word, I wasn't drinking the Kool-Aid.

Didn't matter in the end. After our six-song EP made the rounds internally, EMI passed.

"All right, boys," Bo says, cracking open a beer for himself. "Enjoy yourselves, but go easy until our meeting with Ira is over. Syd!" he shouts at the top of his lungs.

Syd throws open the door and at least a dozen people rush in, drinks in hand. As if the rest of us are invisible, the majority of the crowd rushes right up to Drexel.

It must be good to be the front man.

I duck out of the room and into the corridor that leads from dressing rooms to the stage. The entourages of four hungry bands are on a major high. Beer is flowing. Shots are downed. The smell

of weed—good weed—fills the air. Despite the rivalries, cama-
raderie is high. We all kicked ass. There's an electric crackle of
something good buzzing. It's hope, and it's contagious.

I like moments like this, when people, me included, are
brimming with positive energy. Tonight, we all believe that destiny's calling, that there's something just over the horizon so
good that it's terrifying. Some people like to talk it up during
moments like this. Boast. Beat their chests. But not me. I keep
these moments to myself. Tuck them away. There sure as hell
aren't many of them.

I walk by the members of the Pontius Pilots. Jeremy Bayre, the
drummer, hands me an open fifth of Jack. I take a big, fat swig.
It burns delightfully and I get a little shiver as it slides down the
hatch. Further down the hall, I cross paths with Barbie and her
twins. We awkwardly get in each other's way as we try to pass.
We laugh.

"You're really good," she says.

"So are you."

She giggles. Sounds perfectly ditzy.

"Enjoy the show?"

"I love you guys," she says.

God, up close her tits are even bigger than I thought. "I'm
Kane."

"Wendy," she says with a killer smile and nary an ounce of
brainpower.

"Can I get you a drink?" I ask.

"Vodka?"

"I think that's doable," I say, taking her by the hand and leading her back to our dressing room. As soon as we walk in, the
other guys start ogling her. I hate letting Wendy out of my sight
for the twenty seconds it takes me to dig Bo's bottle of Belvedere
out of the cooler and fill a red plastic cup.

Just as I hand Wendy her drink, Bo enters and lets out a piercing whistle. "Attention! Guys, Ira wants a word."

"I'll be right back," I tell Wendy. "Help yourself to the Belvedere." Troy, Drexel, Jay, and I follow Bo into the corridor where Ira Bowersock is waiting with a smile. This guy oozes success. Late forties. Salt-and-pepper hair. Five o'clock shadow. Jeans. Untucked white shirt and navy blazer. George Clooney would play him in a movie.

"Ira," Bo says, hugging the guy. "Glad you made it."

"Wouldn't have missed it," Ira says. He has a deep, DJ voice. He's heard the EP. This is the first time he's seen us live. Here comes the verdict.

He makes eye contact with each one of us. "Look, guys, I'll be brief," Ira says. "You put on a killer show. I liked the EP. You're catchy, but you also have a rev in your engine. It's music to dance to, or rob a 7-Eleven at gunpoint to."

We all laugh. He defined us in three seconds. He's good.

Ira looks at Bo, then at us. "I think if we can put some meat on your bones—lyrically, stylistically—you might pop."

Drexel winces. He doesn't believe he needs an ounce of meat on any bone. Boy needs to find his poker face.

"The rumors are true. I'm starting a new label," Ira continues. "Nothing official yet. Just leased some rehearsal space temporarily out by Van Nuys Airport. I'm building a studio in Burbank."

Bo smells blood. "Congratulations," he says to Ira. "But if you're really interested, we need to know now. Other labels are calling. Tonight's gonna put us over the top." Bo's stretching the truth a little. Now that EMI passed, only a handful of minor labels are still courting us. But if Ira doesn't know EMI passed yet, Bo's strategy might just work.

"Let me get away and think," Ira says. "I'll be in touch this week."

Holy shit, it's a maybe. "When's your next gig?" Ira asks.

Bo hands Ira a flyer. "Friday night. At the Whisky."

"I'll be there," Ira says.

Bo plays it cool. "You and many others."

I study Ira as he walks away. He doesn't stop to talk to any of the other bands.

I have a good feeling about this guy.

"I don't know," Drexel whines again.

"Listen to me," Bo says sternly. "I know the lay of the land. If this guy is serious and we get in on the ground floor, this is an elevator that won't stop climbing."

We stand there silently for a few minutes.

Bo breaks the tension. "Work is over," he says. "Go have fun."

We all go separate directions. I'm about to make a beeline back to Wendy, but Syd stops me short of our dressing room. "There's some fat old dude out front who won't leave," Syd says. Says he's a friend of yours. Should I let him come back?"

"No," I snap. I'm not mixing worlds. Ned's not welcome in this reality. "I'll go out and see him. Do me a favor," I say. "Go pour Wendy Whoppers another Belvedere on the rocks and tell her what a genius I am."

He laughs. "Yeah, right."

I walk down the crammed hallway to the stage. Look down. There he stands in front of the stage, all two hundred eighty-five pounds of him. Dr. Ned Ross. Ghost from the past. He grins. "Look at you. Eric Clapton up there. Guitar Hero. Big rock star—can't respond to emails or phone messages?"

"Sorry, it's been a crazy year," I say, extending my hand down. He grabs it, plants his foot on a chair, and I pull him up onstage. "Fuck, you're heavy," I groan. "What happened to that blood type diet you were on?"

"I did what it said. It didn't work."

"You can't lose weight eating roast beef every day. It's fucking impossible. It doesn't matter that you're O-negative."

"I'm thinking about getting that lap band."

"Just lay off the Funyuns and pizza. Get a dog and walk him. It's not rocket science."

"If it were as easy as rocket science, I'd have washboard abs by now," Ned says.

And with that, we're right back in our groove.

"Why'd you come?" I ask.

Ned takes in the view of the ballroom from the stage. "To hear the music."

"And?"

"I wasn't disappointed. Your band doesn't suck. Actually—truthfully—you're pretty good. You're the nucleus . . . and I'm not just saying that 'cause you *used* to be my friend. You really nailed 'Layla.'"

"Thanks," I say.

"I also came to talk shop. I might have something for us. Could be big." Ned looks at me intently. I don't flinch.

"I'm done with all of that. I told you."

"Just hear me out."

I still like this guy, but I want to turn and run. "No."

"You still have the soul trap, right? You didn't destroy it?"

"It's right where I left it."

"I may need it," Ned says.

I'm getting jittery. I need to get away from him. Away from my past. Back to the band—to Wendy.

"What's the problem?" Ned asks, impatiently. "It's me. It's Ned. We're still friends, right?"

I don't answer. I'm having trouble breathing. My pulse is racing. The hair stands up on my arms. I feel like I'm being watched from behind. That old feeling is back.

"I mean, why does it have to be all or nothing with you?" Ned demands to know.

"You have to understand something. This . . . ," I say, raising my arms and glancing around, ". . . is my present. You're a reminder of the past."

"That stings," Ned says. "Got ice in your veins, Kane," he adds, chuckling in disbelief.

"No offense," I shoot back. "When past and present collide, it fucks me all up."

"We've been through a lot," Ned adds. "I have feelings, you know."

Christ, take a hint already. "I know," I say. What does he need me to do—write it in blood for him? He's not getting back in. I feed him some bullshit: "You know me—I'm not good at balancing things." Then, the truth: "You know me—I'm an asshole."

He laughs. "Yeah, I know you. And I've sure as hell missed you."

He is not going away. Ever. "You wanna talk? Catch up? Fine. But not now."

"When?" he asks.

"We rehearse almost every night. Next week?" I can turn next week into next month.

"How about tomorrow? You rehearse on Sundays?"

May as well get it over with. Whatever. "Fine. Tomorrow night works."

"I'll meet you at that bar by your apartment. What's it called?"

"The Frolic Room."

"Yeah. Nine o' clock. Okay?"

I haven't been to the Frolic Room since I throttled the bartender. It was the day I kissed off my past. Kind of miss that jukebox, that smell of rot. "Okay," I tell him.

"Bring the soul trap."

It's a demand, not a question. I flinch. Even though I haven't touched it in almost a year, it's still mine. I'm the one who uses it to hunt down, capture, and send ghosts from this world to the next. I'm the one who risks my hide, scrambles my brain to project my soul inside the trap to face the spirits I trap. It's the coolest fucking toy in the world, and like a bad kid, I don't like sharing it with anyone, even the guy who helped design and build it.

But if I keep it, I'll never escape from my past. I'll never bury the ghost hunter persona that defined me for a decade. "All right," I finally say. "I'll bring it."

"Okay, then," he says. Damn, he picks up on my reluctance. He knows me too well. "I'll let you get back to your festivities."

"I'd invite you back for a drink," I lie, "but—"

"Nah," he growls. "I'd stand out like a turd on a wedding cake."

I laugh. I kind of miss that.

Ned clumsily jumps off the stage and lands on his feet with a thud. "That hurt," he groans. "Damn knee."

I watch him limp across the ballroom. He stops and turns. Yells, "Thanks, Kane."

And then I get a shiver. There's a spirit in this old theater. The minute I tuned back in, I felt it.

I kind of miss those shivers.

I wave good-bye and head toward the dressing room. Hopefully, Wendy's plastic cup is empty and she's ready for a night of fun. Syd stops me short of the dressing room door. "You may not want to go in there," he says.

I ignore him. Walk in. Drexel's making out with Wendy, one hand on her ass, the other up her Kings of Leon tee.

Goddamn it, Ned.

Wendy sees me out of the corner of her eye and totally ignores me. Starts nibbling Drexel's neck like a vampire toying with her prey.

I turn and aimlessly wander. Syd's laughing. "I told her you were a genius," he teases. I give him the finger. "Twenty bucks says he bangs her on the premises."

I walk away. A few minutes later, I see Syd waving madly at me from down the corridor. "She's blowing him," he mouths at me, slowly and deliberately, as he points to our dressing room.

It must be really good to be the front man.

Two

Feels weird to walk the streets again with the soul trap in my backpack. Felt trippy just seeing it again resting in its lockbox. It's almost a year to the day since I tucked it away behind a drywall cutout in my bedroom closet. It has power. No matter where I am in that shitty apartment, I feel its presence—its pull. I give myself kudos for pushing it down.

It's less than a five-minute walk from my dump on Yucca to the Frolic Room at Hollywood and Vine. Feels like forever since I've stopped to bask in the light of the iconic neon sign above the door. It was my North Star for years. Feel like I should genuflect on Gary Cooper's sidewalk star before walking in.

I cross the threshold.

I'm home.

I take a deep breath. Still dark. Still the size of a shoe box. Still as stale and musty as a closed casket. Still haunted.

"Friend of the Devil" greets me. Surely a Deadhead Ned juke-box pick. There he sits, his back turned to me, a gin and tonic in hand. I take a seat next to him. Back in my favorite corner stool against the mirror.

The bartender sees me, raises his hands in mock praise. "Behold. Rejoice. The prodigal son returns." Gabe's his name, I think. Still a smart-ass. No wonder I choked him. He walks over bearing gifts—a bottle of Jameson and a Harp. "Still drinking the Irish?" he asks.

I nod and extend my hand. He fills my shot glass with a flourish. He looks trimmer, healthier. His curly blond hair is grown out. His doughy face is leaner. "You dropped some poundage," I say.

"I'm in training," he says.

"La Brea Bakery must be out of business."

Ned laughs.

"How's life, Kane?" the bartender asks. "Haven't seen you since when?" He pauses for effect, strokes his chin sarcastically, "Oh yeah . . . since that day you almost crushed my windpipe?"

"Seems like just yesterday."

He laughs and walks away.

"What?" Ned asks. "You attacked the bartender?"

"He had it coming."

"Do you actually want to go to jail, or do you just feel you have to?"

"It was a bad day."

"When?"

"Guess."

Ned gets it in a second. "The day you had it out with Eva? The day the article appeared?"

Nod. Drink.

He keeps going. "The day . . . after Donna and Ollie—"

"Don't push it," I snap.

"Sorry." He holds his glass up. "Cheers."

We clink. "Cheers."

After "Friend of the Devil," "Rainy Day Dream Away" by Jimi Hendrix plays. I down my shot.

"I saw this one on the jukebox and remembered that drive we took to Lompoc. You really dug this song."

Nod. Drink.

"I only played three tunes," Ned says. "You missed the first one."

"What was it?"

"Bertha," he says, all proud of himself.

I revive our normal tired shtick. "You and the fucking Dead, already. You oughta be ashamed."

He volleys back—same as ever. "One day, when you grow up, you'll understand."

I get up and make my way to a genuine Hollywood power spot—the Frolic Room jukebox—and feed it a five. Ned started something with "Friend of the Devil." I'm gonna finish it. Make my selections carefully. Try to ignore what's playing—a despicable three-song selection played by some douche bag trespassing on my turf.

Unbearable.

Michael Bublé followed by Jack Johnson, followed by the founding father of all wuss rock, Dave Matthews.

Unforgivable.

I return to my stool where a fresh round awaits. My songs kick in. First selection: Van Halen, "Runnin' with the Devil."

"You picked this one?" Ned asks.

Nod. Drink. "So what did you want to talk to me about?"

"I don't know—a lot of things. Ever straighten things out with Eva?"

Shot glass shakes in my hand. Drain it. "None of your business." I look away.

Ned spies me through the mirror. "You know, she was telling the truth. She didn't write that story."

I stare back at his reflection. Big gulp of beer. "I don't care."

"There was a brouhaha at the *Times* over it. That Cross guy got shitcanned."

Turn and give him the evil eye. "I. Don't. Fucking. Care."

Second song kicks in: "Devil Inside"—INXS. Ned holds up his gin and tonic and looks at it in the dim light shining from a saucer lamp above. "This glass is dirty."

I look at his stained sweater. "Are you kidding me?"

"It's all right," he says. "I think I'll have a margarita after this. I'll ask for a clean glass. Think that bartender makes a good margarita?"

"Highly doubtful."

Then, out of nowhere, he has the balls to say, "You really kind of blew it with her. You really should look up Eva and sort things out."

I squeeze my empty shot glass. Eyelids twitch. I shoot off the barstool. "I'm outta here."

"Come on," Ned says, grabbing my arm and pulling me back. "Sorry. I'll shut up about it."

"Don't mention her again. Understand?"

Tense silence for a couple minutes. Finally the third song starts. "Devil with the Blue Dress" by Mitch Ryder and the Detroit Wheels. Ned smiles. "I get it," he chuckles. "You're a clever little shit." He drains his gin and tonic, plucks the lime out, gives it a suck. "Always entertaining with you, kid. You should be a DJ. Have your own show on XM. *Kane's Rock and Roll Theme Hour.* Can't wait to hear what's next." Against my advice, Ned goes with a margarita.

Fourth song is a fun little throwaway: "The Devil Went Down to Georgia." Ned loves it. Rocks to the beat and taps along on the bar. Tequila's going straight to his head. "You happy in that band?" he asks me.

"Yeah."

He asks gingerly, "Do those guys know anything about your previous career?"

"They googled me. Found the article."

"And?"

"They got a kick out of it. Felt a lot more comfortable when I assured them I gave up that line of work . . . for good." Take that, Ned.

"Astral Fountain," he says, all slow and dramatic. "Weren't you in a different band a few months ago?"

"Yeah. And it was ten months ago."

"What happened?"

"Astral Fountain's been around a couple of years. They were on the verge, but their guitar player was holding them back. When they finally booted him, I got invited to audition."

"So you bailed on your other band?"

"We weren't going anywhere. I went from having a hobby to a real job. I did the right thing."

"Still stay in touch with that Pat guy—the EMT? Wasn't he in that other band?"

"Yeah." Ned's pushing all my buttons tonight. Pat and I didn't part on good terms.

"Do you return his calls or did you cut him out of your life, too?"

I'm off my stool again. "Look, we all know I'm a lousy friend—a general shitbag. OK? You win."

"Sit down," Ned says, all innocently. "Just busting your chops."

Another stiff bout of silence. Beck's "Devil's Haircut" is up next. The bartender strolls over. Pours me another shot. "Kane, I've got a helluva supernatural yarn for you. Good versus evil stuff. Tell me when it's a good time."

I look at my watch. "How about fuck you o'clock?"

He winks at Ned and warns, "Don't piss this tough guy off," before sauntering away.

I need to take control of this drinking session. Formulate an escape plan. Now. Get Ned talking. Pour margaritas down his throat. He'll drone on for an hour about nothing and then doze off. "How's your job?" I ask him.

Ned licks salt off the rim of his dirty margarita glass. "Same as it's been for twenty-plus years. Ingrained. I could teach my classes in a coma."

"Retire then. Consult."

"Nah. A few more years till my financial ducks are in a row. Plus, I keep hanging in to see if I ever meet a kid as smart as me." He takes a big sip of his margarita and shoots me a sad look. "Never happens."

"Never will."

"It's weird," he says. He wrestles with saying something or not, then blurts out, "I've been down in the dumps lately."

"Depressed?"

"I guess so. Feels weird. For me."

"They have pills for that, you know."

"Ahh . . ." He waves that notion off. "Get on the prescription train and you never get off."

Ned—depressed? "What's the matter?"

He thinks about it for awhile. "Nothing specific. Just bored. A little lonely. Getting old. More tired than usual."

What? Ned? "This does not sound like you talking."

"Tell me about it."

"You could see a shrink."

"Please," he says, all dismissively. "It'd be like Stephen Hawking telling his troubles to a chimp. I'll snap out of it."

"Get some exercise. That'll help."

"How would you know?"

Springsteen's "Devils & Dust" is up next. Ned changes the subject. "How are you getting by?"

He hit my sore spot. As always, I'm broke. "I make a little gigging. Not much. Burned through almost all of the money from that priest in Lompoc."

"I still can't believe I had to lean on a priest to get paid."

"He was pissed about that article," I remind him. "Who can blame him?"

"A deal's a deal—that's all I'm saying. Just because he's a priest doesn't mean he can stiff us. So that money's gone?"

"I'm racking up credit card debt as usual," I admit.

"How much?"

"Just shy of twenty grand. Put last month's rent on my MasterCard." Damn. Now I'm saying more than I should. Booze has loosened my vocal chords. "Eating a lot of mac and cheese."

"No Lean Pockets?"

"Too expensive."

"Seriously," he says, making it a point to make eye contact, "if you need some money—"

I cut him off. "No." The last thing I need is to owe Ned money.

"I can front you some cash. No problem. Just a loan."

"No," I say, firmly. "But, thanks." Try to joke it off by saying the unthinkable. "If this keeps up, I'm gonna have to get a real job."

"Can't happen," Ned says, chuckling. "The world would stop turning."

"Sympathy for the Devil" starts just as Ned asks, "Did you bring the soul trap?"

Here we go. Finally. The real reason for this un–happy hour. The bartender derails our conversation yet again by pounding out the opening bongo solo of the song on the bar. He belts out a couple of Jagger-like "Yows!" I wave on another round. I'm one drink away from being able to cope with where this conversation is headed.

"The trap's right here," I say, kicking my backpack on the bar rail.

Ned leans over, picks up the backpack, and looks inside. "It's vibrating," he says.

"It always vibrates in here," I tell him. "Place is haunted."

"Should we do something?"

"Yeah. Let the ghost drink in peace."

Gabe the bartender has Superman ears. Strolls over from ten feet away with our drinks. "You talking about the spirit in here?" Guy never learns.

"Yeah," says Ned. "What about it?"

Gabe refills my shot glass and says, "There's something here all right. I've seen him in the mirror." He's not bullshitting us. Once, when I was sitting by myself at the bar, I saw the reflection of my face change. Someone else was looking at me. A man. It happened in a flash. Can't tell the bartender, though. He'll talk our ears off about it.

"Private conversation," I snap at him.

"Got it. Customer's always right," he says, walking away.

Ned inspects the backpack again, whispers to me, "So I can take it? You're okay with that?"

"I brought it here, didn't I?" I whisper back.

He grins at me. "You're curious. I know it. I can tell."

"Screw you. What do you know?"

He holds up the backpack. "I know the soul trap is as much a part of you as that guitar."

I don't answer. That about says it all.

"I'll tell you what's cooking—"

"Don't."

"I have to tell you. Just hear me out."

"Whatever," I say. But he's right. I'm curious. "Fine, but be concise."

"Shout at the Devil" by Mötley Crüe plays.

Ned's two drinks behind me, but fading fast. His margarita isn't going down smoothly. His blood sugar's whacked. Put a fork in him. He slurs a little as he says, "Does the name Barrington ring any bells?"

I think about it for a few seconds. "I don't know—Barrington Gardens in Pasadena—"

"Right," he says. "And Barrington Library and Barrington Boulevard and the Barrington Arms Hotel and so on in Pasadena. . . ."

"Okay. So?"

"So? So, an assistant to Mildred Barrington—the grand dame matriarch of the Barrington family—contacted me. Mrs. Barrington wants to talk to us."

"Talk to you."

"Talk to us. She read that *Times* article. She wants you."

My ego instantly inflates. Someone important knows my name. But I can't give Ned an inch. "Forget it," I announce.

"She won't talk to me without you."

"Tough shit."

Ned hits his margarita like it's a magic elixir that'll make him more persuasive. "Listen to me," he implores. "This is a billionaire. A damn-near hundred-year-old billionairess. Could be a fucking gold mine."

Kid Rock's "Devil Without a Cause" kicks in.

"Sorry. Not interested," I say, even though I am. Fight the temptation. I need to focus on the band and nothing else.

Ned slumps, looking glum. "Alcohol depresses me," he says. "I should know better than to drink with you." It's an act . . . I think. He's trying to bait me. But maybe not. "I have three more years at Caltech prison. I am so bored . . . so burned out, sometimes I don't think I'm gonna make it. If I can land us a fat deal, maybe I can get out early."

Don't look at him. Stand your ground. I glance away, but catch sight of his reflection in the mirror. He is getting old. He's not well. It's not an act.

Shit.

"Just tag along," he says. "Help me land the gig, and I'll take it from there."

I drink up, grab my phone and keys off the bar. Stand. Feeling pretty dizzy.

"Please," he says, so seriously, it unnerves me.

"Devil Woman"—Cliff Richard—plays next.

I'm way drunk.

Goddamnit, he pulled it off. He got me thinking about ghosts again. He won. A couple of sad looks and I caved. Pussy. "When and where." I can't believe I hear myself ask.

"She lives up north, in Pebble Beach—Seventeen Mile Drive. Some mansion."

"That's a friggin' hike," I gripe. "Are we flying?"

Ned perks right up. "It's a nice drive. What's your week look like?"

"Bad," I say. "Rehearsal every afternoon, except tomorrow." Could kick my own ass the second I say it. Served up the opening on a platter.

He perks up. "So let's go tomorrow."

Shake my head, wave that notion off. "We're rehearsing Tuesday at noon."

"Hell, let's leave right now," he says, grabbing his keys. "We'll get everything we need at your place, drive out to my place, load the camper, hit a 7-Eleven for coffee. I'll scarf down some donuts, sober up, and drive. You can crash. We'll be there by dawn. I'll call the assistant back first thing and get us a meeting." He rattles it all off so fast my whiskey-soaked brain jams.

Some nice jazz plays. My last selection: "That Old Devil Moon." Never heard it before.

Ned stops, listens, identifies it. "Is this Miles?"

I nod. The bartender loves it, yells down from the other end of the bar, "Did you play this, Kane?" I nod. "Good man. This is my kinda music. Listen to that trumpet. Only two trumpet players better."

He's dying to tell me the others. Screw you, pal.

"What do you say?" Ned asks. "Sound like a plan?"

"What if she can't meet?"

"I'll play hardball," Ned promises. "It's tomorrow or never."

"But don't you teach?"

"I'll call in sick." Ned's fired up. "Let's do this. Spur of the moment."

I run the facts through my boozy head. "I swear to Christ, if you don't have me back here in twenty-four hours—to the minute—I'll release my flying monkeys all over your fat ass."

"Deal. Start your stopwatch."

I actually do—the one on my iPhone. Look at my reflection in the mirror. *This is probably yet another big mistake.* I'm pissed off at myself for another minute, but then I move on. "Okay, what do I need to know about this woman?"

Ned puts down his drink, counts off on his fingers as he speaks. "One: She's obscenely rich. Gave up a career in show business and married the heir to an empire. Two: She's old—ancient.

Ninety-eight, but still Energizer Bunnying it along. Three: She's powerful. Smart. Demanding. Ruthless in business. Shockingly tight with a charitable buck. Warm and fuzzy would not describe her. Now that I think about it," he says, finishing off his drink, "you'd probably get along with her."

"And if I go along with you, what do I get out of this?"

"Fifty-fifty, as usual."

"No!" I say it way too loud. I'm really drunk. "I'll help you get the job—that's probably all I can do. I'm not going to fuck my chances up."

"A consulting fee then. How does ten percent sound?"

"Fifteen percent," I counter.

Ned smacks the bar. "Deal."

"And you pick up this tab," I add, "and pay for everything on the road trip."

"Done." Ned waves for the check. Pulls out a wad of cash. Leaves the pain-in-the-ass barkeep a twenty-dollar tip.

"Blessings be upon you, my friend," Gabe says, shaking Ned's hands. "Good to have you back, Kane," he says to me. "With you back in here drinking, we can pay our rent for sure." I fire him a murderous look. "I know," he says, throwing up his hands in mock surrender. "Shut up and pour."

My legs are shaky on the way out. "My car's over there," Ned says. We cross Hollywood Boulevard and enter the parking lot where the Brown Derby once stood. Ned pops the hatch on his Subaru Outback and pulls out something I recognize in a second—a vintage guitar case. "This is for you," he says, handing it to me, "for helping me out."

Holy shit. A Gibson Les Paul '57 Goldtop Darkback Reissue. An exact replica of the guitar that Skydog Allman, among other legends, played. I hold it aloft like Excalibur. I swear it glows.

Ned's got a dumb grin on his face. Like a dad on Christmas morning. "That's it, right? The one you went on and on about the last time we were drinking."

"Yeah," I say, stunned.

"It's yours now," he says, proudly. "Let's hear you make it talk."

Speechless. The mother of all gifts. Aggravation melts away. The booze makes me all gooey. Like amnesia dissolving, I remember—here stands the only person who gives a shit.

"This lists for five grand."

"More or less," he says.

"I can't accept it."

"Who are you kidding? Now put it away before someone mugs us."

I get choked up. Too much Jameson. Too much emotion. Reach for a smart-ass remark, but I got nothing. "Thanks."

Ned speeds down Hollywood Boulevard. I look at him in the dashboard light. "If I would have said no and meant it, would you still have given it to me?"

"Shit," he says, laughing, popping open the center console, and grabbing the receipt. "Why do you think I held onto this?"

Three

When we get to Carmel in the morning, we find out Mrs. Barrington is hosting a political fund-raising luncheon and can't meet us until early evening.

I end up killing the day with Ned, who talks my ear off, and getting a helluva good look at the other side of the tracks. Carmel oozes money, but not in an obvious Beverly Hills way. Everyone just stepped out of a J. Crew catalog. Tons of dogs on leashes, and even they look rich. Lots of quaint shops selling stuff no one needs. Tree-lined streets with art galleries and cozy little restaurants. Walking around in my jeans, leather jacket, and boots, I get a few suspicious looks, a few double takes, like maybe I'm a rock star or actor in town for a visit. Maybe someday. Sure as hell not now. I spy the price tag on a sculpture of a nude woman trapped in glass that stands in a gallery window—$38,900.

I don't belong here. Never will.

I'm grumpy as hell as we lumber into the La Playa Hotel in Carmel just after seven PM. It's quaint. Feels a little musty, but homey. The centerpiece of the lobby is an ornate marble fireplace. They're burning pine. I can tell by the crackle and the scent. My dad used to love to burn pine in our fireplace when I was a kid. Made the whole house smell like Christmas. Cheers me up a little.

Cute girl behind the desk points us toward the bar. We walk down a corridor, but a sign in the entrance of the bar reads: *Closed.* "What the fuck?" I bitch. "You got the place wrong?"

"No, I didn't," he assures me. "I see a bartender in there, come on."

We move the velvet rope and step into an old school bar with brass fixtures and more wood than a porn shoot. It's dimly lit, moody. Historic photos of Carmel hang on the walls along with geographic survey maps from the town's construction. A bartender in a white tuxedo jacket fills bowls with nuts. High-end bottles of liquor are neatly lined up on mirrored shelves. Two angels—intricately carved in wood—face each other. They seem to stand guard above the cash register.

The place is empty save for two geezers at a corner table. I'm in a scene from *The Shining*. Guy Geezer waves us over.

Introductions are made. Lady Geezer is Mildred Barrington, but we can call her Millie. Ninety-eight, but looks seventy. Still got a spark in her green eyes. Dyed hair. Dressed to the nines. Silk, lace, pearls around her neck and on her fingers. Her mind and eyes are young.

Guy Geezer is—amazingly—Ronald Barrington, Millie's son. Pale face, black suit—he looks like a corpse who crawled out of his casket. Can't be. Spider veins on his nose, chronically bloodshot eyes. That sickly little chemical kind of musk that heavy vodka drinkers ooze. A top-shelf alcoholic.

The bartender approaches and takes our order. Me: Jameson on the rocks; Ned: Glenlivet; corpse: Grey Goose on the rocks; Millie: vodka gimlet, extra limes.

"Surprised there's not a crowd in here. Very nice bar," I offer, as an icebreaker.

"I had the bar closed," Millie says, matter-of-factly. "To give us total privacy." She says it all formal—prih-vah-see.

Geezer guy adjusts his jacket collar, coughs out, "Mother owns the hotel."

Millie pats my hand. "You remind me of a young Bob Mitchum," she says. "You have that same worn-out look."

I guess I'll take it as a compliment.

"I knew Bob Mitchum," she boasts.

"Really?"

The geezer's all slurry when he says, "Mother was an actress."

"And a singer and a dancer. Tell them, Ronnie." She snaps her fingers at him.

"Mother was in nine movies," Ronnie says, finishing his drink. A lot of vodka down the hatch.

Millie leans forward in her chair. "I costarred in a film with Don Ameche. I acted on Broadway. And I danced in Paris—summer of 1937."

As if he's reading her bio, Ronnie blurts out, "Mother was a presence of stage and screen," Ronnie says. The bartender walks over, almost without notice, and refills Ronnie's tall glass—nearly to the rim.

I notice a framed Hollywood magazine cover from the early thirties on the wall across from us. My eyes dart from the cover to Millie. "That's you."

Millie sips her gimlet. Nods. "I retired from show business in 1941—when I married Harry. I could have been a millionaire on my own," she boasts. "But a billionaire . . . that required matrimony." She laughs, gravel and soot in the throat—a career smoker. Winks at me again.

Ned seems amused.

Millie turns in her seat and sizes me up. "So you're the mystery man from the newspaper article?" she asks.

"Kane." She says it with gusto and lets it trail off. "Splendid name. I knew Orson Welles," she says. "Fancied himself a great lover, but he was hung like my pinkie."

Ronnie chokes on a cashew. "Mother, please."

Millie looks me right in the eye. A hardcore stare. Doubt is in her voice when she asks, "Did you really rid that church in Lompoc of its ghost? Is the story true?"

"More or less," I say.

"I've met many liars," Millie says. "Even married a few of them."

"I'm not lying."

She flashes a phony smile while she studies me hard. I maintain eye contact. "Do you have this device—this soul trap—with you?"

I hold up my backpack. "Right here."

"May I see it?" she asks, politely.

I look around—no one, except for the bartender. I take out the trap and lay it on the table. It vibrates, beeps—the monitor flashes. I kill the beeper.

"Is it a gun? What's it doing?" Ronnie asks, looking at me nervously.

"It's picking up a presence. This hotel is haunted."

"Is it? How exciting." She laughs like I'm bullshitting her, nods toward the trap. "Tell me, how does it work?

I look at Ned—*all yours, buddy.* He gives me a little nod of reassurance, then walks them through how we capture and interrogate ghosts. He starts getting too technical. I interrupt and simplify. I'm concise. *Soul Trap for Dummies.*

When I'm finished, Ned looks for clarification. "So I take it you want us to rid the hotel of the ghost or ghosts haunting it?"

"No," she says.

"Then why are we here?"

"You're both from Los Angeles. Surely you know the Colorado Street Bridge in Pasadena."

"Driven over it a million times," Ned says. "I live in Pasadena."

"I've seen it," I say.

"Did you see the *L.A. Times* article week before last—about the girl who jumped off?"

Haven't looked at the *L.A. Times* since that article, since that day with Eva. "No."

Ned shakes his head. "Didn't hear about it, but I know it happens there a lot."

Millie finishes her gimlet. The bartender is right there the moment she sets her glass down. We all nod yes to another round. "Two Sundays ago, a seventeen-year-old girl leapt off the bridge.

Her name was Anna Burrows. I saw her picture in the newspaper. A beautiful, young thing. Seeing her face, pondering her sad and unnecessary end. It moved me."

We all clam up until the bartender delivers our drinks and leaves. Then Ned chimes in. "It's nicknamed Suicide Bridge. It's had that moniker since its construction in 1909. At least a hundred people have jumped."

Ronnie corrects him. "The number is closer to two hundred."

Millie taps her finger again. "Whatever the number, I want it to stop with Anna Burrows. Enough is enough."

Don't know whether to say what's on my mind. I walk on eggshells as I say, "No disrespect, but what do you care? You don't even live in Pasadena anymore."

"The bridge has become a blight on my city."

"And when mother says 'my city,' she means *my city*," Ronnie says.

"But every town has a dark side," I say. "Why do you take it personally?"

She bristles. Doesn't like talking back. "Pasadena is my crown jewel," she says. "I spent my best years building, crafting that city. I gave that town my heart and soul. The bridge means a great deal to me personally," she says.

"Why?" I ask.

A little smile that seems genuine. Her body language suggests reluctance to elaborate, but she tells me more. "The bridge and I are the same age—give or take," she says. "We're dear old friends. Sisters. We're intertwined. It's always been a special place for me. Back when I was a child, it was as much a pedestrian bridge as traffic route. People strolled there. The views at sunset were breathtaking. There were no ugly railings. No traffic whizzing by. My family walked the bridge; we had picnics beneath it."

Her voice cracks with emotion. "Of all the many things written about me—bad and worse—no one ever wrote this: my late husband Harry proposed to me on that bridge."

"Really?" Ronnie and I say simultaneously.

"Yes, really," she says. "We were in the dead center of the bridge. Looking out at those majestic San Gabriel Mountains, I said, 'Yes.' Together, we built a life, and a city."

Immediately, Ned pisses on the emotional moment. "I hear ya'," he says. "Great story. But there's a suicide bridge in practically every town in the US," Ned points out. "You'll never stop people who are down and out from killing themselves."

Millie ignores Ned, stares me straight in the eye. "Understand me. I want the suicides to end."

"Sorry, but we're not psychologists," I say.

Millie grows weary. More reluctance as she says, "A late friend once told me the bridge was haunted. That this was a supernatural issue, not a psychological one."

"A psychic?" I ask.

"That's a . . . *loose* term, dare I say a vulgar one, in my book," Millie says. "Let's just say my friend seemed to be genuinely sensitive to these things.

"And you believed her?"

"Frankly, no. I've always been a skeptic. I believe in the here and now. But as the years have passed, and the suicides have continued, and I've marched steadily toward my own mortality, I've allowed myself to revisit the subject, to become more open-minded about the possibility."

"There are ghost stories in books—all over the web—about the bridge," Ned says. "Any place with that much negative energy is likely to be a hotbed of paranormal activity. I almost guarantee you it's haunted. Probably by a number of spirits. We need to know exactly what it is you want us to do."

Millie taps her fingers on the table, no doubt issuing a direct order. "If there are spirits at the bridge, I want them gone. Someday I mean to have my ashes scattered there, and I don't intend on sharing the bridge with anyone, or anything that is causing people to take their own precious lives."

Ned looks at me. I look the other way. It's a huge job. Would eat up lots of time. I told Ned I couldn't promise him anything. He so wants me to look at him, to give him a read, but I won't. Ned finally answers her. "Okay, I get it. Like I said, it could be a difficult job. We should discuss our fee."

At the mention of money, Millie's pearly white dentures gleam. She takes a dainty sip of her gimlet, stares us down, and says, "Don't pull any nonsense on me. I may be old, but I'm not stupid. I'll only say that once." She glares at me, then Ned. "So what's your fee?"

Ned completely chokes. He is so psyched out he doesn't know what to ask for.

Millie smiles. "Let's discuss this in stages." She just schooled Ned, the genius.

Ned's eyes beg me to save him. I'm silent.

"You claim I have a haunted hotel here?" Millie asks.

I'll at least answer that. "For sure," I tell her. "There's a ghost. Right here in the bar."

"Then make this skeptic a believer," she says. "Capture this ghost. Tell me why it's here. Get rid of it."

Ned's chuckle drips with sarcasm. "You want us to audition?"

"Heavens no. Working for free is not good business," Millie says. "Tell me what it will cost."

Ned looks at me. I'm all poker face. "Ten thousand dollars," Ned blurts out.

Not a second ticks off the clock before she says, "Fine. Do this, and I'll decide if a larger project warrants discussion."

"Can I have a minute with my partner?" Ned asks.

"By all means," she says.

I follow Ned into the corridor outside the bar. "Forget about the big job—the bridge," Ned whispers. "This ghost right here is easy pickins'."

He's right. The ghost is stationary. Two phantom fences before it knows what hit it, pull the trigger, and it's toast. "I think I can nail it in a few seconds."

Ned grins. "Then let's do it. A quick and dirty 10K."

Follow Ned back to the bar. One thing bothers me—I don't have my lucky necklace. I never ghost-hunt without it. Haven't worn it since I put the trap away last year. I didn't think I'd need it tonight.

Ned turns to tell me something when we enter the bar, but I shove him aside, grab the soul trap off the table, and fire at the spot where the spirit hovers. Take a wild shot at catching the soul by surprise. Squeeze the trigger and fire. There's that sound— huge, otherworldy, powerful. A slow build up as the energy fields converge and then, *Boom!* Haven't heard it in a long time.

I kind of miss that sound.

The blast just misses the bartender. He runs for cover. Glasses shatter from the shock wave.

The sound rumbles from the bar, through the corridor, and into the lobby.

"Mother of pearl," Millie cries when she hears that unforget- table roar.

Check the monitor. Missed. Fuck. I'm out of practice. Track the soul on the monitor—it's darting around, fast. The tiny bulbs lighting the liquor shelves blow. It's pissed off. *Whoosh.* Ghost is gone—on the run.

We take off after it.

Son of a bitch. Here I go again.

Soul keeps us running up and down the stairs of the four- story hotel until we finally track it down and pin it inside the bar with two phantom fences. The bartender fled long ago. But Millie and Ronnie Barrington are still there.

One by one, the liquor bottles topple off the mirrored shelves and smash on the floor. The glowing orb manifests again before our eyes and darts toward the doorway. When it runs into the phantom fence, it crackles with energy. It's stunned.

"Now!" Ned shouts.

I raise the soul trap and aim. An unseen force guides the barrel left, then a little right. The crosshairs on the trap's monitors blink red. Targeting tone rings out. I pull the trigger.

The roar is deeper this time. Millie shrieks. Ronnie's under the table. The sound echoes for several seconds. "What happened?" she asks when the room finally settles.

"We got it," I say.

Ronnie struggles to get to his feet. "What now?" he asks.

We take Millie and Ronnie to the camper, show them the equipment, walk them through the process while I stretch out on the bed above the cab and get wired and ready to go in. Feels like I'm slipping into a second skin as I don the electrodes, the NuMag helmet, the Ganzfeld goggles, and earplugs. I lay back in silent darkness. I reach up and feel the ceiling of the camper a foot away.

Ned sends a current of electricity. It circulates around the rim of the goggles. The helmet vibrates. My skin buzzes. I begin my routine—breathing, relaxation techniques, meditation. Have a hard time settling my mind. Thoughts pop like loud little firecrackers.

Focus.

Concentrate.

It's not working. The camper is too crowded. Can't calm down. Can't project my soul.

I ask Millie and Ronnie to step outside for a few minutes. I start over. Focus on nothing but my breath. In one nostril, out the other. It's working. Surround myself with a white light of protection. Meditate. Recall a fond memory—a conversation I had with Donna Lonzi inside the trap. My chakras energize. My soul vibrates, rises. Darkness is illuminated by a rainbow of colors that swirl gently in my third eye. I'm floating away. The vibrant colors blend into a single shade of purple. I hear the electric hum and the high-pitch ringing. I made it.

· · ·

I open my eyes.

The last time I projected my consciousness into the trap, Ned skinned the interior like a '50s diner. Now it's back to interrogation central. A metal table, two metal chairs, a single lightbulb and the big door to the hereafter. A guy in a tuxedo stands in the corner. Looks to be in his late thirties. Black hair. A long, narrow face. Olive complexion. Tall and thin. A sad look. Reminds me a little of Adrien Brody.

"Who are you?" he asks. "Where am I?"

I ignore his questions. Order him to take a seat.

We sit at the table across from each other.

I stare at him until he's good and nervous. "What's your name?"

"Stanley Tekulve. What's yours?"

"Never mind. Why are you haunting this hotel, Stanley?"

"So I can watch Millie Barrington grow old and die," he answers, coldly.

"Old grudge?" I ask.

"We were lovers."

"When?"

"Most of the forties. When I was the manager at La Playa."

"Banging the boss, huh?"

"It was more than that," he says. "We were in love." He pronounces everything too precisely, just like Millie. "She told me she would leave her husband for me. That she'd give up her fortune. That we'd be married."

"And?"

"She lied. And when she was done with me, she sacked me. She drove me to despair. She's evil, I tell you. Ours was a love spell that became a curse." I want to puke. He's phony. Talks like a talentless actor delivering his lines in a bad '40s movie.

I don't like this guy. Want to smack him a good one. But on he drones. "Her betrayal ruined me. My mind became fragmented. I lost hope. I was drawn to do something I would have never dreamed of doing before I met that witch."

"What?"

"I took my own life."

That one catches me by surprise. It's the first soul I ever trapped who committed suicide.

Stanley's voice is full of regret when he tells me, "When Millie left me, I went down to the beach, walked into Carmel Bay, and let the current sweep me away."

I knock on the table to get his attention. "Sorry to hear that, but it's time for you to move on."

He sits up and shakes his head in protest. "No. No. I'm not walking through my door until that wicked witch is dead. I watch her get older and uglier—every day. I see the light in her becoming eyes dim."

"You don't get to make the rules today, pal. Millie does. And Millie says you're moving on." I press the button under the corner of the table. The crystal-handled lever materializes by my side. The steel door to the hereafter appears right behind Stanley. It startles him. He panics.

He knows he's fucked. "No!" he sobs. "I'm not ready."

"Sorry. Last call, Stanley."

He weeps, his head in his hands. "I'm afraid I'll go to hell for what she made me do."

"Should have thought about that before you pissed your life away." End of discussion. I yank the lever. The door inches open to the sound of heavy chains. I brace. You never know what's on the other side. I back away, expecting to see the orange glow that signifies a one-way ticket to hell. But there are no demons, no blasts of foul, hot air. There's nothing but a thick gray fog and eerie silence. The fog creeps into the room toward Stanley. No voices. No one waiting to welcome him. Stanley tries to grab onto the table, but the fog pries his fingers loose one at a time. He cries out. He tries to stay rooted, but the fog envelops him and pulls him steadily toward the door. He's paralyzed, unable to resist, but his eyes bug wide as he says, "I'm warning you." He screams at me before the fog carries him away, "Get too close to Millie, and you'll lose your heart and soul."

The door slams shut. The cheesy old movie dialogue is gone with the fog.

My exit door appears behind me. I leave.

I'm on my back, convulsing. Fighting for breath. My heart races. I'm drenched in sweat.

"Is he all right?" Millie asks, alarmed.

"It's normal," Ned says. "He's a little out of practice."

My lungs start to function. Ned stands on the ladder, peels off the electrodes, and yanks off my helmet. I see two of him. He helps me climb down, one slow step at a time. I'm wickedly dizzy. I gulp down a bottle of water, take a seat at the table.

"Well?" Ronnie asks.

"Ghost is gone," I choke out.

"Tell me," Millie says. "What was his name?"

"Stanley," I say, coughing.

Millie's jaw drops. "My God," she says. She knows now. She shoots me a spiteful little smirk. "And what did that fool have to say for himself?"

"You knew it was him?"

"I wasn't entirely certain, but I had a strong feeling."

"You could have told me that," I snap.

Millie laughs—that Shirley Temple four-packs-a-day giggle. "Tell me. Tell me everything he said."

"Let me think," I say, still a little muddled. Millie gets impatient. "Tell me" she barks. "Every word of it."

Did I mention I pretty much hate everyone? That includes people who always get everything they want and old ladies who think they can jerk me around. Screw you, Millie. You kept a secret from me, I'll keep one from you. "It was a little hazy," I lie. "The gist of it was that you jilted him."

Ronnie shakes his head and grins. "Oh, Mother, not another one of your dalliances."

Millie opens her bejeweled handbag, takes out a letter written on La Playa Hotel stationary, yellowed with age. She hands it to me. I read it aloud:

> *My Dearest Mildred,*
>
> *It is finished. You got what you wanted. I am gone from your hotel. I am gone from your life. Gone from all life.*
>
> *How could you, Millie? How could you fake such a deep and lasting love for me when all the time, I was just your puppet?*
>
> *Your betrayal is the devil's dagger that darkened your soul and pierced my heart. May you never forget that your wickedness drove me to this. And you will have to live with it for the rest of your life.*
>
> *Let the sea swallow me.*
>
> *Yours, Stanley*

Before I'm even finished, Millie is laughing. "Stanley—what a romantic sap."

"So," I say, rereading the line, "how did you how manage to fake such a deep and lasting love?"

She shoots me a look like the answer is obvious. "I am an actress," she says. "A damn good one."

Time to knock her down a peg. "Stanley enjoyed watching you grow old. He wanted to see you die."

"Stanley loses . . . again," she says, dentures gleaming. "And I win." She looks at me all serious. "I make it a point to always win."

Damn. She really is a nasty old bird. Ronnie looks at me and Ned with unfocused, bloodshot eyes. "Well, I'd say you passed the audition."

"With flying colors," Millie adds. "Let's retire to the hotel bar for more cocktails, so we can discuss our next project."

Three hours into our ride back to L.A., I'm still feeling like shit, and we're both still giggling like teenage girls. I'm clutching an envelope stuffed with ten grand in cash, but that's just chicken feed. "I can't friggin' believe it," Ned keeps repeating.

"Me neither," I laugh. "200K for the bridge job!"

"And she didn't even bat an eye," Ned says. "I didn't know what to say. I mean how much is too much for people like that? Maybe I should have asked for a million, huh?"

"She's tough. Just be happy with what you're getting."

"What we're getting," Ned says, looking over at me.

The band flashes through my brain. "I don't know," I say. "I don't have the time."

"I won't do it without you," Ned says. "She only gave us a month. Come on, we're a team."

$200K. I can get out of debt. Get my credit report out of the shitter. Buy a new car. Finally get the hell out off Yucca Street. I'm so sick of being broke. Tired of choking on bills. Shit, who am I kidding? I'm all in.

But I make Ned sweat a little. "I don't know," I repeat over and over.

"Come on, we'll do it as your schedule permits. It won't infringe on the band. I mean, how bad can it be? Couldn't be any worse than last year."

"If I go along with this, I run the show."

"As always," Ned says all reassuringly.

"The band comes first."

"Of course."

"You have to promise not to be a pain in my ass."

"I promise. I'm turning over a new leaf."

I sit silently, let him sweat for just a few more minutes.

Ned finally breaks the silence. "Are we back in business?"

"Yeah," I say, handing him half the cash in the envelope. "Fifty-fifty."

"All right!" Ned shouts. "The man is back!"

Four

Ned drops me off at my apartment at 6:30 AM. Schedule for the morning: Shit, shower, shave, nap. Hit the bank and make my deposit. Pay a stack of bills. Leave for rehearsal at 11:30.

I open the door to my apartment and everything looks different, though it's all the same. I've ignored all the hardware that supports the trap for nearly a year. But when I turn on the light this time, I see it all, right there. The Tesla supercomputer, the monitors, the gurney, the IVeR—it's all covered in dust, but suddenly looks new again.

I'm tempted to power everything up, run all the software updates, make sure it's all still working, but I need sleep. Strip to my briefs and crawl in bed. My mind won't settle. The excitement of Millie's $200K wears off. I can't stop thinking about the way she laughed at Stanley's suicide. She's ruthless. She calls the bridge a blight on her city, but in truth, the bridge is probably the only thing in "her city" she can't control, and that's what bugs her. Do I really believe she was moved by a news story about a teenager jumping or by memories of her youth? People that rich only care about two things: making more money and gaining more power. But who knows? She's at the end of the road. Maybe she's softening. Getting sentimental. I can't fully read her. What does this old lady want?

And what exactly was Stanley trying to warn me about? I toss and turn for almost an hour. Try to recount the conversation, but

I didn't listen all that closely. Couldn't get past what an asshole Stanley was, spouting the same bullshit as every loser who gets dumped and wants to blame the other person. Guy deserves what he got. Right?

I give up on sleeping. While my pot of coffee brews, I down a jumbo Red Bull and a big bowl of Frosted Cheerios. Nuke a container of mac and cheese. I need to know more. I sit down at my Mac and google Millie Garlington. It would take me a week to get through all the entries, but I dig in as best I can.

Millie is listed on a few conspiracy websites that tout her as a member of the Illuminati, part of the Merovingian bloodline, which can supposedly be traced back to the pharaohs in ancient Egypt. Don't put much credence in any of that. Most billionaires and political leaders are on that list. The ultrawealthy are always obvious and easy targets for paranoid conspiracy geeks broadcasting from their mothers' basements.

Then I come across fragments from a 1950 two-part exposé in the gossip rag *Confidential* about L.A.'s richest people. The Barringtons are mentioned. Millie and her husband were known to pay their servants handsomely. But they were also known to work their staffers to the bone, demand utter loyalty and complete confidentiality. Their housekeeper, a woman named Helena Maldanado, made headlines when she sued her former employers for wrongful termination and back wages. An upcoming issue of *Confidential* promised an explosive tell-all interview about shocking secrets behind the gates of the Barrington estate. But the trail dead-ends there. I can't find any trace of the follow-up interview.

I find a fat, two-hundred-plus-page document posted by an author who was outlining an unauthorized biography of the Barringtons in 1997. It mostly focuses on the Barrington fortune. The family invested in dozens of local SoCal companies in the forties and fifties and made a killing in the aerospace industry and in freeway construction. I jot down a list of the companies mentioned in the interview. I've heard of a few of them—Lock-heed, Hughes Aircraft, Northrop. What follows is a lot of detailed financial information. Boring. Too dense. I move on.

Two hours pass in what feels like twenty minutes. I could get lost in Millie's amazing life, but I stop myself. Can't let precious time get sucked away. I have to focus on my music. I bookmark a couple dozen sites. Paste links into an e-mail. Scan my page of notes and send everything to Ned with a terse email:

> I started this. U can finish it. Don't know if I trust her. Need 2 know more.

Let Ned earn his keep and do the grunt work. The band is priority one.

I turn off my Mac. Glance around. The equipment calls to me. Shit, I just can't resist. I switch everything on. Connect the soul trap to the Tesla. It all works.

Power up the IVeR. I dig the crystal goblet that once belonged to British occultist Aleister Crowley out of my kitchen cabinet. Drank out of it once or twice, but haven't energized it or used it on the IVeR since I shut everything down and walked away last year. The goblet may still have a faint supernatural charge. I place it on top of the IVeR and listen as it hums to life. I tune the ectometer and search for the disembodied voice of a spirit named Karl. I still have no idea who or what he is. "Karl? Karl, are you still out there?"

I finesse the tuner. A voice sings an eerie tune. It's a Beatles song for sure. Karl loves the Fab Four. This song is creepy. About a fog in L.A. People losing their way. What's the title? Something about a blue jay. "Blue Jay Way." "Karl?"

"Howdy, stranger," Karl says, slow and deep, almost robotlike, through static crackles.

"Colorado Street Bridge—Pasadena," I say.

"A bridge over troubled water," Karl says. "It's a long way down—as you will see."

"What does that mean?"

The IVeR fries out. I'll have to carve out time to recharge it.

I've had a recurring dream about falling off a bridge for years. Does Karl know that? Or does he see something else? Shit. I'm sick of Karl always fucking with me like this.

Text message alert rings. It's from Bo:

> Rehearsals cancelled this week. Drexel resting throat until gig Fri. I have meetings with indies incl. Epitaph Records.

A week to myself.

I'm inspired. I practice—all day. Work on my solos until my fingertips are raw.

The whole time my mind keeps going back to that conversation I had with Ned at the Frolic Room. The one about Eva. Ned's positive she told me the truth about that article. In the back of my head, I think I believed her all along. There was just too much emotional baggage that day, and my coping skills suck.

I wanted her. By the time she got around to wanting me, I wanted someone else . . . someone dead. I accused her of being jealous of a ghost. I fired insults with both barrels. She fired them right back. It got ugly.

I really fucked up.

She didn't deserve what I dished out.

She was good to me.

She cared about me.

These thoughts stay with me all afternoon.

• • •

I drive downtown. Park myself at a Starbucks sidewalk table directly across the street from the *L.A. Times.* Text message from Ned:

> Will dig deeper into grand dame's life. Did a prelim
> sweep of the Col. St. Brg yesterday. Have lots of info.
> Let's go there ASAP.

Now that rehearsal is off, I text back:

> Tomorrow morning?

Not three seconds pass before he fires back:

> Meet in Parking Lot J of the Rose Bowl at 10.

I drink enough coffee to get shaky, kill time with a Charlie Huston ebook, and glance up every two or three seconds in case Eva walks out.

She doesn't.

Six PM.

Stay or go? . . .

Can't believe I'm doing this.

I walk in the building, feeling like a dwarf under the huge globe in the lobby. Eyes go straight to the towering murals. Lots of people leaving, but no sign of Eva. I take the elevator to the newsroom. A pretty receptionist stops me, dials Eva.

I see her head pop up from across the open room jammed with desks. She walks toward me with purpose like she always does. Jeans, black leather jacket. Her hair is longer, straighter than last year.

She's not pleased. "What are you doing here?"

I smile at her. "Hi, Eva."

Nothing. She glances at the receptionist, uncomfortable. She still hates me. I can tell. "Can we talk?"

The receptionist is pretending not to listen. Long silence, then, "Sure."

I follow Eva across the wide-open and chaotic newsroom. Pass desk after desk, crammed tight with monitors, stacks of paper, and personal mementos, namely photos of spouses and kids. Feels like I'm looking into prison cells without the bars. She never glances back at me, but I can see her mind racing. No doubt constructing the clever string of insults she's about to unleash on me. She passes her desk and leads me to a glass-walled conference room, the faint smell of coffee in the air. She closes the door hard behind her.

I'm gonna get my ass handed to me. I take a seat. It feels like an electric chair.

"Okay," she says, matter-of-factly. "I'm not interested in speaking to you." She won't even sit down.

"Come on," I urge, pushing out the chair next to me.

"No."

I try to look her in the eye, but she looks at the L.A. skyline out the window. "Two minutes. Then I'll leave. I just want to say some things. Please, sit down."

She freezes. She's close to bolting, but she stops, composes herself. Sits down. "Two minutes," she says.

I've got nothing rehearsed. It's straight from the hip and delivered slowly. "I owe you an apology. I'm sorry."

"I told you," she says quickly, "I had nothing to do with that article."

"I should have believed you. I was just watching a wrecking ball destroy my life, and you got in the way."

"Exactly. I was in the way. You were in love with someone else."

"I was a mess." She nods at that. "You were nothing but great to me. I'm sorry."

A little smile. "Okay."

And some of the tension lifts.

"So, do you think that we—"

She cuts me off.

"Not. A. Chance."

"What?"

"You know what."

"No, I don't. You didn't let me finish. I see you're still good at that."

"Go ahead, finish your sentence."

"Do you think that we might still . . . work together?"

She at least pretends to think about it before saying, "I don't think so."

"Listen, Ned and I are doing one last gig together. It might interest you."

She's at least tempted. "No," she insists.

"Come on—let's go have a drink. I'll tell you about it. Just hear me out, then you can tell me to fuck off and I will." I look way into those blue eyes, the color of Tiffany gift boxes. "One drink?"

"You can't stop at one."

She's got me there.

"Forget it," she says. "I can't stomach watching you try to express yourself through jukebox selections."

Ouch. "Okay, we'll stay here in this glass cage and catch up."

And that's what we do, but it's all forced and uncomfortable. I tell her about the band, invite her to our next gig. She tells me about a story she wrote about five homeless people who live under an overpass of the 110 Freeway. Says she got nominated for a Los Angeles Press Club award. I tell her she's a shoe-in.

I start babbling. Need a drink bad. Tell her I haven't dated anyone since the last time I saw her. Neglect to tell her about the seven or eight hookups or the working gal I kept in business all last summer. She tells me she's been in two mini-relationships, neither of which lasted more than a month. She's available. Fuckin' A.

I tell her about Millie Barrington and the Colorado Street Bridge gig. It's sure a small world, because she actually wrote the write-up in *The Times* about Anna Burrows. I ask her if she wants to join me and Ned at the bridge in the morning. Tells me she'll think about it. Progress.

We run out of things to say. She looks at her watch.

"I have to go," she announces.

"I'll walk you to your car," I say.

On the way out, I stop and admire the globe in the lobby. Must be fifteen feet tall. "So," I ask, "is it a big world or a small world?"

"Both," Eva says.

We don't say a hell of a lot on the walk through the parking garage. When we reach her car, I say, "It was good to see you again."

"You, too," she says, not at all warmly.

Then I pull a huge douche move. I lean in and hug her. "Any chance at all we can rewind and hit Play again?"

"It happened the way it was supposed to happen," she answers.

"You really think so?"

"Yeah."

"Sorry to hear that."

"You had your chance," she says.

"Give me another one and I won't screw it up."

"No."

"So this is it?"

She thinks about it as she gets in her Volvo. "I don't know. I guess we can still be friends."

"Friends?"

"Yeah. Maybe we'll get back to work on your story."

"Friends . . . and colleagues?"

"Yeah."

"Right back where we started?"

"Yes."

"I'll take it," I say.

She smiles.

"Will I see you at the bridge in the morning?"

"Don't know. Maybe. Call me in the morning. Do you still have my number?"

"Of course," I say.

Sure she hates me now. But I'm gonna get this girl back. And this time, I'm not going to fuck it up.

Five

I don't even need my alarm clock. I'm up early to the baritone opera of two guys schtupping in the apartment above me. Moans, groans—sounds like a damn Abu Ghraib "interrogation." I fumble through my dresser drawer until I find my lucky necklace. It's cumbersome and heavy—a hodgepodge of religious medals and talismans that I've collected over the years. It's got definite mojo and emits measurable energy when I'm around spirits. It protects me—at least I think it does, and that's what counts. I double-check to make sure the trap is charged and working, pack it carefully in my backpack, fill up my travel mug with coffee, and hit the road.

I'm surprised to see Eva's car parked next to Ned's camper in Lot J. They're all smiles, chatting away as I pull up. Ned's wearing Caltech sweats and his tweed cap. He looks like a hobo who just rolled off a boxcar. I tell him as much. Eva's all stylish casual as usual. A Nike ad. The girl could wear a Hefty bag and look great.

"I scoped the entire area out Tuesday," Ned tells us. "There's a walking trail up the road about a quarter mile. It takes you down into the Arroyo Seco. Trail runs right along the stream. About a half mile down that trail, where the stream feeds into the concrete river channel, is the bottom of the bridge. You up for a little hike?"

"Sure," Eva says. She ties up her hair, ready to roll.

Oh, fuck. Ned's in tour-guide mode. I thought we were going to get right to work, but I know what's coming next. A full walkthrough where he tells us everything he's learned in excruciating detail. Christ. I don't want a fucking history lesson. I just want to knock this job out and get my money.

Just when I'm about to tell Ned to shut up, Eva looks over and gives me a half-friendly smile. It calms me. I'll shut up. I can't get off on the wrong foot with Eva now that I got the door open again.

Jackass Ned failed to mention we'd be hiking. While Eva and Ned are sporting sneakers, I'm wearing my black leather boots with the silver skull buckles. But I can't wuss out in front of Eva, so I grab my backpack. Ned picks up his duffle bag. "What do you have in there?" I ask him.

"Standard gear. Thermal cam. Digital recorder. First aid kit. Water. And some snacks."

Snacks? Jesus. I'm in for a long day.

Ned's already breathing heavy by the time the road meets the dirt trail. The first part of the walk is uphill. Then we hit a dirt trail and downhill into the thick brush alongside a slow-moving stream. A few joggers pass us.

"Not much of a river," I say.

"Flooding has always been a big issue," Ned says. "The water flow is controlled upstream at Devil's Gate Dam."

"That's the dam right off the 210, right?" Eva asks. "The one below NASA's Jet Propulsion Laboratory?"

"Right," Ned says. "The water from the dam flows under the freeway, drains into a concrete river channel along the golf courses at the Rose Bowl, and then feeds into here. Actually this little area we're in now is only one of two spots in the stream's whole forty-five-mile trek that's still in its natural state."

We stroll past a guy fishing with his young son. I steal a peek in their bucket. Nothing. Down the trail, I catch sight of a massive bridge. "That must be it," I say. "It's huge."

"Nope," Ned says. "That's the Pioneer Bridge. It runs right alongside the Colorado Street Bridge. Built in the '50s when the 134 Freeway went in. Our bridge is just beyond that one."

The trail takes us right under the freeway. The sound of traffic echoes off the underbelly of the bridge—a steady roar. There's a homeless encampment at the front of the massive pylons of the freeway bridge. I spot two guys sleeping in close-quartered squalor. They don't even stir as we pass.

Ned glances at the encampment without sympathy. "The bums will always lose," he says.

"Shit, that's harsh," I say. "Did Millie Barrington coin that phrase?"

Ned chuckles. "It's a line from my favorite movie—*The Big Lebowski.*"

We trudge up the trail. A big wet spot appears on the back of Ned's sweatshirt. He's struggling.

We finally catch sight of the bridge. Compared to the Pioneer Bridge, the Colorado Street Bridge looks like a priceless antique. From below, the structure appears graceful and old. The concrete arches have the look of Gothic cathedral windows. It's a long, skeletal structure. Beautiful.

We gaze at it silently.

"Look at those arches," Eva says.

Know-it-all Ned chimes right in. Him and his goddamn photographic memory for Wikipedia entries. "Those are called Beaux-Arts arches."

"I have to say," Eva responds, "you could transplant this bridge to Paris and it would fit right in."

"It's long," I say. "Stretches the entire length of the canyon."

"Just shy of fifteen hundred feet," Ned says. I'm shocked he doesn't have the exact footage.

Something about the elegance of the bridge strikes me as feminine. I turn around and point to the Pioneer Bridge we just walked under. "That bridge is an ugly guy. This one," I say turning toward our bridge, "is a pretty woman."

"A strong, powerful woman," Ned adds, "with many secrets."

"What's that building?" Eva asks, pointing beyond the bridge. Framed in one of the wide arches stands a building that is six stories tall. Two wings jut off a central tower with tall arched windows. The tower is topped with a black-and-gold zigzagged dome. If you ignored the neighborhood and just looked at the tower and dome, you'd swear you were staring at a European cathedral.

Whatever it is, the building oozes history. I can feel it all the way down here. "Looks like a hotel out of a Stephen King book," Eva says.

"Used to be. Built in the '20s. Called the Vista del Arroyo Hotel. Owned by the Barrington family, like pretty much everything else in Pasadena. When the depression hit, the Barringtons shut it down. They sold it during World War II to the war department and it became an Army hospital for returning soldiers. Remained a hospital until 1950. Government used it after that. It became a courthouse in the '70s and that's what it is today. One of the few that Kane hasn't been tried in," he adds.

I don't laugh. My feet are killing me. I can feel blisters forming. We march on. I see another building, this one directly under the far end of the Pasadena side of the bridge. "Looks fairly new," I say.

"Condos," Ned says. "Major shitstorm when the building went up. Purists were pissed off."

"They'll build housing anywhere in California," Eva marvels. "Even under a haunted bridge."

We finally reach the bridge. "Those light posts are so huge when you're driving past them. From down here, they look tiny," Eva says, pointing.

Beneath the dead center of the bridge, the natural stream flows into a little dam that drains into a fifty-foot-wide concrete river channel. Ned traces a path in the air with his hands. "That flows the whole way through Pasadena and South Pasadena and eventually dumps into the L.A. River just past Dodger Stadium."

Twenty feet or so above the dam there is another, much smaller bridge. "Look at that," Eva points out. "A tiny bridge under a huge bridge. That's a good vantage point. How do we get up there?"

"We don't," Ned says. "City property. No trespassing. Department of Water and Power uses the small bridge as a perch to monitor floodwaters during big rainstorms."

"There must be some way to get up there," she says.

Ned shakes his head. "Nada. The gate to the small bridge is on South Arroyo Boulevard at the top of the ravine, but it's chain-locked. Forget it. Already checked it out."

We're dwarfed standing next to one of the massive support columns. I look up. Whoa. Ned had his fucking answer ready before I even ask the question.

"About a hundred eighty feet up," Ned says. "We're at the very bottom. We're standing on the spot where most jumpers land. Including that girl who jumped week before last."

We look around. Bad energy pulsates in this sad, silent spot.

I glance up again for a closer look and notice what appear to be platforms jutting out. "Look at those," I say pointing them out one by one, every hundred feet or so. "They look like diving boards."

Ned pulls a folder full of papers out of his duffle bag. "Let's debrief. I have some stuff to show you."

Shit, I'll gladly listen to him drone on if it means resting my feet. We walk to a couple of boulders and sit. Ned passes around articles he printed off the web and starts recapping. "I went to the newspaper archives yesterday at the Pasadena library and wrote down the few confirmed facts I found amongst a sea of bullshit and urban legends on the Internet. Fact: the bridge was built in 1913. Fact: trouble started right away. August 1, 1913. A crew is pouring concrete into the forms when the segment they're working on drops out. They tumble down the side of canyon with all the wreckage landing on top of them. At least one of the men died—John Sullivan. He may or may have not have actually been poured into the concrete on the bridge when the span gave way. Conflicting reports on that. Two more might have died a few days later. I couldn't find the newspaper for August 3. Fact: the first suicide was 1915. After that, the floodgates opened. Can you guess when the most suicides were?"

"Disco era," I say.

No one laughs. My surliness must be rubbing off.

"Great Depression," Eva guesses.

"That's a fact," Ned says, in that teacher-to-student way I hate. "Ninety-five suicides between 1920 and 1937, a dozen in 1935 alone. Sometimes it wanes, but never ceases. There's been one so far this year, three last year. According to my count, we're up to 198 jumpers.

"Any survivors?" I ask.

"Only one. In 1937, a despondent woman went to the bridge, threw her three-year-old daughter over the side, then jumped. Mother was splattered right over there. Cops found the little girl wandering around near her mother's body without a scratch."

"How could that be?" Eva asks.

"A tree limb probably broke her fall," I say, looking up at some of the dense pockets of trees surrounding many of the archways.

Ned continues. "Ghost sightings out the wazoo. There have been lots of paranormal investigations over the years. Full-body apparitions seen on top and below. EVPs. Orbs."

I stand up, walk around the pond, still within speaking distance of Ned and Eva. "Do you feel the air down here," I ask them. "It feels thick. Heavy. There's trapped energy here."

"I feel it, too," Ned says. "When I was scoping out the place, let me show you what I filmed."

Ned takes out the thermal cam. Shows us a strange clip he shot not far from where we are. Red heat signatures pulsate between the beams on the underside of the bridge. Another clip he shot on the regular video camera shows a green mist darting directly in front of the lens. We can hear an audible *whoosh*. "I didn't see or hear that when it happened," he points out. He plays two EVPs from the digital recorder he used. I hold it close to my ear. Very distant and muffled.

I finally perk up. "Those are cries for help," I say.

Eva looks scared, pale. "I feel dizzy," she says. "I don't like it down here."

I take the soul trap out of my backpack and power it up. It hums and vibrates the second it boots. There's definitely something here. I follow the signal and isolate it. It's coming from above us. Way up in a corner nook tucked between beams in the undersurface, just where Ned shot the thermal-cam footage.

"Too far up to target." Ned says.

"How do we get up on top?" I want to know.

Ned gives us two options. Either return to the camper, drive to the Eagle Rock side of the bridge, park, and walk about a quarter mile to stairs leading up to the bridge, or walk from where we are. The walk would be straight uphill—steep in spots—for about a mile to where the bridge starts on the Pasadena side. It's a toss-up. Both options suck when you're wearing leather boots. "Let's just go from here," I moan.

We follow a steep dirt trail to a makeshift stairway of stones from the riverbed. It's not an easy hike. My blisters are raw. Ned points out a locked iron gate with *No Trespassing* signs just off the road. Through the gate I see the access road to the small bridge. Ned's right—locked tight.

We take the sidewalk up South Arroyo Boulevard past the condo building "This is a perfect place to park next time we come," I point out.

Eva notices I'm slowing down. "Your feet aren't enjoying this, are they?" Eva asks.

"No friggin' wonder," Ned says, pointing to my boots.

"You didn't say we'd be mountain climbing," I say, all pissed.

"Quit bitching," Ned says. "I'm not having any fun either."

Just past the condos, the road snakes seriously uphill. The climb has no effect on Eva. Goddamn spring in her step as I limp along with blisters the size of crucifixion wounds and Ned staves off a coronary.

Twenty minutes later, we make it to the top. We have to dodge some fast-moving traffic to finally reach the bridge. "They sure as fuck don't make it easy to get up here and kill yourself," I say.

From below, you can't appreciate how much the bridge curves. But from up here, it's definitely a winding road. "I thought bridges were supposed to be straight," I say.

"Proved too tough to find solid footing in the riverbed," Ned points out. "They ended up planting their way across the canyon one arch at a time. It really is an engineering marvel."

"It is a beautiful view," Eva says. She stops to admire one of the fifty or so cast-iron Victorian lampposts, each with five white light globes.

"I love driving by here at night," Ned says, "when it's all lit up."

We walk the Rose Bowl side first. I stop and grab a bar from the six-foot metal railing atop the concrete ledge. People would have to work to get up and over it. "Millie said there wasn't always a fence here."

"Added in '93, when the bridge reopened after a major overhaul. Before that they had a chain-link fence. After the depression, they even topped it with barbed wire. Still, people found a way to climb over and jump. Imagine how much better this looked in Millie's day—when there was nothing but this original railing." He points to the concrete railing, under which stretches a balustrade of concrete columns the entire length of the bridge on both sides. Looks like a thousand urns lined up all nice and neat.

Every fifty feet or so, we pass little alcoves tucked between the light posts. Benches were built right into the original railings. These were the areas that looked like platforms from below. Ned tells us, "Most people jump from these."

I stop at an alcove. "Wonder if this is where Millie got engaged."

"She said it was in the center," Ned says.

When we reach the Eagle Rock side of the bridge, we walk down a stairwell to an underpass lit by a two dim yellow lights.

A few cars zoom by as we set out to cross the tunnel to another staircase.

Ned turns on his thermal cam, leads the way. We follow a few steps behind. "A couple of paranormal websites say there's an evil spirit in this underpass." As if a ghost responds on cue, the ceiling lights flicker and die. So does Ned's thermal cam. "Fuck," I hear him mumble. "Battery drain."

Eva grabs my arm. I grab the soul trap out of my backpack. It vibrates and hums the entire minute it takes to trek to the opposite stairwell. Then the signal fades and dies.

We climb up to the opposite side of the bridge. "At least we have one hotspot back there to investigate," Ned says. He checks the thermal cam. "It's up and running again. Go figure. Whatever entity drained it is pretty powerful."

We continue to walk and monitor our signals. When we reach the dead center of the bridge, the soul trap goes haywire. "Something's right under our feet," I tell Ned. I jump the barrier on the sidewalk and cross to the other side. Fuck. I check the trap and confirm the readings. "The signal stretches the whole way across. Massive energy. Same spot we targeted from below. I've never seen anything this immense."

Ned looks through the bars of the railing. "How can we get under here?" he asks.

"You tell me."

Eva chimes in. "You might be able to rappel down."

"I don't know shit about rappelling," I say.

"I do," Eva says. "I know a lot about it."

"No way," I tell her. "Too much traffic up here. Someone would call 911 in ten seconds if they saw anyone up on that railing."

"I can't get arrested again," I say.

I look over the edge. "If we're going to get under the bridge, it has to be from below, late at night. No one will see us down there in the dark."

"Let me noodle it," Ned says.

We walk the rest of the way across the bridge. The trap is silent. "Whatever it is," I recap, "is big and clustered in that one spot back there."

"I'll figure something out," Ned assures me.

"I can help," Eva says. "I've done a lot of climbing."

I've mentally prepared my feet for further torture, when Ned says enough's enough and calls a cab to take us back to the Rose Bowl parking lot. "My treat," he assures us.

While we're waiting, I just have to ask, "Are you really this big of a lazy ass?"

He stands tall. "Yes, I am."

A few minutes later, a cab picks us up at the corner of Colorado and Orange Grove. Cab driver is pissed off he's only taking us a couple of miles. On the ride back, my phone rings, interrupting a conversation Ned and Eva are having about rock-climbing gear.

It's Bo. "Mandatory band meeting at five PM," he announces.

"Where?"

"The Rainbow."

"What's it about?"

"Be there to find out," he says.

Six

My mind races in the car. Definitely news. But good or bad?

Got a guitar riff on the brain. Trying to place it. Maybe the Ramones or the Clash. It's playing over and over again in my head, driving me nuts.

I thought for sure I'd have time to swing by my apartment before the meeting, but double whammy: major accident meets early rush-hour traffic. The 101 is wall-to-wall. Head straight to the Rainbow.

I walk past the floor-to-ceiling pictures—forty years of massive, nonstop partying. I'm proud. My picture's in there somewhere—taken last Halloween. After that shiteous drive, I need a drink. I catch sight of Drexel and Jay sitting in the corner booth in the dining room. Screw it. I'm still a few minutes early. I pretend like I don't see them and hang a right into the bar.

The Rainbow is a rock-and-roll museum. The Hard Rock Cafe, only real. Gold and Platinum records hang in places of honor. It's packed with floor to ceiling memorabilia—autographed group photos, guitars, and drum heads. It covers the walls in the bar and the dining room. There's a club upstairs. We've played there a half-dozen times. But it's not open this early. We'll be stuck in the main dining room with the tourists.

The downstairs bar is a cavern—a dark, cramped, musical mecca faintly lit by a plasma TV, an aquarium that stretches the length of the back wall, Christmas lights, vintage cigarette machine (fully functional), and the glow from a pair of Pac-Man machines. The whole place smells like the inside of an old guitar case.

The barstools are all occupied, including the one Troy has his ass planted on. Just the way he grips his beer bottle, looks at me, and says, "Hey, bro," tells me he's been here all afternoon. I elbow my way next to him and order a shot and beer.

I feel a slap on my back. Bo and Ira Bowersock are standing behind me. Shit, this is serious. "Do follow," Bo says.

Troy and I trail Bo and Ira to the shadowy dining room—another seriously red place. Red curved booths, red tablecloths, red carpet, red candleholders, red light fixtures above every booth. Add the fireplace, front and center, and it feels like the devil's private banquet hall.

We huddle in the back booth—the same table where John Belushi ate his last meal. I get stuck sitting next to Troy. He's been on a bender. Liquor oozes from his pores. Smells like Lindsay Lohan's water bottle. Jay drinks coffee; Drexel, a Red Bull. Bo and Ira order scotch.

We order a shitload of bar food—one notch above a truck-stop diner. Greasy fried stuff. Big portions. Decent pizza. A spaghetti-and-meatballs kind of place.

Uncomfortable small talk commences. Drexel won't take his Ray Bans off. Douche bag.

A threesome of girls—a blonde, a brunette, and an Asian—walk in. Two of them wear shamelessly short dresses and heels. The brunette has skinny jeans and a see-through blouse under which she sports an impressively filled black lace bra. Troy nudges me. I've seen them before, at a gig we played at the Troubador. They insist on taking the booth next to ours.

This is the buzz.

Food arrives and we feast. Ira avoids shoptalk while we're chowing. He wears a hell of a poker face. Bo doesn't force the issue. We talk about movies and TV shows. Ira's subtly getting more of our back stories, pulling information out of us.

"Why do you want this?" he asks each one of us.

Bo's first. Glad I'm not. "I want to take a band to the top. I've taken more than a few pretty far, but I want that feeling."

Drexel's turn. "Sex, money, and rock and roll."

"Spoken like a true rock star. But no drugs?" Ira asks him.

"Clean and sober," Drexel boasts.

"Good. Smart."

Troy's turn. He points at Drexel. "Ditto on everything he wants, but throw in the drugs for me." We all laugh. Ira doesn't know Troy's not kidding.

Jay has the most articulate response. "I love music. I want to spend my life doing something I love." Good answer. Can tell Ira likes it.

All eyes on me. Rack my brain. How do I sum it up? A few nervous uhms, then my mind flashes back to when I was thirteen or fourteen. "There was a sign on the wall of the music room when I was in eighth grade. A quote from Plato. '*Music gives soul to the universe, wings to the mind, flight to the imagination, and life to everything.*' That's how I feel when I'm playing." Ira nods. He knows the quote. A look in his eyes says he lives the quote.

Ira's ready to move on, but Bo nods at him, says, "Your turn."

"I want to get back to my roots," Ira says. "I've accomplished a lot. Success. Money. But somewhere along the line, I think I lost myself."

Honesty? Wow.

After we've stuffed our faces like pigs at a trough, Ira finally gets down to business. "You're probably wondering why I'm here."

We brace ourselves.

"Bottom line, I want to sign you."

We breathe a collective sigh.

"You're good," he says. "I think, with some direction, you could be great. That's as much ass kissing as I'm going to do, so if you need more, we're probably not a good fit."

"Our egos are in check," Bo assures him.

Ira breaks eye contact, glances down. Uh-oh. "I want a one-week exclusive option," he says.

Drexel sighs. "What does that mean?" he asks, like a bratty kid.

"It means I wire twenty-five K to your account right now and you allow me to close my financing and put this deal in place. A dozen investors have bought in and it's all on schedule, but I won't bullshit you. Sometimes crazy shit goes down in the eleventh hour. I need a few more days."

If Bo's disappointed, he's hiding it well. "So, if after seven days, you fall short . . ."

"You keep the twenty-five grand and we start over or you move on. And if all goes according to plan, we'll sign papers and the twenty-five grand will roll into your advance."

Bo look at us, then at Ira. "I'll have to discuss it with the band."

"Of course," Ira says. "A couple of issues I want to get on the table and I'll be off."

Issues? Uh-oh.

"Your name," Ira says first. "Sounds a little New Agey for your sound."

We never discussed beforehand who would do the speaking. Just assumed it would be Bo. But Drexel gets defensive and defends the name. "Nothing New Agey about it. It's Hollywood. When Jay and I met, I was living in a guest house on Astral Drive. Jay was living in a dump on Fountain."

Ira rolls it around. "That's a good story," he says. "Press likes anecdotes like that." Gives it some silent thought. "Let me think about it."

"That's the name of my band," Drexel insists. He shakes his head. Sarcastic little chuckle. Fuck. He's gonna blow it.

Ira lets it roll off, shoots Drexel a slick little smile. "Gonna tell me who your father is?"

Drexel smirks back. "You've been reading too many websites."

"Good," Ira says. "Don't tell anyone. The mystery . . . that'll play."

Drexel takes it as a compliment. The tension eases.

"What else?" Bo asks.

Ira looks right at me. "You need another guitar."

No one protests. "Kane's a great lead." I'll take that compliment to the bank. "But you need a rhythm guitar," Ira continues. "And Jay's bass is too distorted. He needs to play one instrument, not a hybrid of two."

"I see wisdom in that observation," Bo says. What an ass kisser.

"Harmonies," Ira says next. "I want to hear them in these songs. But they're not there." Fair enough. "We need a voice—or voices—to wrap themselves around Drexel's amazing vocals." He phrases it just right. "Can't you hear it?"

"Maybe," Drexel says. Ira's good. Disarmed Drexel the same instant he fired a shot.

Ira directs the next one right at Drexel and Jay. "The lyrics."

Porcupine spikes go up. "What about the lyrics?" Drexel snaps.

"They're good," Ira assures him. "But they're not great."

More tension. Bo shoots Drexel a *shut the fuck up* look. "That's your opinion," Drexel says. "EMI thinks differently."

Ira smiles. "I'll bet they do." He knows that EMI passed. "Do you write together—as a group?" Ira asks.

"Jay and I write everything," Drexel says.

"I suggest opening the process up. Write together. Write individually. Write what you know and what you're feeling. Don't write what you think entitled kids on the Sunset Strip want to hear. You're shortchanging yourselves . . . and your audience. You can express any thought, any worry, any dream, any emotion you're feeling in a four-minute song. Challenge yourselves."

"You make it sound like we suck," Drexel says.

Ira breathes in deep, exhales hard, looks like a dad losing

patience with his three-year-old. "Come on, Drexel. You're sitting here with me. We're talking a deal. Don't make me baby you."

Drexel stares at him blankly.

Ira takes out his BlackBerry. "What's your schedule?"

"Playing the Whisky Friday night," Bo says. "Maybe Club Spaceland in two weeks, but that's not final."

"Good. Don't commit to anything else yet. I want a big launch. A lot of hype. So do you."

Drexel perks up.

"That's it, gentlemen," Ira says. "Thanks for hearing me out. Call me with your decision." He shakes our hands and is out the door fast.

Pitchers of beer arrive, courtesy of the girls next door.

Bo stares at us before speaking. I can read his mind—*Oh shit.* He wanted a deal tonight. Despite the chicks eye-fucking us from the next table, there's tension in the air.

"We should go back to EMI," Drexel tells Bo.

"They passed," Bo says.

"Then make them un-pass," Drexel demands. "You work for us. I want EMI."

Bo snaps. Whisper-yells, "Well, EMI doesn't want you!" Silence hangs heavy. There's palpable anger between us that shouldn't be there. We're on the verge of a deal. We're still alive. Why does it feel like doomsday?

It's Drexel. It's always him. He sucks the life out of everything. Creates stress. Did I mention I pretty much hate everyone? Especially my backstabbing, soulless prick of a singer.

"I told you before—EMI wasn't right for us," Bo continues. "We're better off with Ira's start-up. I say we take the option. That's if he'll still sign us . . . after your fucking shitty attitude. So, let's put it to a vote, now so I can call him back."

"No," Drexel says. "We're better than a start-up."

"This guy's a heavyweight," Jay says. "I say we take the twenty-five K," Jay says. Drexel looks surprised. "What's a week?"

"Here, here," Troy says.

I refill my mug and chime in. "I think Ira's the real deal," I say. "I vote yes."

"Done," Bo says. "I'll call him now."

Drexel finally takes off the Ray-Bans, points them at me like he's aiming a revolver. Then he fires, point-blank: "You're work for hire. It doesn't matter what you think."

That stings, but I pretend it doesn't.

"You only have a ten-percent stake, and you're lucky we gave you that. Don't fucking forget where you sit on the totem pole."

I'm ready to take down Eddie Van Halen's guitar off the wall and use it to cave in his skull. Maybe that's what he's trying to do—bait me so I snap, then fire me. But I've wrecked my life before and I'm not gonna do it again. Despite every fiber of my being itching to fight, I swallow Drexel's shit. I even try to make light of it by saying, "His majesty has spoken."

Drexel laughs. "Lighten up, dude. Go smooth out your solos."

Idiot. My voice cracks. "Go find a mirror to stare into."

Silence. The girls next door put down their appletinis and crane their necks to see if we're going to fight.

"Enough," Bo says. I keep my eyes locked on Drexel. "Be at the Whisky by six PM, gentlemen. Arrive early. Arrive sober. And be ready to play your asses off in the cathedral of rock."

I bolt from the table. I need alcohol—now. I head back to the bar, order a double Jameson, knock it down, and order another. Hits me hard and fast. I climb the stairs to the men's room. It ought to be condemned. Gang tags and band stickers all over the walls and stall doors. The only thing cool about it is that every rock star has pissed here at one time or another.

Someone sneaks up on me and hits me in the back while I'm whizzing. Drexel. "What are you up to now?" he asks.

"I'm just standing here holding my dick thinking about how much it reminds me of you."

He laughs. "Don't get all bent out of shape. All good bands have internal drama."

"You're an asshole," I tell him. I'll play nice around the others, but one on one, I'm through biting my tongue.

He checks himself out in the mirror. "I know," he says. "And I don't apologize for it."

Drexel follows me back to the bar. My drink is waiting. Down the hatch. "Mmmm, that tastes good," I say, rubbing it in. Dick move.

"Jay had to bolt. You want to hang out?" Drexel asks.

I'd rather have a root canal. Same time, wouldn't mind straightening things out with him before it gets worse. "What do you have in mind? Don't say an AA meeting."

Drexel nods toward the dining room. "Those chicks want to take us out. Come on—bounce with us. We'll have fun. Tear it up."

"One more drink," I say. Actually two more drinks. Another double. Just flew past a nice buzz and crash-landed in Drunskville.

It's all a blur.

We're piled into a white Escalade. I can't even tell what direction we're headed. Drexel and I dub them the Triplets of Melrose. The driver is Kinsey. Cool name. Tall blonde, supermodel face. The brunette, Natalie, stands, head popped out of the sun roof. She's screaming, "Sayonara, motherfuckers!" over and over. I'm in a leather captain's seat right behind her, staring at her perfect ass. Drexel's in the third row nailing the Asian chick—Nikki, I think she said her name was. USC student. She's moaning. Sounds like a Vietnamese cathouse in here.

Natalie plops down in the seat next to me. Says she's twenty-one. Already had a boob job. Nursing student by day, stripper at Crazy Girls by night. She hands me a bottle of Grey Goose and a bong. Monster hit. Killer weed. Check out her prescription bottle.

Weed's called Grape Ape. She tells me I'm a better guitar player than John Mayer and goes down on me. Another monster hit. I chug vodka.

I'm fucked up something fierce.

While the Triplets of Melrose load up on top-shelf vodka at Highland Liquor, I puke in the parking lot. Applause from pedestrians walking by. Drexel runs over, hands me a Red Bull and two blue pills.

"Man up," he says.

"Pills? I thought you were clean."

"Prescription meds," he snaps. "Cialis." Rings a bell. Too fucked up to think clearly. "It's boner juice," he says.

"I don't need these. I hope you don't."

"Take them. You're fucked up bad," he says. "If you can't get it up, you'll embarrass the band."

Then it hits me. He's sober. He's behaving like Bacchus with a crystal-clear mind. No excuses. Cool. Newfound respect for the lad. Grab the pills out of his hand and wash them down with a 40-ounce Bud I yank out of the cooler. Scarf down two Slim Jims. Tell the girls to pay. Liquor-mart sustenance.

We're in Kinsey's high-rise condo on Alta Loma. Can see the Hollywood Bowl from the hot tub on the sixteenth-floor balcony. Cialis rules. Pound Natalie from behind while she and Nikki go at it. We switch it up. I'm as hard as a bust of Shakespeare, but so fucked up I have no sensation in my action zone. Like someone shot my junk with Novocain. Away I pound, though, like a jackhammer stuck on high. It gets pointless after a while. Natalie gets tired, calls time-out, so I crawl out of the hot tub. Dry off, wrap a towel around me and search for the bathroom. Still pointing due north. Fucking comical.

The hallway bathroom is locked, so I peek in the master bedroom before throwing open the door. Kinsey is on all fours. Drexel snorts an eight-inch line of coke off her ass.

Smile, you're on *Candid Camera*.

Duck straight out, but he knows that I know. It's an image that'll still be there even after my head lands back on my shoulders in the morning. Twelve-steps, my ass. Twelve steps maybe, but not in a straight line.

I head back to the balcony. Kinsey comes out, strips, and jumps in the hot tub with me. Good Lord—legs like stilts. She's cool—does most of the talking. We both love Clapton. She loves *Ghost Hunters* and *Paranormal State*. I laugh. She knows a few Hollywood ghost stories. We hit it off. I like her best. We talk a lot faster after we knock off an eight-ball of coke. The condo is hers, a gift from her father—an Oscar-winning producer with an office on the Warner Brothers lot. Name sounds familiar, but I forget it the second I hear it.

She tells me how much she loves Astral Fountain. Thinks we're gonna hit it big and wants to come along for the ride. She tells me I can crash at her place—anytime, as long as I want. I thank her—tell her I live just down the street. "Where?" she wants to know.

"Wrong side of the tracks," is all I divulge. I climb out of the hot tub for a minute to grab an ice bucket, apologize for my persistent woodrow. Says she doesn't mind at all then jumps all over it.

Yep, I like her best.

When I wake up on a patio sofa, the sun is up. I get dressed and check on Drexel. He's snoring in the bedroom, Nikki and Natalie under each arm. I'm out the door without notice. Less than a mile to my place.

I jump in the shower and wash away my sins. Drink a bottle of grape Pedialyte, a gallon of water. Swallow three Tylenol. Turn my phone off. Set my alarm clock for 4 PM and drop down on my bed like a boxer hitting the canvas. My heart races—all that coke.

Assessment: I'm alive. That's good.

Feel like the poster boy for that TV commercial warning: *if you have an erection that lasts for more than four hours . . .*

Let there be no doubt—I'm in the right profession.

Seven

Other than getting up twice to piss, I sleep hard. Wake up just before sunset when my phone rings. Blocked number. I answer anyway and hear, "Hold please for Mrs. Barrington."

A few seconds later Millie greets me with a bright and cheery "Good evening, Kane." More like good morning. "So tell me about your progress," she says.

I clear my throat, hack some poison out of my lungs, and tell her—not all that coherently—that we've scoped out the bridge, deemed it haunted, and are formulating a plan.

Millie is none too pleased. "Really, I expected some more action on your part," she says, like a grannie bitching out a grocery store clerk. "I'm not a very patient woman."

"Well, you'll have to be, Mrs. Barrington," I say, annoyed and hung over. "This is major. The bridge is teeming with supernatural energy. We'll get the job done, but it may take some time."

"At my age, time has become a very scarce commodity."

"Duly noted," I say.

"What's this I hear about you being in a band?" she asks.

Whoa. "How did you know that?"

"You don't think I'd pay someone a small fortune without learning more about him," Millie says with a knowing chuckle. "I do hope your musical aspirations don't interfere with our business arrangement?"

"They won't," I tell her.

"So you're a guitar player?" she asks.

"Yep."

"Like my dear boy Eddie Van Halen?"

Can't believe what I'm hearing. Grumpy grannie knows Van Halen? "Don't tell me you're a fan," I say.

"Hardly," Millie says with a laugh. "But Eddie and his brother Alex and that wild singer in the tight pants and the other one whose name escapes me—they're all Pasadena-raised. I couldn't help but take an interest in them. And I gave them a helping hand along the way."

"No kidding?" The alarm bells go off. What is she getting at?

There's a long pause before Millie says, "Maybe I can help pry a few doors open for you—after you help me, that is."

"I'll be in touch," I tell her.

"Try not to keep me waiting," she's says all phony friendly before hanging up.

"Goddamnit, I get the point," I shout to myself. The call rattles me. The old bitty applies pressure, then dangles a carrot. She's going to be a pain in my ass.

My night is off to a shitty start and it gets even shittier when I realize there are three voice messages from Ned. Call him back. Three rings, then, "What? I'm knee-deep in research."

"You called me."

"Millie Barrington's had quite the life. Just started to dig into the stuff you sent me."

"I just got off the phone with her," I tell Ned. "I want to move on this fast."

"Me, too," Ned says. "I've been noodling it with Eva. We came up with a way to get you under the bridge."

"Tell me." Shit. Big mistake. He'll babble for an hour. Can't deal with it right now. "You know what, scratch that, whatever it is, I trust you."

"Good," Ned says. "It involves danger and peril. So when do you want to go?"

The sooner the better. I want that money. Strike that—I need that money. "Tonight."

"I'm game. Did you talk to Eva about it?"

"Nah. You call her," I tell him. No way can I talk to her after I just banged three groupies.

"What if she can't go?" he asks.

"Make up a line of bullshit—tell her the electromagnetic fields are favorable tonight or something. Let's just get on with it and get paid."

"Call you back in five."

I'm trying to gag down a bowl of Lucky Charms when Ned calls back.

"We're on," he says. "But she can't be there until eleven."

"Okay."

"We need to prep you. Might take an hour or two. I scouted around for a place where the camper won't attract attention. There's a parking lot behind a little restaurant called the Stoney Point Grill. It's about a half mile short of the bridge on Colorado, just past Eagle Rock. There's a little nook between the restaurant and the parking lot. I'll be parked there."

By one AM, we've downed two pots of coffee and Ned and Eva have walked me through the process of top-rope climbing. Showed me a 400-foot rope. Showed me the harness I'll be wearing when they elevate me a 150 feet up underneath the bridge. I don't need coffee. I need drugs, booze, friggin' laughing gas.

They don't know it yet, but I can't do this. I hate heights. I've been having a recurring dream of falling off a bridge since I was a kid. While they argue about how to best equalize the belay anchors, I sweat like a bastard.

Eva studies pictures from on top of the bridge. "We have to use these little concrete urn things for support," she points out to Ned. "We can create a perfect three-point anchor system and equalize it so his weight is evenly distributed. It'll make it easier to lift and lower him."

"I don't know," Ned argues. "I think it'll work better if we tie off the anchor knots on the metal railing."

"Just trust me," Eva snaps. "I know how to do this."

"I don't know," Ned says, all doubtful.

Her cheeks flush. "I've climbed Point Dume and Joshua Tree. Where have you climbed?"

"I'm just saying—"

"No, Ned, I'm saying, so shut up and listen for once. I actually know what I'm talking about. It's not something I just read about on Wikipedia. It's one of my hobbies. You've just read about it over the last couple of days."

Ned doesn't like the scolding. "This is Kane's life we're talking about!"

"You don't think I know that?" Eva shouts. "Jesus Christ!"

"Fine," Ned barks. Then he shuts up. An all-time first.

I'm dumbfounded. "You're my hero," I tell Eva.

Figuring everyone needs to calm down, I say, "I need some air." On my way out, I tell them, "Just figure it out. I'm not good with heights. Tell me what to do when the time comes. The more I know now, the more chance I'll fuck it up, so give it to me in small doses, okay?"

They nod.

I take a walk around the block. It's a chilly night. I'm nervous. Queasy. When I check back in, Ned and Eva are practicing tying off knots on the camper's kitchenette table legs. Tensions have eased. They're playing well together. Ned is actually listening. When Eva starts talking about carabiners, I duck out again.

They call me in a few minutes later. They're ready. The plan: I'll drive. Drop them off on top of the bridge. They'll set up the anchor system and drop the rope down from the bridge to the ground. Figure it'll take them less than five minutes. When the prep work's done, I'll double back and pick them up.

"Doesn't someone have to be with the ropes on top?" I ask.

"No—it'll all be secure," Eva promises.

We drive to the condo parking lot under the Pasadena side of the bridge and head down the ravine trail to the dry riverbed beneath the bridge.

3:20 AM.

We throw the camper in park in the underpass by the stairs. Ned and Eva dart out. I drive up the steep hill on South Arroyo Boulevard, hang a right onto Orange Grove, and another onto the bridge. Ned and Eva wave me past. Not ready yet.

Another full loop. This time I get a thumbs-up.

"We're good?" I ask.

"Ready," Eva says.

I pull into the parking lot, kill the engine and lights, and dig my lucky necklace out of my backpack, quietly take a few deep breaths, and put it on. I feel calmer.

Ten minutes later, we're under the bridge, flashlights in hand. Eva spots the rope. Yanks on it with all her weight. "Solid," she says. Must look like I'm about to shit my pants when I look up because Eva says, "You're gonna be okay. We have three anchors up there combining to form a single, equalized anchor. I went way overboard." Eva secures the rope to the harness and hands me a helmet. "Even if we both let go of the rope, the anchor systems and belay loops are designed to prevent you from falling. You'd fall a little, then hang. But that won't happen, so don't worry about it."

"Better not," I tell her.

Eva helps me step into the harness and secures it around my waist. Ned fastens the buckles around my legs. "Want me to tickle your balls while I'm at it?" he asks.

"No, but Eva can." She doesn't laugh.

"Now what?" I ask.

"We hoist you up," Ned answers as he hands me the soul trap. "We're called the belayers."

Eva rolls her eyes. "Jesus," she mutters. "You're Wikinsufferable."

"What do you weigh?" Ned asks me.

"One eighty-five, give or take," I say.

"You're kidding," he says. "I weighed that in the sixth grade," Ned says. He sizes me up. "My sciatic nerve's gonna love this," he bitches.

Voices mutter. It's pitch-black. No moon. We hear whispers. Eva grabs my hand and squeezes. Jesus, don't be the cops.

"Who's there?" Ned whisper-shouts.

Two figures emerge from the darkness. Homeless guys. We walked past their encampment the first time we visited the bridge. They approach slowly. One of them is Hispanic and short, late thirties. Long hair and salt-and-pepper goatee. The other is midfifties, at least six and a half feet, tall and skinny like one of the light posts up on top. A scary-looking giant in a filthy Lakers cap. We scan them for weapons, but their hands are empty. They're just curious.

"Beat it," Ned orders.

"What are you doing?" the short one asks, all serious.

The skinny one eyes up the soul trap in my hands, the climbing harness. "That's a big-ass barrel on that gun. You a bunch of terrorists?"

"We're S.W.A.T. team members," Ned says. "We're conducting training exercises."

The short one points to Ned's midsection, "Not with a gut like that."

Ned doesn't miss a beat. "I'm the brigade commander," he says. "My actual swatting days are about twenty years in the rearview mirror."

Ned eyes up the two guys and nods at me. "Horsepower," he whispers. Says to them, "You guys wanna help?"

"Do what?"

"Help us pull on this rope, that's all," Ned says. "Five minutes, tops."

"What do we get?" the tall one wants to know.

"What do you want?" Ned asks.

"Twenty bucks a man," the short one says. "And a ride to 7-Eleven."

"Done," Ned says. "What are your names?"

"This is Mike. I'm Tall Kevin," the beanpole says.

Ned winks at me. "Not to be confused with Short Kevin." He claps his hands. "All right, gentlemen, just remember to pull your weight."

They grab handfuls of rope along with Eva and Ned, who don gloves. I pull Eva close, whisper in her ear. "Keep a close eye on these guys. And don't let go of the rope."

"I won't," she promises. "Don't look down." She points skyward. "You may rock a little up there. Don't freak. You're secure."

Eva cracks a couple of glow sticks and drops them on the ground. Mike and Tall Kevin look eerie in the green glow. "Let's do it," I order. I put on the gloves Eva hands me, grab the rope above my head, and squeeze. It dawns on me: My life is in the hands of a woman who can't stand me, two loons, and Ned. Make that three loons. Jesus.

"On the count of three," Ned says. "One . . . two . . . three . . ."

They pull. My feet are off the ground. Twenty feet up, I'm in complete darkness. Clutch the soul trap and rope. Scared shitless. So dark, all I can see is two tiny slivers of green light. I focus my gaze on a lamppost up top. I'm inching toward it.

"Looking good," Ned shouts up. "You're halfway there."

The lamppost gets bigger, brighter. A stiff breeze kicks up. I sway. Clutch the rope tighter. Heart races.

Thirty feet from the top, at the base of an arch, my ascent stops. Can't believe I'm a 150 fucking feet in the air. "Are you in range?" Ned shouts.

I steady myself. With one hand on the rope, I throw the switch on the trap. It hums to life, vibrates with such force it nearly flies out of my hand. The monitor on the butt end strobes. Never saw a signal this strong. Can't lock in on a single target. It's either malfunctioning or there are more targets than it can process. An unseen force pulls the barrel in all directions. I feel light-headed. Vertigo. Gonna drop the trap. Panic. Gonna fall. Living my recurring nightmare. Can't catch my breath.

Get a grip. Do this.

I let go of the rope, dangling in mid-air, and grab the trap with both hands. I steady the barrel, aiming at a bright, strong pulsating ball of energy at the very bottom of the cluster. I squeeze the trigger. Wall of sound blasts off the underside of the bridge and echoes off the ravine walls and down the riverbed.

I've definitely trapped something. "Get me down!" I shout.

I clutch the trap to my chest and grab the rope. Feel myself being lowered. Lock eyes on the lamppost and watch it shrink. Finally, hands around my waist, earth beneath my feet. Hallefuckin-lujah.

Can't shed the harness fast enough. "I aimed at something bright at the bottom of the energy mass. I've got something in the trap," I tell them. "Let's get out of here. Pay those guys."

Ned looks annoyed as he hands each bum a twenty.

We're on the move. Eva and Ned are right behind me. "What about our deal?" Tall Kevin asks.

I stop. "What?"

"7-Eleven," he says.

Ned looks at me. "We've got to get out of here. We made a big racket."

I wave the bums over. "A deal's a deal."

Ned fires me a dirty look.

"We don't need enemies down here," I point out. "And I need all the good karma I can get."

Mike stays put. "I'm in the mood for a good biography. Gonna use my cash at Vroman's Bookstore," he says.

The rest of us hike up the steep path to the top of the ravine, then power walk up South Arroyo Boulevard to the camper. I drop off Eva and Ned on top of the bridge to get the climbing gear.

I drive Tall Kevin to 7-Eleven and watch him blow his twenty on malt liquor, cigarettes, and snack cakes. He can't decide between *Hustler* and *Barely Legal*. I chip in so he can buy both. Merry fuckin' Christmas.

On the ride back, Tall Kevin's so happy he dances in the passenger seat. "How'd you end up under a bridge?" I ask him.

He tears open the pack of Ho Hos. "I don't even remember," he says. "I think it was the voice that told me to come here."

"What voice?" I look at him but he won't make eye contact.

"It talks to me sometimes."

"Male or female."

"Female."

"Happy or sad?"

"Neither. More like angry. She doesn't like me."

"Where are you from?"

"Tempe, Arizona. That was another life ago." Ho Hos gone in two bites. "I played basketball for the Sun Devils—no shit."

"You went to college?"

"Graduated with honors." He laughs. "I know, man. Fuckin' trippy. I was a gym teacher at Coolidge Elementary. I was married. Had a daughter."

"What happened?"

Out of nowhere, he gets angry, yells at me, "Don't ask me! Ask the voice."

We drive the rest of the way without a word. He just hums. I give him an extra ten bucks, drop him off at the top of the ravine, then loop back to where Eva and Ned are waiting.

I ease back into the little parking lot behind the Stoney Point Grill at 4:20 AM. Ned wants to call it a night. I want to go in the trap now. "But we're all beat," he moans.

"Make another pot of coffee while you get me wired up. I'm ready now."

While Ned powers up the equipment, Eva helps place the electrodes and fasten the NuMag helmet. Ned sends the electrical current. It's smooth. As inviting as an electric blanket in an igloo. It takes all of my will and focus to fight off sleep during my breathing routine. Doze off a couple times, but Ned jolts me back with hand claps and hollers. Eva steps up on the ladder, holds my hand, and squeezes when she sees me falling asleep.

There's a split second where I think I'm dreaming. Turns out I'm journeying. My field of vision goes purple. I hear that familiar electronic hum.

When I open my eyes and focus, I see something I've never seen in the trap before and freeze. Get such a scare, I let out a "Whoa!"

Do I approach or run?

Eight

I approach cautiously. In the dim light, it looks like a nude, bald, featureless mannequin. I move closer. It's moving. It's a human body in a skin-tight, head-to-toe gray bodysuit with thin black pinstripes. No holes for eyes or mouth.

I inch forward for a closer look. Female curves. It's a she.

A foot away, she senses me and cowers. Reaches out blindly, shakily. I reach out and touch her head, a gentle pat of reassurance. The bodysuit feels rubbery and ice cold. I see mouth movement under the fabric. It looks like she's talking, but I can't hear a sound. She clutches my arm. I get a sturdy grip on her wrist and yank the rubbery fabric until it rips. I peel the fabric away, exposing a hand. Black wristband with silver studs. Black nail polish.

I grip and tear the material from around her mouth. There's a huge gasp, then, "Get me out of here."

"Breathe deep," I tell her. "I'll work on getting you free."

She hyperventilates. Panics. Digs her nails into my arm and breaks the skin.

"Calm down. Relax," I say, sending out peaceful vibes. "Everything will be all right. Think of something nice. Hum me a song while I get you out of this suit."

She hums. Muffled at first, then clearer, louder. She begins to breathe easier. I recognize the tune. "The Middle." I tear away the material below her waist, freeing her legs. I see a pair of faded jeans, checkered Vans, and a dolphin tatt on her ankle. "You can't hum anything better than 'Jimmy Eat World'?"

She gives me the finger. I tear the rest of the bodysuit off. She's a teenager. Big green eyes. Emo hairdo—black with red streaks. Heavy black eyeshadow. Red lipstick. Nose stud. Her black hoodie that says: *This is not a photo opportunity.* She wears a rope necklace with a pewter medallion. The imagery on the medallion rings a bell: an all-seeing eye, dove, burning chalice. An occult symbol. It'll come to me.

She coughs up thick phlegm, chokes out, "Who are you?"

I tell her.

She blinks, squints. Her eyes focus on my Led Zeppelin tee, the one with the cloaked hermit. She stares at it with a look of relief and a little knowing smile. What's that about?

I lead her to the table. We size each other up.

She speaks first. "Where are we?"

"Somewhere between life and death."

"I'm dead?"

"Yeah."

"And you're dead?"

"Not exactly." Give her a quick explanation of the trap. Tell her we don't have time to get into details. "Who are you?"

"Anna Burrows."

"You're Anna Burrows?"

She looks surprised. "How do you know me?"

"I read about you in the newspaper. You jumped off the Colorado Street Bridge a couple of weeks ago."

"How did I end up trapped in that suit?" she asks.

"You mean you don't know?"

"No. The last thing I remember was climbing up and grabbing one of the lampposts on the bridge. I remember staring up at the dome of that big building across the way. Then I jumped. It was like I jumped off the high dive into a pool or something. Didn't hurt. Felt like someone fished me out of the bottom of a pitch-black lake. I couldn't see or hear shit. After that, I guess I passed out. And woke up in here."

"Did you hear anyone? Anything?"

"No."

"See anyone?"

"No. But, sometimes, I kind of woke up for a second or two. There were definitely other people around me."

The energy cluster under the bridge—it must be made up of individual souls. Anna's soul must have attached itself at the bottom.

"Are you taking me to J.D.?" she asks.

"Who's J.D.?"

"My boyfriend."

"Why would I be taking you to him?"

"Because he did it, too."

"Did what?"

"Offed himself. We had a pact. We'd do it separately, then meet up here on the other side."

A suicide pact. Stupid-ass kids pissing away their lives.

"Where's J.D.?" she asks.

"I don't know."

She gives me a worried look. "He was like so sure we were going to meet right up."

"What about your parents?" I ask her.

"My dad's dead," she says. "Is he here?" Pick up a hint of anticipation.

"No," I tell her.

She looks disappointed. "Figures," she says, rolling her eyes. "Fucktard."

"You didn't get along?"

"No, we got along all right."

"Then why is he a . . . ?" Can't bring myself to say fucktard.

"'Cause he dropped dead running the L.A. Marathon. I mean, what kind of lame-ass tool runs twenty-six miles?"

"What about your mother?"

"I hate her."

"Hate?"

"Yes. *Hate* her," she insists. "I don't use that word lightly, though I use it a lot. I hate everyone. I hate my friends. I hate school. I hate pretty much everything."

A kindred spirit.

"Is that why you jumped?"

"Maybe a little. But not really. I jumped for J.D."

"Were you depressed?"

"Sure. Who's not? It's all a big fucking nothing. But I told you—it was me and J.D., makin' our statement."

I really don't want to hear the fucktard answer, but I still have to ask, "What's your statement?"

She gets pissy, like it's so obvious. "That we figured it out. That we're better than everyone. That we piss on the rules. That no one tells us what to do. That we do what we will!"

It's the way she says "we will"—spitting venom and false courage. Like a cymbal crash. Her medallion. That crest. I remember now. O.T.O. Ordo Templi Orientis. A secret society founded by Aleister Crowley in the early part of the twentieth century. No wonder she looked relieved when she saw my Zeppelin shirt. Led Zeppelin was grounded in Crowleyism.

Don't even get me started about Aleister Crowley. Drug addict, anarchist, sex fiend, and major practitioner of the occult. A lot of people claim he was an outright Satanist. Seeing as he referred to himself as The Beast, the number 666, and the wickedest man in the world, and that there are volumes of quotes in which he trashes any and all religions, they might be right.

I got curious about Crowley when I was seventeen or eighteen—about Anna's age. Hit me hard, my little dark phase. It was all seductive to a kid like me. It started with Crowley's fat mug on the *Sergeant Pepper* cover. Then I read a Jimmy Page interview in *Guitar Player* magazine. Jimmy bought Crowley's castle in Scotland. Like a million other wannabe guitar heroes, I figured if it worked for Jimmy, it might work for me. Started reading books, but stopped short of conducting rituals. Knowing what I know today, I'm glad I did. Those books used to pulse with dark energy. Always felt a little sick when I held them. Tossed them all by the time I dropped out of high school and moved to L.A.

Now my mind's racing in all kinds of directions. The fact that Crowley's crystal goblet showed up on my doorstep last year still weirds me out. My buddy Seamus got it from somewhere in Ireland. Sometimes I think I should have just tossed it. I'm not entirely comfortable owning something that belonged to Crowley. But the goblet powers the IVeR like nothing I've ever seen. It works, so I'm not messing with a good thing.

My assessment of Mr. Crowley: though definitely dark and depraved, he probably wasn't the Antichrist he claimed to be. Wasn't even an anarchist. More like a carnival huckster. Way ahead of his time. Built most of his pseudo-religion on getting laid—open sex with whoever and whatever. Promoted wife swapping before it was cool. Also built his religion in the tradition of freemasonry—advancing through countless levels, each level costing a tidy fee that went right in his pocket. Fucker raked it in and spent it just as fast on wine, women, and song. "*Do what thou wilt shall be the whole of the law*" was his mantra. And a lot of horny fat cats said: "*Where do I sign up?*"

Crowley died in the late forties, but the dude lives on in music, movies, and loads of dumbass kids with no self-esteem looking for shortcuts or confidence boosters.

Case in point. This dumbass kid. I shake my head in disgust and say to Anna, "Don't tell me this is about Aleister Crowley."

The little brat's temper flares. "Jesus Christ, for the last time, this is about me and J.D. And what do you know about Aleister Crowley anyway?"

"I know a lot. I know his teachings can muddle your mind."

She laughs. "You're just afraid. You're probably some kind of born-again Christian."

"Listen, kid, I had my little Crowley phase, too. You mess with that stuff, it's hard to wash off." Suddenly sound a lot like Ned when he lectures me.

Little know-it-all pain in the ass scoffs at me. "I get my power from magik—and that's magic with a *k*." Crowley claimed his rituals summoned ancient magic, but he spelled magik with a "k," to signify it was genuine and not an illusion. I always thought that made Crowley a bit of a fucktard.

"I've read the same books you read."

"But you didn't perform rituals like I did?"

"I was smart enough to know better."

"Big pussy. That's where the real power lies. I cursed my ex-friends. I cursed my enemies."

"But they're alive right now and you're dead. Hmmm . . ."

"Fuck off."

I feel like washing her mouth out with soap, but I feel bad for her at the same time. I look at her and see myself at seventeen. Obnoxious. Unbearable. Stubborn. Stupid. Nothing but hormones and conflict. "You didn't know any better," I say.

"Know what, asshole?" she yells.

"Know that seventeen's as bad as it gets. Know that you just have to hang on because it gets better a little farther down the road."

She leaps out of her chair. "Oh my God, dude, you are so retarded."

Did I mention, like my little friend here, I pretty much hate everyone. That includes every teenager on the planet. Note to self: *get a vasectomy—fast*. I press the button under the corner of the table and a crystal-handled lever materializes by my side. A cold steel door fades in behind Anna and scares the shit out of her. She screams. Then she tries to laugh it off and act tough, but she's worried.

"You need to go through that door," I tell her. "Now."

"What's on the other side?"

"I don't know?"

"Is J.D. there?"

"I don't know."

"Will I go to hell?"

"I doubt it."

"Too bad," she says.

I shake my head and look her in the eye. No nonsense. "Better take that remark back—before it's too late."

Don't need to tell her I've seen hell. My eyes say it. The tough little sorceress just melts. She softens. Sounds like a little girl when she says, "I want to go home now."

Block it out, Kane. Do your job.

"You can't," I say.

A half sob, then: "Please, dude, take me home."

"It's too late. You're dead."

Tears in her eyes. Regret. "You mean, like, my body is buried?"

I nod.

She cooks up a vivid image in her mind that steamrolls her. Her legs buckle. Looks at me pleadingly, and says, "This really sucks."

"I know."

She breaks down. At this point I stand up. There's nothing I can do or say. Then—damn it—she looks at me and holds her arms open like a little kid. I hesitate, then hug her—good and hard. She buries her head in my chest and sobs. "You tell me when you're ready," I say.

Black streaks pour down her cheeks. "I'm scared."

"Remember that song you were humming? Everything will be all right."

She cries another minute or two. Looks up at me and says, "I guess I'm ready."

"Any messages you want me to deliver?"

She wipes smudged makeup from her cheeks. "Find J.D. Tell him I love him. Tell him to find me."

"What's his last name?" I ask.

"Harlan."

"A-n, e-n, or i-n?"

"A-n."

"Where do I find him?"

"If he's dead, find him however you found me. If he's still alive, he lives in Azusa. Find him there or on Facebook."

"Facebook?"

"That's how we communicated. We fell in love with each other's words. We never met for real."

"You're kidding me?" Social networking reaches as far as the soul trap. "Did you at least speak to him?" I ask.

"We talked on the phone a couple of times, that's all. Mostly we wrote to each other."

Wait till Eva hears this story. "So, you hate the world, you're depressed, you follow Aleister Crowley, but you ended your life over a virtual Facebook boyfriend?"

"Pretty romantic, don't you think?" She's proud. "Virtual is better than real any day."

Wow. Tragic. Stupid. Impulsive. All of the above. "Anything else?"

"Tell my dumbass mom . . . sorry."

"Okay."

"It wasn't always so fucked up between us," she admits. "Sometimes, when I was little, we had fun." She smiles at a memory.

"What?" I ask.

"*Velveteen Rabbit,*" she answers.

"What's that?"

"My mother kept forcing this book on me when I was a kid," she says. "It's about a toy rabbit who wants to become real." Then she laughs.

"What? Tell me."

She perks up. Cute smile that's been hiding. "We went to San Diego Zoo once when I was maybe five. I'm marching around with my little stuffed rabbit having the time of my life. We walked up this hill to this gigantic caged-in habitat thing where they kept these eagles. We looked around—couldn't see anything. Then, there was this rustling and out of the trees flies this mean-ass-looking eagle. Lands five feet from us. Has a big white rabbit in his talons. It was feeding hour. Some zoo attendant forgot to post the sign to block off the path up to the cage."

"Oh shit," I say.

For a normal kid, that might be a traumatic memory. But not Anna. She starts laughing. She really is a twisted kid.

"I mean, this eagle starts feasting. My mom's going apeshit. My dad's covering my eyes." She's belly laughing. "So much for the *Velveteen Rabbit*."

Her laugh is infectious. "What happened?" I ask, grinning.

"Well, my mom marched off to Guest Services and went ballistic. Probably saw it as a golden opportunity for a refund or a free-meal voucher. But my dad did something I'll never forget."

"What?"

"He took me by the hand while my mom was ranting and raving and walked me to the gift shop. He took a big stuffed eagle off the shelf and we just sat there for a few minutes and played on the floor of the shop. He was the lonely eagle who wanted to be friends with my scared bunny. Then Mom came and found us and took a stuffed panda off the shelf. The three of us played in that shop for a long time."

"Sounds like a nice memory," I say.

"Tell Mom I loved her in my own fucked-up way."

"I'll tell her," I promise.

I pull the lever. The door inches open. I wait for a thunderous blast. Nothing but eerie silence. Same as it was for Stanley Tekulve, the spirit I ejected in Carmel. Gray fog creeps past the threshold, envelops Anna, pulls her toward the stark, colorless abyss.

As she drifts away, she looks at me, full of fear. "Daddy? Where are you?" she whimpers. I close my eyes and imagine Dorothy clicking the heels of her ruby slippers. When I open them, Anna's gone, taken by the fog.

What a waste of life.

I'm slammed back into my body. Everything in the camper spins. I've got wicked vertigo. It takes five minutes before I can sit up without feeling like I'm falling off the edge of the earth. I debrief Eva and Ned. Eva takes notes on her laptop. Types as fast as my words come out. Almost drops her pen when I tell her why Anna jumped. She tells us she'll run a background check on J. D. Harlan.

"There might be a story in this for you," I tell her. "Romeo and Juliet in cyberspace."

"Already thought of that," Eva says.

No doubt.

My lungs erupt. Major coughing jag. Ned gives me glass after glass of water. "That energy cluster—that's the souls of the people who jumped off the bridge."

"You're talking two hundred individual souls, give or take, bound together." Ned says. "We've never encountered anything like that."

"And what's the deal with the bodysuit?" I ask. "We've never seen that either."

"Maybe it has to do with suicides," Eva guesses.

Ned's antsy. He paces. Needs a salty snack. "So what do we do now?"

Only one solution I can think of. "We clear the souls out, one at a time."

Ned shoots it down. "You can't. That many trips inside will kill you." He noodles it. "Sometimes we've had two souls in there at once. Depending on their energy levels, we can maybe get three in there. But even if we could do that consistently, you'd still be looking at 66.6 trips inside."

I laugh out loud when he says the number. Takes a second for him to get it. "Evil number or not, it's still too big."

"Then think of another way," I tell him. "I want that money."

Ned loves a challenge. "Give me some time to think," he says.

"Now what?" Eva asks, looking at me.

"I deliver a message to Anna Burrows' mother. And you track down J. D. Harlan."

"Don't you have a gig tonight?" Ned asks.

"Yeah, you guys wanna come?" I give them the details.

I can tell Eva's curious. "Sure."

"Nah," Ned says. "I doubt the Whisky has an AARP discount."

"Come on," I urge, "I want you there."

Ned air guitars. "Then I'll be there."

Nine

Am I dreaming? Is this real? I'm standing under a spotlight on the same stage that Clapton, Hendrix, Townshend, Zappa, and Jim Morrison played on. The Whisky a Go Go, baby. The heart and soul of Hollywood.

And I feel like death. Got a good seven hours of sleep, but it didn't do much good. I feel worse than I did when I came out of the trap. Headache, nausea, the runs. My hands tingle. And my vision is blurry.

My time with Anna Burrows was toxic.

This is not good.

Before we start our sound check, Drexel pulls me aside, whispers to me, "Dude . . . the other night . . ."

"I don't remember much," I say, lying my ass off. That's a night seared into my memory bank for life.

Drexel grabs my collars, shakes me. "That was epic, dude." I nod and smile. "But . . . what happens in Vegas . . ."

"I hear ya. No worries."

"I mean it," Drexel stresses. "Jay would kill me."

"Bo would kill us both," I add.

"I fell off the wagon, just for a night, but I'm right back on."

"Good," I tell him.

"We cool on this, bro?" he asks.

"I've got your back." We bump fists.

A breakthrough. Invisible band glue. Blood brothers in debauchery.

We run through our first two numbers. I'm stiff, but manage to deliver. My stomach burns. Gotta be careful jumping around. Ass might blow. Gotta play it calm and steady.

The Whisky's sound and lighting systems are awesome. Drexel's in fine form, voice is strong. I tune my Les Paul and set my amp. Guitar's ready. Not so sure about me.

"We're golden," Bo says, when Syd gives the thumbs-up that we're wired and ready. Bo gathers us center stage. "Anyone want to offer a prayer to the god of rock and roll?"

"Bless us and make us rich so we can drown in pussy. Amen," Drexel says, head bowed.

"I've got a prayer," I say. Start strumming some chords. Then I play a bluesy riff—real slow. You can tell they know it, but can't place it. Then I sing it—the opening of "Peace in the Valley." Always liked that song. Had a nutty religious foster mother when I was twelve who played Elvis' version over and over. It stuck.

Keep riffing. Jay puts down a great bass line. Troy joins in—mostly on cymbals, but with an occasional thump of the bass drum. I sing the words. Drexel stands next to me and repeat-sings them. Puts his brilliant stamp on them. We play the first verse four times back-to-back. Nice pace—low and slow. A magic moment. Bo throws his hands up. "Fucking brilliant," he says. "Open the show with it—just one verse."

We look at each other. Why not? Feels right. I work with Drexel until he has the lyrics down. I make him a cheat sheet and tape it to the monitor.

We go backstage to rest until show time.

A wave of nausea pummels me. I hit the john and vomit. Shouldn't have gone in the trap last night. Idiot. Too much on the line tonight.

A Subway tray arrives and I heave. Can't stomach a bite. I duck out to buy a bottle of Mylanta at Rite-Aid. Chug half the bottle at the cash register.

Bo wakes me up from a catnap thirty minutes before show time. My stomach feels a little better but my head still throbs.

Syd leads us to the stage. The house lights go out. The crowd roars—the best damn sound in the world. Three hundred people sound like ten thousand.

They're ready. This is it.

Drexel sees I'm wearing his Ray-Bans. "What the fuck?" he says, annoyed. He takes off his Wayfarers and glares at me. "You're copping my act?"

Too late to argue. Syd shines the flashlight, lights out path, and shoves us onstage. Troy counts off and we go. The Les Paul feels like a weapon in my hand. I simulate shooting the audience with it. This guitar has power. Songs hide deep inside it.

As usual, it takes me awhile to look around. Even with sunglasses on, I can't miss Ned. He's behind the plastic curtain in the jam-packed smoking room—cigarette in mouth, gin and tonic in hand. The fat fuck cracks me up. Behind a wall of smoke, he looks like a mental patient in an asylum that just caught fire.

I catch sight of Ira Bowersock at the bar. Poker-faced. As usual, I can't read him. I cross the stage and play to the left side of the room. Lots of hands in the air.

Three-quarters of the way through the set, I spot Eva hugging the wall halfway back. It's impossible to miss her. Hair down. Wears a gray minidress and black high-heeled boots. Sipping vodka and rocking to the beat. Best-looking girl in the room, and that's saying a lot for a Saturday night in Hollywood. We make eye contact. She smiles. Somehow, I manage to nail my solos despite my fingers feeling like Popsicles. Eva grooves nice and slow while I play. Drexel notices. Singles her out. His voice goes all slithery and velvet. Try to show him up with my final solo, but I'm the Invisible Man next to him. Eva's locked in on him. So is the rest of the crowd. It's all Drexel. His piercing vocals hit the crowd like taser shots. My guitar and his voice meld. He's never been better. He's carrying us on his back. God, how I love to hear this little prick sing.

I spot a breathtaking woman along the wall. A head taller than any female on the floor. Thirty, maybe thirty-five. Black leather miniskirt. Long black hair and muscular legs. Smokin' hot. While everyone around her is bopping up and down in unison, she's cool, barely moving. This lady in black eye-fucks me for the duration of the song. Those eyes energize me. I start playing to her. Then Eva. Back to the lady in black. Then Eva again.

The final two numbers go off without a hitch. Ira Bowersock is on his feet, applauding.

Offstage, a dizzy spell strikes. Syd shoves me back for the encore. I play the shit out of my solo just for Eva. Drexel circles me, nudges me back. It's his turf. I stand my ground. He reaches out and slaps my Ray-Bans off. They fly into the crowd. Ready to club him like a baby seal, but remind myself of what's on the line and regain composure. I drop back to my normal spot on stage and end the song without incident.

Syd leads us back to the dressing room. The door slams shut behind us. Coolers are full. Grab an icy beer and chug. Then a wave of exhaustion rolls over me. A trapdoor opens and everything drops. My blood pressure is low. Breathing is shallow. Collapse on the sofa. Troy hands me another beer. Überdizzy. I'm hanging on by a thread.

"No speech?" Jay asks Bo.

"A short one," Bo says. Three words: "You nailed it."

"So now what?" asks Drexel.

Bo looks at the locked door. "We wait."

I close my eyes and doze off in an instant. I'm startled awake by a knock. My stomach rumbles. Gonna puke. Hang on.

Syd opens the door. Ira Bowersock enters.

Bo point-blanks it. "Well?"

"Incredible," Ira says. "Memorable."

Bo treads lightly. "Any news?"

Ira is silent. Looks each one of us in the eye, then says, "Twenty-eight hours straight with lawyers and investment bankers, but my financing closed this afternoon. Gentlemen, let's make a deal. Welcome to my new label—Deep Lever Records."

"I like the name," Bo says.

"And you're my flagship act," Ira says.

We stand. Hug. High-five. I so wish I could enjoy this moment. Bo pops champagne.

"To Astral Fountain," Ira toasts.

"To Deep Lever," Bo adds.

We clink plastic cups. Mission accomplished.

Bo looks at Ira. "Next steps?"

"Don't schedule any more gigs," Ira says. "I have a plan, but I'll spring it on you next week—after the deal sheet."

"When do we do that?" Bo asks.

"Let's meet for breakfast at the Chateau Marmont at eleven," Ira tells Bo. "I'll have paperwork. For now, go enjoy yourselves."

Syd throws the door open and our dressing room floods with friends and fans. Too many people. Too much energy. I feel claustrophobic, like a panic attack is coming. I wander out of the dressing room. Spot Ned. Beeline straight to him. He hugs me. "Fantastic, Kane," he says. I practically collapse in his arms.

He drags me down the hallway, opens the emergency exit door, pulls me into the alley behind garbage bins full of empty bottles.

I'm instantly on my hands and knees vomiting water and bile. My head feels like it's gonna blow. I pass out, come to a few minutes later. I'm on my ass, sitting against the building. Ned is over me, opening my eyelids, checking my pupils.

"I've gotta get you home. We need to track down that creepy guru guy."

"Master Choi," I say.

"Right. Good idea."

I need a major dose of prana healing. It saved my ass last year.

"Can you stand?" Ned asks.

"I think so." I struggle.

Ned helps me to my feet. "Let's go," he says.

"Wait," I say, waving him off. "I have to say good-bye."

I lean on Ned and he opens the door. I steady myself and take baby steps back inside to the dressing room. Drexel and Bo are chatting up Eva. When she sees me, she walks straight over. "There you are," she says. "You were awesome."

"Thanks for coming," I tell her. My voice is weak.

Ned gives her a look. She sees I'm hurting. "Are you all right?"

"Yeah," I say. "Just some side effects from last night."

Ned shakes his head. "Let me introduce you to everyone," I say, leading Eva around the room. All eyes are on her. Especially Drexel's. What a prick.

Bo comes over and whispers in my ear. "We're going to the Rainbow. Gonna tear it up tonight."

"I'm spent," I tell him.

"You?" Bo asks, shocked.

I laugh it off, but I'm pissed inside. Gonna miss the party I've dreamed of my whole life.

"We'll drink your share," Bo says. He glances at Eva and says, "The blonde—she with you?"

"We're just friends."

"Drexel was asking, that's all."

Fuck. Just then, Drexel moves in on Eva. "Tell him she's out of his league," I whisper to Bo. "I mean it. Do something. She's a friend. I don't want Boy Wonder harassing her."

"Okay. But no promises."

Stagger straight to Eva and Drexel. "Rainbow, dude," Drexel says to me. "Remember last time we partied . . ." He grins. Shit, don't spill it. Not in front of Eva.

"Not tonight," I say.

"Our dreams just came true, and you're gonna bounce?"

"You owe me a pair of sunglasses," I say.

He laughs. "Fine. I'll send you a truck full when the first check clears." Drexel nods to Eva. "Kane, here, tried to steal my act. Had to teach him a lesson." Eva smiles uncomfortably.

I ignore him and look at Eva. "You want to go somewhere?"

"No, I have to go home," Eva says. "I'll call you tomorrow."

"Be on your way, Kane," Drexel says, "so I can talk Eva here into joining the party."

I would love to bitch-slap him into next week, but I can't feel my hands. Ned can read my body language. He grabs my arm and pulls me away. We're out the emergency exit door and I'm leaning on him on the way to the car.

Walk past my '96 Mustang, so rusty it looks like it went through atmospheric reentry. "What about my car?"

"Leave it. We'll get it tomorrow." Ned stops to marvel at my piece-of-shit ride. "Maybe you'll get lucky and someone will steal it."

"Don't worry about Eva," Ned reassures me. "She can spot an asshole a mile away."

Collapse into Ned's Subaru. I dial Soon Choi on my phone. Apologize for the late-night call, explain the situation. He agrees to get out of bed and drive from Santa Monica to my place. Guy's an angel.

"We can't do this a hundred times," Ned says. "Hell, you probably can't do it ten times. There's something about the energy of these suicides. It drains you more intensely."

"I'm just out of practice," I tell him. "I'll get used to it again. It's more money than we'll ever see. I'm not blowing this chance. I'll manage."

"You can't spend money inside a coffin."

"So what are you suggesting? Call it off?"

"Maybe I can go in," Ned says. "We can split the load."

"We've already had this discussion," I snap. "If it does this to me, it'll kill you."

"Then how about Eva? She's young and fit."

I'm silent. She'd probably jump at the chance to do it.

"Come on, it's a good idea," Ned says. "You know it."

"Let me think about that," I tell him before slamming the door.

• • •

Master Choi arrives just after two in the morning. He spends a long time just staring at me. He's reading my aura. He tells me to put out my tongue, studies it carefully, and looks alarmed. I stretch out on my bed. He places a bowl of water with Hawaiian rock salt at his feet. Runs his hands six inches above my body from head to toe. He stops every few seconds to identify energy blocks. He glances around, troubled.

"What?" I ask.

"Nothing," he says. "There's dark energy around you."

"Yeah," I say. "We're in the middle of Hollywood."

"It's not that," he says. "I'm not sure what it is, but it's close to you. It's blocking your energy flow. Depleting you."

Ned's right—the energy of suicide victims is doing way more damage.

Choi spends three hours raking my aura with his fingers and flicks the diseased energy into the saltwater. He gives me specific instructions about psychically protecting my apartment, my car, and my astral body. He tells me to cleanse my apartment by burning sage in every room, and to place a bowl of sea salt by my front door. I must meditate daily, starting now, in hopes of bringing peace to my angry, unsettled mind. And when I feel my spiritual energy waning, I'm to envision myself wearing a white suit of protective armor that makes me impenetrable to dark energy. If I do these things, he tells me, I'll be shielded from the negative energy.

I would love to see Ned's face right now. New Age bullshit, he'd say. But I promise Choi I'll do what he says—despite all the craziness going on in my life.

Choi demands silence and meditates over me. A wave of peace washes over me, and I drift into a deep sleep.

Ten

I wake up six hours later and it feels like I slept for a week. A note on my desk from Choi reads:

> Your aura is repaired. Your chakras are energized.
> Rest. Heal. Protect yourself.

I'm hungry. I nuke a breakfast sandwich and wonder how the after-party went. I think about what Ned suggested in the car—Eva going inside the trap. She's been in there before—the time she went in behind my back to meet Donna Lonzi. She has the ability to project herself. She's tough. It's not a bad idea. And—if nothing else—it guarantees me more time with her.

I grab my phone and call her. She sounds groggy. "Sorry, did I wake you?"

"Yeah," she groans. "How do you feel?"

"Feeling better," I say. "Did you have fun last night?"

"Too much fun," she says. "You guys were great."

"Thanks. What time did you get home?"

"I don't know—after four, I think."

"You went to the Rainbow then?"

"Yeah."

Fuck.

"Your singer twisted my arm," she says.

Motherfuck.

I can hear her stretching. "It's a fun group of people."

I make a fist. Bite it. All the healing just got flushed. "I should have warned you about Drexel," I say with a halfhearted laugh. "I'll bet he spent the whole night telling you what a genius he is."

She laughs and lets out a cough—a hangover hack. "He's a character," she says.

"More like a caricature." Sit. I wait for her to tell me what an asshole he is. Nothing. Too classy for backstabbing? Or . . . ?

"He's got some charm," she finally says.

Ouch. Silence.

"And Jay," she continues, "amazing bass player. Really nice guy."

"Uh-huh."

"They really love you. You're like their big brother."

Silence.

"I'm happy you have friends," she says. "You need that." Oh geez.

I come about a centimeter from telling her all I need is her, but I chicken out. Not time. Not yet. I shift gears and tempt Eva like the serpent tempted Eve. I offer her the chance to go back into the trap and help me free the souls under the bridge.

"Yes, yes, yes," she says over and over. "I'm so in. When? When are we going?" Like a kid counting down the days to Disneyland.

"Soon. I'll let you know when," I tell her.

"I'll be waiting." I can hear her hop out of bed. "Oh, by the way, can't find anything on J. D. Harlan. No obituaries. No news. No listings in Azusa."

"His Facebook page has been removed," I tell her. "I have a feeling he's dead."

"I'll call Azusa High School next," she says.

I turn on my Mac. Takes about a minute to snag a name and address on peoplefinder.com. Teresa K. Burrows, age 39, 9876 Creemore Road, La Crescenta, CA, and a number. Anna's mother.

Maybe tomorrow I'll go see her. Over the phone she'll think I'm a nut.

I dig for more info on Teresa Burrows. Can't find much. No profiles for her on LinkedIn, Facebook, or MySpace. She's mentioned as a plaintiff in a lawsuit against a company called Vizer Technologies. Looks like it never made it to court. I google Vizer. Vitamins, supplements, energy drinks. Can't find information on how the case was resolved.

I check out Anna Burrows' Facebook page. It's set to private. All I can see is her photo. Google J. D. Harlan. A handful of them out there, but no teenagers from Azusa. Can't find a profile that matches.

There's a big accident on the 101. It takes me almost an hour to go the lousy twenty-mile trek from my place to La Crescenta. Teresa Burrows' house is tucked up in the foothills. I spot a good-looking brunette getting into a silver Lexus parked in the driveway. Must be her. She drives away.

I follow her from a distance all the way from La Crescenta to Northridge. She parks in a student lot at Cal State Northridge. She must be a student at CSUN. I park three spaces from her. She climbs out of the car. She's petite with long, straight black hair. My guess—Hispanic, but not full-blooded. Red blouse. Tight jeans. Good genes.

She's thirty-nine, but still fits in on a college campus. She throws a backpack over her shoulder and walks into a building called Manzanita Hall.

What to do now?

I decide to drive back to her place and wait. I position the car so I can see her returning in my side mirror. I dive back into Charlie Huston's novel. Just shy of two hours later, the Lexus pulls back into the driveway. I open my car door, but freeze. Cold feet. How the fuck do I even start this conversation? Maybe I should call instead.

I grab my phone and freeze again. Sweat.

Don't overthink it. Just do it. I punch in the numbers. It rings. I sweat harder.

"Hello?"

I stammer. Cotton mouth. *Grow a sack already.* "Is this Teresa Burrows?"

"Yes . . . who's calling?"

"My name is Kane Pryce."

"Sorry, I don't—"

"This is about Anna."

Dreadful silence, then, "What about Anna?" Her voice cracks.

I draw a blank. Finally blurt out, "This is gonna sound crazy . . ."

An abrupt "I have to go."

"Please. Anna has a message for you."

Silent anger, then, "Do you have no shame?"

"Just hear me out."

"I'm hanging up now."

Totally choking. Gotta pull a rabbit . . . of course. "San Diego Zoo. An eagle feeding on a rabbit. You and Anna and the *Velveteen Rabbit.*"

She gasps.

"How do you know about that? Who are you?"

"I'll tell you, but please, just hear me out."

A long pause, then, "Okay."

I don't get into specifics. Tell her I've spoken to Anna's spirit. That I have a message to pass on. Give her the details of the zoo story. Tell her how Anna summed it all up—that it wasn't always so fucked up between them.

She doesn't say a word.

"Can I speak to you in person?"

Prepare to hear click. Instead, "Okay."

"Now a good time?"

"Sure."

Even though I'm looking at her house in my rearview mirror, I ask, "Where do you live?"

"Meet me at Starbucks in La Crescenta," she says. "It's on Foothill and Boston." She wants to meet in public. Smart woman.

"Okay. I can be there in thirty minutes." I can be there in two. "What do you look like?" I could give a police description.

"Dark hair. I'm wearing a red blouse." She hangs up. A few minutes later, I spy her leaving the house. Read another two chapters of *Caught Stealing*, then drive to Starbucks.

I walk in. Coffee smells good. I spot her instantly, but glance around for effect. She stands. Tiny. Five feet and change. We shake hands. My eyes go straight to the cleavage. Ginormous rack for such a petite woman. And they're not fake. Force my gaze upstairs. She dyes her hair. Some definite mileage around her dark eyes, but a perfect olive complexion. A four-star MILF. Already banged her in my mind. Shameful. Guess I've visited one too many cougar porn sites.

Two venti lattes and we settle in. I start by stammering my way through a disclaimer: I'm not a psychic or a fortune teller or a medium. I'm not out to milk a dime from you or take advantage of your grief.

I'm overselling it. It's not working.

All she says after my feeble speech is, "What about Anna?"

Give her a tight overview—soul trapper 101. Tell her that Anna's soul has moved on. She looks at me like I'm a loon.

I take out my iPad and show her what's posted about me on laghostpost.com. Let her read the *L.A. Times* article from last year. "Most everything you've just read is true," I tell her, "but I'll deny it." This adds legitimacy.

"I remember this article," she says. She agrees to hear me out.

Second round of venti lattes. I tell her about the Colorado Street Bridge gig, my encounter with Anna.

Tears well up. She dons her sunglasses, blows her nose.

"What did she want to tell me?" Teresa asks.

"First, she's sorry. Second—she loves you."

Teresa grabs her keys. "Anna would never have said that. That's not her." She stands to leave.

"What she said exactly was, 'Tell my dumbass mom, sorry.'" Teresa puts the keys down. "Then she said, 'Tell her I loved her in my own fucked-up way.'"

"That's Anna," Teresa says, laughing and crying at the same time. "Why did she do it?"

"You don't know?" I ask.

Teresa shakes her head.

"A boy."

Teresa sighs, rolls her tear-filled eyes. "Oh, no."

"She knows she screwed up," I say. But what comfort is that to a mother who will never see her daughter again?

"Anything else?" Anna asks.

"She missed her dad after he died. I could tell."

"She did," Teresa confirms.

"How did he die?"

Teresa leans forward and puts her chin in her hands. "Mile sixteen of the 2009 L.A. Marathon. He was only thirty-eight."

"You've been through a lot."

She breaks down. People at nearby tables shoot us worried looks. I'm not sure what to do. I reach over and give her tiny hand a squeeze.

"After Tony died, it just all fell apart between us. She hated me. She was so angry. She abandoned her friends, made new ones that she kept secret. She got into trouble. She became someone else."

"She was involved in some pretty dark things," I tell Teresa. "Did you know that?"

She looks surprised that I know. "I told her to get those occult books out of our house. She wouldn't listen. I gave up."

"Must have been hard."

"God, we were at each other's throats all the time. It was awful." Through sobs, she says, "I failed my little girl."

"No, you didn't."

"I did," she insists. "I should have saved her. But I couldn't. She was obsessed with death and the afterlife. She kept saying that somewhere past death was real life. She drew some kind of presence to our house. I was terrified."

"There was no stopping her," I say. "Dark energy has power. Don't blame yourself."

Caffeine hits us both at the same time. Teresa regains her composure, gently pulls her hand away from mine. "Who was the boy?" she asks. "Did she say?"

"J. D. Harlan."

A vacant look. "I never heard Anna mention him. But no surprise there."

"Can I see her computer?" I ask.

She looks alarmed. "Why?"

"I want to find this J. D."

"No," Teresa says. "I've heard you out, but I don't think—"

"Please," I say. "For Anna."

Teresa looks way into my eyes. Mulls it over. "Okay," she says. "I live close."

Wonder how creeped out she'd be if I told her she could follow me.

Teresa's house is modest but neat. A three-bedroom, single-story ranch. One of a million valley houses with the same floor plan. Sympathy cards on the mantle. Wilted flowers from family and friends are on their last legs.

Teresa leads me to Anna's bedroom. A pentagram sticker on the door welcomes visitors.

"I need to take this off," Teresa says, embarrassed. She opens the door and turns on the light. The first thing I see is Aleister Crowley's fat, evil face on a wall poster. She should have been getting out of her boy band phase. Instead she sports posters of Marilyn Manson, assorted demons, and occult symbols.

I scan the bookshelf above her desk. *The Book of Law* and six other Crowley books, including *Goetia*, a hard-core, demon-summoning book that's hard to come by. Also a book called *Freedom Is a Two-Edged Sword*, by someone named John Whiteside Parsons. Pick it up and glance at a couple pages. It's occult, too.

Seeing these books drums up bad memories.

Anna was deeper into this shit than I thought.

Teresa looks around. "I need to pack this room away," she says. "I don't want to remember Anna like this. I just can't bring myself to do it."

All I have is a cheesy cliché. "It takes time."

Teresa boots up Anna's Mac. We go to Anna's Facebook page. It's set to auto login, thank God. I wouldn't have wanted to sit here and try to guess a mental teenager's password. We examine her page. What a friggin' personal statement. Her last entry is dated the day before her suicide. It shows a recent close-up photo of a too-brightly-lit, ancient-looking David Lee Roth. Beneath it a banner headline:

GO AHEAD, JUMP!

"I never saw this," Teresa says. She stands over my shoulder. I scroll down and we both read.

ANNA BURROWS
Current City: La Crescenta, CA
Hometown: Hell
Sex: Female
Birthday: October 26, 1994
Interested in: Anything with a dick. People in my area who want to get stoned and weird.
Religious Views: Order of Thelema

Bio: I'm 17 going on 27. I'm the wickedest girl in the world. Don't call me chubby—I beat anorexia, that's all. I'm smokin' and beefy n' all. There's Magik in this young girl's heart. I can hurt you without being there, so watch out, bitches. I have 7 piercings—nose, tongue, ears, come find the rest. Three tatts. I think random thoughts and speak only when I have something to say. Just cause I'm quiet doesn't mean I'm shy. I don't need therapy or anger management. I just need to quit living in a world of assholes. I like guys. Hate girls. Hate school. Love weed. Love tequila. My dad is dead. My mom might as well be. I love to fucking swear. Trust is the funniest word in the dictionary. Freedom is a two-edged sword.

Who I'd Like to Meet: Aleister Crowley, Marilyn Manson, Gerard Way, Jenna Jameson, 72 demons,

Education: Who needs geometry when you have Magik?

Employer:

Blockbuster—Fired

Target—Fired.

Krispy Kreme—fired (one hour! North American record!)

Professional Hater—Employee of the Year

Interests:

Penises. Drugs. Evil. Rock and Roll. Anime. Vintage seventies porn with those big bushes. Ouija boards. War. Did I say penises? BIG penises. Emo. My Chemical Romance. Taking Back Sunday. Disfiguring the Goddess. The hidden messages in everything. M&Ms. Cats. Colbert Report.

Hating everything. Seriously.

Just a few things I hate:

School. Sports. People with laptops in Starbucks who think they're writers. Coozes pushing strollers into Starbucks. Fucking Starbucks in general. Farmville and Mafia Wars and all other junior twatsy little games for

geriatrics and newbies. MMOs. Fat-ass World of War-
craft fucktards can shove their spells up their asses and
choke to death on their Doritos. Big budget video games.
Fuck Grand Theft Auto, go kill someone for real. Rock
Band. Guitar Hero—play for real, you douches. Cholos,
Gangstas, Lezzes, Homos, Christians, Jews, Buddhists,
Muslims—I hate you all equally. Cheerleaders. Goth.
Wicca (pussies). Anyone over 25. Jackasses who ride
mountain bikes in Spider-Man costumes and faggoty
helmets. Plastic surgery—you're old, accept it. Skinny
people—eat a Western Bacon Cheeseburger, you fucks.
Twilight (You want to see immortals? You can't handle
immortals!)

Favorite Quotes:

No one here gets out alive.—Jim Morrison
Do what thou wilt and that shall be the whole of the law.
—Aleister Crowley
Ordinary morality is for ordinary people.—Aleister Crowley

I laugh at some of it. I don't know what to say to the person
who gave birth to someone even more cynical than me. I go with,
"Too bad. She would have outgrown this stuff."

We read her wall, then her private messages. Pretty close circle.
A lot of messages exchanged with someone named Frater Lieber
last year. Almost all sexual. She was meeting up for late-night
rendezvous with him in the warehouse of his plumbing business.
Ditching school and meeting him in motels for lunch hour sex.
What isn't about sex is about Crowley and magik. Whoever this
guy is, he comes off as Anna's dark guru. We click on his profile.
It's set to private, but his profile pic is a shot of Aleister Crowley.

All of the current exchanges are with J. D. Harlan. His profile's
been removed. He looks like a little prick in his profile pic—long,
sandy blond hair, peach fuzz goatee, smirk. We sift through back-

and-forth volleys of messages. Teresa gets uncomfortable, turns her back, and sits on the bed. "I don't want to see this anymore."

"Do you mind if I look for just a minute longer?" I ask.

She nods with major reluctance and looks out the window. This is so painful for her. I gotta be quick. Speed-read. Painful for me, too. Dumb kidspeak—like nails on a chalkboard. The exchanges—occurring over the course of six weeks—are all over the map. I compartmentalize them in my mind. The early friendly ones, like:

J.D.: u seem cool
A: u 2

and:

J.D.: u look cute.
A: U R hot!

and:

J.D.: I <3 Stratego U?
A: Decent band. I'll turn u on 2 Disfiguring the Goddess.

The ones where Anna reveals her obsession with the occult:

A: I will teach u Magik.
J.D.: u r bad, girl!
A: sacred, sexual magik.
J.D.: i'm so in.
A: read the book of law
J.D.: will find it. read it 4 u
A: u will be my dark angel

The light, funny exchanges full of trash talk:

J.D.: shut up, slut! transformers 3 rocked!

A: shia labeouf has a mangina!!

J.D.: wrong!

A: dude, you are so retarded

J.D.: I am so right, u hoebag!

The down-and-dirty talk, with their elaborate system of codes:

J.D.: what will u do when I ˆ * your 7Y7?

A: duh i'll scream so loud we'll wake up the dumb-ass neighbors

J.D.: Will u #*$ my (I)? :)

A: I will so 4200 your big fat !!

Then, near the end, it gets all twisted:

J.D.: we'll be Romeo and Juliet. Hitler and Eva Braun! u and me 4 ever

A: u think so?

J.D.: shit, yeah. we'll be famous

A: gonna be a movie.

J.D.: fuck this world.

A: and everyone in it!

J.D.: you in?

A: I'm in. on to the next life. how will u do it?

J.D.: My secret. Will make a statement. u?

A: A leap of faith

J.D.: I'll find u

A: I'll be waiting over there

The last exchange:

J.D.: not gonna wimp out?

A: no way

J.D.: u ready?
A: I am so dead tonight.
J.D.: when?
A: 3:30 the evil hour
J.D.: <3 u 4 ever :x
A: <3 u See you through the looking glass :x.

I feel drained. "Stupid-ass kids," I whisper to myself.

Teresa leaves the room and returns with a note. "It's her suicide note," she says, handing it to me. It reads:

> *To whom it may concern:*
> *Fuck you all!*
> *Sincerely,*
> *Anna K Burrows.*

A pisspot right to the end. I hand the note back to Teresa. "I want to find out what happened to J. D. Harlan."

"No. Let it go. It doesn't matter now."

"It matters to me," I say.

She's firm. "I told you—no! This is private. It's over. She's gone. I'm getting rid of this computer. Getting rid of all this stuff."

Way to go, Kane. Idiot. I've pushed her too far. "I'm sorry," I say. "I'll leave you alone now."

She looks relieved.

"Just know," I tell her, "that Anna still exists. That she's moved on. That she didn't really hate you."

"Yes, she did."

"She just thought she hated you," I tell her. "The last thing she did before she moved on was to call out for you."

Teresa looks startled. "Really?"

"Really."

Teresa walks me to the front door. I offer my hand. She takes it. "It was nice to meet you," I say. Then, surprising myself, I hug her, whisper in her ear, "I'm sorry for your loss. Your losses."

She tears up. Smiles at me. "Thank you."

The door shuts behind me. I close my eyes. I see J.D.'s smug little profile pic in my mind. *You better be dead, kid, because I'm coming for you.*

Eleven

First stop today—Hollywood Forever Cemetery.

I stop at Johnny and Dee Dee Ramone's tombstones to pay my respects, but pick a different spot to recharge Aleister Crowley's goblet. I plop down next to a tombstone with a carving of a sexy female vampire. It belongs to Maila Nurmi, a.k.a. Vampira, the TV host of horror movies in the '50s and star of Ed Wood's cult classic *Plan 9 from Outer Space*. She died a few years ago in her eighties. With her skin-tight black dress, jet-black straight hair, pale white skin, and enormous rack, she became an icon. Elvira totally ripped her off. Vampira rules—definitely deserves to rest in peace within visual range of the Hollywood sign.

What few people know is that she was buds with James Dean. Claimed to be able to speak to him after he drove his Porsche Spyder down the road to glory. Bullshit? Who knows. If it's not true, it should be. If it is, maybe there's psychic energy crackling bubbling up from below. I lean Crowley's goblet against her nifty tombstone and let it bake. I pull my iPad out of my backpack, don my headphones. I can't think of any vampire songs, so I play the late great Amy Winehouse. Sit back and listen to "Back to Black" while I surf. Here's to you, Vampira.

When the album ends, I wonder if Vampira is present. My iPad's battery drains prematurely. I shut down and grab the goblet. It's scorching hot. Mission accomplished. I stand up and brush the grass clippings from my jeans.

Back at my apartment, I test the goblet. I set it atop the IVeR, and power it up. See if Karl has anything to say.

I rub my finger around the rim of the goblet until it hums its menacing tone. I tune the ectometer and find Karl quickly this time. "Help," he says slowly and deliberately. Then, "Help!" with more urgency. Yep, another Beatles tune. It's him.

I'm ready to sing along to "Help!" with him. But he lets out a guttural moan of pain and then a long, disturbing scream. It startles me. The scream fades away. The IVeR tunes itself. What the hell?!

"Karl? Karl?" I shout.

A new voice breaks through the static. A first. Karl's is the only voice I've ever heard. This voice chatters away, but is too muffled and distant to discern. British, I think. Maybe Irish. Too tinny to say. High-pitched and sing-songey. Holy shit. It sounds a little like John Lennon.

The voice gets a little clearer. Make out the words, "hate you . . ."

"Who are you?" I ask, loudly and clearly. "Where's Karl?" Feedback squeals. Ozone in the air around me crackles. The hair stands up on my arms.

The voice sounds nearer. It's still hard to make out, but it's singing, slow and off-key. "Don't know why I hate you, but I do . . ."

"Who are you? Tell me your name."

It just keeps singing. "Don't know why I loathe you, but it's true."

I try to engage it. "What's that song? It's not the Beatles."

Through pounds of static, the garbled voice responds, "You know."

"I don't know," I say. "Tell me."

The signal grows stronger. The voice distorts, but is clear: "It's your song."

"What?"

"You wrote it."

Now the hair on my head is standing up.

His words make me dizzy. Total mindfuck. "What are you talking about?" Are my eyes playing tricks on me or are little orbs of light streaming out of the IVeR and hitting me in the head? I bury my face in my hands. My head buzzes. I hear the voice in my head now. Singing. It's clearer. It can't carry a tune. Definitely British. "Don't know why I hate you, but I do." It sounds so familiar. It's the Clash—maybe the Ramones.

I breathe deep and glance up. A jellylike substance bubbles around the rim of the goblet. When I touch it, it scorches my finger tip. The IVeR shorts out. The static energy surge wanes.

What the fuck?

I grab the goblet but it's hot. Too hot. I drop it. The goo hardens. It only takes a minute for it to crumble off the crystal like dried-out Play-Doh. I try to power the device back up, but the goblet is drained dry.

That song rings in my ears. Maybe it's not the Ramones—might be Art Brut. Don't think it's the Sex Pistols. John Lennon solo? It's somebody—I know it. Gonna drive me nuts until I figure it out. I google the lyrics. Nothing.

What the fuck?

I know this song. Focus. I'll play the guitar riff and it'll come to me. That'll solve it. I grab my Blackie Strat. Plug into my AmpliTude iRig, slap my earphones on, crank the volume, and play. The opening riff pours right out. Play a few recognizable licks that I know come from that song.

I throw off my headphones. Pour through my iTunes library, old CDs. Google some more.

Nada.

Can't find it anywhere.

What the fuck?

Grab my guitar again. Don the headphones. Close my eyes, feel it somewhere deep inside me, and play it beginning to end without as much as a pause—intro riff, verse, chorus, riff, verse, chorus, riff, verse, chorus, solo, verse, solo, finale.

It rocks. Simple. Clean. Timely, but comfortable—dashes of retro punk sprinkled all through it to give it a familiar coziness.

What the fuck?

I grab some sheets of blank paper out of my printer and a pen. Start with what I heard:

> *Don't know why I hate you, but I do.*

Write a second line:

> *Don't know why I loathe you, but it's true.*

That's the chorus.

Get stuck. Now what? I can't write. I close my eyes, breathe, hear the words. In my mind, I see foster parents from my ugly past. See Drexel slapping my sunglasses off. See a parade of people who I've crossed paths with in my life. My pen starts to move. My hand is being guided. First it's scribbly lines, then words—a lot of words.

The words just flow. The pen is on autopilot. Only a few words get scratched out and replaced. I'm not doing the scratching. It takes less than ten minutes. Then the pen stops. I pick up the paper. It's not my handwriting. It's elegant. It's all there. Four verses and the chorus. It's amusing and violent—the misery of seeing the ones I hate; the many ways I'd like to see them die. I pick up my guitar and play it. Add a bridge. The lyrics to the bridge pour out:

> *An ounce of love, a pound of hate*
> *Carries you to the devil's gate.*
> *A pound of hate, a ton of bliss*
> *This love hate thing, I will not miss.*

• • •

It's titled "Pound of Hate."

What the fuck?

I'm suddenly compelled to launch Pro Tools. I record the music. Tweak the solo till it clicks. Lay down a screaming vocal track with some distortion. I try to give it as much feeling as Cobain did when he builds to screaming in "Smells Like Teen Spirit." Can't wait to hear this fucker with a rapid-fire drum track.

I play it back. An homage to punk. Simple. Silly, but surly. My favorite bands thrown into a blender and mixed on High. I burn it and load it on all my Apple devices.

What the fuck is going on?

Is this the spark that people who create for a living talk about? That flash of knowing? That ability to reach out into the ether, lasso something fully formed that's always been, yank it down to earth, and stamp your name on it? If it is, I'm hooked.

Only takes two hours, but I'm exhausted. Buzzing without drugs or booze. Which reminds me . . . pour a megashot of whiskey into Crowley's goblet. Raise my glass to the IVeR. "Thanks . . . whoever you are." Down the whiskey.

Ned calls. "We need to meet at the bridge ASAP."

"I'm ready to go back. So is Eva. I was thinking about what you said. It's a good idea to send Eva into the trap."

Ned sounds stressed. "No," he says. "We need to talk."

"About what?"

"I've dug a lot deeper in my research." He pauses, then blurts out. "I think we have to call this whole thing off."

"Why? What are you talking about?"

He's evasive. "There are things you need to know about the bridge, about the area around it . . . about Millie Barrington. Meet me first thing in the morning. This isn't something I can explain over the phone."

"I'll be there at nine. This had better be important," I warn him. "And short."

"Bring your iPad," he tells me. "I'll email you some links in the morning, but promise not to open any of them until we're together."

"Whatever," I say, annoyed.

I hang up and listen to "Pound of Hate."

I smile. I have arrived.

Twelve

Ned and I are standing under the bridge just south of the condo parking lot where our cars are parked. I've got a dull headache. Feels like a hangover headache, but I wasn't boozing last night. Ned, as always, looks bad. Even fatter. He's wearing sweats again. I can smell Egg McMuffin on his breath.

"I really can't handle another grand tour or three-hour lecture," I warn him. "I just want to finish this job and collect our money. Figure out what we need to do and let's get on with it."

"No. This is important," Ned says.

He's dead serious. "All right," I snap. "What has you so rattled you want to call this off?"

He looks around and says, "A lot of things, really. I know you think I talk too much, but hear me out this morning. Okay?"

"Fine."

"Some of the stuff I'm going to tell you is stuff I've heard—working at Caltech and living in Pasadena and all. Some of it, I just learned since you sent me those links to research. So our field trip this morning starts right here."

God, here we go. Ned opens a folder and hands me a copy of the front page of the *Pasadena Star-News*, dated June 18, 1950. Photo of two Pasadena cops standing over a body under a sheet. Ned and I are standing right where the photo was taken over sixty years ago. The headline reads:

DISGRUNTLED BARRINGTON SERVANT LEAPS OFF
COLORADO STREET BRIDGE

I scan the article. The victim's name: Helena Maldanado. Mrs. Barrington's housekeeper. He just got my attention. "She was the former employee who was set to give the big, shocking, tell-all interview about the Barringtons to that gossip rag."

"She killed herself," Ned tells me.

"No wonder I couldn't find the interview anywhere."

"Two people that we know of who worked for Millie committed suicide," Ned says. "One of them died right here. Millie's known to be a tough boss, but still, doesn't it sound weird?"

"Maybe," I say.

"Tuck that info away for now," Ned says. He starts walking. "Follow me."

On the other side of the bridge, we stop and look up at the domed courthouse on the hill above us. Ned points to the building.

"You already told me about it," I remind him. "Courthouse that used to be a veteran's hospital that used to be a fancy hotel for fat cats."

Ned tells me to take out my iPad and open the first link he emailed me. It's a Wikipedia page for the Richard H. Chambers United States Court of Appeals. "Read the Building History section," he orders. "Specifically, the first building that stood on the site."

The original La Vista del Arroyo Hotel was opened by a woman named Emma C. Bangs in 1882. "All right, so what?"

"Open the second link," he says.

"Come on—this is bullshit?" I snap. "Just tell me what you need to tell me."

"I could tell you, but . . ." He's getting annoyed, too. "Ten years around you, I figured something out: You don't listen. You pay more attention, absorb things more when you're learning for yourself."

"Is that right?" I scoff.

He gets mad and yells, "Look, you said you'd hear me out!"

"Whatever," I shoot back. I hold the iPad a couple inches from my eyes. "Happy?" I open the link. It's a national register of historic places nomination form with a date stamp of February 19, 1981. Ned has me scroll down to page 6. Mrs. Bangs' hotel, which opened in 1882, was considered "healthful for consumptives" and the facility included a "spiritual healing" cottage. Got to admit, that sounds a little too New Agey for 1882.

"Next link," Ned says. I open an *L.A. Times* article about the building from 1983. Ned points to the paragraph he wants me to read. Emma Bangs moved from Boston to Pasadena in 1881, with her daughter, who suffered from tuberculosis. Mrs. Bangs brought with her extensive knowledge of "metaphysical healing."

"You're doing good," Ned teases. "One more link. It's a Wikipedia page for the Massachusetts Metaphysical College, an institution founded by a woman named Mary Baker Eddy in 1881. She taught metaphysical healing. Called it Christian Science."

"Always wondered what Christian Science was," I say.

"Just another thing to tuck away for now. We'll come back to it later. Right now, let's go for a short ride."

Fifteen minutes later, he pulls into the parking lot of Hahamongna Watershed Park, a couple of miles north of the bridge beyond the Rose Bowl.

"There's no easy access to the top of the dam from the road," Ned says as he pops open his trunk and pulls out a pair of Hush Puppies. "We have to walk it."

"What's a dam have to do with this?"

"You'll see."

Ned plops down on the bumper. Bends over and grunts as he swaps shoes.

"Hey, Mr. Rogers," I say, "how far are we hiking?"

"About a mile, round-trip."

We take a walking trail that becomes a horse trail littered with rocks and surrounded by thick brush. Halfway down, we stand aside as four horseback riders pass. Three of them are kids wearing Camp Hahamongna shirts. The leader—decked out in cowboy attire and mirrored sunglasses—must be their instructor. He tips his cowboy hat as we pass. "Howdy."

At the top of the embankment we pick up a pedestrian bridge atop the dam.

We walk halfway across the dam that stretches three hundred feet across a deep gorge between two steep cliff walls. One of the cliff walls was blasted smooth when the dam was constructed. But the cliff wall on the opposite side is in its natural state.

I can feel the soul trap vibrating through my backpack. "What is this place?" I ask.

"It's called Devil's Gate Dam."

That's weird. The words *devil's gate* are in the lyrics of "Pound of Hate." Jung's synchronicity fucking with me again? "Why is it called that?"

Ned beckons me to the railing. I hate heights, but look down. It's at least a hundred-foot drop straight into a dry riverbed. Ned points to the cliff wall to our right, the one still in its natural state. "There's one reason," he answers.

I see it almost instantly. The jagged rocks of the cliff wall form a face—an evil face. Eyes. Nose. Mouth. It's huge—must be forty feet tall. Striking. Obvious. Gives off a sinister vibe. "Holy shit."

"And take a look down there," he says, pointing to an enormous boulder at the bottom of the gorge. I squint. It's a hundred yards away, but unmistakable. Another devil's head. Abstract, but three-dimensional. Even has horns. The rock is smooth and gray. Massive—at least twenty feet tall.

"They have to be man-made," I say.

"Nope," Ned says. "Open that second link."

I take a seat on the curb. The link sends me to a page buried in arroyoseco.org. Old photos of the dam's construction and vintage postcards from the twenties and thirties. Ned points to an aerial shot taken in 1920, looking down at the half-constructed dam. "That photo was taken before they blasted the cliff over there," he tells me.

Look over at the smooth cliff face. It's so obvious, I laugh. A ginormous devil head—almost as tall as the entire hundred-foot cliff wall. This formation is more straight on. Eyes, nose, mouth. Even has ears.

Shake my head in disbelief. "This place is like Mount Rushmore in hell," I say.

Ned laughs. "Good one. Next link," he says. Before I click on it, he explains, "That's a photo from 1888, long before the dam was here." The old photo is taken from the banks of the river below. Water flows directly between the bizarre rock formations. The place emanates evil. "The Indians were scared shitless of this place," Ned says. "No wonder. That's how it looked when they were around. It was a forbidden zone for the Gabrielino Shoshone Indians. They thought this place was the gateway to the underworld."

I hand Ned my backpack. It shakes in his hand. "What the hell's going on?" he asks. "What's the trap picking up?"

"I don't know," I say. "Any guesses?"

Ned looks around. "I think this whole place is a massive magnetic vortex. There's got to be huge deposits of magnetite and other minerals buried underneath here."

The trap vibrates so intensely, I think for a minute it might explode. "Can't tell what it's reacting to," I say. "But we better get out of here before it fries."

"But we're not done yet," Ned says. "Turn around." He points toward the mountains.

Across a blanket of tree tops that span a mile-long trek of riverbed I see a campus of generic, unmarked buildings at the base of the foothills. It looks totally out of time and place against the rugged mountain range behind it. "That's NASA, right? I've driven past here."

"Right," Ned says. "NASA JPL—short for Jet Propulsion Lab.

Long before NASA absorbed it, JPL evolved from a small start-up company called Aerojet, founded in 1942."

"Okay, so?"

"Take a seat on the curb over there and type *Founder JPL* into Google. Read the first entry." Ned's smart. Knew just how to hook me. Do as I'm told with no argument. "I can't wait to see your face when you read this," Ned says all eagerly. He lights a cigarette and lets me read.

Open a Wikipedia page for a guy named Jack Parsons. Full name: John Whiteside Parsons. Died at thirty-eight. Rocket-propulsion researcher. Associated with Caltech. Cofounder of Aerojet. Then my jaw drops. Occultist. Thelemite. Disciple of Aleister Crowley. Leader of Crowley's American Ordo Templi Orientis Lodge. Author of a number of books on Crowleyism and the occult. Wait a minute. Anna Burrows had one of his books on her bedroom shelf. Look at Ned. "Are you shitting me?"

"I shit you not."

Google Parsons' name. Open a half-dozen websites and give them a quick glance. He invented solid rocket fuel. Summoned demons. Had some kind of close relationship with L. Ron Hubbard, founder of Scientology. There's a crater on the moon named after him. Goddamnit, I have to dig deep into this guy's life. "He's a legendary black magician," I say to Ned. "How is it I've never heard of him before?"

"Because you're a good Jedi," he answers.

I sum up what I just read. "He's a rocket scientist by day. Occultist by night."

Ned hums the *Twilight Zone* theme. "I've been reading all about him. He conducted rocket tests in the late thirties right in that riverbed," he says pointing to a spot between the dam and the NASA campus. "And according to a book I just finished, he carried out black magic rituals right here at the dam. Was personally tapped by Aleister Crowley to run his Order of Thelema Lodge in America. Crowley treated this guy like a son."

"It's doubly weird," I say, "because the goblet that's powering the IVeR belonged to Aleister Crowley."

Ned looks shocked. "You never told me that." He says it like a scared kid.

"I didn't?"

"No."

"Sorry—I guess I should have."

"Yeah, I guess so." Fear and annoyance as he says, "Why are we messing around with an object like that?"

"Because it's powerful," I say. "It works. Works better than any crystal we ever used. Isn't that what counts?"

"I don't know about that," he says, ominously.

"What else can you tell me about Parsons?"

"I'll give you a book about him. Read it. Called *Sex and Rockets*. But I'll give you a couple of highlights to chew on right now. Crowley's Order of Thelema Lodge was set up in Parsons' mansion on Orange Grove Boulevard."

"Shit, that's right by the bridge," I say.

"Nine blocks to be precise," Ned adds.

"What else?"

"Parsons supposedly summoned demons. Spent months trying to summon one in particular."

"Got a name?" I ask.

"Babalon," Ned says. "Parsons and Crowley spelled her name with an *a* instead of a *y*."

I try to remember that name from my demonology books. "Babalon . . . Babylon . . ."

Ned points to my iPad. Next link. Passage from an online bible. "She's in the Book of Revelations," Ned says. Read from Revelation 17:3–6:

> Then the angel carried me away in the Spirit into a desert. There I saw a woman sitting on a scarlet beast that was covered with blasphemous names and had seven

heads and ten horns. The woman was dressed in purple and scarlet, and was glittering with gold, precious stones and pearls. She held a golden cup in her hand, filled with abominable things and the filth of her adulteries. This title was written on her forehead:

MYSTERY
BABALON THE GREAT
THE MOTHER OF PROSTITUTES
AND OF THE ABOMINATIONS OF THE EARTH.

I saw that the woman was drunk with the blood of the saints, the blood of those who bore testimony to Jesus.

"So what happened?" I ask Ned. "Did Parsons summon Babalon?"

"No one knows for sure. Some say he pulled it off. It all took place in 1946. Parsons called it the Babalon Working project. . . . And, oh . . . ," Ned says," remembering something else. "The guy who assisted Parsons in the ritual was none other than L. Ron Hubbard."

"What?!"

"It's true. Hubbard was Parsons' right-hand-man in all this Crowley sexual magik thing."

"So the father of Scientology is linked to Aleister Crowley? Are you shitting me?"

"I shit you not."

"How did I not know this stuff?" Note to self: *Study harder.*

"Hubbard lived with Parsons at the mansion on Orange Grove," Ned says.

"How long was this before Hubbard founded Scientology?"

"Five or six years," Ned says. "But during the time in between, Hubbard skipped town with a big chunk of Parsons' fortune and Parsons' wife. Bought himself a yacht in Florida, sailed off into the sunset with Mrs. Parsons, and went into hiding until just after Parsons died in '52. Suddenly reemerges and founds Scientology."

This tale is just too fat and juicy.

"You think Scientology is grounded in Crowleyism?" he asks me.

I shrug. "Pretty much everything I know about Scientology comes from a *South Park* episode," I admit. "Really can't say."

"Practical question: Do you think any of this explains why Tom Cruise freaked out on Oprah's sofa?"

I laugh. Fucking Ned.

"So what do you know about Christian Science?" he asks next.

"Even less," I admit.

"Well, it's got a lot of weird baggage, too." Ned says. "Lot of websites out there say it's also grounded in Satanism."

"Come on."

"See for yourself," Ned says. "Mary Baker Eddy, the founder of the religion, rewrote the entire Bible because she said there were 30,000 errors in it. She was way out there. Radical stuff like there is no devil or hell. There is no sin. The body really doesn't exist, so there is no such thing as illness. The biggest error in the Bible, according to her, was that Christ never died on the cross. Essentially he faked his death, hid out in his tomb, and waltzed out three days later the savior of the world."

"Denying the existence of evil. Mocking Christ. The Holy Trinity—yeah, that's demonic doctrine," I say. True Satanic messages basically take religious fundamentals and turn them on their ear.

Don't know if it's the information overload, but I'm getting a bad headache. It's like the dam is emanating dark energy. I'm feeling confused. But I need to know more. Need to hole up and start researching right away. "So," I summarize, "you have some form of Crowleyism for sure, plus some early ties to Scientology and Christian Science. Three controversial—possibly dark—religious cults all casting a shadow on our bridge?"

"Freaky deaky, my friend," Ned says. "Coincidence . . . or something more?" He says it just like Rod Serling.

"Do you think all this stuff about Jack Parsons is true?" I ask him.

"Sounds crazy, for sure," Ned says. "But there are so many sources. And they all say the same things." He stares at the sterile-looking NASA buildings on the hill. "Being inside Caltech for twenty-five years—I've heard Parsons' name bandied about all over the campus. I've crossed paths with some real old-timers who knew him. They used to talk about this stuff. I thought they were senile old fossils. Not anymore."

"What happened to Parsons?" I ask.

Ned sits on the curb next to me. "Made a fortune. Seems to have blown most of it. Bad investments. Plus Hubbard robbed him of a big chunk of it. He married a woman who claimed to be the personification of the demon Babalon, then died in an explosion in his home laboratory in 1952. The blast was so powerful it rocked the bridge and all of Pasadena. Yet he never lost consciousness, despite the fact the explosion blew off his arm, shattered his other limbs, and tore half his face off. Took the bastard three hours to die."

"Sounds like it's right out of a *Tall Tales of Terror* '50s comic book."

"I know," Ned says. "But that's not the end. Gets even weirder. The night Parsons died, his mother committed suicide. In a house she was renting one block from the bridge. OD'd on pills."

"She killed herself the same night?"

"Yep."

"So what caused the explosion?"

"No one knows for sure," Ned says. "A lot of speculation. Experimenting with a new rocket fuel? Creating smoke effects for a Hollywood studio? Summoning a demon? Murdered by the FBI? Even one theory that Howard Hughes had him killed for stealing company secrets from Hughes' aerospace company."

"What a fucking story," I say. "A man who grew up, lived, and died on the same street. Fortunes made and lost. Black magic meets visionary technology. All within the confines of the Arroyo Seco."

"It's a doozy," Ned says, "but I haven't told you the punch line."

"What?"

"Remember that list of Aerospace companies you emailed me—the ones Millie Barrington and her husband were early investors in?"

"Yeah."

"Guess what company is on that list?"

I get chills. "Don't tell me—Aerojet?"

"Yep," Ned says. "Now do you smell a rat?"

I think it over. "I don't know," I say. "The Barringtons invested in a lot of local companies. Probably a hundred or more."

"Fine," Ned says. "But what if this old lady knows more than she's letting on? I mean, do we trust this woman? What if we're being set up?"

"Set up for what? Let's not get paranoid," I urge. "She's paying us to do a job."

"I'm just playing devil's advocate—here at Devil's Gate Dam." He smiles.

"We have one more stop to make," he says.

"There's more?" I marvel.

As soon as we put some distance between ourselves and the dam, my headache subsides. We take the horse trail back to Ned's car. It's a quiet walk back. We're both thinking.

Ned drives back across the road that parallels the dam, heads north into the foothills. He hugs the windy canyon streets until we reach a road near the rugged mountain range.

"We're on Loma Alta, right?" Ned asks me.

I check the next street sign we pass. "Yeah."

After a series of sharp turns, Ned pulls off to the side of the road and turns off the ignition.

"Why are we stopping here?"

"You'll see."

I glance around. Straight ahead, the road crests a hill. A huge man-made debris basin drops off to the right. To the left, a house stands on a hill above the road. Beyond the house, it's nothing but the steep and rocky San Gabriel mountain range. "Why are we stopping here?"

Ned lights a cigarette. "You mind?"

"No."

He puffs away. "Did you ever hear of Gravity Hill?" he asks.

"No. Where is it?"

"Right under your ass," he says. "Watch this." Ned puts his Subaru in neutral. Instead of rolling backward down the hill, the car rolls forward. Up the hill.

By the time the car reaches the crest, my headache is back. "What the fuck?" I ask. Soul trap vibrates off the charts again. "What is this place?"

"You tell me," Ned says.

"We're rolling uphill. How is that possible?"

"I'm a genius and I can't explain it."

"Well, try."

"The theories run the gamut," Ned says as his car rolls steadily up the hill. "Teenagers have been telling ghost stories about this place for a century. One says an old Indian was killed here and his spirit pushes cars out of harm's way. Another says a bus load of kids were in a wreck back there around that wicked bend. Some of them died, and their spirits push cars up the hill."

"Stop the car," I say. Ned slams it back in park. I climb out, soul trap in hand. Stand in the center of the road and scan the area. No identifiable targets. Yet the trap goes apeshit.

Ned rolls down his window. "What do you got?"

"It's not a soul—or a group of souls. But it's something. Something huge."

Ned looks in his side mirrors. "A lot of people say this is just an optical illusion—that we're really going downhill instead of up."

"Come on, we know uphill," I say. "No way this is downhill. Right?"

"Not a chance," Ned says. "I think it's another electromagnetic vortex," Ned says. "I'm feeling the same sensations I felt at the dam."

"Me, too."

Ned flicks his cigarette butt out the window, lights up another. He grabs an empty bottle of Mountain Dew from his backseat floor, opens the car door, and drops the bottle on the road. It rolls up the hill, picking up speed as it goes.

"Does that look downhill to you?" he asks me.

"No."

"Everything is being pulled up. Do you feel it in your solar plexus."

A twinge of vibration in my chest. Feels like I'm being subtly pulled, like I'm wearing a suit of armor and there's a big magnet at the top of the hill. "I feel it," I say.

"Get in," Ned orders. Jump in and Ned takes off. Once we're over the hill, the odd physical sensations pass for us both. "Felt like my head was crackling back there," Ned says.

"Me, too."

As we barrel down the meandering roads toward the freeway, my head clears, but my thoughts are still a mess. The Colorado Street Bridge. Devil's Gate and its demonic rock formations. Aleister Crowley and his disciple, Jack Parsons. Rocketry. Scientology. Christian Science. Gravity Hill. My fucking head spins. "What's really going on here?"

I want answers, but Ned doesn't have them. "I don't know. "We have the Jet Propulsion Lab with an occult past sandwiched between two electromagnetic vortexes. And all that energy flows straight downstream to a suicide bridge where two hundred souls remain trapped."

My mood sinks. I'm agitated. The energy from the dam and Gravity Hill has knocked me way off-center. I'm like a kid on the verge of a tantrum because his jigsaw puzzle pieces won't fit.

"It can't all be a coincidence. There has to be a connection to all of this. What is it?"

Ned looks sullen. "I don't know. But I'm telling you—I have a feeling Millie Barrington might."

"Get her on the phone," I tell him. "Let's find out."

Ned pulls over in a parking lot by the Rose Bowl. He gets out of the car and walks in big circles while he speaks on his cell. I stay in the car, study some of the research material he printed.

When Ned comes back, he looks worried.

"Well?" I ask.

"Spoke to Ronnie Barrington. Millie is ill. According to Ronnie, very ill. She can't speak to us. The way he talked—she may be on her way to the big adios. I hit him with a laundry list of questions, but Ronnie played dumb. I don't think it's an act. He claims he knows nothing about Aerojet, his parents' old business dealings, or the maid's suicide in 1950. The guy's a drunken buffoon. I can see how he might have been out of the loop."

"So now what?" I ask in frustration.

"Now? Now we call this off. We don't know what we're dealing with."

I kick the glove compartment. "So just quit, that's your solution?"

"How can you not smell a rat, Kane?" Ned scolds me like a kid playing with matches. "We have to be more careful. We just can't go walking into places without knowing what kind of spiritual energy might be lurking there. We go looking for one thing, we might end up stumbling upon something else, something we can't handle."

I get straight to the point. "We're never gonna get close to this kind of money again."

"I told you once—you can't spend money from inside a coffin," Ned yells.

It's like the two hemispheres of my brain are locked and fighting each other. One voice says, '*Just walk away and focus on the band. You never wanted to do this in the first place.*' But another voice shouts, 'Money, money, money!' And there's a third voice in there, too, whispering about secrets that need to be uncovered. I battle my will daily, but not like this. There's something deeper calling me, pulling me. I should walk. I know it. But I just can't.

"I'm not convinced we should quit," I tell him.

"Forget it, Kane. I watched you die once—"

"And I survived," I remind him.

"Talk to Eva," Ned suggests. "She's smart. Let's see what she thinks."

"Good idea," I say. Way better than good. Any chance to see Eva sounds like a fucking brilliant idea.

When I'm in my car, I dial her. Straight to voicemail. Shoot her a text:

I need to talk to u.

A few minutes later, I get one back:

Me 2. Have news. Out of town. Swamped. Meet Thurs before work. 8? Starbucks across from office?

I text back:

It's a date.

Just seeing the word *date* gives me hope. Two seconds later, she responds:

Date? In your dreams.

Shit.

Thirteen

I get up early and put the morning to good use. Practice hard. Haven't heard a word from Bo or any of the band. Hope to hell the record deal is being hammered out.

My first stop today—the 101 Coffee Shop. Lunch with Detective Cliff DuPree. Last time I saw him was a year ago, right at this table. He looks exactly the same. Think he's even wearing the same tie. Still sporting his Magnum P.I. pornstache.

He's pleased I've kept my nose clean and focused on my music. I tell him I'll invite him to our next gig. He tells me he'll wait for the CD.

"Wonder where that waitress is that had the hots for you," I say, digging into my Cobb salad.

"I got her pregnant and had to kill her," he says, all serious. My fork freezes in place. He keeps eating his catfish sandwich. Doesn't crack a smile. Keep staring, waiting for him to blink. Takes a long time for his pornstache to curl upward. "Bad cop joke," he says.

"I've got a story," I tell him.

"I wondered why we were here."

"Teenage shitbag boy meets teenage fucked-up girl on Facebook. They start chatting, nonstop. Shitbag boy proposes a suicide pact. Teenage girl buys into it. She offs herself. He pussies out. Or maybe he just did it for kicks."

To DuPree's annoyance, his catfish falls out of the bun. "So? What do you want to know?"

"How bad can I beat shitbag boy's ass?" I'm amped up on coffee and songwriting.

"Assaulting a minor? While on probation? Nah."

"Is what shitbag boy did a crime?" I ask.

He dabs Cajun seasoning off his mouth. "Don't know for sure," he says. "Maybe."

"I'm gonna track him down today."

DuPree dips an onion ring in ketchup and points it at me. "Not a good idea. One wrong move, and you're back in jail," he reminds me. "Just give me a name."

"J. D. Harlan," I tell him. "Seventeen, maybe eighteen. Azusa High School."

He jots the info on a napkin and shoves it in his shirt pocket. "I'll run a search," he tells me. "You keep your distance."

"If nothing else, the little shit can apologize to the girl's mother."

"Stay out of it," he warns.

I nod, waving the waitress over to ask for an extra helping of bacon bits.

DuPree gives me a suspicious cop look. "Why are you doing this?" he asks. "Did you know this girl or something?"

"Not when she was alive," I say.

Now it's a look of disappointment. "Shit, Kane, I thought you gave that up."

I keep eating.

"You're going to ruin your life if you don't wise up and destroy that thing," he says.

Not going there. End of lunch. End of discussion. A 'check, please' wave. "How's your family?" I ask.

I walk back to my apartment. I can't get Millie Barrington out of my mind. I should practice my guitar, but I'm drawn to my computer, tempted to dig into Millie's life some more. I give in. Poke around some websites, return to that dense online document posted by the author who abandoned his Barrington biography in '97. I speed-read most of it, but dig into a short, glossed-over section about Millie Barrington's hidden generosity. She made several large, anonymous donations to Pasadena causes, all the while being portrayed as a Scrooge-like figure by the press. The author even notes that she went to great lengths and great expense to see that a mentally ill housekeeper received the best psychiatric care money could buy. This has to be a reference to Helena Maldanado. I pinpoint the date. Bingo. 1950.

I'm about to call Ned when my phone vibrates. Text message from Bo:

MANDATORY band meeting. Rainbow. 7.

Uh-oh. There's news. I study the message. No hint whether the news is good or bad, but I don't like the way he capped the word "mandatory." My imagination goes all gray and shadowy. The deal got blown. I know it. With crystal-clear imagery, I imagine filling out applications at restaurants all over Hollywood. Waiting on assholes. Counting down the days until I die.

Come on, Kane—a little positivity for Chrissake.

This time I visualize us in a high-rise conference room with a view of the Hollywood sign. We're signing a contract using a ceremonial pen that Drexel says is the same pen his bastard father used to sign his band's epic, life-changing recording contract. Champagne corks pop. The Triplets of Melrose pour the bubbly and pass around the crystal champagne flutes.

It's working.

I'm so inspired, I kick the positivity up a notch. On my way to the Rainbow, I stop by 1600 Vine, the luxury apartment complex just south of Hollywood and Vine. I take a tour of a model unit. Sweet Baby Jesus. It's only a few blocks from my dump on Yucca, but it's another world. Brand-spanking-new. Hardwood floors. Two bedrooms. Could build myself a little studio. Fireplace.

Washer and dryer. Balcony patio. Killer view from the master bedroom. You can see the Frolic Room up the street. Way off in the distance, rain clouds roll in over the Hollywood sign.

I tour the grounds. Oh my God. Rooftop terrace with a pool and spa. Zen garden. Fire pits. Health club. Coffee shop. Dry cleaner.

Rent is three grand a month, give or take. This isn't a pipe dream. This is doable . . . almost.

I dick around dreaming about stainless-steel kitchen appliances so long, I'm the last one to arrive at the Rainbow. On the drive over, the skies open up. Park and hustle two blocks in the pouring rain. I'm drenched. Everyone is in the back corner booth except for Troy. Bo has documents spread out in front of him. When he sees me, he says. "Okay, let's get started."

"Aren't we waiting for Troy?" I ask.

No one answers.

"Are we ordering food?" Jay asks.

Bo looks anxious. "Let's just get through this first."

"Hurry up then," says Drexel. "What's the deal?"

"Five-hundred-thousand-dollar advance on signing," Bo says. I think we all let out a collective gasp. "Royalty percentages are standard. And remember, a third of the album budget comes out of that, so get the notion of buying mansions in the hills out of your minds."

Jay breaks out in a sweat. He grins wide. "Still," he says, "it's finally some decent money in our pockets."

"We get paid another two hundred grand when we deliver the record. We get tour support, though we aren't even close to finalizing the details on that. We're also guaranteed six hundred thousand on the second and third records, but Ira gets the option to drop us after the second album if certain sales thresholds on the first two records aren't met."

"Fuck it all," Drexel shouts, "this is a million-dollar deal!"

We all hug, bump fists, and raise glasses.

"Frankly, I was hoping for more," Bo says, donning his reading spectacles with a sigh. "Now for the terms of Ira Bowersock's offer. One—"

Drexel interrupts him. "One: We all have to sell our souls to Satan." Jay laughs.

Bo picks up the term sheet and studies it for comic effect. "That's not on the list," he says, smiling. "One: We can keep our name. I'm quoting Ira here—the name has a good story behind it. It's not too heavy. Two: We add another guitar."

"Totally agree," Drexel says, almost instantly.

Bo awaits my reaction. I'm okay with it. "Fine," I say.

Bo returns to the term sheet. "We add keyboards to the recording sessions. And maybe the live show."

Again, no arguments.

"Three," Bo continues, "Ira chooses the producer."

"Makes sense," I say. Drexel and Jay sit silently. They don't like it, but have one million three hundred thousand reasons not to gripe. Bullet dodged.

"Done, then," Bo says, checking it off. "Four: We're open to songwriting input from our entire inner circle."

Drexel throws off the Ray-Bans. "Bullshit," he snaps. "Me and Jay write the tunes."

Bo bristles. "I'm quoting Ira again—it's time for the band to grow up."

"What's that supposed to mean?" Drexel barks.

Bo throws down his pen. Turns red, and whisper-yells, "It means—don't fuck up my deal."

"Whatever," Drexel says. "Tell the prick whatever he wants to hear. I'll school him after my check clears."

"And last," Bo says, "Troy goes."

"What?" I ask. Wait for the punch line. Drexel and Jay just sit and look straight ahead. This is old news to them. "Why?'

"You know why," Bo answers. "He's not good enough." I'm about to defend him, but Bo cuts me off. "And he's never sober."

I shake my head in disgust. "We got here with Troy, and now we're just gonna Pete Best him?"

"This is nonnegotiable," Bo says. "And I agree with Ira on this one. Come on, be honest. You know we could do better."

Can't deny that. Troy's a character, a fun guy. But he's only a notch or two above mediocre. And lazy as hell.

"Good riddance," Drexel says.

Smug prick. I feel like tossing my beer in his face. "You don't have to be an asshole about it," I bark.

He puts his sunglasses back on. "Yes, I do," he says with that little smirk of his. "I'm a rock star."

"We're all in agreement then?" Bo asks. "Speak now or forever hold your peace."

We're all silent.

"Done," Bo says, putting the documents back into a manila envelope. "I'll call Ira tonight."

"Practical question," I say. "When does Troy go?"

"Termination is effective immediately," Bo says.

"Then who's our drummer?"

"Which leads to the next item on our agenda," Bo continues. "A drummer. Floor is open for discussion."

We all toss out names. It's a short list. Only three or four drummers with the chops to pull it off. And they're all in bands already. Bo jots down the names and guarantees to track them down tonight. We pick next Monday for auditions. That gives everyone a chance to learn our material.

Drexel shits all over Bo's plan. He just spews negativity. He whines that it'll take months to find a new drummer. No way will any of the drummers mentioned part ways with their current bands. No way can we go into a recording studio with someone we've never played with.

"Let's take it a day at a time. Don't forget, we have a deal,"

Bo reminds Drexel. "Every drummer on the Strip will kill to get with us."

For once, I'm with Drexel. It won't be easy to integrate a new member into the band. And then it pops in my mind like a fire-cracker—Joanie Soral, the drummer in my last band. Best drummer I've played with. She buries Troy. Does session work all over town, so she adapts quickly. A musical sponge. She totally nailed the drum tracks to "Layla" for me in one night last year.

"I want to throw out another name," I say.

Bo takes the paper napkin he jotted the names on out of his pocket. "Shoot."

"Joanie Soral."

"A chick," Drexel says, like she's a leper. "No way."

"Never heard of her," Jay says. "What band is she in?"

"I don't know. Haven't talked to her in four or five months. She was in my last band," I tell them.

"What—she your girlfriend or something?" Drexel asks.

"No, she's a pro," I shoot back. "A session drummer. Top shelf."

"No way," Drexel says. "A chick will throw off the band."

I ignore him, look at Bo and Jay. "I'm telling you, she's great. Just let her audition. You'll see."

"She really good?" Jay asks.

I nod. "Trust me."

"Where can I reach her?" Bo asks.

"I'll take care of it. Let me call her right now," I say.

When I get up to leave, Drexel starts pouting. Bo does his best to ignore him by thumbing through the paperwork.

Outside, the rain has died down for the moment, but I hear a distant crack of thunder. I stand on the rain-soaked sidewalk right under the famous Rainbow sign, and dial Joanie. Picks up on the second ring. "To what do I owe this honor?" she says.

Traffic zooms by, splashing water my way. It's tough to hear. I'll save the chitchat. "Care to audition for Astral Fountain?" I ask.

"Are you kidding?"

"No joke," I say. "We need a drummer—fast."

"What happened to Troy?"

"The record company doesn't want him."

"So it's true—you landed a deal."

"It's true."

"I know how Troy feels," she says.

Ouch. She's still pissed at me for bolting from our band when I joined Astral Fountain.

"I'm sorry it went down the way it did," I say, not really meaning it, but hoping it's what she needs to hear.

"You did the right thing," she says. "We weren't cutting it."

"So you'll audition?"

"Fuck, yeah," she says with a laugh. "When?"

"Monday. Noon."

"Shit—that fast?"

"Yeah. Can you play any of our stuff?"

"I've been to a few of your gigs. I have your EP. I'll start right now—slay it by Monday."

"Fuckin' A."

"Any other advice?" she asks me.

"Yeah," I tell her, "Put on your hottest outfit, an extra coat of paint, and kiss the singer's ass."

I pocket my phone. The rain comes down harder. I catch sight of a woman standing in front of a sushi joint directly across Sunset. Amazon tall. Buff. Skin-tight black leather pants and jacket. Long hair, pulled back. Big red lips. She's stares me down. She's oblivious to the rain. She must recognize me. Do I know her? No way. Wouldn't forget a woman that hot if I had Alzheimer's. I give her a nod and a smile. Nothing. Wave. She just keeps staring at me as the rain pelts her. Screw it. She can follow me back inside.

I return to our table. "Joanie'll be there on Monday," I announce.

"Great," Bo says. "I just got a hold of the others. They'll be there, too."

Drexel slams his hand on the table. "We're fucking rushing this," he says.

"I disagree," Bo says. "Look, we all know it's one of the three or four people we mentioned, or it's nobody. It's not like there are a hundred drummers to audition. And it's good to live on edge, to throw someone into the fire."

Drexel keeps pouting. "You're gonna fuck this up," he says.

Bo breathes deep. I can see him turning over appeasement strategies in his head. "If we don't connect with him . . . or her . . . we'll keep searching. And we're not going to worry about the rhythm guitar or keyboard slots until a drummer is in place. Agreed?"

Jay and I nod. Drexel ignores us, plays with his fork.

"Who's going to tell Troy?" I ask.

Drexel points at Bo. Bo gestures compliance. "It's my job," he says. "I'll go see him right now."

"I'll go with you," I say.

Drexel snickers. "Sucker," he says to me.

"Let's go," I say to Bo.

I have one foot out of the booth when Drexel decides to make an announcement. "I'm throwing a blowout at Voyeur Saturday night. You're all invited. Bring chicks." Shit, that's a pricey club. Drexel's serious about letting the good times roll. Drexel grabs my arm as I'm leaving and says, "That girl, Eva. You have a number or email?"

It hits a nerve like a dentist's drill. "Not for you," I tell him. I walk away but glance back at him right before I leave. He's shooting me that fucking smirk.

Bo and I track down Troy at Crazy Girls on La Brea. He's getting a lap dance from Natalie, one of the Triplets of Melrose I banged during my last night of debauchery. We sit at the bar and order a round. When the dance is over, Bo waves over Troy and his hard-on.

Troy has a shit-eating grin on his face. Bo hands him a beer. "You guys were right," Troy says to me. "That chick is smokin' hot."

"We need to talk," Bo says.

"Is the deal done?" Troy asks him.

"Yes, the deal is done," Bo answers. "But . . . I'm really sorry to say it doesn't include you." Wow, just like that. No buildup, no small talk. Just dropped the bomb on Hiroshima. Clearly not the first time he's done this.

Troy laughs. "What did you say?"

Bo eyes up the stripper on stage. Remains disconnected. "You're out, Troy."

Troy looks at me and laughs. "You're fucking with me."

This sucks. I don't know what to tell him. "Sorry" is all that comes out.

He's standing there with a beer in his hands waiting for a punch line that doesn't exist. Then it hits him. "Just like that?" he says. Tears well up in his bloodshot eyes.

Bo lets out a big sigh.

Then rage kicks in. "This is such fucking bullshit," Troy says. A big tear streaks down his cheeks. He looks right at me. "I thought you were my friend."

I find the balls to make eye contact. "I am," I tell him.

"And you honestly think I'm not good enough?" he asks.

"Yes," I say. "I'm being honest because you are my friend." I sound like a douche. What kind of shit am I spewing? What do I know about friendship—or honesty.

Troy gets right in my face. "Fuck you," he snarls. "And tell those other two pussies to go fuck themselves."

Troy is at the crossroads. He'll either work harder and get better or drink himself to death in a year. I could tell him a lot of things that would be true: to practice more, to lay off the sauce and the pills, to take his instrument more seriously, to get some help if he needs it. If I were a real friend, I could buy him drinks until dawn. Get him laid. Take him to dinner, watch him stuff his face, and listen to him vent. I could do all that. But I don't. I don't do a thing. Don't mutter a word.

I zone out as Bo gives him the details of his meager severance package. Natalie walks over. "Wanna party tonight, Kane?" she whispers in my ear.

Just what the doctor ordered. But I can't. "Rain check. Gotta work tonight," I tell her.

Bo nods at me and we make a beeline for the door. Right before I pass through the black velvet curtains at the exit, something tells me to glance over my shoulder and give Troy an honest, sympathetic look.

I don't.

I don't sleep well. Lightning flashes illuminate my room. Thunder booms. Such a foreign sound in L.A. It's been four years since the last thunderstorm I remember. Totally unnerves me.

Just before five AM, my phone rings. Don't recognize the number.

"Hello."

"Hello, Kane," says a woman, all slow and sultry. "Sleeping?"

"Who is this?" She has a sexy voice. I'm interested.

"It's Millie Barrington," she says. "How are you this fine morning?"

Gross.

She coughs—a heavy cough from deep in her chest. "Ronnie told me you called. Said you had questions. That it sounded urgent." The vitality she just had in her voice drains away. She sounds old again.

"Ronnie told me you were ill," I say.

"I'm feeling much better tonight," she says. "But at my age, a cold could kill me, so I don't get my hopes up."

"Thanks for calling me back."

"Telephones bore me. I tend to lose interest fast, so go ahead . . . ask your questions."

"You were an investor in a company called Aerojet."

"Aerojet?" She thinks. "I don't recall. That must have been in the early forties. My husband and I invested in dozens of aerospace companies. We made a fortune. I don't remember the names. I do remember Howard Hughes wining and dining us. Strange man. We invested a bundle in him."

"Did you ever meet a man named Jack Parsons? He lived and worked in Pasadena."

She thinks. "Hmmm . . . doesn't ring a bell."

"He was one of the founders of Aerojet. The company was based in Pasadena. You were one of the first investors."

"If I ever met him, I don't remember. You have to understand, Kane, I met at least fifty influential people a day back then. And Harry did most of the business glad-handing."

"Parsons was born and bred in Pasadena. He had strong occult ties. You're sure you never heard rumors about him floating around Pasadena?"

A long pause. "Was he the rocket scientist who died in an explosion?"

"Yes."

"I vaguely remember that story in the papers. What happened?"

"He died under mysterious circumstances. You're sure you never met him?"

"I can't be sure," she says. "I may have. But I don't recall. Is this somehow related to the bridge?"

"That's what I'm trying to find out."

"I'm sorry I can't be of more help."

"Then tell me about Helena Maldanado."

She goes silent. I can tell I caught her off-guard. "You've certainly done your homework."

"She was your housekeeper?"

"She was more than that. Helena was a dear friend and confi-dante. She was the old friend I mentioned—the one who told me the bridge was haunted." She sighs. I can tell she's settling into a comfortable chair. "You asked if I believed her. I didn't because Helena was also a very mentally disturbed woman. Always a tad unpredictable and emotional, but very honest and hardworking. Quite loyal to me. But as her condition grew worse she exhibited violent mood swings. She heard voices, became paranoid and suicidal."

"She claimed you ruined her life. Said she knew secrets about you. She was trying to sue you in her final days."

"She was a paranoid schizophrenic," Millie snaps. "By the end, she saw everyone as a threat. Just what are you accusing me of?"

"You drove her to the brink, then fired her, didn't you?"

"I don't remember—I probably did. I don't tolerate disloyalty."

"I don't get you, Millie. Why are you lying to me?"

"I'm not lying."

"You tried to get Helena the best psychiatric care your money could buy."

Millie's shocked at first, then mad. "How do you know that?"

"Like you said, I've done my homework."

Millie's anger flares. "The poor woman needed my help. But she leapt off that godforsaken bridge before I could see to it that she was properly cared for."

"I know," I say. "I also know that you're a lot more generous than you let on. Why the coldhearted act, Millie?"

"Because I don't much care for people," she says. "But I know that with my wealth, I have some responsibility to contribute. Not a lot, mind you. We all play the game, Kane. Just because I won the game doesn't mean it's my responsibility to help all the losers across the finish line. So, yes, sometimes I help. But I do it when I want to do it, not when someone tells me I should. And I sure as hell don't want to be praised for any help I provide. Good Lord, if that happened, I'd never find a moment's peace. When I die, I want the pundits to ask, 'How could she have lived a century with such poison in her blood?'"

"You have a heart inside you, Millie. That secret is safe with me, provided you're not keeping other secrets from me about the bridge."

"You know everything I know on the matter," Millie insists. Her voice cracks. "Helena's suicide still haunts me. It's that bridge," she says. "She was right. It's haunted, isn't it."

"Yes."

"And you're going to make it right," she says.

Silence hangs. "I'm working on it," I say.

"I trust you'll continue to do so. . . ."

Decision time. Walk away or see this through.

I knew there was another reason she called us. Something she was hiding. Helena Maldanado. She lost a friend to the bridge. She didn't miss a beat when I asked her about Jack Parsons. She never got nervous, never stammered. Can never be totally certain, but I think she's telling me everything.

"Yes," I finally answer. "I'll keep working on it."

"Good." Thunder booms. "Is it storming?" Millie asks.

"Yeah."

"I love when it storms in Los Angeles. Such a rare treat."

"Me too."

"I take it you're all alone in bed on this stormy night."

Where is this going? "Yeah," I say.

"No lady friend?"

"Not tonight." She better not start talking dirty.

"Why is that? You're a handsome fellow. Even with your lonely eyes."

"Still searching, Millie."

"Remember, Kane, you're playing the same game I played."

"What does that mean?"

"It means, you could meet a nice woman of means—twenty,

twenty-five years older than you. Inherit a fortune while you're still young enough to enjoy it."

I chuckle. "Was *Sunset Boulevard* on tonight?"

"I'm serious," she says. "If you don't know any women who fit the bill, I might be able to arrange some introductions."

I laugh. She's just fucking with me. I think.

"Do you have a grandmother?" she asks.

"Not that I knew," I admit.

"May I give you some grandmotherly advice based on hard-earned experience?"

"Please do."

"Marry rich. But if you don't, at least marry someone who will do for you before they do for themselves. If you do either of those things, you'll emerge the victor."

"The victor?" I ask, amused.

"The game, Kane. You either win or lose."

"Isn't the point of love to both win?"

"Impossible," she barks. "Don't leave it to chance. Make it a point to always win."

I can't help it—I like this old lady. Seventy years separate us, but we're kindred spirits. "God, Millie, that's probably the worst advice I've ever heard."

Now Millie laughs. "Live a hundred years—you'll see."

Fourteen

I finish off my coffee. "So that's the story," I tell Eva, after dumping all the new info Ned uncovered about the bridge and the surrounding area. "Ned is cautious, thinks we should probably pack it in. I think we should keep going. So what do you think?"

She doesn't even take a minute to answer. "I agree with you."

"You're not just saying that because I'm giving you a chance to go back inside the trap?"

"No," she says too quickly. I look her in the eye. "I don't know . . . maybe," she says. "I can't help it. I'm too curious. And those souls—they need help. And the money . . . come on."

"I have to warn you," I tell her, "being that close to suicide is draining."

Eva's getting emotional; tears well up, but she fights them back. "It's just unimaginable to me how you can stand up there and jump. I mean you just step off, and that's it. Over and out."

I just want to reach over and touch her. I feel closer to Eva than ever. I've wrestled with these same questions. "There's something so yin and yang about suicide."

She fumbles in her purse for a Kleenex. "What do you mean?"

"It requires genuine cowardice to just give up on life. But it also requires real courage to actually go through with ending it."

She thinks it over. "I see what you mean," she says. "It takes self-awareness to put the question of life and death to yourself, and then weigh all the factors. And then you turn around and destroy that supreme self-awareness."

"Exactly." She just said what I've been trying to say. Damn, she's smart. I so want to have conversations like this. It's her brain as much as her body.

"When do we go back to the bridge?" Eva asks.

"Friday night. Midnight. Let's meet at the same spot. I'll call Ned and set it up."

I grab two more coffees. Before I even sit down, Eva's on to the next topic. "J. D. Harlan," she announces.

"Did you track him down?" I ask.

"Spoke to the principal of Azusa High School—Mr. Pepper."

"Is he a doctor?"

Eva's too focused to laugh. "No students named Harlan. Had him check back five years. Nothing. What do you make of that?"

Shrug. "Using a fake name? Or lying about where he lived and went to school?"

"You said Anna Burrows never saw him, right?" Eva asks.

"Right. Spoke to him a couple of times, though."

"What if it was someone fucking with her?"

"Why?"

Eva's imagination runs wild. "Maybe he's one of those creepy predators. Maybe she had an enemy that was posing as this guy."

"Maybe he did kill himself," I say. "Just somewhere else." Run it all through my mind again. "I read all the emails and text messages," I tell her. "It felt authentic—just like a real, dipshit kid. I think J. D. Harlan exists. I have a call in to a cop friend. We'll find him."

"I never got a chance to ask you—did you ever go see Anna Burrows' mother?" I nod. "How did it go?"

"Tense. Sad. But I think I convinced her I was telling the truth."

"That's 'cause when you want to be, you're genuine," Eva says. I tuck the compliment away.

"I want to help her," I say. "I have to find the little shit that did this to her daughter."

Eva packs her notebook and phone in her purse. "I have to get to work."

"Oh, speaking of little shits," I tell her, "my singer Drexel wanted me to give him your number. Fucking guy's unbelievable."

"He didn't need you," she says. "He found me."

"What?" I squeeze my coffee until it squirts out the lid.

"He called me last night."

The urge to smash the window at Starbucks is great. I bite my tongue. Silence for at least ten seconds.

"What?" she sort of giggles. I think she's enjoying this.

Can't hold it in anymore. "Fucking little prick," I grunt. People next to us look over.

"This had better be your protective big brother side coming out," she says, with a sliver of alarm, "because I can handle myself."

"What did he want?"

"He asked me out."

"You said no . . . right?"

She stands and looks at me. "I said yes. We're on for tonight."

I'm sinking. This can't be happening. I bite my tongue. *Just shut up, Kane.*

"What's he like?" she asks. "Tell me."

Don't answer. Silence hangs.

"Tell me," she repeats.

"A spoiled child," I say.

She starts with her sleuthing. "He's talented. You said so yourself."

"L.A. is full of talented assholes."

"He's cute," she adds.

"Cute?" Anger just spiked up to friggin' homicidal rage. "So he's your type? Spoiled trust-fund brat."

"He has a trust fund?"

I snap. I start pointing at her like my finger is one of Freddy

Krueger's blades. "You don't tell him a thing about the soul trap—or what I do. Do you understand?"

She looks at me all surprised. "Don't talk to me like that. What are you so pissed off about?"

"What do you think?"

"Oh." She should just shut the fuck up now, but she doesn't. "I told you already . . . you and I—"

Cut her off. "Mention any of this and I will write you off."

She's ready to rumble. "A threat?"

My phone rings. It's Detective DuPree.

"Hey," I answer, hoping Eva thinks it's a girl.

"I ran a pretty thorough check on your boy Harlan," he tells me.

"And?"

"Nothing. I don't have a single hit for a J. D. Harlan, age sixteen to twenty, in Azusa. Or anywhere else in L.A. for that matter."

"You're sure?"

"I do this for a living," he says.

"So that's it?" I ask, stumped.

"I got in touch with a detective from Pasadena. He wants to question Teresa Burrows. Right now. Her place. Thought you might want to be there."

"All right. I'll get there as fast as I can."

I pocket my phone. I wait for Eva to ask who it was, but she doesn't. I crack first. "That was a detective I know from LAPD."

"Is he one of the many cops who arrested you?"

"Ha, ha. He ran a search on J. D. Harlan."

"And?"

I drag it out nice and long. Make her wait. "He doesn't exist," I finally say.

"Where are you going?"

I walk away first. "None of your business. You can come to the bridge Friday night. Or not," I say with a chill. "I really don't care."

"Count me in." Eva shoots me a weird, deliberate semismirk. She knows I care. She's glad I care.

I call Ned on my way to La Crescenta. Tell him we're on for the bridge Friday night. He argues, but I shut him up fast—tell him Eva and I are in agreement about going in, that I spoke to Millie Barrington and I think she's telling us the truth. End of discussion. Then he starts groaning. I make the mistake of asking him what's wrong. He starts telling me about his bum knee—in brain-numbing detail. There goes the entire car ride. So much for unwinding with some tunes.

I ring Teresa's doorbell just after six.

DuPree is already there, along with a lanky Hispanic guy about my age. Teresa's an emotional wreck. DuPree called her before they arrived, so it wasn't a total surprise. She has no idea why I'm there with detectives from two different police departments. She doesn't want to talk. Who can blame her?

DuPree introduces the stranger. "This is Detective Leo Alvarez from the Pasadena Cyber Crimes division." Shake his hand. Bad shirt and tie. Crew cut. A scar on his forehead. Mustache. What is it with detectives and mustaches?

"And you're a relative of Mrs. Burrows?" he asks, confused by my presence.

Look at Teresa. What am I? "A friend," I say, phrasing it more like a question.

Teresa nods. "Yes, he's a friend."

DuPree fills Teresa in. I came to him with the name of Anna's boyfriend. He ran a search and found out the guy didn't exist. He alerted the Pasadena police because it falls under their jurisdiction.

"But this is La Crescenta," Teresa says. "I don't understand."

DuPree shoots Alvarez a look like which one of us should explain. Alvarez nods to him. "Anna died in Pasadena," DuPree explains. "Her death isn't just a suicide. It's a crime."

"Crime?" Anna asks.

"A homicide," Alvarez says. "Someone's responsible for her death. And I need to find him."

DuPree looks at everyone. "This is the point where I officially have to duck out. Detective Alvarez will take over from here." DuPree shakes Anna's hand. "My condolences," he says.

Alvarez asks to see Anna's bedroom.

I walk DuPree to the door. "Keep me in the loop," he says. "Interesting case. I'm curious."

"This guy any good?" I ask him.

He shrugs. "Don't know. Police departments everywhere are adding these tech-savvy types. It's all too new for me to say." Shake his hand. "Keep your nose clean," he tells me. "Think before you act."

"That's the same thing you told me when I was eighteen."

"Maybe you'll finally listen."

I join Teresa and Alvarez in Anna's bedroom. Alvarez is disassembling Anna's PC, labeling the components.

"I already wiped it clean," Teresa tells Alvarez.

"Not a problem. I have some pretty impressive data retrieval resources at my disposal. Are there other computers in the house?"

"Just my laptop," Teresa answers.

"Did Anna use it?"

"No. Never," Teresa says.

"Did she have a cell phone," he asks. Teresa nods. "Can I have it please." Teresa leaves the room, returns a minute later with a phone. Alvarez tags it. He asks me for a hand and we transport the equipment to his car.

We regroup on Teresa's back patio for Alvarez's litany of questions. Alvarez types notes on an Android as he questions Teresa.

"I can't believe anyone would do this," Teresa says over and over.

"Teenagers can be ruthless," Alvarez says.

It's feeling too much like an interrogation. I decide to chime in. "There's a period where they have no problem bad-mouthing each other to their faces," I say. "Then something happens and it all becomes backstabbing. That's the worst time."

Alvarez nods. "Did Anna have any enemies?"

"Enemies?" Teresa says with a tinge of anger. "That's exactly what she called them. It used to piss me off so much. How can a seventeen-year-old kid have enemies?"

"But she did have significant conflicts with her peers?" Alvarez asks.

An emphatic "Yes."

"Who?" he asks.

"Everyone," she says.

"Everyone?"

"Starting with her former best friend," Teresa says, "and it goes from there. Every friend. Every teacher. Every relative became her enemy."

"What's her former best friend's name?" he asks.

"Piper May."

"Do you have her address?"

"She lives across the street. Things got ugly between them."

"When did this fallout occur?"

Teresa looks exhausted—in need of painkillers. "Late 2009. After her dad died. After that, Anna underwent a significant personality change." She starts to cry. "I can't really do this—I'm sorry," Teresa says.

Alvarez is pushy with a heart. "I know this is very painful," he says, "but, Mrs. Burrows, I need to know everything."

Teresa cries, waves him off.

"Why don't I tell you what I know," I suggest. "Teresa, you can fill in the blanks." She nods, blows her nose.

I take my time. Tell Alvarez everything—Anna's father's death, her deep involvement with the occult, her sexual relationship with someone on Facebook named Frater Lieber, her involve-

ment with Aleister Crowley's O.T.O., her bizarre cyberrelation-
ship with J. D. Harlan and their suicide pact. Alvarez's fingers are
flying.

Anna looks relieved. She composes herself enough to give
Alvarez a list of a dozen of Anna's former friends and teachers.

"Who were her current friends?" Alvarez asks.

"I don't know," Teresa answers. "We stopped communicating."

"Was she gone a lot?" he asks.

"Not really. She spent most of her time in her room on the
computer or reading."

"I think I have enough information to get started," Alvarez
says. He offers her the box of Kleenex. "We'll find out who did
this," he assures her.

"How?" she asks. "It could be anyone."

"We'll investigate on two fronts," he explains. "The old
fashioned way—interviewing friends, teachers. And," he says,
"we'll analyze her computer, investigate all of her online activities." He holds his hand up. "Digital fingerprints," he says. "As
incriminating as the real ones." Alvarez sees that Teresa is spent.
"I think we've accomplished enough today." He stands, offers
his hand.

I don't know whether to leave with Alvarez or not. I decide to
stay. I pull Alvarez aside before he's out the door and whisper to
him, "Can I call you for updates?"

He's suspicious.

"Why? Who are you to this woman?"

Don't know how to answer.

"A friend."

"Good friend?"

"Yeah."

"*Gooood friend?*" he asks, grinding it out.

"That's out of line," I say.

"She seems a little fragile. Maybe you can be a go-between if
I need one."

I nod. Wish I had a card to hand him. Always wanted one of those. "I'll email you my contact info," I tell him.

I close the door on Alvarez. I turn and look at Teresa but don't know what to say. Neither does she. She looks broken. But hot. And I love that hint of a Hispanic accent. Goddamn, this is way inappropriate. We keep staring. She's giving me a look—I think. But maybe it's the tears. I break the silence, crack the tension. "I need a drink," I say. "And I'm starving. Wanna grab a bite?"

I follow Teresa to Pepe's, a Mexican hole-in-the-wall on the main drag in downtown Montrose. She lands a parking spot right in front. I circle around and find a spot a few blocks away in front of a Christian Science Reading Room. Great little neighbor-hood—tree-lined streets, a real retro feel. "I like this place," I tell Teresa when I reach her on the sidewalk. "Looks like Main Street at Disneyland."

"They shoot a lot of movies here," she tells me. "Because it looks like it could be anywhere."

We order top-shelf margaritas before our asses even hit our chairs. They arrive in a flash. Scarf chips and salsa. I unwind. Hold my big glass aloft. "Cheers." Goes down nice and smooth.

"Why would anyone want to hurt Anna?" she asks.

"I don't know," I say. "Maybe someone was trying to get even with her."

"For what?"

"Who knows? Teenagers are fucked-up creatures."

"She could be so vicious," Teresa says.

I smile, recalling my short time with Anna. "I only knew her for a few minutes, but she knew just what buttons to push. Had a lot of venom in her."

"I don't know where it came from," Teresa says. As if she needs to defend herself, she says, "Not from me. Not from her father."

We order. A carne asada burrito for me. Fajita salad for her. Two more margaritas. She's still tense. She stares down into the salsa bowl and says, "I don't know what happened. Why we couldn't get along. Her friend, Piper, across the street, she and her mother are like Siamese twins. They do everything together. They're silly—like best friends."

"More seventeen-year-olds hate their parents than like them." I'm talking out my ass, but making it sound like I know a thing or two.

"Were you that way?"

Down the hatch with margarita two. Go there or not? Hold my glass up and wave on another. "I was an orphan—after the age of ten."

"That's terrible," Teresa says. "I'm sorry."

I finish, my third margarita arrives, and, despite that voice in my head screaming, *"Shut up!"* I tell her about my past. When the fuck am I ever going to learn?

Finish my third margarita. Teresa nurses her second. "Another?" I ask.

"I shouldn't," Teresa says. "I'm too old to drink like this."

"You're not old, believe me," I say. My eyes go straight to her cleavage. She catches me looking. Busted.

"I'm going to be forty next month," she admits. "Forty, but sometimes I feel seventy."

"You don't look forty," I tell her. There. Said it. Conversation just took an interesting U-turn.

"What about you?" she asks. "You might be thirty. But I doubt it."

"I'll be twenty-nine in a few months."

"And you make a living as a supernatural . . . ?" She doesn't know how to phrase it.

"As a paranormal investigator?" I finish.

She nods.

"No, I'm also a musician."

"Really?"

"I'm in a band. We just got a record deal."

"That's exciting. Congratulations."

Overly cocky when I say, "We just played the Whisky."

"That's major," she says. "I saw the Chili Peppers there in 1990." That news requires another margarita and leads to a twenty-minute discussion about the early nineties music scene on the Strip. I'm chowing my burrito and soaking up her college stories about seeing Guns N' Roses and Nirvana in their prime.

Tequila's knocking me on my ass. She's looking really fine. I like her. I want to do more than just bury my head in that cleavage; I want to get to know her better. "How about you? What do you do for a living?" I ask.

"Nothing, right now," she says. "But I'm working on it."

I say nothing.

"After my husband died, I went back to school."

"For what?"

"Working on two degrees," she says. "Psychology. I'm going for a PsyD at the Chicago School of Professional Psychology."

"In Chicago?"

"No," she laughs. "There's a branch in Westwood."

"A psychiatrist?"

"No—I'll be a licensed, practicing clinician." Look at her stumped. "A therapist," she explains."

"Specializing in what?"

She pokes at her food. She's hardly eaten a bite. "I'd like to focus on families affected by suicide."

Noble. Smart. "How long until you hang your shingle?"

"I'm at least nine months away from finishing my dissertation. But I'm logging hours, doing an internship with patients at Gateways," she says.

"I'll bet you have some stories."

She pushes around salad greens. "I do. Some very sad ones."

"Any funny ones?"

"Not really."

"What else are you studying?" I ask, hitting bottom on the third margarita.

"Screenwriting," she says. "At UC Northridge."

Damn liquor. I come about an inch from slipping up and telling her I already know she goes there. Shit. *Slow down.* She'll think I'm a stalker. *Go easy.* "So you're a writer?"

"It's just a hobby," she says. "Something I love to do. I know the odds are slim. Can't rely on it to make a living. But we all need to dream." Nod my approval. Clink her glass. "I just want to earn my degree," she says. "Finish something I started a long time ago."

"Which is . . . ?"

"I was working on an English degree at USC. Wanted to be a screenwriter way back when, but I got pregnant my junior year."

"Spring break gone awry?" I joke.

"Entire junior year gone awry. Dan and I got married. I never finished college."

"A psychologist screenwriter?" I say. "You'll have lots of material to write about."

Two more margaritas. We kick around our favorite movies. Mine: *Pulp Fiction.* Hers: *Thelma and Louise.* Never saw it. She lights up when she talks about it. "We'll have to watch it together," she says.

Yes! Sofa time.

I'm genuinely curious about something, but I don't know whether to ask or not. If I were sober, probably wouldn't. But here I go. I begin with a disclaimer: "Don't mean to get too personal . . . but how does one without a job pay for an education? I only ask because it's something I should look into someday."

Question catches her off-guard. She takes a minute to gather her thoughts. "When my husband died, there was a lawsuit . . . and a settlement."

"Oh." My body language invites her to elaborate.

"Dan was a serious runner. Over thirty marathons. He was taking a supplement that affected his heart."

"Like ephedra?"

"Along those lines," Teresa says. "He took handfuls of pills every morning. Drank shakes. He'd take anything if he though it'd make him run ten seconds faster. Anyway, it led to his death."

I think back to my days and nights locked away in isolation during marathon guitar sessions. "When something makes you feel good, it's easy to get obsessed."

"I never understood his obsession," she says. "He'd put his body through hell. For what—a nice medal? He should have been spending all those hours with me and Anna."

I remember that flash of disappointment in Anna's face when she realized her father wasn't with me in the trap. "I don't think Anna ever got over his death."

"She was a daddy's girl," Teresa admits.

"How about you?" I ask. "Have you gotten over it?"

"I don't know," she says. "When someone that strong is there in the morning and gone that night—without any warning. I don't think anyone gets over something like that. But I'm trying."

"It's good that you have the . . ." Stammer. Bite my tongue just shy of saying *money*. Rephrase it more tactfully. ". . . Resources to continue your education."

"It wasn't a million-dollar settlement or anything like that. But it was enough for me and Anna to start over. And now she's gone."

"You must have other family," I say.

She shakes her head. "Only child. My parents are gone." Tears well up. "Three years ago, I never had a minute to myself. Now, I'm all alone."

When she says that, I get sucked in. We're kindred spirits. Fellow members of the Lonely Hearts Club. I reach over and squeeze her hand. "I know how you feel," I say, and mean it.

"Don't like your salad?" I ask, changing the subject.

"I haven't been eating much," she says. "There's been so much food in my refrigerator—from neighbors, friends. Weird how food gets associated with death. Turns me off."

"Your appetite will return."

"I won't starve," she says.

It's time to go. She's drunk. One more drink and we both might wreck on the way home. I wave for the check. She grabs her purse, wants to pay. I insist and hand the waiter my plastic.

I feel compelled to say something meaningful, but I'm half in the bag and, as always, my brain, heart, and mouth are all disconnected. I give it a shot, though: "You've faced a lot of death," I say. "You're still standing. And you'll make it through this."

This time she reaches over and squeezes my hand. "I'm so tired," she whispers. "I just want to take a yearlong nap, wake up, and start over."

"I'm not a psychologist," I say, "but what you just said there is really healthy."

"What?"

"A lot of people would have said, *'and never wake up.'* But you said, *'wake up and start over.'*" She smiles at me, nods. "Starting over is good," I say. "It means you're still in the game."

I walk her to her car. An awkward moment. I feel like kissing her. Too sleazy? I think she's thinking about it, but not sure. She's an emotional wreck, after all. I open the car door for her and settle on a hug. She kisses my cheek. "Thank you," she whispers in my ear. "You have no idea how badly I needed an evening like this."

She gets in her car. "You okay to drive?" I ask. "Those margaritas were potent."

"I'm okay," she says. "Just up the hill."

Closes the door and starts her car. Knock on her window. She lowers it. "Call me when you hear from that cop," I say.

"Okay."

A long shot, but what the hell? "You're probably not up to it," I say, "but my lead singer is throwing a shindig Saturday night in Hollywood . . ." I let it hang. Wait for a reaction. She's polite. She gives me a look like she's at least thinking about it.

"I don't think I'm ready for something like that," she says. She smiles. It's genuine. "But thank you. That's sweet of you."

I watch her drive away. It was worth a shot.

I weave my way back to Hollywood. When I get home I can't get Eva out of my mind. Drexel? Is she fucking serious? I kick my sofa across the room. Then I pour myself a glass of Jameson and sulk.

Feel lonely. If I had a friend, I'd drag him out to a diner. Make him watch me drink coffee and listen to me vent.

Instead, I settle for whiskey and the most depressing music I can think of in my iTunes library.

Fifteen

I head over to Pasadena and kill Friday evening at Barnes & Noble and Pasadena Guitars. Nice little guitar shop. I wander around, play a little. Seriously thinking about buying a Martin D-18 acoustic.

I pop in a pawn shop on Colorado that has some used guitars on the back wall. Play some more. No standouts. I wander around. Come across a box full of old postcards. Thumb through. I pull one out—it's of the bridge. It's yellow and weathered. Flip it over. Dated 1946. A note from a young soldier, just returning from the war, to his mother in Pittsburgh. Tells her he's standing on this "grand bridge" wondering what the future holds and hoping for the day he can move his parents west to join him. His name: Charles Galbraith. Wonder what ever happened to him.

The postcard moves me. I have to have it. Don't know why. Something tells me he might have been a jumper. Or is it just my imagination? Price tag: five bucks. Offer the owner two bucks. He says no. I shoplift it. Feels good.

I hit a bar, down a couple of beers. Grow surlier by the second thinking about Eva, so I quit drinking. Drive across the bridge to the Stoney Point Grill parking lot where Ned is waiting. Eva is already there, climbing gear in tow. I can't even look at her without seeing Drexel's smirk.

"Same game plan tonight as last time," I announce. No friendly chitchat. I'm all business. "Fair warning," I tell Eva, "clear your calendar tomorrow. You're liable to get pretty sick."

She rubs a hand over her flat stomach. "I remember how I felt that first time," she says.

I remember, too. I was good and pissed off that she went into the trap behind my back. Blew my chances with Eva right then and there. I push that bad memory below the surface and spend the next half hour walking Eva through the psychic protective measures Master Choi taught me the other day. It'll be rough going for both of us, but for me, at least, it should be easier than last time.

"How did your date go last night?" I ask her.

A little smile, then, "Great. Hey, I'll be at Drexel's party tomorrow night. You'll be there, right?"

Goddamnit. My world is crumbling.

"Here," Ned says, handing Eva an orange vest and hard hat. "I got us these for when we're on the bridge," he says. "Might be enough to keep a do-gooder from calling the police. Got some traffic cones, too."

Just like last time, I drive, drop Ned and Eva off on top of the bridge with the climbing gear. I brood. Circle around twice, seething, getting angrier by the second. Imagine drowning Drexel and Eva in their own bodily fluids.

I totally overestimated her. I was right when I dumped her the first time. She actually buys into Drexel's act? So pathetic. They can both rot.

I maintain my silence after I pick them up. I don't mutter a word the whole time we're parking or hiking down the ravine.

Eva cracks first. She pulls me aside right before we reach the bottom. "What's wrong with you?" she wants to know.

There's hate in my eyes. I gulp down a wide and colorful rainbow of insults. Push her aside. Keep walking.

I can feel my temper ready to blow the entire time I'm donning the climbing vest. I get distracted when our homeless pals reappear out of the shadows. "You're back," Mike says. He unzips his Warner Brothers sweatshirt and tosses it on the ground. "Need another hand?"

"Sure," I say.

"Another twenty?"

"Talk to my accountant," I say, pointing at Ned.

"Sure," Ned says.

Mike grabs the rope. Tall Kevin stands motionless, silent. He stares up at the bridge, glassy-eyed, a vacant look on his face. Unnerved, I ask Mike, "Is he all right?"

"He's having an off day. He'll sit this one out." Mike takes Tall Kevin by the arm and leads him to the shallow pond, where he takes a seat on a rock and begins rocking in place. I can tell Mike cares about this guy.

"You watch out for him, huh?"

"I try to," Mike says. "Tall Kevin's a good guy."

"No offense," I say, "but you seem kind of together. Why are you living down here?"

Mike's porcupine needles go up. "You don't really want to hear another sorry-ass tale about a failed actor, do you?" he asks.

"No," Ned says.

"I do," I say.

"Me, too," Eva adds.

Mike shakes his head in disgust, talks fast. "It was law school or acting. I chose to follow my dreams. But there were heroin dealers along my yellow-brick road. The companions I met along the way lacked heart, brains, and courage. And the yellow brick road ended right under this bridge. That's the elevator pitch. And that's all you're getting. So heave ho—up you go, motherfucker."

Eva, Ned, and Mike send me up on the count of three. I spot the lamppost I focused on last time. Stare at it. Focus. Nice and steady. There's a three-quarter moon tonight. I can see more than last time. Not good. Goddamn, I'm *way* up here. The urge to look down is overpowering, but I stave it off.

"All right," I hear Eva yell up. Stop in midair. I'm swinging like a pendulum. I steady myself. I put a big white bubble of protection around me, mentally don my white armor, get my breathing nice and steady, finger my lucky necklace, aim the soul at the top of the cluster, and pull the trigger. *Ka-boom!* The soul trap vibrates violently, but I hold barrel steady and don't get rattled. I'm shaking, swinging, but I won't take my finger off the trigger. I stretch the blast, milk it dry. Finally my hand feels forcibly yanked away. Don't know how many souls I trapped, but it's definitely more than one. "Lower me," I yell down. Smooth ride down, but my hands burn.

I'm out of the harness and packed up in a matter of minutes. Now my hands get cold. "Pay him," I tell Ned. He looks all annoyed handing over a twenty to Mike. "Give his buddy over there a twenty, too. Karma and all."

Ned peels off another twenty and hands it to Tall Kevin, who still seems oblivious. "Don't know whether to claim these guys as dependents or write this off as a charitable deduction," he bitches.

Then Tall Kevin looks up blankly and says, "That voice—it's talking to me again. Right now."

"What's it saying?" I ask.

He points at me. "It says, '*Kill him.*'"

Ned backs away slowly. Eva rushes to my side and clutches my arm. I grip the climbing bag tight. Prepare to swing. This white armor better do its magic. We're all frozen, staring at each other.

Mike helps Tall Kevin up. "He's just talking out his ass," Mike says. "Don't listen to him."

But I'm listening. "How do you answer the voice?" I ask.

An absent stare on Tall Kevin's face, then: "I tell her I ain't killing nobody."

"I told you," Mike says. "He's a good guy, just fucked up is all."

When they disappear into the darkness, Ned says, "Let's get the fuck out of here."

We double-time it to the camper—all uphill. Eva and I barely break a sweat, but Ned is huffing and puffing. I stop and pretend to take a rock out of my boot just so he can catch his breath.

"We're not coming back here without a big fucking gun," Ned says. "Jesus, did you see the look in his eye?"

I climb behind the wheel. On the ride to the top of the bridge, Ned quickly connects the trap to the Tesla and confirms there are five souls inside—our most ever. I drop them off and wonder who we'll be meeting next as I loop around twice before picking them up.

I pull into our nook at Stoney Point. My palms are blistered. The windfall of souls came with a price.

When it comes time to go in, I stall. None of us have any idea how intense the journey inside will be with multiple souls present. If one soul can scramble your brain and make you sick, what will three do?

Eva insists on going in first. Her reasoning: she's cautious—way more cautious than I am. If she senses trouble she'll bail, whereas I would stubbornly stay. Second, she thinks Ned and I are far more experienced at monitoring vital signs than she is.

They're both good arguments. If she goes in first, I can watch her vitals like a hawk. Pull her out at the first sign of trouble. Know better what I'll be dealing with when I go in.

It's a huge risk, but we all agree—Eva will go in first.

It feels completely alien to be the one wiring up Eva for the journey inside. I tell her I'm worried she's not going to have the strength to tear off those eerie bodysuits.

"I can handle it," she assures me. She grabs my arm, digs her fingers in, and squeezes.

I'm extra cautious, making sure every electrode is precisely applied. When it's time to place the electrodes on her chest and lower abdomen, I tell her to unbutton her blouse and jeans. After that, it's goddamn impossible to concentrate. Not an ounce of fat. Flawless tits—not too big, not too small—just friggin' right.

I take my good old time applying the last of the electrodes before she buttons up and dons the NuMag helmet and Ganzfeld goggles. I swallow down my anger at her and carefully walk her through the protection exercises. I make her describe her white protective armor. She's way serious and does exactly what I tell her.

Guide her through the projection routine step-by-step. She's an A student. In less than half an hour, she's gone.

Ned monitors her vitals, eyes locked on the dual monitors. "Dude, this is a weird feeling," I say.

"I'll bet," Ned says. "Just relax. She'll be fine."

I never take my eyes off her. Every so often, her head rocks or her limbs twitch. There's an inhuman quality to her spastic movements. "I'm a fucking nervous wreck," I say.

Ned laughs. "Now you know how I feel."

"Everything okay?" I ask.

"Vitals all look good," Ned says, studying the monitors.

Ten minutes later, I hear a beep. "What's that?" I ask, keeping my eyes locked on her.

"She's triggering the lever," Ned says. "Here we go. . . . Lever activated."

"Well?" I ask about a minute later.

Ned's silent for another thirty seconds. Then he says, "Soul ejected. Atta girl, Eva."

Breathe a little easier. One down, one to go.

We're silent for the next several minutes. Then Eva signals for the lever. Ned sends it. A few seconds later, her twitching intensifies. She goes rigid. Monitors sound shrill alarms.

Ned leaps up in a panic. "Jesus Christ, her pulse is tanking," he shouts. "We've got to get her out of there! I think it's trying to take her with it."

I grab Eva's hand, stroke her forehead, and whisper in her ear, "Stay calm. Stay calm."

Ned drops back in his seat, grabs the mouse. "Exit door activated," he says. "Come on, Eva—get your ass back here."

She convulses. I'm on top of her, ready at any second to perform CPR if she flatlines. Adrenaline racing, waiting . . . waiting . . . and then the spastic tremors stop. Her breathing steadies.

Color returns to Ned's face. "Her pulse is back up," he says, still breathing hard.

Then her eyes open wide, her back arches, and she gasps for breath. I pull off the helmet and goggles, grab her face in my hands, inch in close, and let her eyes focus on me. "It's okay," I whisper. "You're back."

She's melting down. Weeps as she tears off the electrodes plastered on her body. Then she sits bolt upright and her projectile vomit covers me. I don't even blink. I hold her head steady and let her unload. Ease her down on her back when she's emptied the tank. Ned tosses me a cold cloth and I apply it to her forehead. I hold her hand silently until she's calm enough to speak.

"What happened?" I ask, equal parts urgency and calm.

"I got scared right away," she says. "The dim room. Those bodysuits. It was terrifying."

"I know. It took guts to go in there."

She takes the cloth off her forehead and dabs around the corners of her mouth. "The first one was only seventeen years old. He thought it was still 1974."

"Did you get a name?" I ask.

"Denny Stetson. Sweet kid. Shy."

"Did he tell you why he did it?"

"Jumped after he didn't get accepted to Stanford. I guess UCLA was a fate worse than death."

"You're kidding?"

"Father told him he was a disgrace."

"Poor kid."

"When I opened that door," Eva says, "a fog poured in and took him away—just like you said. Where did he go?"

I shrug. "I don't know."

"I don't think it's a good place," she says with a sad look.

"Neither do I," I admit.

Eva sits up, looking at me pleadingly. She squeezes my hand. "The second one was . . ." She lays back, rolls on her side, buries her face in the pillow, and sobs. "She was the same age as me. Mavis Royer." Eva can't get it out.

I pat her shoulder. "You have to tell me," I say. "Just take your time. What has you so upset?"

"She's the person Ned told us about the first time we visited the bridge. The woman who threw her three-year-old daughter off and then jumped." Eva curls up and weeps.

"Oh, man." No wonder she's a basket case. "When did that happen?"

She mumbles something. I have to ask her to repeat it twice. "May 1, 1937."

"Why did she do it?"

Eva looks at me like I'm an idiot. "She was insane. You could see it in her eyes. Hear it in her voice. She was frantic . . . violent. She attacked me. Thought I was keeping her daughter from her. I had to fight her off until the fog pulled her off me."

"Did you tell her her daughter survived?"

"I tried to, but she didn't believe me," Eva says. She begins to regain her composure. She sits up again. Looks worn. "It's so draining to be in the presence of that kind of madness."

"I know," I say.

She grabs my arm. Looks to me for an explanation I don't have. We stare at each other in silence. "It's just so fucked up," she finally says.

That about sums it up.

"You need some water and fresh air," I say. I glance at Ned and give him a nod.

"Come on, Eva," he says. "Let's go stretch our legs."

We both help Eva down the ladder. She's unsteady. Ned leads her outside. It's just me and a bed full of vomit. Puke in the camper is nothing new. At least half the times I come out of the trap, I lose my lunch. Ned has a big stash of cleaning supplies on hand. While they're out strolling in the moonlight, I strip the bed, toss the sheets in a dumpster behind the restaurant, Lysol, and spray down everything with 409. When it's spic-and-span, I open the door and summon them back in.

Eva is weak. Pale. Ill. She looks around, smells the disinfectant. "I'm sorry," she says, breaking into tears again. "I'm so embarrassed."

"Not a problem," I say. "I've been there."

She climbs back to the bed and falls asleep instantly.

I look at Ned. "I'll go in and deal with the rest of the souls."

"I'll get everything ready," he says.

Here we go. I wire myself up. After watching what Eva just went through, I spend extra time meditating, protecting myself, and energizing my chakras and aura before I commence with my normal entry routine. The extra effort pays off. My mind settles and I'm on my way quickly.

I hear the hum. Open my eyes. Three mannequin-like figures walk aimlessly, like lunatics walking in circles in an asylum. They occasionally bump into each other, or a wall, or the table and chairs. They're all men. I approach slowly. They sense my presence when I step near—freeze. I gently guide one of them to the table and help the other two take seats on the floor against the far wall. One of them seems to relax when I treat him gently. The other one bristles, pushes me away.

I take the hand of the soul at the table, give it a few reassuring pats. I grab a handful of the skinlike material at the top of his head and yank so hard it drives him to his knees. Tear the cowl away. Expose a face. A Japanese guy—slight, midthirties, glasses—looks up at me. He's confused. Deeply suspicious of me. Thinks it's still 1942, the height of the war. He has a fiancée back in Japan. She can't visit him. He can't return to her. He's despondent. Speaks good enough broken English.

"Is that why you jumped?" I ask. "Over a woman?"

Tears well up in his eyes. "That's not why," he says. "I give up because they took me from my home. My job."

"Who did?"

"The US army," he says in Engrish. Comes out like "almy."

"Took you where?"

"To prison camp in Santa Anita."

"Why?"

"Because I am Jap."

"Were you a spy or something?"

"No. I wasn't spy or soldier. I had nothing to do with the war. I was mechanic with good job."

"So why did they take you?"

"They took us all."

"When?"

"Last month. All Japanese were ordered to Rose Bowl. We were taken on buses."

"So what happened?"

His voice cracks as he recalls painful memories. "I am not animal in cage," he says. A tear streams down his cheek. "I do nothing wrong. I love America. I love Roosevelt. Why am I prisoner in my own country?" I look at him and shrug. "It's insanity—this war," he cries.

"How did you end up at the bridge?" I ask.

He plots it out on the tabletop for me with his hands. "I escaped. I was hunted. Running. Alone. Nowhere to go." Hopelessness emanates from him. "I ended up on bridge. Nowhere left for me to run. It was the edge of earth. So I jump."

His own brand of Hari Kari.

"I am not Japanese. I am not American," he cries. "I am just me." He thumps his chest.

Spoken like a very old soul caught in the wrong place at the wrong time.

"I hurt no one. Why must I be hurt?"

He grabs my arm, pleading for an answer. "I don't know," I say, "Because we live in a shitty, unfair world."

I press the button under the table. The lever appears. "Come on," I say, helping him up and leading him to the door. "You have to go now." I pull the lever. The door opens. Silence. He's scared. Shivering. Fog rolls in and takes him away.

The door slams shut. The dissipating fog smells stale.

I never even asked his name.

By the time I yank the bodysuit off the next one, I'm spent. He's a sweaty ox of a guy in the prime of his life. Brown hair, a handlebar mustache, and cement-stained overalls. Looks like an old bare-knuckle fighter from the turn of the twentieth century. I give him the run-through.

Through an Irish brogue as thick as his forearms, he introduces himself as John Sullivan. "Call me Johnny," he says. Tells me it's a blazing hot day—August 2, 1913. He and his sixteen-man crew were just laying concrete forms on a new span of the bridge when the scaffolding they were standing on collapsed. Sullivan and at least two others fell into the fresh concrete, which gave way and collapsed 150 feet to the streambed below.

"What's the last thing you remember?" I ask him.

"Billy Thum was laughing his bollocks off. I'd just recited a limerick." He's grinning, recalling it: *"A mortician who practiced in Fife, made love to the corpse of his wife. 'How could I know, Judge?—She was cold and did not budge—just the same as she acted in life.'"*

I crack a smile. Fucking Irish and their rhymes. "That's it? That's all you remember?"

He shakes his head. The smile vanishes. "I remember the sound of the wood cracking—like a forest of oaks snapping like twigs—all at once. Landing face first in the wet cement, trying to crawl out of it when the bottom dropped. I remember the fall. Remember telling myself to kiss my arse good-bye."

"You were the first person to die on the bridge?"

"Two others joined me a few seconds later," he says.

"Why didn't you leave through your exit door after you died?"

"What door?" he asks. "There was no door. Only darkness."

"Did you hear anything? See anything?"

"No. Felt like I was blindfolded, dragged, and strung up like a sock to dry on the line. Then, I think I just went to sleep."

The lever appears for the third time. "Road's rising to meet you, Johnny," I tell him. "Time to move on."

"I wish I could say good-bye to me dear wife and child."

"Yeah . . . well." Don't tell him they've probably been dead for decades. He can be surprised if they're waiting.

Johnny looks at me, grins, and winks. "I'm on me way to Heaven," he says. "Jesus will welcome me."

"You lived a good life then?" I ask him.

"Surely not," he replies. "But Jesus was an Irishman like me."

I laugh. "Didn't know that."

"It's true," he says. "He lived with his mother until he was thirty-three, never had a job, and thought he was the son of God." He grins.

I pull the lever. The door inches open more slowly than before.

I shake Johnny's hand. "May you be in heaven a half hour—"

"—before the devil knows you're dead," he finishes. Smiles wide and gives me a playful slap on the shoulder. Lurch forward. Fucker's got a strong handshake.

When the door opens completely, I expect the fog to roll in. This time, a soft blue light penetrates the darkness and a cool breeze flows through the room where we're standing. It's a warm and welcoming light. Then—distant at first, but steadily increasing in volume and intensity—I hear the sustained, calm, vibrational tones that welcomed Donna and Ollie when I released them last year. A melodic reverberation that oozes peace. Unseen, but present somewhere in that blue light, awaits Johnny's family. Voices beckon. Johnny's soul radiates. I get hit with a blast of it. Feels good. "I'm on me way," he says, excitedly, before dissolving into the light. A few seconds later, I hear him shout, way off in the distance, "Glory be—there's whiskey over here!"

The hypnotic blue light fades into black. The door closes gently and steadily.

Silence.

I help the last one up. He doesn't flinch. I tear away his bodysuit. He's about my age. Blond crew cut and goatee. Short and wiry. Denim shorts, sleeveless white tee, sunburst tattoo on his left shoulder. He scratches at his arms, looks me in the eye with big, polka-dot pupils. Drug addict for sure. Probably meth. Looks crazy. He's a badass.

"So this is hell?" he asks.

"Not quite. Not yet."

I tell him where he is, who I am. He laughs. Thinks it's cool. Has this crazy look, like he might lunge at me. Note to Ned: *Make a set of handcuffs for ghosts like this.* He asks me for a cigarette and gets pissed when I tell him his smoking days are over.

His name is Jimmy Bleyer. As soon as he says it, it rings a bell—a newspaper article. I read about him in a pile of information Ned gave me. He was out on parole in '99. Found out his wife ran off with another guy, chased her down, and shot her and her mother in the head in front of his two kids. Led the police on a thirty-mile chase to the bridge, where he got out and jumped.

Did I mention I pretty much hate everyone? Especially drug-addicted murderers. *Just press the button and pull the lever.* But I can't fight the urge to ask him the one question that bugs me.

"Why did you drive all the way to the bridge? Why didn't you just shoot yourself?"

Jimmy looks at me, his eyes bugging wide. Rocks in his chair nervously, thinking about it. "Not sure," he says. "I'd never even seen that bridge before. But someone was telling me to go there. Dude, it was freaky—like my car was driving itself."

Suddenly the door behind us inches open by itself. I haven't activated the lever.

What the fuck?

Then it flies open. A familiar, chilling sound booms. Moans. Static. Demonic wailing. A blast of noxious air knocks us on our asses. Suddenly I'm choking on the taste of sulfur. My eyes are flooding. I glance over. Through watery eyes, I see Jimmy sling-shotted into the darkness.

I struggle to get to my feet. The darkness glows burnt orange. Two giant hands with long black fingernails burst through the door, grab me by the neck, and drags me through the door into the ash and smoke beyond it. I see that burnt-orange glow.

It's a demon.

I'm fucked.

Sixteen

I'm dead. Again.

I see my door for just a few seconds. Bright red with a crystal doorknob. I want to open it, but it blows right past me. Vanishes. Smoke dissipates. Nauseating stench fades. Orange glow dissolves into a dense gray fog.

I'm gliding along, then walking. Taking steps. Feeling my way forward, lost in the blanket of fog.

I'm alone.

And so fucked.

I hear a voice calling for help through the mist. It's the Japanese guy I just ejected. I shout out, "Stop walking! Keep calling out. I'll find you."

I follow his voice through the blinding gray cloud. Filled with a gripping anxiety that my next step will be my last, right off the edge of a cliff. I'm covered in a cold, wet mist. I keep reaching out. Nudge forward. Grab a shoulder. Found him.

"Where are we?" the Japanese guy asks.

"I don't know," I say. "But let's stick together. What's your name, dude?

"Tatsuo. And yours?

"Kane."

We shake hands and keep moving.

I hear a noise. Movement. Four figures pour out of the fog and surround us. They're gray-haired, faceless, featureless, wearing stark-white jackets and pants. Three male, two female. I try to barrel past them, but their touch paralyzes me. I'm frozen on my feet. Tatsuo is behind me, screaming for help. One of the faceless figures gets right in my face. I feel warmth radiating from the blank canvas face. I'm dizzy. Two figures grab me by the arm and lead me forward. I can walk—barely.

The fog thins enough to reveal a sterile-looking, unmarked white building. It's bland. There's no earth beneath it. We're floating in a storm cloud. Devoid of signage. Looks like a newly constructed hospital doused with glossy white paint.

Tatsuo and I are led inside. "Don't leave me," he pleads.

I see long white hallways with doors on both sides, most of them shut. I glance in a few of the open doors. People wearing white hospital gowns are either asleep or sitting on the floor in empty white chambers. The conscious ones look all vegged out.

I break away from my guides—or guards—long enough to peek inside the window of a closed door. A faceless white figure like the one escorting me holds an unconscious woman in her thirties in her lap, like a mother holds a baby. The faceless figure strokes the woman's hair tenderly.

I get a chill.

Don't like it here.

I pass an open door and hear, "I know you." It's Stanley Tekulve, the hotel manager I ejected from the trap in Carmel.

I freeze.

My guides beckon me forward. I resist. They try to drag me. I fight back. Throw wild punches. A couple of them land. Two of them drag Tatsuo away screaming. I discombobulate the other two long enough to duck into Stanley's room and slam the door shut.

There's no apparent lock, but the guides can't seem to enter. They bang on the door. Yank it. It won't budge.

"What are you doing?" Stanley demands to know.

"What is this place?"

"The Medicantium," he says. "They're Cleansers," he says,

pointing to the white-clad faceless being trying to pry the door open.

"What goes on here?"

"All of these people—everyone—they did what I did."

"Suicide?"

He nods.

"It's a wonderful place," he says. "I thank you for sending me here. Please—just open the door and let them in."

I smell a rat. Stanley was self-absorbed and melodramatic when I met him. There's something different about his voice. He's too calm. "You're not like yourself," I say. "What happened to you?"

"I was a broken soul. My Cleanser is fixing me."

"How?"

"Touch. Reflection. Discussion. Isolation. Studying. My Cleanser touches me. She loves me. I relive my life. See the instances where the breaks occurred."

I'm not even sure it's really him. "You're not the same person I met. So who are you?"

"No one . . . yet. I am being remade."

"What are you talking about?"

"I understand so much more now, Kane," Stanley says. "My Cleanser helps me rest. Heal. I sleep and am rewired. Made new."

"You sound brainwashed," I say, grabbing and shaking him. "Or else you're a demon fucking with me. But you're sure as shit not the vindictive prick who loved the idea of Millie Barrington growing old and dying."

"Don't you understand, Kane? I was broken. We're all broken. We need to be fixed. The Cleansers help us wash away the shame of our self-destruction, wash away all that's bad so all we're left with is the good we've managed to hang onto in life."

"This is your punishment, right?" I say. "You're being forced to say this?"

He shakes his head, looks at me all calm and hollow. "Cleansers don't punish. Yes. It's a violation to the universe to squander the gift of life. But I punish myself when they show me the opportunities I lost, the opportunities many others lost because of my suicide."

My mind shoots back to hell—that cold cavelike nook I was trapped in. Seeing my life. Living lost opportunities. Experiencing the consequences of my poor decisions. The pain of the flames and the beatings from the demons were nothing compared to the pain of that self-reflection. Maybe I'm back in hell—just in a different wing.

"Is this hell?" I ask him.

"Hell is for souls who hate God and goodness. When there is no goodness left, when the badness can no longer be washed away, a soul's light is extinguished. Hell is for those dark souls—souls like Millie's." There it is, alive and well—a trace of his hatred still burns. "But for us," he says, "everyone here—there's still hope, still light in our souls."

"So all that talk about suicide victims going to hell is wrong?"

"It's just man-made religious doctrine meant to instill fear. The Medicantium is a place of healing—not damnation. There are reasons behind every suicide. Misguided as most of these reasons are, each one of them is weighed according to each person's circumstances. Only by thoughtfully evaluating every reason can a soul heal."

"But this place doesn't feel peaceful," I say. "I don't like it here."

"It's peaceful," Stanley says. "But perhaps not pleasant. You must resolve your problems. And that's not easy. My affair with Millie and all the other problems that drove me to my hopeless state didn't go away after my death. They followed me here. My suicide was an act of procrastination, not finality. Having failed to overcome my problems in life, suicide was, I thought, my only recourse to erase them. But now I know. The only way I can rewire and repair myself—to live again—is to face my problems. Overcome them."

"Live again?" I ask. "Reincarnation?"

"We live and die and continue on until our souls shine bright or go dark."

Why don't I believe him? Why do I have such a bad feeling? It's cold here. Lonely. He's talking all stilted. This is all wrong—like *Stepford Wives* or *Invasion of the Body Snatchers*.

"I'm getting you out of here."

"I won't leave."

"Suit yourself," I say.

I throw open the door, barrel past the Cleansers. I'm not ending up here. No one's erasing me.

I run down a flight of stairs. Sprint through another corridor. A head peeks out of a doorway. "Kane, help me. Get me out of here."

Anna Burrows.

"Come on," I yell.

We make a run for the front door. Four Cleansers block our path, but our joint panic and fear and rage startle them enough that we can shove them aside and escape the building. We run straight into the fog.

"Where are we going?" Anna asks.

"Away from here."

I stop. There are footsteps close behind us. "Run!" I grab Anna's hand and bolt forward.

"I want to go home," Anna cries, trying to keep pace with me. "I shouldn't have died when I did."

"Join the club."

We run until we're winded. Stop. Listen. Silence. I can't see a foot in front of us. "Thanks, dude," Anna whispers.

I shush her. Listen. No footsteps. "Thanks for getting me out of that place," she says.

"Are you okay?" I ask her.

"Shit, I can't be fixed," she says. "I don't want to be fixed. No fucker's washing away my darkness. I worked hard for it. It's what makes me me."

There's the author of that wicked Facebook profile—still alive and well.

"I talked to your mother," I whisper.

"Was she pissed off?"

"Sad."

"Really?"

"More than you'll ever know. Shhhh." Listen. Silence. Maybe we lost them.

"What about J.D.?" she says, too loudly for me.

Turn an imaginary volume knob down in her face. "Quiet," I whisper-yell.

"J.D.—did you find him?" Shit. An ugly can of worms. Not here. Once we get out of this fog, I'll tell her there is no J.D., pick her brain, try to find out who set her up.

"No" is all I say. Then I grab her hand and we run again into the mist until we plow straight into a huge steel door. It's the door to the trap. I'm back. Just may get out of this yet. I bang on the door and scream for Ned.

I hear murmurs in the fog. Footsteps approaching.

Boom! Boom! Pound on the door. "Ned?"

Door cracks open; fog begins to rise. One foot past the threshold.

A half-dozen Cleansers emerge out of the fog. They grab Anna by the arm, pull her toward them. Clutch her other arm. It's a tug of war. She looks at me, panic-stricken. "Please, no—don't let go."

"I won't." As soon as the words are out of my mouth, her arm is yanked from my hand. She vanishes into the fog with the Cleansers. Her screams blend into someone else's.

Eva's.

Wham.

I'm back. Flat on my back. On the floor of the camper. Eva's kneeling over me. She breaks the suction of her mouth over mine.

My chest is on fire. She was performing CPR—on me. Ned—pale, flop sweat—looks like he's a few seconds away from a coronary. He stares down at me. "Holy shit. Can you hear me?"

I choke out a "Yeah."

Eva can't catch her breath. "Oh my God. Oh, my God! You were dead."

Ned gets in my face. "This fucking stops here! We're done with this. All of it!"

I sit up. I'm woozy. Tank is on empty. "I've been where they go."

"Hell?" Eva asks.

"No."

"Where then?" Ned wants to know.

I spend the next several minutes clearing my head and telling them about the souls I encountered, the Medicantium. Shit, for being dead over two minutes in Earth time, I'm doing pretty well. Sitting. Eating crackers. Drinking water. It took me forever to rebound last time I died. Am I getting used to it? Was it the fact that I journeyed to hell that savaged me last year?

Eva looks wiped out. Worse than me. It's the third time she's saved my life. I wish I would've left the anger I felt toward Eva and Drexel somewhere over there, beyond that door. But I didn't. Still, I'm polite enough to say, "Thank you."

She leans over and hugs me. It catches me off guard but I hug her back. It's not a hug hug, though. Just a hug.

I lost.

Drexel won.

I'm cool with it.

I guess.

Suddenly Eva goes limp in my arms. She's faint. Her journey inside, the adrenaline rush of watching me die—it's all too much. I guide her up the stairs to the bed of the camper. She's asleep in a minute.

"She can't drive," I tell Ned.

"How about you?" he asks.

"I'm toast."

"We'll stay put tonight," he says. "I'll keep an eye on you both. We'll head out at dawn's early light."

I nod, yawn wide.

"We're done here," Ned says. He grabs the trap and points it at me. "We're done with all of this," he snaps, holding it up like it's a cursed object. "For good."

"We'll talk about it later."

"No. You'll talk and I'll listen and shake my head. And you'll get what you want—like you always do. Those days are over, Kane. I say we destroy the trap now. Enough is enough."

I'm too worn out to argue. "Let's sleep on it."

Ned sits at the table—invites me to join him. "You want a beer?"

"Abso-fucking-lutely."

When it comes to beer, Ned never splurges. Two cans of Bud Light. "Cheers," he says. We tap cans.

"What do you make of the fact that that construction worker who fell ascended and the others vanished in that fog?" I ask him.

Ned takes a long sip of beer. "Must be because he died in an accident and the others killed themselves."

Sip my beer. I'm queasy. "That's my guess, too."

"That place—the Medi—whatever. What is it?" Ned asks.

"I don't think it's hell. It's not like when a demon comes for a soul. And it's not like when loved ones come in that blue light. The fog is gray and silent."

"Doesn't sound nice."

"It's not."

Ned pops the cap on another beer. When he drinks faster than me, I know his nerves are shot.

"What do you make of all this?" I ask him.

Usually a question like that elicits an hourlong diatribe where Ned tells me he has it all figured out. He knows every goddamn thing there is to know, after all. I kind of secretly hope this is one of those times because I'm clueless.

This time Ned just shrugs. He's as tired, and stumped as I am. "I was over at Barrington Library this morning doing more research. There are folders locked in a case that detail the entire history of the bridge. You can't take any of the stuff out of the library—or copy it—but you can look though it under supervision. It's a hodgepodge of information going way back. Time periods overlap. No order to it. More weird shit."

"Like what?"

"Like there was an Indian camp down there, up until the late 1700s when the missionaries arrived on the scene. The Gabrielino Shoshone Indians. Maybe there's some kind of Indian curse on the land."

An interesting theory. I'd be clueless on how to combat something like that. Know next to nothing about Native American shamanism.

"A hundred years later, an industrialist from Chicago named James W. Scoville buys the land and builds a big mansion down there. Builds a dam and a pump house to irrigate his orange and avocado groves. After moving west to Pasadena, he was one of the early trustees of Throop Polytechnic, which went on to become Caltech—employer of yours truly."

"What do you know about him?" I ask.

"Not a lot. A big philanthropist. Beloved. But who knows with captains of industry like that? Look at Nicky Lonzi. He was Mr. Wonderful to the world. But we found out what was behind his veil."

"What year are we talking?"

"Scoville lived down there with his family all during the 1880s. Died in 1893. I dug around and it turns out he's distantly related to three American presidents."

Come on, not more sacred bloodlines of the Illuminati shit. Sorry, I just can't bring myself to believe that the most successful, powerful, and überwealthy people are all connected. But I have read some convincing arguments, mostly from author David Icke, who can really screw with brains on this issue.

Ned chuckles at something. He's getting tipsy on a couple cheap beers and total fatigue.

"What?"

"I found an unbelievable story in that folder. You probably don't know who William Holden is."

"Give me some credit," I snap. "I was just talking to Millie Barrington about *Sunset Boulevard.*"

"Turns out Holden's from Pasadena," Ned says. "When he was seventeen, he walked the entire perimeter of the bridge—both sides—on his hands, to win a bet with his friends."

I imagine Holden up there, cheating death, but going on to live the Life of Riley. Anna Burrows, Denny Stetson, and William Holden—all up on that bridge—same ages, different fates. Life ain't fair.

"What's the official suicide count?" I ask.

"It's not something the record keepers in Pasadena like to broadcast. But according to my count, 197."

Ned's eyes are getting heavy. "Get some sleep," I tell him.

He stands and pulls the small bed out of the table bench he's sitting on. "You wanna flip a coin for it?" he asks.

"Nah," I say. "There's room up there," I say, pointing to Eva.

When I'm halfway up the ladder, Ned says, "If you pull your head out of your ass, I think you would have a shot with her."

"No comment," I say.

Crawl up and lay next to Eva. She seems to sense my presence and stirs. She curls up in a ball next to me.

And then it hits me: I'm finally in bed with Eva.

Too bad we're both half-dead.

Seventeen

Before I even stir, Eva's up and gone in the morning. Ned's still snoring when I leave. I feel a deep loneliness on my drive back to Hollywood. Colors just blaze. Everything seems more real. I should be happy to be alive. But I'm not.

I go home and crash. My phone wakes me up. I'm discombobulated. Is it day or night? I squint at the phone. 6:30 PM. Don't recognize the number or voice. Finally put two and two together when he mentions Anna Burrows—it's Leo Alvarez, the cybercop from Pasadena.

"I just updated Teresa Burrows," he tells me. "Would you like to hear what I told her?"

"Definitely," I say, sitting up.

"We were able to retrieve all the data from Anna Burrows' computer. Analyzed her Facebook profile. We've been working with Facebook on the J. D. Harlan profile."

"And?"

"It's fake. We already knew that. What we found out, though, is that the Harlan profile wasn't generated on a PC or a Mac."

"What then?"

"It was all done from an iPhone. We're working with Apple right now. Should ID the phone pretty quickly. I'll keep you and Mrs. Borrows posted."

"Thanks."

I take a shower and dress for Drexel's party. Can't bear the thought of seeing Eva and Drexel together. I'll need a lot of alcohol to cope with that.

In the stairwell, I cross paths with Pat Boreo, neighbor and former bandmate. We were just getting Lucid Fear off the ground, when I bailed and joined Astral Fountain. There's a palpable, god-awful silence when we almost kind of stop and talk, but don't, and then try again. Finally, Pat says, "How's it going, dude?"

"All right, I guess. How about you?"

"Good. Busy," he says. "Off to work." Along with being a killer guitarist, Pat's a certified EMT. He saved my life last year.

Silence again.

"Congrats on the record deal."

"How did you find out?"

"Joanie."

More silence.

"Look, I know it kinda got weird between us at the end. But . . . I'm glad for you. Really, I am."

"Thanks."

Pat's a decent guy. Takes his guitar playing really seriously. I left him high and dry and here he is, still talking to me. "I mean, at first I was pissed off, but, hell, I would have done the same thing."

Should just shut up, but I stammer, start sounding like an asshole. "It wasn't you—or Joanie or Cliff. You're all great." Sound patronizing. Just speak the truth. "It was a better opportunity. Astral Fountain was ready to break. They had a buzz."

"I know," Pat says. "Takes years to build that kind of buzz. We didn't have it."

Yet more silence.

"So we're cool?" Pat asks.

"We're cool."

"Let's hang out soon. Talk some music. It's always a blast."

"I got the Les Paul," I tell him.

"Sweet."

We shake hands. I feel a whole lot better.

I hop in my car. End up where else but the Frolic Room. It's early. Me, two drunks, and Gabe the bartender. Slug the jukebox and take my normal seat in the corner by the mirror.

Bartender walks over, Jameson bottle in hand. I drink a couple of rounds in peace, before he finally starts his yapping. "You look depressed," he says.

"I am," I say. "Always."

He tickles his earlobe. "Go ahead and bitch. I'm listening."

Only dumbasses unload their problems on bartenders, but then again, dying last night was a bit of a special occasion. "You believe in the afterlife?" I ask him.

"Believe in it," he says. "I've seen it. Had what's called a near-death experience."

"And?"

"I returned," he says.

"Was it a bad trip?"

"No. Heaven's a great place." He refills my shot glass and gets me a bottle of Stella. "Then there was the time you almost killed me . . ."

"You're exaggerating."

"Easy for you to say. You were the one doing the choking." "My Funny Valentine" by Chet Baker plays. The bartender listens and grins. "Did you play this?"

"Yep."

"Well done, sir."

"You said once there are two trumpet players better than Miles Davis. Chet has to be one of them, right?"

"Number two," he says.

"Who's numero uno?"

"You're looking at him."

"Bullshit."

"You're not the only guy in a band, Kane."

"Really? Trumpet?"

He nods.

"Where do you play?" I ask.

"All over town."

"Cheers," I say, knocking down my shot. He pours another, tends to the drunks at the other end, returns a few minutes later.

The whiskey tastes extra good tonight. Out of left field, I ask him, "Did you ever think about killing yourself?"

He shoots me a worried look. "No. Why—have you?"

"No," I lie.

He stands there, frozen, staring. "You're not thinking about it now, are you?"

"No," I laugh. "Just wondering—why do you think people give up?"

"On life?"

"Yeah." I knock down my shot and ask for another. I'm buzzed. Dying seems to have knocked my tolerance level down a peg. I'll need food or I'm in for a long night.

"They lose hope," he answers. "Life becomes meaningless and absurd. They can't take a step back and see things clearly anymore. They can't hear anything except their own voices telling them to die."

"Exactly," I say, slapping the bar. "See, you understand."

"They give up too soon. Always. They forget to remember that tomorrow is another day," he says like Scarlett O'Hara.

"Exactly!"

"Life's not supposed to be easy—or fair," he says. "It is what it is. You just have to keep believing your fortunes can change on a dime because, truthfully, they can. They do. You have to endure."

"Amen," I say, draining my beer. I wave off another. "I'm off to a party."

"Ever been to the Colorado Street Bridge?" I ask him while I pay my tab.

"A time or two," he says. "Suicide Bridge."

"Helluva place to die."

"Ain't they all?"

"Why do people jump off bridges?"

He thinks about it. "They're taking action—showing life who's boss. They're jumping from one life to the next. A clear transition. Breaking the plane, the surface from this life to the next."

I'm amazed. He's as smart as fucking Einstein right now. Or I'm drunker than I think. Tip him twenty bucks. He picks up the cash. "Thanks, but what's this for?" he asks.

"Tuition, professor."

Just after ten, I breeze right past the rope line and two door-men the size of refrigerators. I ring the doorbell. Enter. Voyeur is a trip. Lives up to the billing: erotic nightclub. *Eyes Wide Shut* wood-paneled millionaire's club meets Cirque du Soleil. Superhot topless dancers in Venetian carnival masks perform not only on stage, but in every conceivable nook and cranny in the place, including the ceiling where they roll around in netting. Dance floor is jam-packed. It's hot as a furnace and dark. Dim lights shine on wallpaper depicting vintage pornographic scenes. Everyone's glistening. Place smells like perfume, latex, and sweat.

Drexel's reserved the entire corner lounge—three tables surrounded by leather-studded armchairs and sofas. There he sits surrounded by Bo, Jay, Syd, Ira Bowersock, the Triplets of Melrose, and—fuck me blind—Eva, who's cuddled up next to Drexel on a sofa.

Drexel waves me over. He's riding high. Probably because he is high. I can see it. He orders bottle service at all three tables. Vodka, Cristal, tonic, and orange juice. Christ, this is gonna cost him a fortune—ten, fifteen grand depending on how big the crowd gets. I plan to do my part to put a dent in his wallet. Grab one of the vodka bottles and pour like it's water. Fuck the mixers. Charlie Sheen would be proud.

I take a seat. Pound the vodka. Refill.

Eva gets up and heads toward the restrooms. Drexel slithers next to me, puts his arm around my neck. "Dude," he says, squeezing me around the neck, "my balls are drained dry." He laughs. "That Eva fucks like a champion. What were you thinking when you let her go?"

It's like a porno playing on a fifty-inch fucking plasma in my mind—him and Eva. My blood pressure skyrockets. I don't say a word. Block him out of my peripheral vision. Chug my vodka and refill my glass.

Drexel gives me that smirk. "All I'm saying is—thanks, dude."

Before I can bite his ear off and spit it out, Bo makes an announcement. "Quick powwow before we lose our senses."

A crowd is starting to close in around us. Drexel hands Syd two hundred-dollar bills and sends him off. The music is loud. We huddle close to hear each other.

"First, a toast," Bo says. We all grab our glasses. Ira pours himself champagne and holds it up. Jay holds up his can of Red Bull. Drexel grabs the bottle of vodka off the table and pours a stiff shot in a glass. Jay's jaw drops. "Just one," Drexel says to him, annoyed.

Bo shouts over the music, "Gentlemen, to the end of an era. And the birth of a new eon. Cheers." We clink drinks. "Ira has an announcement," he adds.

Ira shoots us a confident smile. "Who's up for a launch party?"

"Where?" Drexel asks.

Bo looks at Ira. "Tell him."

"The Roxy," Ira says. "Two weeks from tonight. You'll play a full set, then you'll hobnob. I'll invite all the players. Introduce you to the world. Let the press feed."

"We don't even have a drummer," Drexel whines.

"We'll take care of that next week."

"Then what?" Drexel wants to know.

"Then we'll go into the studio and make a record." Ira placates Drexel by adding, "And you'll be on to stardom."

"We better be," Drexel snaps.

I sense impatience in Ira's voice when he tells us, "Just worry about the next two weeks and let me take care of the rest. We'll meet Monday in Van Nuys to audition drummers. And give me a short list of names for the rhythm guitar players you want to audition. Not even gonna worry about it until after the Roxy show, but I want to make some calls."

I flip my cocktail napkin over, grab Ira's Mont Blanc pen, and jot down a single name and number: Pat Boreo. Hand it to Ira who hands it to Bo. "Call this guy," I urge them. "He's good."

Drexel gets defensive. Shouts at me like I'm his manservant. "Give me that fucking pen. I have names, too." He scribbles a couple names and hands them to Bo.

I look over past the dance floor. Syd greases the DJ. A few seconds later, our EP thunders from every speaker in the house. I down another vodka. A small army surrounds us. Meeting adjourned.

I'm drunk. The heat. The volume. Everything starts to blur.

Complete strangers paw at us. People kiss our asses shamelessly. My cock gets grabbed—twice. We're so mobbed, I can't even tell who's doing the grabbing.

This is the buzz.

I duck away to clear my head. Brush up against Paris Hilton. Give her the once-over. She looks back. This is nuts. Somebody says Dita Von Teese just left. Goddamnit!

Eva finds me ogling a masked pole dancer. "Is this how it feels every time you go in the trap?" she asks, with a groan. "I'm so sick."

"Pretty much." Can't even look at her.

"No wonder you're such a surly prick."

I don't laugh.

"I'm just kidding," she says. "Lighten up."

No point in causing a scene. She's gone to the dark side. Good riddance. "I think your reaction was so severe because you were attacked. Happened to me once and I was down and out for three days."

"Are we going back in?" she asks.

"I don't know. Can't think about that now."

Eva glances over at the crowd surrounding Drexel. "There's a story," she says. "Wouldn't you say?"

"What?"

"I think I'll call it *Hollywood Knights*. About a band breaking out from the crowded pack to take the nation by storm."

"You've been listening to Drexel." I wait for her to laugh, like she's delivering a punch line. Silence. Uh-oh, she's serious. "What if the band fails?" I ask.

"Doesn't matter," she says without missing a beat. "Losers and winners both make for great stories."

"So much for the story about the slacker paranormal investigator."

"Yes. The one about the cute, but deeply flawed and obnoxious ghost hunter."

Cute? Hmmm . . .

"That's not just a story," Eva continues, "it's a book. And someday, it'll be a good one." She wanders back to Drexel, but glances back on her way.

She still digs me. I can hear it—*way* back there. I'm still in the game.

For being dead last night, I suddenly feel alive. I walk past a photo booth on my way back from the john. A sign urges: *No inhibitions beyond this curtain.* Someone's inside. Curtain swings open a few minutes later. A way-drunk Sunset slut stumbles out followed by a guy with a big grin on his face. He hands me a photo strip. Close-up blow job pics.

"Nice composition," I say, handing it back.

Someone taps me on the shoulder. I turn. The woman in black. Saw her outside the Rainbow and in the crowd at the Whisky. Busting out of skin-tight black leather pants and vest. Just the medicine I need. We lock eyes. She hits me with a nasty little smile, pushes me inside the phone booth, and kisses me deep and hard. Deal sealed.

Walk my prize back to the party. Lock eyes with Eva. *Watch this*, I say without saying it. Grab a hand full of leather ass and offer my new friend a bottle of vodka. "Drink?" She looks at the bottle, then at me. Eva takes in the six-footer with perfect milky skin and eyes as dark as two open manhole covers. The lady in black snatches the bottle out of my hand and knocks a half-dozen gulps down. Think I'm in love. "I'm Kane." Wait for a name, but only get that beguiling smile. "Gotta name?" I finally ask her.

"Got a lot of them," she answers. "But tonight, you can call me anything you like." She has a low, slow, dusky voice with a hint of a Middle Eastern accent. "So what do you want to call me?"

"Mine," I answer.

Nothing but a sly smile. She hands back the bottle. "Let's do this," she says.

Let there be no doubt—I am in the right profession.

I grab her hand and march her by Bo and Ira like she's a Doberman in a dog show. Walk her out slowly so Eva and Drexel can get an eyeful. "I don't live far away," I say. "My place?" She doesn't answer.

We walk down Edinburgh Avenue. When we reach my shit-box Mustang convertible parked in front of an apartment building, I apologize. "We just signed a record deal. I'm buying a Ferrari," I assure her.

"Right here," she says, grabbing my collar and kissing me.

"Right here?" I confirm. Look around. A little privacy afforded by a row of jacaranda trees, but still out in the open.

"On the car," she clarifies, pulling me down on top of her right on the hood. We turn the heads of a few people walking up the sidewalk on the other side of the street.

I love it. Pure rock and roll.

We go at it from all angles. Rough. Hardcore. Fun as hell. Have her bent over the hood. She whirls around. Grabs me and slams me on my back. Climbs on top and rides me like I'm Secre-fucking-tariat. Bang away. Hood's dented. Couldn't care less.

Close my eyes. Groan. Then it's a blur. I'm in the air and

slammed straight through my ragtop into the backseat. A second later two hands—surrounded by a glowing aura—grab me by the neck.

I see black fingernails.

Oh, fuck.

She tears me through the flattened wreckage of my roof, holds me aloft for a second, then slams me facedown on the hood of the car. My rib cage buckles. The hood caves in. She plants her spiked heel against the back of my skull and applies pressure. Searing pain.

I'm gonna die.

She leans down. I feel the heat of her breath in my ear. Then a growl starts to form the words, "Stay away from my bridge."

She flips me over, slams me on my back, and drives the heel into my Adam's apple. I get a front-row view of the baddest-looking demon I've seen yet. Murky red aura. Same hair and eyes, but cold gray skin, huge black wings, and badass ornate black battle armor. She carries a long, intricately carved wooden staff with a ribbed metal spearhead and tassels at one end and a battle ax at the other. She could pass for a fifth member of Kiss.

"Who are you?" she demands to know.

I'm speechless.

Heel driven deeper into my throat. "Who are you?"

"Kane Pryce."

"Do you serve him?" she hisses.

"Who?"

"Do you serve him?"

Would plead the fifth if my throat wasn't about to erupt. "No," I manage to choke out. She looks down. Her cold eyes glow red. "You escaped death once. It won't happen again. Return to my bridge again, and you die."

Then she's gone. And it's just me, my boner, and my trashed Mustang wondering what freight train just hit us.

Eighteen

In some nether region between sleep and consciousness, I
hear a heavy drumbeat. Tribal. Menacing. Its beat matches the
throbbing in my temples. Then I hear a guitar. Acoustic licks.
Then electric. Heavy strumming followed by major chords. Then
a mournful solo. It's gorgeous. Carries me into consciousness.

It's not really Clapton. More Page with shades of Townshend.
It's big. Burns familiar. I can't place it. I've been through this once.
Go along for the ride.

I haven't charged the crystal goblet; so I can't power up the
IVeR to find out if the song is another gift from the voice that
reached out to me. I plop on my sofa, close my eyes, and drown
in it. Hear the song—beginning to end. It's a friggin' masterpiece.
Starts out feeling classical. Then rolls into vintage rock.

I leap out of bed and grab my guitar. Dig around for paper and
a pencil. Start getting it down. It's tough to play. A bitch to tran-
scribe. I work at it for an hour. Two. Three. It starts small, then
swells into something meaningful and angry. It's a rock anthem.

No words. I only hear music. Guitar and drums. Can't get
Suicide Bridge out of my mind the whole time I'm working on it.
Also, I see the ocean when I play it—the way the tide ebbs and
flows. Combine the two inspirational images. I visualize a bridge
by the ocean. People jump off this bridge, too. When I'm finished
roughing it out, I hear a title in my head: "Hostile Bridge." Spend
two hours producing a rough recording.

I'm beat.

I finally let my mind wander to the demon. I have no idea what the fallout is from having sex with a resident of hell. What it might lead to, or mean. She warned me to stay away from the bridge. But I'll have to go back to get answers.

Too scared to think about it now. Christ, the look in her eyes.

Three days off. There's no way I can stay here or I'll keep seeing that demon, mope about Eva, wonder how Anna Burrows is holding up in the Medicantium. I'll obsess. And drink.

I need to escape.

I need something.

Not music.

Not ghosts.

Not demons.

Something real. Anything real.

I drive out to La Crescenta on a whim. Pull into Teresa Burrows' driveway. Knock on the door.

No one home. This is stupid. What am I doing?

I head back to my car. Hear giggling from across the street. Two females. One of them bolts into the house with Trader Joe's grocery bags. The other one has her ass in the air, leaning into the passenger side of a Hyundai, grabbing fast-food bags off the floor. I walk over. The girl backs out of the car. She's only a teenager. She throws her hand on her hip and stares me down. What's her name? Paige? Paula? Piper—that's the name Teresa mentioned. Piper May.

"Are you Piper?" I ask. She's the all-American girl—straight blond hair, blue eyes. Long and lean. Unblemished. Get your mind out of the gutter, Kane. "You were a friend of Anna's?"

"Used to be," she says.

"What happened?"

"Who are you?" she wants to know.

"Friend of Anna's family," is all I offer up.

"You're another detective, right," she says. "I already told the last guy everything. Anna went ballistic. She was normal one day and fucking crazy the next. I wrote her ass off."

Play along like I am a detective. "Did she have any enemies? Anyone out to hurt her?"

"I don't know," she says, all pissy. "When she was normal, we hung out. Then her dad died. Then it was like Ouija boards and séances and crazy-ass books. She was in my bedroom one night and made my dresser bounce up and down by itself. That was it for me."

"Get away from her," a voice shouts from the front door. Piper's mother charges straight at me. Same blond hair and blue eyes, but skin that's been in the sun too long and a few extra pounds of junk in the trunk. Fake boobs. Lots of makeup. A few spider veins around her calves, but generally holding her own against Father Time. Definitely doable. Gotta love these foothills MILFs. "What do you want? She's already been questioned," she says, annoyingly loud. Ditzy high voice ruins the package. She grabs her daughter by the arm and leads her inside.

I cross the street. I've got one foot in my car when Teresa pulls in the driveway next to me. "Kane, what are you doing here?"

I'd like to know myself. Play it cool. "Thought I'd say hi."

"You were great last night. I loved your band."

"Really? Thanks." She's nice. Real. I can feel it. This'll do.

Piper's mother marches across the street. She gets in Teresa's face, wicked-witch grimace on her face. "Who is this guy?"

Teresa gestures for the woman to back off. "He's a friend," she says.

The woman points a bony finger in Teresa's face. "Well, tell your friend to stay away from my daughter. And stay off my fucking property or I'll call the police."

Teresa looks at me like: *What's she talking about?*

"Sorry," I say. "I spoke to her daughter." Look at Piper's mother. "I'm sorry."

"Sorry doesn't cut it, *mister*," she says in that shrill voice.

Teresa waves her off. "Go back home, Bridget."

Bridget doesn't budge. "This is such bullshit," she moans. "You're harassing Piper. I already told you, Teresa, I'm sorry about what happened to Anna. But you go and give the police Piper's name? Send them to our front door? What's wrong with you?"

"Enough, Bridget," Teresa says firmly.

"It's not Piper's fault that you didn't—"

Teresa's turning red. "Enough, Bridget," Teresa repeats.

If Bridget's index finger was a pepper shaker, Teresa would be sneezing. "All I'm saying is that Anna had major problems—"

Teresa slaps Bridget's finger away from her face and follows it up with a backhand to her face. "Did all that silicone make you deaf? Or do you need me to kick your fat ass across the street for you?"

The look on Bridget's stunned face is priceless. Cheeks puffing—practically hyperventilating. "Fat ass?" she rages. She has a lot more dumb shit on the tip of her tongue, but thinks better of letting it fly. She retreats. I watch her booty sway all the way across Creemore Road.

"Nicely done," I say.

Teresa shakes with rage.

"Sorry for stirring up shit. Should have minded my own business."

"Can you believe we used to be friends?" Teresa says.

"I'm so sorry," I say again. Pause and add, ". . . that you were friends with her."

That brings a smile.

We stand there in the driveway, staring at each other. "Why did you come here?" she asks.

"You left last night before I could talk to you," I say.

"I'm sorry. I just wasn't ready to be around that many people. I hope you understand."

"Sure," I say. "I'm just happy you were there."

"Is that why you came here—to tell me that?"

"No. I came here to see you."

"Why?"

Try to tell her with my eyes.

We keep staring.

She's figuring it out.

Inch closer. She inches back. "I had a nice time with you the other night at Pepe's."

"Me, too."

Take a few steps toward her front door. She takes a few steps back.

I go out on a limb. "I like you."

She smiles, but glances away. "Me, too."

"Watching you kick ass like that. I'm kind of dying here," I say.

"Me, too." She shakes her head, looks away. "I haven't done this in so long."

"It'll come back to you."

I follow her inside.

"I so needed that," she says.

"Me, too."

"You? Find that hard to believe. You've had plenty, I'd suspect."

"Had the wrong ones," I say.

We find our way to the kitchen. She makes eggs. I notice a big manila envelope on her kitchen table marked "Pasadena Police Department." "What's this?" I ask.

"The detective we spoke to sent that to me," she says. "I'm supposed to read it to see if I recognize any of the people she was writing to. I just can't do it."

"Can I look?"

She nods. Screen captures of Anna's Facebook profile. Transcripts of her IMs. Same stuff I read the day I met Teresa.

"Would you do me a favor?" she asks.

"Sure."

"Throw it away."

"Really?"

"If I keep it, I'll read it. And it'll break my heart."

"But maybe—"

"Please."

"Okay."

I take the envelope outside. I open the lid of the trash can but can't bring myself to toss it. It's like tossing a part of that smart-ass kid I kind of liked. Walk over to my car and toss it in my trunk. Tuck it away in the same crate where I tucked away Donna Lonzi's photos and home movies.

I go back inside. "It's gone," I tell Teresa.

"Thank you," she says.

I debate whether to tell her about Anna. The Medicantium. The chase. What's the point?

"Are you gonna leave now?" she asks.

"Do you want me to?

"No."

And we're off to the races again.

We blow it all off—her classes, the band, the bridge. We do this:

Bang.

Swap stories/get to know each other.

Order takeout.

Watch a movie.

Have a drink.

Lick our respective emotional wounds.

Repeat.

We agree to keep the movies light. *The Hangover* (lived that one). *Wedding Crashers. Old School.*

It's nice. It'll do.

I ask her on a real date. We pick Lucques. She gets all dolled up. Looks like money. Heels. Perfume. Cleavage popping. A gorgeous, edible beauty mark on her right breast. We pull off Melrose and knock off one more. Four-course tasting menu. Four bottles of wine. Six hundred bucks with tip. Charge it. Who cares?

I take her to my place. Afterward, I show her everything—the IVeR, the soul trap, the hardware and software. Think she finally believes me—that I did speak to Anna. Play guitar for her.

I'm into her, I guess.

She's into me, I think.

Important thing is Eva's in the rearview mirror.

Teresa pores over my collection of movies. Everything's violent, depressing, or XXX. She likes chick flicks. Asks me if I've ever seen *The Devil Wears Prada*. I ask her if she has a concussion. She doesn't laugh. We do it again.

Between romps, we sit on the fire escape, half-naked. Watch an alley-cat toy with a mouse. Mouse tries to run. Cat stops it, knocks it around, holds it hostage. Sometimes the cat and mouse just sit, exhausted, side by side like old chums, before the sick game resumes. Fascinating. Cruel. The mouse's best chance is to dart straight into traffic on Cahuenga. He's small, agile. Might actually make it across. The cat might get all flustered, chase him, and be plowed by a passing car.

Teresa roots for the cat.

Shit. It's that first ding in the brand-new car.

I root for the mouse. The mouse darts into traffic. Teresa jumps up and screams. Her towel falls off. We're drunk. She's naked. Cheering. That prick of a cat spends two lives, dodges traffic, and brings the mouse back to the sidewalk on the corner.

He plays with it for an another hour before he gets bored and finishes it off. Just enough time for the Viagra to kick in.

More sex. Good sex.

Teresa's woefully out of touch when it comes to music. I lay a mega-playlist on her. She's overwhelmed. I'm like Einstein teaching Algebra I. I burn her CDs. Gift her songs. She tries to convince me Dave Matthews is great.

Ding.

I tout "Layla" as the ultimate love song. Play it for her. Play her some of the band's songs. Play her the new one—the instrumental. I explain it to her.

She pretends to get it, but doesn't.

Ding.

We go back to her place.

She asks me if I'll bring some paint cans in from the garage and help her paint Anna's room.

Ding.

"I'm so happy," she says the next time we catch our breath.

We watch an Austin Powers flick. She makes me pause it. Bitches and moans—in the nude, mind you—about how offensive it is for Fat Bastard to want to eat babies.

Ding.

Shit, Kane, lighten up. Stop with the dings. She's not perfect, but who is? It's okay. Sure as shit better than being alone.

More dumbass comedies and date movies. I can't take it. I wanna throw darts at Bradley Cooper's face. Will Ferrell can blow me.

• • •

We're naked at the breakfast nook eating waffles. "You ever think of leaving here?" she asks me.

"What—L.A.?"

"Yeah."

"Not really. I don't know. Maybe . . . someday."

"So you're not rooted?"

"No. No soil down here," I say, pointing to my feet.

"That's good."

What is she getting at?

Ding.

Time to go. She stops me at the front door, pulls down my jeans. Guess I'm staying.

Later, when she's in the shower, my phone rings. Eva.

"I'm occupied," I say.

"I'll bet. Hard to miss the woman you left with."

"Who?"

"The leather goddess."

"I'm not with her," I say.

"Who then?" she asks, curiosity genuinely piqued.

"You wish."

"Not at all."

"What do you want?"

"I couldn't get Mavis Royer out of my mind."

"That's because she attacked you."

"I just couldn't get over the fact the little girl lived—it's an amazing story."

"Sure is. That's a long way down."

"I spent my sick day researching on our online archives. Read everything I could about the story. The little girl—Geraldine— was discovered by a policeman a few minutes after her mother jumped. She was wandering around down there. She had some scratches, but no broken bones—no serious injuries."

"That was one lucky kid."

"Wanna meet her?" she asks with the cutest smile.

"Say again."

"She's still alive. Seventy-nine years old. Tracked her down on peoplefinder.com. Just reached out—asked her for an interview."

"So that's why you're calling me?"

"Why else? Look, it's an important part of the story," she answers. "Do you want to sit in or not? I really don't care."

Using my own words against me. She's good. "Count me in."

"I'll email you after I set up the interview."

Let myself out before Teresa gets out of the shower.

The nice little three-day detour ends. Eva just pulled me right back into my life.

Nineteen

For pushing eighty, Geraldine Molek looks fantastic. I'd peg her for mid-sixties. She's short, a little pudgy. Her short gray hair still has traces of blond. She wears thick, tinted eyeglasses. Has a boisterous laugh that bounces off the ceiling of the San Gabriel Mission Church and reverberates through the two-century-old walls. Eva and I are seated next to her in the first row of pews. Despite Eva offering to take her to the restaurant of her choice, Geraldine, who tells us to call her Gerri, selected this church as the location for her interview. I figured she must be a religious freak, but she's not preachy. She even peppers the small-talk portion of our conversation with a few choice profanities.

Gerri was an hour late. That left Eva and me to kill time walking the grounds of the mission. There was nothing but prickly silence between us. And now I'm pressed for time. Gotta get to rehearsal in less than an hour. Can't miss the first drummer audition.

The church is one of the oldest structures in L.A. A plaque in front says it was built in 1775. Place feels that old. Cold and hard—cavernlike. Six life-size statues stand in two rows against the back wall behind the altar. Wonder how many prayers have bounced off them.

We settle in the front row by the old wooden pulpit with a windy little staircase leading up to it.

I can sense it right away—there's a ghost on the pulpit looking down at us. I can feel the energy. No big surprise. A place with this kind of history and emotional energy is bound to attract ghosts. While Eva and Gerri chat, I open my backpack and nonchalantly inspect the trap. It's vibrating. My hunch was right. Strong presence in range.

I can't stop looking at my watch. Gotta leave soon. Hurry up, Eva.

The small talk finally winds down. Gerri's a talker. She gives us a snapshot of her life. Widow, mother of two, and grandmother of five. Taught grade school in Temple City for thirty-eight years.

She's one of those people I can never quite trust because she's seemingly content, genuinely happy. She and Eva hit it off. Eva's doing her charming-pushy thing. Jotting down notes in her tablet. Gerri is spilling her guts. Please. Do I really need to hear about her hysterectomy in '84?

Every time I look at Eva, I see her with Drexel. I suspect that when I look at him this afternoon, I'll see her, too. Gotta get away from her, let her go. This is not healthy.

I glance at my watch again. Shit, Eva—speed this up. Gotta be on the road in fifteen minutes tops.

"Do you remember your mother?" Eva asks. Finally.

Gerri looks up at the pulpit as if she senses the presence there. "No," she answers. "I wish I did."

I can see the heavy weight of Eva's thoughts. She came face-to-face with Gerri's mother—stared into her crazy eyes. The madness she encountered terrified Eva, left a mark. There's a lot she could tell Gerri. Or not. I'm curious to see how she plays it.

"Why do you think your mother did what she did?" Eva asks.

"She wasn't in her right mind," Gerri says. "From what my aunt used to tell me, she hadn't been in quite some time. She heard voices. Suffered from hallucinations. My father left us. My mother believed the world was an evil place. She wrote a note saying she was trying to protect me."

"Sounds like paranoid schizophrenia," I say.

Gerri nods. "Today, she'd probably be diagnosed with that. But in 1937—at the height of the Great Depression, psychiatry was considered unorthodox. Mental illnesses weren't discussed."

"What would you tell your mother if you could?" Eva asks.

"I'd tell her to rest in peace," Gerri answers. "I harbor no anger, no resentment toward her. In her mind, it was an act of love. I can appreciate that. She loved me."

Eva tears up a little. "I know she did." That's all Eva says. Doesn't elaborate.

The ghost in the pulpit moves. I sense it now in the pew behind us.

I check my watch. Hourglass just ran out of sand. I have to be there for every guitarist's audition. Can't let Drexel sway the decision-making process.

"You were only three and a half. Do you remember anything from that day?" Eva asks.

"It's my first memory," Gerri says. "My most prominent memory."

"Tell me about it," Eva says.

Despite the fact that she's talking about being hurled off a bridge, Gerri has a warm little smile on her face. "All I remember is the fall. It seemed to last forever. Then, he caught me and guided me down."

I start to walk away, but stop. "Who?" I ask.

"Him," Gerri says pointing to the top-center statue above the altar—a blond-haired winged figure clad in white. An angel. "That's who caught me," she says empathically. "The Archangel Gabriel."

I size her up more closely. She doesn't seem crazy at all. An angel?

"It was him," Gerri says, sensing my doubt. "That's why I invited you to meet me here. This is my favorite place in the world. I owe my life to Gabriel."

I have to go. Damn, just when it got really interesting. I stand and say good bye. Grab my backpack. Soul trap is still vibrating wildly. I give Eva the phone-to-ear sign. Double-time it out the front door of the old church.

True to his word, Bo has brought together three of the best drummers in L.A. Little do they know I'm bringing in the best of them all—Joanie Soral.

I step out into the hall littered with drum cases. Ira Bowersock strolls in smelling of good cologne. He walks right past me and the drummers waiting in the hall without making eye contact. Game face on.

Bo calls the band together. Our instructions: jam hard. See if any of them can: a) keep up and b) fit in.

First drummer up—Jeremy Bayre—from the Pontius Pilots. Big guy. Big Tama drum kit. Arrives with his own drum tech and it still takes him twenty minutes to get ready. Uses Lars Ulrich's standard setup. Even brings a huge-ass Chinese gong. For our sound, we don't need a show-off with a megakit.

We start jamming. He knows a few of our songs. Is lost on others. He's locked in with Troy. Holds a beat. He listens and his fills are tasty. But he's not a great improviser. When he's lost, there's no chance for recovery. Better than Troy, but something doesn't click.

While he tears down and we huddle and compare notes, Ken Rossen, from the Kleptos, sets up. A nice, compact DW Pacific seven-piece set. We start with a simple jam, move into our opener: "Creed." He's creative at playing simple beats. Has a real dynamic range—can play it somewhere between soft and full-on loud naturally. But he rushes when he gets excited and he doesn't know at least half of our songs. We spend lot of time interrupting to walk him through. Can't get into a sustained groove.

Next up is Joanie. All five feet two of her marches in like she owns the place. She's dressed like she's ready for a brawl—jeans and a black leather jacket. Petite and strawberry blond. Midthirties, but still radiates a skanky hotness. She'll age well thanks to good genes, clean living, and a love of her work.

I help her set up her Tama double-bass kit. She asks me to set up a mic. She's gonna sing?! I spy Drexel with Bo and Ira Bowersock. He's already trash-talking her.

The band hits the floor. Joanie is presumptuous enough to count off the opening of "User." We ease right in. She knows the song. She knows all the songs. Gets all the stops and starts right. Plays with authority. Sings nice unobtrusive background vocals without ever losing a beat. This female voice adds something incredible to the mix without ever treading on Drexel's precious toes. Our miniset builds. She amazes us with her odd timings and ghost notes. Personality and flair ooze.

She doesn't get in the way; she guides us.

It's magic.

We play for forty minutes and she never seems to miss a beat. If she does, she rebounds so gracefully, none of us know. By the time we finish, Bo and Ira are applauding.

I feel totally energized. Could keep playing all night.

Next, Johnny Antinori enters with a handler who helps him set up a gorgeous maple Ludwig kit. After Joanie, the rest of the band is kind of spent, but two songs in, we get a second wind and pick up the pace. Johnny's younger than Joanie, but he looks forty. Hard living.

He's played in dozens of bands around Hollywood—even did a stint for Ozzy. Huge toms and kick drums. Heavy hitter. A deep, menacing sound that's a shade too dark for us but that could wake up John Bonham in his casket. Nice sharp rimshots and hi-hat work, but too tight. Too on the beat. And he rushes when he gets excited. He just looks too old and hairy back there. And the neon glowing drumsticks and special drumming shoes are just plain dorky.

We cut it short after five songs. Drexel says his voice is strained.

After the drummers are packed and gone, we have our pow-wow. Normally we'd all sit here and flex our nuts, pinpointing every minute detail we liked and disliked about them all—showing off, batting around lingo, trying to upstage each other. But we're all too exhausted after an afternoon of really hard work. Bottom line—any one of them is way better than Troy, but only one blew the doors off my barn.

"Cast your vote," Bo says. He looks at Drexel first.

"Cancel the gig. Keep looking," Drexel says.

"Where?" Bo says, all annoyed. "Keith Moon and Bonzo are still dead and Dave Grohl is booked. So fucking pick one."

"The dude from Pontius Pilots then."

Bo looks at me.

"Joanie," I say. I'm going to leave it at that, but I add, "We can go onstage with her tonight and we'll all be better for it." Drexel shakes his head and laughs.

Jay looks at Drexel, then me. "The chick," he says. "She's fucking scary good."

Bo raises his hand. "Joanie then," he says. "I never heard the band play better."

Drexel is about to pipe up, but Ira casts his vote before Drexel can get his words out. "She's a perfect fit," says Ira. "Those harmonies were incredible. I got chills."

"Are you deaf? She throws off the whole dynamic," Drexel yells.

Bo shoots him a murderous glance.

"I'm not deaf," Ira says calmly. Drexel slumps in his seat, pouting. "I know what sells," Ira says. "And today, that's it."

Yes sir, Mr. Trump, sir. I'd laugh in his face if Drexel would quit moping and look up at me. Welcome to the world of enslaved employment, bitch. The boss has spoken.

"Call her up and get her back in here," Ira orders.

I dial her up. She's only a few miles away. U-turns it and is back in five minutes. Just before she gets there, Bo informs me he's getting bumped to twenty percent and I'm getting fifteen percent ownership. Joanie is offered five percent. She's through the roof. She would take this gig for free.

Right before we're ready to raise our glasses and toast to a new beginning, Joanie stops us. "I have to tell you something." The way she says it—feels like trouble. Damn. "I'm gay," she says without wavering. "There, I said it," she says. "Deal with it—or not."

No news to me. Big effing deal seems to be the consensus.

"I like it," Ira says. "A black guy, a lesbian, a brooding misanthrope, and . . . ," he pauses looking at Drexel, "an asshole." Everyone laughs hard except for Drexel. He stands up and bolts for the door. "A brilliant asshole," Ira adds, but Drexel keeps marching.

Boom! The door slams shut behind Drexel. Bo smiles, but looks worried. Ira's not sweating it. He's seen bigger egos.

While we wait for Drexel's tantrum to end, Joanie talks music with Ira. I glance over and she mouths the words *thank you* to me. I smile and wink.

Drexel rejoins us fifteen minutes later. I think I smell beer on his breath when he walks by.

When it comes to rehearsing, Ira finds out fast that we're more efficient than passionate. We're usually done in just over two hours. No one lingers. Routine is ingrained. We jam for fifteen minutes or so. Just try to find a groove. During our jam, Drexel warms up his voice. He sings little bits of everything—a hodgepodge straight out of his head. From gruff and down-low Johnny Cash to smooth Sinatra to up-in-the rafters Robert Plant or Axl Rose. It's like he's channeling different spirits as he speeds through his routine. Amazing so many singing voices can come out of one person.

When Drexel's ready, we run through seven or eight songs from our set. We look for breakdowns, point out our screwups to each other. Tighten things up. It all goes smoothly considering we're breaking in a new band member. Joanie's a pro. We work through the stumbling blocks until we have the gist of both sets down. Drexel never says a word to Joanie. Won't even look at her.

Bo calls it a night. Something tells me now's a good moment to share my song—"Pound of Hate." "Hang on," I tell everyone before they pack up. "I have something I want you to hear."

I grab the disc out of my backpack, hand it to Bo. He cranks it. Toes tap. Looks of vague familiarity. I see a big grin on Jay's face when he tunes into the lyrics. Drexel squats, head down. He listens closely. "I know this song," Jay says. "Who is this?"

Wait until the song ends to answer. "It's me."

"What are you saying?" Drexel asks.

"I wrote it," I answer. "Made a demo of it the other night."

Bo plays it again. "Where the fuck have you been hiding, you little shit?" he says.

Steam's coming out of Drexel's ears. He paces.

Ira pats me on the back. "Nice," he says. "Old school."

Drexel's a cobra ready to strike.

"Let's go play this fucker," Jay says. "Can't wait to get my bass on it."

Joanie grabs her sticks. "Gonna play it just like Topper Headon." Yes. It feels like the Clash.

Drexel finally speaks. "You think you're gonna sing?"

"Fuck no," I say. "You are." That diffuses some of the tension. "You're the man. Go put your fingerprints all over it."

Kissing his ass hurts.

"So what—you're gonna try to own the song, bleed us for royalties?" Drexel asks.

"What are you fucking talking about," I yell. "We don't even have a deal and you're worried about that? I'm in a band, fuck-stick. One for all and all that horseshit. It's our song. And it won't be any good until you sing it."

"That's cool," Drexel says.

Kissing his ass really hurts.

We play "Pound of Hate" for the first time.

The song just pulls us in. It's easy and fun to play. Takes less than three run-throughs to make it our own. Drexel gives it a comic edge with punk-inspired primal screams. "We've got to end with this one," he warns, "or I'll blow my voice out."

Not sure when, but at some point Eva showed up. I catch sight of her in the corner, dancing and grinning. She likes the tune. I nod to her during my solo. Drexel belts it out right in front of her. He screams the chorus. Shades of Cobain—equal parts madness and brilliance. He's fan-fucking-tastic. When we finish, Eva cheers.

"That's it," Drexel announces. "Voice is toast."

The room buzzes.

"This is a hit record," Ira says.

He's right. I know it. I feel it. And I created it. Probably the best moment of my life. I'm riding high. Feeling proud, confident.

Then the trapdoor opens. Drexel puts his arm around Eva and smirks at me as they head out the door. Fucker loves skewering me. I watch them go, imagining a big target on Drexel's back as my song plays in my head.

Don't know why I hate you, but I do.

Twenty

After rehearsal Thursday, everyone seems a little down, drained. I figure it might be a good time to introduce my new instrumental, "Hostile Bridge." I ask for ten minutes. Gather everyone around and pull out a CD.

"What's this?" Ira asks.

"Something I wrote." I say.

"Another one?" Bo asks. "You're kidding?"

I press Play. They listen. Body language in the room says everyone likes it. Even Drexel. Ira's excited—I can see it in his eyes. He can smell a good song a mile away. When it ends, he says, "Play it again."

After three run-throughs, Ira says two words: "Memorable. Big."

I lay the title on them.

"Any words?" Jay asks.

"Not yet," I say. And throwing out a peace offering to Drexel, I say, "I thought we could write the lyrics together—as a group."

Everyone likes the sound of that. Little half smiles and nods.

"All I can tell you is that it's about a bridge by the sea," I say.

"Why?" Drexel snaps. "Why can't it be about . . . a castle . . . or a fucking space station?"

"It's the image I saw in my head when the music came," I tell him.

"So?"

He's really pissing me off, but I answer him calmly. The answer is clear in my head, but hard to articulate. "It's already written out there in the ether," I say waving my hands in the air. "Everything already exists. When you pull it down and claim it, you claim it all. You respect the spark, the initial vision."

"What the fuck are you smoking, New Age Boy?" Drexel says, with that mousy little laugh of his. "Fine. It's about a bridge. Don't want to fuck with the universe and all."

"A bridge," Joanie says, thinking.

"Think about it," I tell everyone. "Let it stew. Maybe we can try to get some words down tomorrow."

Drexel and I cross paths going in and out of the men's room. "So you liked the song?" I say. I come off needy. I could boot myself in the ass for asking.

"It's all right," he says. "I can make it better."

Little prick. Should know better than to give him a pitch to hit.

"That chick you were with after the show," he says, "the badass in leather. Who is she?"

"Forget her," I tell him.

"Tried to, but it ain't happenin'," he says.

Stare him in the eye. "I thought you were with Eva."

"Yeah, Eva's my go-to," he says. "But that chick in black—" He groans and grabs his junk. "Come on, who is she?"

"No one. Just stay away from her."

He pats me on the shoulder. "I'll find out one way or another."

I ask Joanie if she wants to grab a drink, but she has a date with a stripper named Sienna. Blast the White Stripes on my car ride home. Each time the *boom boom boom* of Meg White's bass drum thumps at the beginning of "The Hardest Button to Button," I imagine smashing my fists through Drexel's eye sockets.

I wake up later from a nightmare. I'm on the bridge. It's night. The demon is there. I see her shadowy form on the dome of the Federal Courthouse building. She takes flight. Can't see her in the darkness of night, just long shadows and the sound of wings beating above and around me. Then I hear that voice whisper in my ear, "Stay away from my bridge."

I get up and crack a beer. Pore through the book Ned gave me about Jack Parsons. Read it cover-to-cover in one sitting. Born with a golden spoon in his mouth. Supposedly invoked Satan at the age of thirteen. Tons of pictures of rocket experiments in the riverbed just north of the Devil's Gate Dam. A detailed account of the twelve-day ritual that Parsons and L. Ron Hubbard conducted in 1946, as they attempted to summon the demon Babalon. Copies of letters exchanged between Parsons and Aleister Crowley. A photograph of the mansion on Orange Grove Boulevard, near the bridge, where Parsons founded Crowley's US Order of Thelema Lodge. An account of Parsons' final years—years in which he seemed to descend into madness. Years when he openly referred to himself as Belarion and the Antichrist. A police photo shows Parsons' home laboratory in ruins after the explosion that killed him in 1952. A ten-foot-high black devil's head was painted on the pink walls. Black lace was draped over the bookshelves. Photos of two notes, written by Parsons, were found in the debris:

> *And in that day (the manifestation of Babalon) my work will be accomplished, and I shall be blown away upon the breath of the father;*

and:

> *Let me know the misery totally. And spare not and be not spared. Sacrament and crucifixion. Oh my passion and flame.*

An account of Parsons' final words: *I wasn't finished.* I pore over accounts of detectives finding spent syringes with traces of morphine. Photos of detectives combing through bottles of chemicals Parsons had stored at the site. Another police photo of a "magik" black box that was uncovered in the aftermath of the explosion. It's adorned with a pentagram, snakes, dragons, and other occult symbols and contained God knows what.

There has to be a connection between Parsons and the demon who warned me away from the bridge.

I have to find out.

"Stay away from my bridge," I hear echoing around my brain.

Since when did I ever heed a warning?

Just after four AM, I wrap up Crowley's goblet, pack it with the trap in my backpack, and venture out.

I park just off Orange Grove Boulevard and walk onto the bridge. An occasional car drives by, but I largely have the bridge to myself. I walk to the center and place Crowley's goblet on the railing. A peace offering. We'll see what happens.

It feels eerily like the nightmare I just woke up from. I look up toward the dome atop the tower of the courthouse. Swear I see something shadowy moving up there. Maybe this wasn't such a great idea.

This is my nightmare. It's happening. Hear wings flapping around me. Soul trap vibrates off the charts. I see a shadowy figure at the far end of the bridge. It descends down the stairs to the underpass below.

This is the moment of truth. Do I follow or run?

Wrong decision could cost me my life.

I pick up the goblet and follow.

I descend into the underpass. No traffic. Just me and a red orb that slowly takes shape. It's her, in full battle armor, surrounded by the murky rust aura that signifies her demonic nature.

I'm scared shitless. She knows it. "I warned you," she finally says.

"I know," I say, tiptoeing on thin ice, "but I need answers."

She stares at me with those black eyes. Her wings twitch. She clutches her spear tighter.

"What happened between us . . . I need to know what it means."

She takes flight. Skims the roof of the underpass and lands behind me. I flinch and wait for a spear in the back. She darts around, close enough to touch. Her stare burns my eyes. "You were inside me, and now a little part of me will always be inside you."

I feel nauseous. Start to panic. "Who are you?" I demand. "Is your name Babalon?"

Nothing but that mind-numbing stare.

I act tough. Yell at her, "In the name of Jesus Christ, tell me your name."

A little smile. "Threatening me?" She points the spear at my throat. My head buzzes. She's in my mind, rooting around. "You invoke the name of Christ, yet you carry Crowley's crystal." I'm genuinely stumped. As if she senses danger, she glances around suspiciously. Sniffs the air. She's tense. On high alert. Here's my chance. I grab the spear out of her hands. It transforms into a metallic ball that fits in my palm. It's icy cold. I stare at it, dumbfounded. It's mesmerizing. She snatches it back out of my grasp. It morphs back into her badass spear with a flash of red light. She's rattled. Black eyes scans the tunnel, then lock on me. "You have the mark of hell on you," she says. "Where did you get it?"

Must be something that identifies my journey to hell, my battle with the demon, Alastor. "I've been there," I tell her. Try to be boastful about it.

"Yet here you stand."

"Here I stand."

She eyes me up. Seems to put two and two together. Says finally, "You are the one? The one who shamed Teeraal? The one who scarred Alastor?"

Word gets around, I guess. Small underworld. "Yes," I answer.

I anticipate a spear through my throat, but instead get a half-respectful glance. "So you came on his behalf—to battle me this night? Like you battled Alastor?"

"I don't know who you're talking about," I say. "Whose behalf? God? Some saint? I'm not here on behalf of anyone. I don't even know who you are."

She's reading me.

"Tell me your name," I shout at her.

A chorus of voices, in different voices and accents, say what sounds like, "Hetu-Ahin, Cally, Babalon, Philatanus."

"Which one are you?"

"All of them," she says. "Different names in different times and places."

Babalon I know from the Parsons' research. Philatanus. I've seen that name somewhere in my demonology book, but I can't remember specifics. Get them all confused. There are so many.

An early-morning jogger runs through the tunnel. He nods at me. "Morning," he says. Runs right through Babalon. Doesn't even blink. Only I can see her.

"Did Jack Parsons or L. Ron Hubbard summon you? Is that where you came from?"

"Summon me?" she says, spitting contempt. "They didn't summon me. They served me. I was here centuries before them."

"But you're the one trapping these souls under the bridge, right?" She doesn't confirm or deny. "Why?"

"To lure him out of hiding."

"Who?"

"My enemy."

"Who is your enemy?"

"You know."

"I don't."

"Gabriel," she growls.

"The archangel?" At last—confirmation that beings playing for the other team really exist. Been waiting forever to find out if it's true. I get excited. "He's here? Where?"

"He's wounded. Hiding," she says with contempt. "But he can't escape. I'll finish him." She moves closer. Stops inches from my face. Her stare is tortuous. I try to look away, but my head is paralyzed, our eyes locked. "Look at me," she says. "Do you serve Gabriel?"

Searing pain in my head. She's reading my thoughts. "No," I scream, head throbbing. She's sucking the truth out of me. Couldn't lie if I tried. What I say next surprises me. "I serve the souls you've trapped here."

"They're just my bait, my prisoners," she says. "Gabriel hears their cries. He'll come back to free them—when he's healed. We'll battle again—for the last time."

"Why do your prisoners wear those bodysuits?"

She smiles. "Think of them as prison uniforms. The suits brand them mine, humiliate them. They suit the faceless, mindless beings they, and all humans, are."

I'm nauseous. Seeing double. She's right. I'm powerless against her.

She points the spear at me again and says, calmly and deliberately, "You don't have the power to stop me. Or to free my prisoners. You have been warned for the last time. Leave here now or die."

In a flash, she's gone.

I'm in way over my head.

I don't feel her presence following me back to my car. But I walk pretty damn fast anyway.

I head straight back to my apartment. Pore through my demonology library. Feeling weak. Need food. Grab the three best books along with my iPad and hit the 101 Coffee Shop. Sun isn't up yet, but I have to eat. Pound coffee. I eat scrambled eggs and read about demons. One of the books, a huge black leather-bound volume adorned with a pentagram, raises the eyebrow of my waitress. She wears a crucifix around her neck. Serves me cautiously. I make a point to give her a friendly smile with each coffee top-off.

I research the names the demon called herself. Hetu-Ahin—an ancient female demon that stalks souls at twilight and dawn in Polynesia and Turkey; Kali—a Hindu demon of dissolution and destruction; Babalon—a demon that personifies female sexuality (she pulls that off, all right); Philatanus—a demon who assists Belial, one four crown princes of hell. Belial's right-hand man, especially helping him corrupt souls toward pedophilic behaviors. Whoever she is, she gets around. She travels the globe. She's ancient. In two of my three books, Philatanus is depicted as a male demon. Only one book, a two-hundred-year-old demonology tome from Ireland, hints that Philatanus may be female and that her partnership with Belial was a marriage of sorts.

Interesting.

Bottom line: she's a major player. Unless I can find her weakness, she's too powerful for me to tangle with. If the angel Gabriel really is out there somewhere, he has his hands full.

Next issue that's driving me nuts. How and why did her six-foot-long spear turn into a tiny sphere in my hand? What's that all about? I got a good look at it. Spear and battle ax in her hands. But in mine—a little ball, not much bigger than a marble. Smooth. Metallic. Three parallel rings around the center. A little dimple above the rings. My first impression when I looked in my palm was: *miniature Star Wars Death Star.*

I start poking around on my iPad. Google all kinds of crazy shit. Sphere weapons. Magic spheres. Mystical spheres. Blah. Blah. I laugh when I see the silver sphere from the movie *Phantasm* pop up in Google Images. Love that cult flick.

Weapon balls. Nothing. Demon spheres. Nada. Demon balls. Nil.

A pot of coffee later, I find it—the sphere I saw in my hand. It's called a Klerksdorp sphere. Decades ago, in a region of South Africa between Klerksdorp and Ottosdal, miners working in the Wonderstone quarries discovered hundreds of these spheres in 2.8 billion-year-old layers of rock deposits buried deep in the earth. They vary slightly in size, but they all look the same—smooth, metallic, three perfectly circular rings around the sphere's equator, as if they were molded. A small dimple on one side. Hard as steel despite the fact the earth they were mined from was as fragile as limestone. Some researchers call them inexplicable, out-of-place artifacts manufactured by intelligent beings. Other geologists claim the objects are natural rock formations.

I read one account from a NASA scientist. He studied a handful of the spheres in 1977. Claimed they were energized. That they rotated on their own axis—two full revolutions per year. Claimed the balance of the sphere was so fine, it exceeded NASA's measuring technology.

All the legends about angels falling to earth pop in my mind. What if the legends are true? What if these spheres are the earthly remnants of angelic weapons used in epic, ancient battles between heaven and hell? What if Gerri Molek is telling the truth—that an angel really did catch her and guide her down when her mother threw her off the bridge?

What's it matter, really? I can't get caught in the crossfire of two warring angels, even if it means finding the answers.

Heavens, no. Hell, no.

Not when I'm about to be a rock star. I don't need this shit.

I got lucky last time. That's all.

Ned's right. The bridge gig is over. We're done.

For the first time in my life, I'm going to heed a warning.

The bridge belongs to Babalon.

Twenty-one

By the time I leave the coffee shop, the sun is shining. I'm so jacked up on caffeine, I decide to call Millie Barrington with the bad news. Even though I like her, I still savor saying no to someone who's used to getting everything she wants.

I call Ronnie Barrington and it goes straight to voice mail. Tell him I have news to share. A few minutes later, Millie calls back.

"Good news to report?" she asks.

"Bad news," I tell her. "I'm dropping the case."

"What? . . . Why?"

"I can't help you," I admit. "I don't think anyone can."

Silence, then she barks, "Unacceptable. Absolutely unacceptable."

"You haven't paid us a dime yet," I remind her. "Let's just part ways and leave it at that."

"If it's an advance you want, just say so. Or is this a ploy to renegotiate your fee?" she asks slowly and suspiciously. "I will not tolerate those kinds of business practices."

"No and no," I say. "There's a force attached to that bridge that's too powerful to stop. You don't want to know more than that."

"Nonsense," Millie shouts. I hear glass shattering on her end. I think she threw something. "You're going to go back to that bridge, and you're going to try harder."

"No. I'm. Not." I say slowly and deliberately.

Millie's voice softens. "But what about your musical aspirations, Kane?"

"What about them?" I say.

"A few phone calls, a few well-placed articles could do wonders for your band," she says.

"Thanks, but we'll handle out own PR."

She laughs. "A few phone calls, a few well-placed articles could destroy your chances for success."

Feels like I've been kicked in the balls. My fist clenches. So full of rage I'm breathing like I just ran a hundred yard dash. "Don't say it—you make it a point to always win."

"I like you, Kane," she says so evenly I believe her. "Let's not let it come to that."

"No," I say. "It's over."

"Sleep on it, my dear boy," she urges. "Better yet, give it one more week."

I don't answer.

"Silence implies consent," Millie says with a little laugh. "I'll take that as a—"

I hang up on her.

Fuck her. She's bluffing.

I think.

Decide to drive out to Caltech to tell Ned I'm pulling the plug. I'll make him do the dirty work and call Millie Barrington with a final no.

I stroll through the bland campus and cross paths with young, eager minds who look more stressed out and overcaffeinated than I do. A competitive environment—Yankee Stadium for techheads. Packed with some of the smartest motherfuckers on the planet—people who think, work, and live about fifty years in the future.

I imagine what it looked like around here in the 1930s, when debonair Jack Parsons walked the campus with a swagger, a notebook detailing rocket experiments under one arm, the *Manifesto of the Antichrist* under the other. It's not a friendly place. Or a calm one. It has a darkness. Parsons must have felt at home here.

I climb the stairs to the third floor of the Sloan Lab building where Ned has a corner office. Knock on his door. Locked. I know on Fridays he has office hours all morning. Bang louder. Maybe he's cranking The Dead with his headphones on.

A head pops out of the office next door. A bald guy with round specs tells me, "Dr. Ross is out sick. Hasn't been here all week."

I trek back to my car and drive to Ned's condo a few miles away. Dial his code at the gate. He buzzes me in.

He doesn't even greet me. His eyes are locked on his computer monitor. He usually looks like hell. Today, he looks worse. Like he hasn't showered in a week. Looks ten pounds heavier. The place is a mess. Curtains drawn. He has his laptop set up on the kitchen table. Stacks of paper surround him. Something's up. He usually keeps things tidy.

He finally glances up with a look that says: *you're interrupting me*.

"You were right—we need to walk away from this one," I say without even asking what's up with him. "I need you to call Millie Barrington and tell her we're definitely out. Get tough with her if she threatens you."

"I'll call her when I get to it."

His framed poster from Lebowski Fest is down. In its place hangs a whiteboard crammed solid with mathematical formulas. He's not sick. He's in the zone—focused. When he gets like this, the world disappears.

I move closer. The room smells of stale farts and Funyuns. "What are you doing?"

He grabs a stack of papers and flips through them furiously before tossing them back on the table. "Okay," he says, "This is a good place to take a break."

He gets up. Stinks like a corpse. "Grab a shower," I tell him, "and we'll get a bite and talk."

"No," he barks. "Fifteen minute break—then I'm back to it."

"What—are you curing cancer or something?"

"I know we're walking away from the bridge gig, but I couldn't help thinking about the dilemma we were facing. Got me thinking." He stretches, then stands at his kitchen counter and addresses me like he's at a podium. "If we can trap three souls, then why not three hundred? It's a matter of power and energy. There might be a way to generate the kind of energy that would require. Do you know about quarks and gluons?"

I stop him. "Please—in English, in a manner my young, fragile mind can digest."

"Okay. Hypothetically speaking, we'd create a new device that can generate more power and harness more energy. Simple enough for you?"

"And that's doable?"

"Maybe," he says, suddenly full of life. "No offense to your dad's memory, but they really should have let me design the trap itself instead of just the UI. Dug my old files out of storage. This motherfucker Tesla was way into things—way deeper than any of us knew." Ned's getting all emotional. "Bottom line—yeah, I think it's possible."

Do I tell him about Babalon or not? He'd just get pissed off that I went there behind his back. Should I tell him I'm done— most likely for good? Look at him. He's all excited. Should just let him keep working.

I decide to play along. "What would it take?"

"Money," he says. "A lot of it."

"Money for what?"

Ned shoots me a boyish grin. "Tesla was closer to his death ray than we really knew."

"Death ray? What are you gonna tell me next—the Death Star is fully operational?"

"Tesla was working on something called a death ray at the end of his life."

"Explain."

"Basically, he was trying to produce a particle beam that could disintegrate anything it was pointed at. To do so, he built a device that produced megapowerful manifestations of immense energy in the open air. Then he devised a mechanism for generating massive electrical force. He accomplished both of those tasks. He was in the process of discovering a way to intensify and amplify this newfound energy and then convert it into a repelling force that could be fired from a cannon or gunlike device."

"And you think you can finish what he started?"

He nods. "I need equipment, though. Pretty unorthodox stuff. It can all be acquired, but it's pricey. I need a big, open space—secluded, gated and guarded. I need some kick-ass research assistants. High-level math and physics guys. Young enough to know better than to ever question me. I need time. Would have to take a sabbatical. I need a hundred fifty K. Maybe more."

"Christ, I could buy a Maserati with that."

He just ignores me and keeps ranting. Point out the obvious Catch-22—that we can't make that kind of money without completing the gig that requires that very technology.

"I know that," he snaps at me. "But I have an idea. I have a pretty healthy 401(k). Maybe I can tap into it—"

"No way," I say.

"We'll find some way to fund this research."

"How?"

"I don't know—but I'll think of something." He looks at me and laughs. "When you're a famous rock star you can take it out of your Maserati fund."

I like the sound of that. Sort of.

"Someday we'll go back and clear the bridge in one shot," Ned says. "That's my goal. We'll prove our technology there. Then there's no job too great. We can clear the fucking battlefield at Gettysburg at ten thousand bucks a ghostly head. We'll recoup our investment fast."

He's so jazzed. No way I'm telling him about Babalon. Odds are he'll never see this through. If he does, I'll bring it up then. Just let him focus on something. It's good for him. I decide to shift gears. "You've been busy," I say. "I'm impressed."

"It feels great."

"It doesn't smell great."

"This state of mind—it's friggin' priceless," he says. "This is what having a brain is all about. Not standing there like a fat ass in front of a pack of entitled little fuckers who can't hold a candle to me . . . and never will."

Ned's not himself. Called himself a fat ass. He's *never* self-deprecating and he never trash-talks his students.

"Still feeling blue?" I ask.

"You have no idea how low I've sunk, buddy. Started after you dumped me for that band."

"Jesus," I hiss, "I thought we were past that."

Ned goes to the refrigerator and returns with two beers. Breakfast of champions. "I had a bad bout of insomnia last August," he tells me. "Some nights, I was talking to the mirror."

"What were you saying?"

"I was saying, 'You wasted your life as a teacher. You're a scientist. A researcher. A . . .'"

He lets it hang. "Go ahead," I urge him. "Say it."

"A friggin' genius."

"Here, here."

Ned slumps. "I was saying, 'You pissed it all away for a steady paycheck.'"

"It wasn't just a check. It was five or six hundred paychecks. Hefty ones. You've had a hell of a career."

"I got lazy," he says. "Now, I don't even know if I have it left in me."

"What?"

"The ability to build something out of an idea."

"You still have it left in you," I say.

He looks around. Sighs. "Look at me. I'm alone."

"That's not such a bad thing," I counter.

No snappy retort. He's way down in the pit. "You know what?" I say. "When this gig next Saturday is behind me, when our record deal is in the bag, I'm taking you out. Musso and Frank. Big steaks. Bigger bar tab."

Nothing. No reaction. He slumps and says, "In the end, I'm gonna die. A few people will remember me for being a prick of a teacher. But I'll have never left a mark. What will it have mattered?"

There, in dim room, in the pale blue light of the laptop, sitting beneath that whiteboard, I see him as clearly as I ever have. He's Ned Ross. Giant pain in my ass. But my only friend. The only person who never gave up on me. My voice cracks. "It'll have mattered," I tell him. He turns his back and walks away. "Everything we've done has mattered," I say, louder.

He stops. His shoulders twitch. Shit, he's crying.

"You all right?" I ask.

"I don't know what's wrong with me."

"You're just tired. Get some sleep. You'll feel better." It feels weird to comfort him.

He nods. Doesn't say anything.

"You want me to get all weepy?" I say. "Fine, I will—go buy me a decent bottle of whiskey."

He composes himself, turns around. Smiles at me. "Musso and Frank, huh?"

"My treat."

"That's a first," he teases.

Lay down the ground rules. "We're not gonna talk about ghosts, or Tesla, or anything that's not of this shitty, mortal world. Cool?"

"Cool," he says. But he gives me this weird look that says it's anything but.

"Just keep figuring things out," I encourage him. "You're the only person in the world who can do it."

He walks me to my car. "Go for a walk around the block," I tell him. "Move your body."

But as I pull away, I watch him walk back inside his building from my rearview mirror.

Note to self: *Keep an eye on him.*

Everyone's grumpy at rehearsal that afternoon. It's Friday. Drexel's late. No one feels like meeting the keyboard player Ira is bringing in. He tells us we're in for a treat. The guy coming in is a pro. Sounds like bullshit to me.

In walks this huge, ripped, brown-skinned, Apache-looking badass with a long ponytail. He wears black jeans and a black leather vest with no shirt underneath. Two equally huge sidekicks carry in a vintage portable Hammond B3 organ and old-school oak Leslie speaker cabinet and get to work on setting them up. The guy brought five hundred pounds of gear to an audition. Way cool.

"Guys," Ira says. "This is Abel Ramirez." The big dude nods at us. "Give us a short bio, Abel," Ira says.

This guy's out in the stratosphere. Deep voice, heavy Hispanic accent. Sounds like Cheech Marin. Tells us he's a descendent of the Mayans. That he's a little light in a world of darkness. That God speaks through his Leslie. That his organ once belonged to Gregg Allman. That it's really not an organ; it's a color instrument, a box of crayons that he uses to color the air. Says he's played organ on twenty records, including tracks by Pearl Jam and David Bowie. He's thirty-four, but looks younger. He's a goddamn character for sure.

We listen as he runs through a half-dozen songs. Totally nails

"Light My Fire," "Pump it Up," and "House of the Rising Sun." I ask him to play the organ part for Hendrix's "Rainy Day Dream Away." Fucker plays it off the top of his head.

He's a music machine.

Drexel comes in toward the end of his solo run-through. He looks bad. Says he's sick. Bullshit. He's fucked up. Droopy eyes. Unsteady gait. Slurred words. I walk by him but I don't smell booze today. Jesus, hopefully it's just pills and not H.

We can all tell. Especially Ira.

Abel, the Mad Mexican, sits in with us during our set. He's prepared. He knows most of our songs. He's right in sync with us. What he doesn't know, he improvises brilliantly. Plays precisely what's lacking. He's got an uncanny ear. Adds a killer little solo to "Pound of Hate." Fits like he just popped in a missing puzzle piece. He doesn't play it all showy. Just the right kind of special sauce that tops off the song.

Five songs in and I'm saying, "Wow." Drexel's way off his game, but it doesn't matter. The band is jamming. Abel fills in holes with little understated dollops of organ riffs—rich and sweet, packed with energy. Smooth chord changes. Plays with his eyes closed, a sure little smile on his face. He's full of soul.

Abel's organ never dominates, but it's ever-present. He's sneaky. Fluid and slippery. Bobs and weaves, plays in and out unobtrusively. Pops up with a flurry of perfect notes then ducks back down below the surface of the song.

He brings a little sound of the carnival to our hard edge.

It fits perfectly.

Ira heard what none of us could hear. He's a genius.

Inch by inch, we're getting there. The band is marching steadily toward completion.

We wrap up after eight songs. Play it cool. Keep our distance. When Abel is packed and gone, we let loose. "Tonight was magic," Ira says.

"So he's in?" Bo asks.

Ira laughs. "A band with Kane *and* Abel—it's fucking destiny." We all laugh. Shit, that never even occurred to me. "We'll get traction with that story," Ira promises.

Abel's in—it's unanimous. He'll join us in the studio. Even Drexel gives him a thumbs-up. He tries to articulate why he liked what he heard, but he's babbling incoherently. Bo keeps cutting him off until Drexel gives up, curls up in a ball in the corner under the mixing board, and starts snoring.

The rest of us hang around, crack open beers (Jay drinks Red Bull), and start brainstorming lyrics for "Hostile Bridge." We throw out images, phrases, rhymes. Mine are all about "Suicide Bridge." No ideas get laughed off. Everyone—Bo and Ira included—participate. Drexel keeps snoozing. A few times we stop and try to laugh off his snoring, but it's not funny and we all know it. It adds a weird tension to the songwriting session. After half an hour, we have some words:

From high towers, mournful wailing
White mist, vapor trailing
A sleepy river, a twilight shiver
Beat of her wings makes me quiver
On Hostile Bridge, I shed my life

A solid verse and we call it a day. Some strong images. Maybe they'll fit, maybe not. It's a start.

Jay wakes up Drexel and drags him out. He's in bad shape. "Sober him up," I whisper to Jay on the way out.

"I'm getting his ass to a meeting," Jay promises.

As soon as I turn the key in the ignition, my phone rings. Teresa. "Want to come by? I need a ride on the Kane train," she says with a laugh.

"Sure."

Why not? A smokin' body like hers can mask a boatload of incompatibility.

I'm on my ways to La Crescenta for lame movies, bad takeout, and crazy good sex.

Suicide Bridge feels like it's a thousand miles from my rear-view mirror.

Twenty-two

An early morning call from the Pasadena cybercop—
Detective Alvarez—ruins my Saturday morning sleep-
in. I roll out of Teresa's bed to take the call. Open the
sliding door in her bedroom and wander into her tiny backyard.
"Wanted to update you," he says. "You'll update the mother, or
should I?"

Look through the sliding door and see Teresa, naked, sprawled
out on the bed. "I'll take care of it."

"What's the relationship between you and her?" he asks.
"Friends or more?"

"Just friends," I lie. Try to change the subject. "Did you find
out who owns the iPhone where the Facebook account was created?"

"Not yet," Alvarez tells me.

"Did you look into the married guy she was having the affair
with last year—Frater something?"

"He was the first suspect on my list," Alvarez tells me. "But he's
clean. We subpoenaed his computer and phone—checked his
phone records. Found mountains of porn and a lot of crazy occult
shit, but nothing that links him to the iPhone or the Facebook
account. Looks like he's telling the truth when he says he hasn't
seen or spoken to Anna in over a year."

"You're sure?" I ask.

"Positive," Alvarez says. "You want to hear what I do know?"
he asks.

"Absolutely," I say.

"All right," Alvarez says. "The phone originally belonged to a guy named Patrick Kennedy who lives in Acton. He closed his AT&T account three months ago and decided to sell the iPhone. Put an ad on Craigslist. Got an offer via email within a couple of hours. Accepted. Received a cash payment in the mail. He sent the phone to: J. D. Harlan, 3666 Military Avenue. That's in Palms—you know where that's at?"

"Yeah," I say. "Down around Culver City—off Sepulveda."

"Right."

"So you nailed your man? J. D. Harlan actually exists."

"Not really," Alvarez says. "Address is a home in foreclosure. Deadbeat owner is a woman named Alberta Tolivar. She hasn't lived in the house in three months. Phone gets delivered to that mailbox. Someone picks it up, makes off with it."

"So trace this Kennedy guy's computer," I suggest. "See if you can find the IP address through the Craigslist order transaction."

"Way ahead of you," Alvarez says. "IP address in a computer owned by a fifty-six-year-old woman in Glendale named Ivana Zaitlin. She's works in the commissary at the Walt Disney Studios."

Wish I had a notebook to jot all this down. "So you think this woman did it."

"Nah. Checked her out. Interviewed her. Confiscated her computer. Our person most likely drove around her neighborhood until they found an unsecure wireless network to jack into. Parked on her street, hijacked her IP address, and ordered the phone on Craigslist."

"Holy shit," I say. "This person's really covering his tracks."

"Crafty prick, that's for sure," Alvarez says. "But nothing too complicated here. Just well thought out. Someone planned this and knew exactly how to pull it off."

"So he got the iPhone," I say. "But he still had to get it activated. Just go to AT&T and trace the new owner."

"Been there, done that," Alvarez says. "The account was set up by someone named Molly Broder at an AT&T store in Sherman Oaks."

"There's your killer," I say.

"Phony identity," he answers. "Had all the right paperwork, though, to activate the account."

"How does one go about creating a fake identity?" I ask. I'm genuinely curious. Hell, I may need one someday.

"A lot of ways," Alvarez says. "I have an idea about how this person snagged this particular identity, but I'm not allowed to disclose that kind of information outside the department."

"Maybe a surveillance camera caught the person."

"Store only keeps archived footage for fifteen days. Clerk's an airhead. Doesn't remember anything. They service hundreds of people a day."

This is some deep and nasty shit. I'm way intrigued. "So how was the bill paid? If it was a check, you'd have a bank account number."

Alvarez likes to answer fast. "Account was managed online from the phone. Money orders for two months, then the account was abandoned."

"Trace the money orders."

"Already did—to a 7-Eleven in a shitty part of Long Beach. No surveillance. A revolving door of clerks who quit as soon as they get shot at. Store processes about a hundred money orders a day. It's the neighborhood bank. And phone carriers—they'll take money from a baby's baptism envelope. They don't care."

I'm out of ideas. "Now what?"

"We're investigating how the phony identity was acquired. But, frankly, that could take months and will probably lead nowhere. We might get lucky, but if someone was smart enough to pull all this off, they were smart enough to cover their tracks when they were poking around public records."

"What about Apple?" I ask. "Can they help?"

"We're working with them. Phone can't be tracked via GPS. They confirmed it. It's off, dead, or destroyed. We know they maintain records that track phone histories, but they're sensitive to sharing those details. That's serious proprietary information."

"Why?"

"Massive invasion of privacy issues. Can you imagine if they're sitting on top of personal information about where you and your phone have been during the last year? Might make you question whether or not to go into that next titty bar."

"What do you think?"

Alvarez is revved up. This is a guy who loves his job. "They definitely have that technology in place. The question is how deep is their archive? How far can they track a phone back to a precise location?"

"How can you find out for sure?"

"We'll subpoena Apple if we have to. But again, we're looking at months—maybe years. They'll fight this one tooth and nail."

"So you're looking for a smoking iPhone," I say.

He laughs. "I'm gonna use that one."

"Keep us posted," I say.

"Will do," Alvarez replies. "Tell the mother to hang in there. Will get this guy—or gal—sooner or later."

I walk back through the sliding door and into the bedroom. Teresa rolls over, covers herself with sheet. "Who were you on the phone with?"

Probably should lie. Hate to start a Saturday morning like this. But I tell her the truth. She sits up. "What did he want?"

I spill it.

She freaks out. Can't blame her.

I take her out for lunch, get a few margaritas in her.

She's scared and can't stop talking about it. Applies all of her psychological expertise to the information Alvarez shared with me. I let her vent and listen. Pretty fascinating to hear her dissect the personality of the person responsible. Bottom line: intelligent and psychotic. Dangerous. She wonders if whoever did this will come after her? Plant viruses. Track her. Try to ruin her life online. I tell her that won't happen. Assure her.

What do I know?

Drop her off. She asks me to stay. "Okay," I say.

We lay around all afternoon into the evening. Don't say a lot. I'm just there for her.

I ask if I can read one of her screenplays. She's all insecure about it. I'd tell her it's good even if it wasn't. Mostly I'm just bored and want something to do. I insist.

She gives me a script for a short film she wrote for a class. A mother and her teenage daughter having lunch. Their guardian angels, invisible to them, but visible to the audience sit next to them and have their lunch. The two conversations play off each other. It's clever. Funny. Even a little sad. Pretty well written. The dialogue is a little stiff here and there, but it's a smart little piece of writing.

I tell Teresa all of this and more. She basks in the praise. It brings her spirits way up. I ask to read more. She says she has some work in progress, but nothing that's readable yet.

We venture out for takeout.

The phone rings. It's Eva.

"What?" I snap. "I'm busy."

"Five minutes," she says.

I step out of line at El Pollo Loco and take a seat at a table in the corner. "Your boyfriend's not looking so good," I say. Try to keep it to a half whisper, but that's hard to do when your blood's boiling. "What's wrong with him?"

"I don't know," she snaps.

"Is it OxyContin or tar heroin? Are you spiking up with him?"

"Fuck off, Kane."

"Do you have any idea how shitty it is that you chose my bandmate to sleep with?"

"That's my business, not yours. That's not why I'm calling you."

"Then what? Calling to tell me you're going to bang Ned next?"

"Enough. Grow up already. I'm calling to ask you why you never called me back after our meeting with Gerri Molek."

"I've been busy."

"I spent over an hour with Gerri after you left. I just finished the article. It's a short fluff piece for next Sunday. You wanna read it?"

"Why not," I say, all sarcastic. "I spoon-fed it to you, with a lot of other stories."

"What are you talking about?"

"Without me, you'd be writing obituaries."

I can feel the steam pouring through my phone. "You are such a prick."

I'm sitting in this chicken joint, so mad I'm sweating through my shirt. I swear I'd throw her on the grill if she were here. "I have more information on Anna Burrows. You should hear it."

I wait to hear a click, but she stays on the line. Silence for a long time. She finally breaks it. "What is it?"

Tell her everything as blandly as possible. Sound like Stephen Fucking Hawking's voice machine. She's lapping it up, though. Every few seconds says something like, "You're kidding."

"You don't print a word of this until Alvarez says you can, do you understand?"

"Of course."

"You're not going to fuck Alvarez or Teresa Burrows over like you fucked me over, right?"

"You're an asshole."

"Why is it, Eva, that I know all of this stuff, but you don't? You're supposed to be the big award-winning journalist and all—not a groupie."

"Fuck off, Kane."

There it is—loud and clear: *Click.*

Twenty-three

Teresa sleeps next to me. The first traces of morning light creep through the venetian blinds. I can't sleep. My mind is racing.

What if?

The soul trailing Eva, Gerri Molek, and me in the old San Gabriel Mission church was powerful. Bold. Fearless. Readings on the trap were off the chart. Came right up to us.

It's an old church. A powerful spot.

What if it wasn't a ghost? What if Gerri's story is true? What if it was the Archangel Gabriel who saved her? Babalon said he exists, that he's near. What if it was an angel watching us from that pulpit?

I wonder.

I crawl out of bed and get dressed. Teresa stirs. "Where are you going?" she asks, still half asleep.

"Out to get coffee and roses," I say.

"Hurry back."

I drive back to my place. Load my backpack with my EMF detector, digital recorder, handheld thermal cam and the trap. At 7-Eleven, I pour a tall coffee and nuke a breakfast sandwich, then hit the 101 North.

Traffic is light and I make it to the mission in less than half an hour. The mission grounds and museum don't open until nine. But there's a seven AM mass underway inside the old mission church. I enter and duck in a pew in the back. The church is half full.

A mostly Hispanic congregation. While a well-fed, gray-haired priest in a purple robe reads the gospel, I open my backpack and turn on my devices. Put the digital recorder and EMF detector in the two breast pockets of the button-down shirt I'm wearing over top of my Jim Morrison tee. Keep the trap in the backpack but put the tricked-out Bluetooth earpiece that Ned built in my ear so I can hear alerts from the trap. I hold the thermal cam in my palm. Do my best to look like a discreet tourist shooting a video while I scan the church for temperature anomalies.

The priest walks to the podium and begins his sermon. I scan around me; point the thermal cam at the rafters. The only heat signatures come from the four ornate lanterns that hang from heavy chains above the center aisle. Old wiring. Other than that, nothing.

Then I feel a chill. The hair on my arms and neck stands up. I feel the crackle of static electricity in the air around me. An alert from the trap beeps through my earpiece. In the other ear, a deep voice whispers something that sounds like, "On it."

I don't see anyone around. But it was a voice. I'm sure. I point the thermal cam. A human-sized heat signature standing motionless, two feet behind me. Can't trap it here. It would cause a ruckus. Whisper to the air around me, "Sit with me." The air crackles. Energy swirls alongside me. Confirm the presence with my thermal cam. Cool. Sitting here during Sunday mass with a soul next to me. "What now?" I ask the air around me.

Voice in my ear says something like, "Keyma." Static energy dissipates. Soul is on the move. I aim the thermal dead ahead. Soul's gliding up the center aisle. It pauses near the front altar, then hangs a right out the side door.

I exit the church. Earpiece sounds an alert. I track the heat signature as it makes its way through the cemetery. A locked gate blocks my path. Grounds don't open until nine.

Screw it.

I jump the gate and follow. An ancient cemetery. Gravestones from the 1700s and 1800s. A wide area of unmarked graves. Read about this part of the cemetery online. Supposedly six thousand Gabrielino Indians are buried here. It's not a big area. They must be stacked on top of each other three or four deep.

Lose track of the soul for a couple of minutes, then pick up the heat signature on the thermal near an old building beyond the cemetery. It's the mission museum, dates back to 1812. Website says it used to be the sleeping quarters for the padres.

Door is locked. I start to walk away when I hear a loud click. The latch raises, door creaks open. I'm being invited in.

I walk from room to room. The thick wood-planked floor creaks with every step I take. Place smells like the inside of an old trunk. I could spend hours strolling from room to room, looking at all the old exhibits, relics, statues, and books locked in airtight glass cases. But I'm trespassing. And I'm still on probation. I need to trap this soul and get out of here fast.

I scan the room. No anomalies. Place feels calm. Then the trap sounds an alert. Follow the signal to a room where the walls are covered with old photographs, religious icons, and paintings. Two large glass cases are filled with old Bibles. Fourteen primitive paintings of the stations of the cross are displayed high on the walls. These aren't traditional religious paintings. They're colorful, vibrant—a Native American feel. Interesting. I read a placard on the wall that dates the paintings back to 1798. They were all painted by a Gabrielino—and they're the oldest pieces of Indian-made Christian art in California. The paint was made from the crushed petals of native California wildflowers.

The most compelling thing in the room, though, is a four-foot-tall crucifix hanging on a wall directly over one of the glass cases. It's carved from wood and painted. I stand beneath it and stare up. Christ is looking down from the cross, straight into my eyes. His face is haunting—a perfect depiction of exhaustion, agony, and sadness. His lifelike eyes are somewhere between life and death. Wounds painted bloodred. Long, straight black hair that looks real. An actual crown of thorns. A sign beneath the cross says:

> Hand carved in the 1790s by the Indian, Ahchancha, later named Gabriel de los Santos. He used his own hair for the hair of Christ.

Air sizzles around me. I pull out my EMF detector. Off the charts—a reading of eighteen milligauss. I take out my digital recorder and turn it on. "Speak into this red light," I say. I ask a series of questions, pausing between each one. "Who are you? . . . Why are you here? . . . Are you a priest? . . ."

I hold the recorder to my ear and listen. There's a voice, but it's garbled. Male. Deep. It's not speaking English. Maybe Spanish. Can't say.

I try something else. "If you can hear," I say loudly, "tap on this glass case once, like this—" I wait for a response. Finally—*tap*. "Good," I say. "Were you a priest who lived here? If you were, tap once." Wait. Nothing. "Were you a missionary?" Wait. Nada. Then I ask the million-dollar question: "Are you Gabriel?" Wait, then . . . *Rap!*

Holy shit.

My heart races. "I need to speak to you. Can you show yourself?" The crucifix rattles on the wall. "There's a way we might be able to speak. Please cooperate. Stand still." Demons are too powerful to trap. Maybe angels are, too. But I have to try.

I reach into my backpack and pull out the trap. The spirit darts about in a panic. "I'm not here to hurt you," I say reassuringly. "I just need to speak with you." The trap auto-targets the ball of energy. Fire! A ghostly roar. The unforgettable sound of time and space tearing is usually followed by a thunderous boom, but this time, the sound of the big rip keeps on ripping. Either the trap can't pull in a spirit this powerful or the soul is putting up a hell of a battle, like a hooked fish that would rather die fighting than be reeled in. The trap vibrates fiercely. I'm afraid it might explode in my hands. Waves of energy fill the room. Everything's abuzz. One of the glass cases cracks. My head throbs, my eyes burn.

Finally—*Boom! Slurp!* Got it.

The room smells like burning hair. I feel nauseous.

I pack up my gear and race out.

Employees from the gift shop are running my way. Shit. I duck into the old winery. Hear the staffers in the corridor between the museum entrance and winery. "Might have been a tremor," one of them says.

"It's the pipes," the other one insists.

They roam around, but leave quickly. I ride it out for an hour, until I hear some tourists milling around outside. I head through the mission grounds to the exit.

Now what?

I call Teresa to tell her I won't be back today. She's bummed, but there's no time to coddle her. I act like I'm in a hurry. I lie and tell her I have band business to attend to. She invites me over later. "We'll see," I say. "Maybe."

I'm going in the trap today, but I can't go it alone.

Ned? He'll wonder what I was doing. Ask me a million questions. Think I'm up to something behind his back. Plus, he's all depressed.

Eva? She's pissed off at me. Plus I don't think I can stomach being around her. I'll only see her and Drexel.

But that's it. It's a short list. Ned or Eva. Evidence of the sorry state of my life.

I dial Eva.

"It's Sunday morning—what do you want?" she snaps. I brace myself, wait to hear Drexel's voice in the background. But I don't. Damn good thing.

"I need a favor."

"Was I not clear when I told you to fuck off?"

"I have a soul. I need to go into the trap."

"Call Ned."

"I don't have the energy to deal with him right now. I'm asking you."

She's shaking off her slumber cobwebs. "You say vicious shit to me, then you act like it never happened."

"This is business," I say. "Can we just put the high school shit aside?"

"As usual, you flatter yourself. Your act is grade school at best."

I won't get sucked down this hole. "What do you want me to say—I'm sorry?"

"That would be a nice start."

"Fine, I'm sorry," I snap. I go overboard. I try to be sarcastic, but I can't pull it off. "Sorry for what I said. Sorry for being a prick. Sorry I blew it. But mostly I'm sorry you're with him."

Silence, then, "That was so John Hughes circa 1985."

"Accept the apology it or shove it up your perfect ass," I say, half-jokingly.

She half-laughs. "Dubiously accepted."

"Will you help me or should I call Ned?" I say, coldly.

"I'll be over this afternoon," she says.

When Eva arrives, she tries some casual chitchat, but I keep it all business. I refresh her memory with a quick run-through of the Silver Cord program, the software that monitors and displays my vital signs on-screen. She asks a lot of questions, makes sure she's clear on everything.

I know I'll be in good hands.

I stretch out on the gurney. Eva helps wire me up. I put on the NuMag helmet and Ganzfeld goggles and start my breathing exercises.

"Give me a thumbs-up when you're ready," Eva says. When

my pulse is down and my breathing is calm and steady, I shoot her a sign. I feel the wave of electricity hit my third eye and circulate around my body in a steady current. Breathe. Meditate. Envision the protective white armor. Surround myself with spheres of protection. All goes white.

I'm gone.

The ringing. The hum. Everything goes purple.

I'm there. But I'm afraid to open my eyes. I'll completely freak if there's a winged angel in white waiting for me.

Go ahead. One eye, then the next.

Shit.

Not an angel. An Indian. Thirty-five, maybe forty. Deer-skin robe. Fringes at the bottom, above his knees. Intense dark eyes. Long, smooth black hair parted in the center. Ornate shell-bead necklace. Beaded belt. A white triangle painted on his forehead. Tattoos of triangular patterns on both forearms. Red, white, and black lines painted under each eye.

He says something in his native language. I hear it inside my head in English. "What is this place?"

He speaks clearly and slowly. "Somewhere between worlds—a place we can talk. Sit down with me." It registers. He hears it in his language. Understands. Cool. Souls transcend human language. One more thing on the "wonder if I can do that in the soul trap" list that I can check off.

We sit across from each other, arms resting on the table. I play it nice and respectful.

"Your name?" he asks.

"Kane Pryce. Yours?"

"Ahchancha. Shaman of the Tongva."

"But you rapped on the glass when I asked if you were Gabriel."

"I was baptized and given the name of my guardian and baptizer—Gabriel de los Santos."

"So what name should I call you?"

"Either."

"Ahchancha, then." Has a nice little bite to it. Fun to say. I recall the name from the placard on the wall. "You're the artist that carved that crucifix—painted those paintings?"

He nods.

"Beautiful work," I say.

"I was inspired by the angel Gabriel whom I served," he says.

"Meaning you served the mission?"

"No. I served the archangel, not the corrupt mission that followed his arrival."

"So he really does exist?" I ask.

The Indian gives me a single nod.

"You saw him?"

"Often."

"When?"

"First, when I was a boy of ten years. He arrived from Heaven with other angels on the great hill at the base of the mountain. He appeared to me."

My brain sparks. Is he talking about Gravity Hill, the place where everything—including a friggin' two-ton camper—inexplicably ascends?

A gateway to Heaven?

"I led the archangel to the Tongva people. He taught that a new age was at hand. That he was sent to this place to ensure that peace would exist between the Tongva and the Spanish, who would be soon be arriving with the message of Christ. To ensure that our two cultures would coexist in harmony. And then they came."

"Who?"

"First, the Franciscan padres, along with the Spanish colonists and army. They were the mission builders. But when they came, so did the chee-sho—the wicked ones."

"I don't understand."

"Demons from the underworld. Belial and his mate, Babalon, arrived in the forbidden stream the stone devils guard."

Devil's Gate Dam and its demonic rock formations?

A gateway to hell?

"What happened?"

"The wicked ones came to hunt and end Gabriel. They lured Gabriel into battle by destroying everything that he had come to prepare."

"How?"

"They darkened souls," he says, with pain in his eyes.

"What souls?"

"All souls," he says. "The souls of the mission padres, who began to use the power of the Spanish army to convert and enslave the Tongva people to their religion and their ways. The souls of the Spanish colonists who schemed to rob my people of our land. And, sadly, they darkened many Tongva souls."

"What happened to your people?"

"For centuries my people knew only peace. There were no conflicts that could not be resolved with reason. But after the Spanish arrived, dissension, rebellion, and violence swept through our tribes. Some chiefs and shamans embraced the darkness. Tongva killed Spanish." Tears well up in his eyes when he says. "Tongva killed Tongva. The chain of missions up and down the coast became shackles that bound the Tongva way. Ten lifetimes of peace were extinguished in the span of my single life. I'm glad I died before I saw the end of the Tongva way of life."

"How did you die?" I ask.

"I died at the hands of the wicked ones."

"When?"

"In the year 1800."

"Tell me what happened."

These are hard memories to relive; I can see it in his eyes.

"With every soul they darkened, Belial and Babalon gained

strength, power. They met Gabriel in battle and nearly ended him, but the brave and crafty archangel escaped. I, along with shamans from other tribes, guarded the badly wounded arch-angel, remained by his side in a safe hiding place."

"Where?"

"A cave. In the cliff wall behind a mighty tower of water. The wicked ones could not pursue Gabriel into the sacred mountains that bore his name. There, in the tiny cave, in Gabriel's presence, the shamans drew paintings on the wall, drank of truth, and saw, in clear visions, how to use the power of the land to drive the wicked ones back to the underworld."

"What happened?"

"We failed. Belial and Babalon were too powerful. They hurled me, and the other shamans, over the cliff at the forbidden stream of the stone devils."

"How did your soul end up at the mission?"

"My spirit cannot rest or leave this realm until the wicked ones are destroyed. Until that day, I am bound within the walls of the place that honors Gabriel. I can venture no farther than the mis-sion grounds. I await a warrior of flesh and blood to accomplish what I failed to do." He gives me a look.

"Me?"

"You have the mark," the Indian says, studying me.

"What mark? What can you see?"

"Your soul is in the balance. Babalon is already working inside you. But so are forces of good."

"What should I do?"

"Choose," Ahchancha says. "Choose to serve the evil ones. Or to fight them."

"How can I fight them?" I ask. "I'm just a person."

"Find the cave. The answer is painted on the cave wall. Burn sage to purify and protect your soul. Drink toloache—the truth. Gaze at the image. Your vision will come."

"What vision? Tell me."

"The vision quest is different for each warrior. Your path—your plan—must come from within your own spirit. You will see your fate . . . and the fate of the wicked ones when you drink truth."

Drink truth? Thought I'd drunk it all. "How do I drink truth?"

"Over a pure flame, brew datura and saltwater with the blood and venom of a rattlesnake from the forbidden stream. A rattlesnake killed by your hand. Drink. See."

Datura? No idea what it is.

I'm about to ask what he's talking about when I suddenly feel weak. My exit door appears. Eva must have a good reason. I must be in some kind of trouble.

"I have to go," I tell Ahchancha. "I'll take you back to the mission. I'll release you there."

I'm feeling more and more drained. I'm in trouble. I need to ask the Indian more, but I can't stay.

I pass through the door.

I can't seem to draw a good, deep breath as I'm blasted back to my body. Eva's freaking. "Your pulse got too low," she says. "I had to get you out."

"Thanks," I manage to choke out. Point to the trash can with urgency. She grabs it and tosses it to me just in time. I puke. Feel a little better almost immediately.

When my head clears and my heart rate stabilizes, I tell Eva everything. She tells me to rest. She goes to the supermarket while I crawl off to shower. My legs are noodles. I'm dizzy.

Eva returns with saltines, ginger ale, and Gatorade. She helps me to my desk. We start researching. She does the grunt work. I mostly sit, fight to keep my crackers down, and bounce about a thousand questions off Eva that she begins to google her way through.

First thing we nail down is datura. Also known as jimsonweed, angel's trumpet, thorn apple, and hell's bells. It's a rare flowering plant that still grows in parts of Southern California. Poisonous at even moderate doses. Big risk of seizures, rashes, and permanent vision problems for anyone stupid enough to ingest it. Major hallucinogenic. No wonder Ahchancha had visions. Stuff is so wicked, even a pro like Hunter S. Thompson was scared of it. Not to mention it's tough to find. It helps that the plant has big white, trumpet-like flowers. There are a number of claims that it grows naturally around power lines in the mountains. One blogger claims to have found a patch of it growing on an overgrown golf course that went out of business up near Santa Clarita. It's worth a look.

We research rattlesnake venom next. Surprising findings. Being injected with it is megadeadly, but ingesting it orally has no major adverse effects. But how the hell am I going to kill a rattlesnake? We watch some YouTube videos. Looks like I'll have to shoot or decapitate it somehow. But the head can bite for an hour—maybe longer—after it's snipped. They're as dangerous dead as alive.

I can see myself ingesting a psychedelic flower that might kill me. But hunting down and killing a wild rattler? No fucking way.

Then there's the cave Ahchancha mentioned, where his pictograph is supposedly painted. Eva pokes around. The nearest natural waterfalls to Gravity Hill are in Rubio Canyon, about a mile and a quarter up and into the mountain. Four different waterfalls cascade down steep cliffs. It's a hotspot for rock climbers. Yet there's no mention anywhere about a cave. We scan images of the waterfalls from dozens of websites. No obvious signs of caves. Search *Indian Petroglyphs*. The only known ones in SoCal are at Burro Flats in Simi Valley, San Gabriel River Canyon, San Clemente Island, Bell Canyon in the Santa Ana Mountains, and Catalina Island. No mention of cave paintings in Rubio Canyon.

"Do you want to hike up to those waterfalls with me? Have a look around?" I ask Eva.

"Sure," she says. "I've hiked there before—three or four years ago. I know my way in and out. Always wanted to climb those falls. Honestly, though, I don't know when I can do it. I'm swamped this week."

"Yeah, you'll be busy polishing Drexel's microphone."

"Don't start," she warns.

"Fine."

"And don't try to go into that canyon by yourself. It's a tricky hike."

"I won't."

"Promise? Not that it's worth much," she zings.

"Promise."

"I have to go," she says. "Are you going to be okay?"

I nod.

"What are you going to do with Ahchancha?" she asks.

"Drop him off in the morning."

Eva reaches in her purse, hands me a CD right before she leaves. "I made this for you . . . before you insulted the shit out of me. It's a Springsteen compilation. Not the greatest hits or anything, just all kinds of interesting stuff that I love."

"Thanks."

"And about Drexel," she says.

Throw my hands up. "Don't."

"It's just—"

Cut her off. "Stop. That's your life over there. And this," I say pointing to my dumpy apartment, "is part of your work life over here. And the two shall intersect nevermore. I accept that. Time for me to stop being the grade school dunce and graduate."

I can't tell if she looks relieved or sad. My vision's blurry and Eva's never easy to read.

She leaves with a calm little "See ya."

I play her CD and get lost in the Springsteen songs. Amazing range of material. Old Dylan-style wordplays. Acoustic numbers. Boardwalk surf band stuff. Dude writes songs that are short stories, maybe even novels. Wish I could tell a story in a three-minute song.

Then there's Eva.

I've burned a thousand CDs for other people. She's the first person who ever burned one for me.

She showed up today.

She took care of me.

She bought me crackers and ginger ale.

I really blew it.

I sit here alone. Ill. Drained. Listen to the Boss belt out "She's the One." I'm too sapped to track down Teresa. She's not the one. Too wiped out even to get up, walk to the kitchen, and grab my fifth of Jameson.

Fuck. Here I go again. Bawling like a little bitch and I'm not even drunk.

Twenty=four

I drag my ass out of bed early and, despite still feeling like hell, drive out to San Gabriel Mission with the trap.

I get there early and I'm the first one through the turnstiles at nine. Find a quiet spot in the sacristy in the back of the church. There's no one around. I press the blue button under the targeting monitor. A blueish white light streams from the barrel. Feels like someone's trying to rip the trap out of my hands. I hold on tight. The stream intensifies, then snaps away from the barrel and forms an orb that darts around the room before slowly vanishing. I feel Ahchancha's presence around me. "I'll be back to see you again," I say.

I head due west on the 210 and drive to the Hahamongna Watershed Park near the Devil's Gate Dam. Park and hike up the milelong horse trail to the top. I stand there looking down and across at those demonic rock formations, feeling the dark energy pulsating around me, with the onset of the dull headache and nausea that accompanies it.

Negativity swirls.

Why am I even here? I'm an idiot. I know nothing about wildlife save for the occasional Nat Geo special when I'm hung over on the couch. I look down at the rocks in the streambed below. Wonder if there's a rattlesnake down there looking for a fight. Even if there was, how could I draw it out? What tempts a rattlesnake the way a hunk of cheddar tempts a mouse? Who cares, really? Because there's that other laughable question: What would I do if I actually crossed paths with a rattler? Shit my pants for sure. Not much else. I don't have a gun. Or a shovel. Or garden shears. Or a first aid kit. Right now, a snake could kill me, but I couldn't kill it. Wasted trip. Note to self: *Come prepared or stay home.*

I take the horse trail back. Stand aside as a five-horse convoy passes. A guy rides in the front—same cowboy I saw when Ned and I were here. Three little kids wearing Camp Hahamongna caps follow, and a teenager in a camp staff shirt brings up the rear. The cowboy looks down at me, tips his shat, and nods. "Howdy."

"Hello again." Here's a guy who looks like he knows the lay of the land. I call out to him as he passes by. "Ever see any rattlers around here?"

He pulls the reins of the lead horse. The processions halts.

"Too often," he says. "At least a half dozen a year."

"This might sound crazy," I say. "But I need to kill a rattle-snake."

"You have a car?"

"Yeah."

"Follow the signs. Drive up to my campground. I'll show you something."

The horse train rolls on. There's a spring in my step on the way back to the car. I wind through the park and take a dirt road to the horse camp, then take a seat on a picnic table. Take in the smell of moist horseshit and wait for the riders to return.

The place looks like a mini dude ranch smack in the middle between Devil's Gate Dam and NASA's JPL campus. There's a little office in a trailer and a larger trailer behind that where someone lives. A dozen or so horse stalls, two corrals, and some small sheds. Beyond that, nothing but heavy brush and the overgrown dry riverbed where Jack Parsons conducted his early rocket experiments.

A friendly black dog approaches, tail wagging. Haven't petted a dog in a long while. Note to self: *Get one of these some day.*

The horse train rolls in ten minutes later. A teenager helps the kids down. The cowboy approaches with a dirty mitt extended. "Hank Hansen," he says. "Camp director." His hands feel like sandpaper. He's got to be forty-five, maybe fifty. Not exactly the Marlboro man. Slight southern drawl. Friendly smile under a black goatee. He walks stiffly—knows pain. A man who's ridden far.

I introduce myself.

"Come over here," he says, leading me toward a wooden shed. He thumbs through a key ring on his belt and opens a big woodplanked door. Pulls the chain on a lightbulb. Hanging from the eight-foot ceiling are seven rattlesnake skins. Big ones. "To answer your question more precisely . . . ," he says.

"You killed them?"

"These are just the ones from this year," he says. Then, a sudden look of misgiving. "You're not an animal activist are you?"

"No."

"It's not like I enjoy killing them," he says. "Have to. Gotta kill anything that can kill my horses. They're my livelihood. My kids. Next time I kill one, I'll give it to you."

"No, I need to kill the snake," I stress. "It has to be me. Do you know where I can find one right now?"

He looks at my suede boots and laughs. "What's a Hollywood boy like you need to kill a snake for?"

"I need its venom and blood."

"For what?" he asks, unfazed.

Jesus, how do I lie my way through this? Medical experiment? Practical joke? This guy can help me. But he wants an answer. I decide on a variation of the truth. No time to think it through. "Do you know anything about shamanism?" I ask.

"Big magic," he says. "Indian stuff. That's about all I know."

"I have Native American blood," I lie. "My ancestors were Chumash." Pull that one out of my ass. "They own the casino in Santa Ynez."

He laughs again. "My horseshit alert just sounded. Indian

blood? You're so fair I'll bet you get a sunburn walking to the driveway to get the paper."

"No, it's true," I assure him. "I'm way into my culture. I need the blood and venom to perform a protection ritual at the new house I bought."

"Where'd you buy?"

No hesitation. "Northridge."

"Struck while the market was down, huh?"

"It was in foreclosure," I volley back. I'm on a roll now. The lies just flow. "Got a wife, and a kid on the way. Want to bless the house right."

"What do you do for a living?"

"I'm an actor."

"Yeah," he says. "A pretty bad one."

Busted.

"You know, rattlesnake venom is deadly."

"I know."

"In careless hands it can kill."

"Believe me, I know. I'm not careless."

"Are you telling me the truth?"

"Yeah."

"You got a number?"

I tell him.

"I'll give you a call next time I cross paths with one," he says, clumsily typing my name and the number into his cell phone. Takes him forever to enter my name in his contact list. "Shaman Kane," he says. "How the hell do you spell shaman?"

Did I mention I pretty much hate everyone? That includes people intimidated by their cell phones.

I get a call from Teresa on my way back to the loaner. "You're up early for being sick."

"What's up?"

"Just got home from class. Had a really lousy morning. What are you doing?"

She's only up the freeway a few miles. Why not? "I'm going to go pick some flowers," I say. "Wanna come along?"

I follow the directions to the abandoned Cascades Golf Course, situated at the base of the mountains where the 5, 210, and the 405 freeways intersect just north of Sylmar. Pretty spot if you ignore the high-voltage power lines zigzagging through an overgrown golf course. Walking up the eleventh fairway, we stop and listen to the sizzle of electricity above us—like bacon frying.

Life ain't bad. It's a gorgeous evening. We're outside. Alone in nature. We should be talking about nice things, but instead it's a bitchfest. Teresa had another bad run-in with Bridget May, her neighbor across the street. Teresa went to apologize for the slap. They had some drinks and things got nasty. Teresa's done with her. That's the Cliffs Notes version. Hers is chock full of mind-numbing detail. She's a writer, all right—with an endless well of words.

She won't stop. "I told her she looked like she lost weight, and she accused me of patronizing her. Then she kept talking about Piper and the prom," she says. "She knew what it was doing to me, but she kept it up." Blah blah blah. Takes as long to recount the story as it took to live it. Maybe longer. I pretend I'm interested and keep my eyes peeled for white flowers in the canyon.

Her negativity is contagious. Pretty soon I'm bitching about Drexel. I stop short of unloading about Eva, though I'm itching to.

I spot something white twenty feet up an embankment in the brush just past the thirteenth green. Creep my way up the hill in my slippery boots through a thicket of jimsonweed. White trumpet flowers. Broad green leaves. Rubbery stems. Right where the blogger said it would be.

"What is it?" Teresa asks.

"Jimsonweed."

"What do you need it for?"

She knows what I do. I could tell her the truth. But why? Too long and complicated. Too weird. I'd sound more like a nut than I already do. "We're going to use it for a photo shoot for a band flyer—an homage to the *Layla* album cover." Good thing I'm not Pinocchio.

"They're pretty," she says. Picks one, gives it a whiff, and winces. "God," she moans. Smells like a sewer."

I stuff a gallon-sized Ziploc full of flowers, leaves, stems—I'll figure it all out later.

Discovery improves our moods. Joint pent-up tensions ease. Then erupt. I turn around. Teresa's undressing. "Anyone for sunset sex?" she asks. Clothes fly. We christen a bench off the fourteenth tee.

Time for a breather. We watch the sun sink into the mountains. I invite her to the gig Saturday night. Tells me she'll be there. Conversation gets deep.

"Did you ever just want to start over?" she asks me.

"Never really got started," I say.

"I'm serious—just start fresh. Somewhere you've never been."

"Not really," I admit. "Do you?"

"Yeah."

"Do it then. You're still young."

"I don't want to do it alone." Oh, boy. Don't respond. I know what's coming. "Take off with me," she says. "Let's just go and live. I have some money. May even end up with a little more."

"Why? Are you close to selling a script?"

"My attorney—the one who represented me before. He says I have a case against Facebook."

I think about it—the depth of her loss. "I'd say he's right."

"But I don't want to go through that again," she says. "I can't handle it—the lawyers and depositions." I nod. "What do you think I should do?" she asks.

I give it some honest thought. "I think you should take whatever you can get. Not that it can replace your daughter."

She looks away. "Just my opinion," I add.

She looks at me. Into me. "So I can't talk you into giving it all up and running away with me?"

I play along. "If the band doesn't make it, I'll be the first one with you on the train out of town."

She smiles. "Promise?"

I don't respond.

We listen to the Chili Peppers on the ride back to her place. Glance over. She does look good. Maybe this is it—as good as it gets. The sex back there was major league. I'll be twenty-nine; she'll be forty. Works when you're naked on a golf course. But what about when I'm still in my forties and she's sixty?

Why am I even number crunching? We don't gel—not really.

We strike a deal: takeout from a chicken teriyaki bowl emporium on Foothill. Then a double feature—our favorite films. *Pulp Fiction* (me) and *Thelma and Louise* (her). Might turn into a decent night.

Dinner and movies get delayed after an hour of solid horseplay.

She's never seen *Pulp Fiction*. It hits her hard. She doesn't laugh when Marvin gets his head blown off in the car. She actually squirms. Thinks Mr. Wolf is an unrealistic character. Duh. She's confused by the out-of-sequence narrative. Thinks Marsellus getting rammed by the hillbilly is "gross."

Ding.

Ding.

Ding.

I feel like I'm in a ten-year marriage that just peaked. Time to wind this down.

We take a break. Pour drinks. Fool around again on the couch. She digs *Thelma and Louise* out of her media cabinet.

My phone rings. It's after midnight. "Sorry to call you late," Detective Alvarez says.

"No problem. What's up?"

"Where are you?"

None of his business, but I'll tell him. Feel weird. But it's not a crime. "I'm visiting Teresa Burrows."

"Good. You can share this with her."

"Shoot."

"We didn't need to subpoena Apple. They agreed to work with us. Turns out their archives aren't as deep as I thought. They only keep precise device-location data for a week. They can track less precise device data by triangulating the general location of the phone from the GSM tower data. We confirmed that the phone has remained in a mile-wide radius of the Burrows' house. Frankly, that didn't help us much. Means it could be any one of her classmates. Or even local members of that sex cult Anna got herself mixed up with."

"So no luck?" I ask.

"Turns out today's our lucky day. We got a hit on the iPhone's GPS. We're taking in a suspect right now for questioning."

I gesture for Teresa to give me something to write on. "Who? Where?"

"Open the front door and look."

Click.

"Who was it?" Teresa asks.

I throw open the front door. Three cop cars—one unmarked, two cruisers with lights blaring—are parked in the driveway across the street. We walk outside in our bare feet. Alvarez, another detective, and two uniformed cops are leading Bridget and Piper May toward the waiting cars. Piper is handcuffed. Bridget is hysterical—throwing a bona fide shitfit the entire neighborhood can hear.

I wave to Alvarez. He motions for Teresa and me to stay put.

Teresa's in a panic. "What's going on?"

"Wait—I'll find out."

I walk a few feet away from Teresa, turn my back and dial Eva. She answers. I can hear Drexel ranting in the background. "Not a good time," she says.

"Shut up and listen to me," I snap. "9879 Creemore Road, La Crescenta. There's a hell of a story ready for you to break. Put the baby to bed and get over here or someone will beat you to it." Hang up. She calls back. Don't answer. It's her prize to win or lose.

Police cruisers pull away; Piper in one car, Bridget in the other. Alvarez walks across the street, waves me over.

"Found the smoking iPhone," Alvarez says. "Piper finally turned it on." Teresa moves closer, hovers close enough to hear. "Number's been on Apple's watch list. They got a hit. Called us a few minutes later with a location. Got a warrant in an hour. Found the iPhone in Piper's bedroom. Confirmed the phony Facebook account was created on it. She's got a sophisticated little app that lets you change your voice on the fly during phone calls. That explains the few phone calls Anna had with J.D. There's even a short recorded conversation between them saved on the phone. Also found a couple forms of identification for Molly Broder, the name used to open the AT&T account."

Teresa puts it together, breaks down. I look back at her, tell her it'll be okay with my eyes. "Did you arrest Piper?" I ask.

"Not yet. Took her in for questioning. But I expect we'll charge her later tonight. Schedule an arraignment."

Teresa walks up to Alvarez, weeping. "Jesus Christ. Did she say why?"

"Not yet," Alvarez tells her. "She's denying it." Gives her a look of genuine sadness. "Mrs. Burrows . . . I know this has to be beyond painful, but at least now you have answers. I hope that brings you some measure of comfort."

Teresa takes a deep breath and lets out a sigh that deflates her spirit. "It doesn't," she says.

Twenty=five

I lie next to Teresa. Another major storm rages outside. We're both restless—in and out of sleep. Sometime, in the middle of the night, I slip into a lucid dream. I'm standing on the ledge of the courthouse dome that overlooks the bridge. Santa Ana winds howl. I'm too terrified to move. Babalon is perched on top of the dome, wings unfurled, armor shimmering in the light of a full moon, spear in hand. She looks towards the mountains, toward Gravity Hill, watching, waiting. Then suddenly, she's at me. "Come to me," she says. A mighty gust of wind knocks me off balance. I try to right myself but I fall—straight down.

I jolt out of bed, soaked.

"What's wrong?" Teresa whispers.

"I have to go."

"I'll come with you."

"You can't. I have to do something. I'll call you first thing in the morning."

I get dressed. When my hand touches the bedroom door-knob, she says, "Kane?"

"Yeah."

"Thank you."

It's 3:17 AM.

The 210 is practically deserted. But the rain-soaked roads are slick, so I take it slow. Still, I'm standing in the underpass at the far end of the bridge in less than twenty minutes. Right away I hear the beating of wings echo off the tunnel ceiling. She's here.

"What do you want?" I ask.

She materializes in front of me. "You," she answers.

"Sorry, I'm spoken for."

"Give yourself to me," she commands.

I stand defiant. "No."

"I can protect you."

"From who?"

"Alastor. Belphegor. Your powerful enemies. When their punishment ends, they will come for you."

I didn't need to hear that, but still, I reject her. "I'll take care of myself."

"I can empower you," she says, moving closer, reaching out and stroking my cheek. She leans in. Our lips almost touch. "Enrich you. I can bring you success."

"And it'll cost me what—my soul?" I say. "The old sell-your-soul-for-rock-and-roll bit?"

"Your body and your soul," she whispers into my ear.

"My body?"

"For me to inhabit," she says with a seductive smile. "Inside you, Gabriel can't touch me. He doesn't have the power to end a mortal life. Together, we can lure him out. And this time, I'll finish him."

"This time? How many battles have you two had?"

"Many."

"And you battle with that?" I say, pointing to her spear. She lets me hold it, but hovers closely. It transforms into a Klerksdorp sphere in my palm.

"Each sphere, forged at the time of creation, is unique, can only be used against one predestined enemy. This one," she says, taking it from my hands, "can end Gabriel."

"And Gabriel has the one that can end you?" I ask.

"And Belial," she answers.

"Two against one. Doesn't sound fair."

Apparently I hit a nerve. "Belial and I were joined," she growls at me.

"So where is your better half?"

With rage and traces of sadness Babalon says, "Extinguished."

"Gabriel defeated him?"

She looks away.

"When?"

"Belial was personified in the body of Jack Parsons. During the ritual—at the moment of transference—Gabriel struck. He ended Belial."

"Was that the explosion that killed Parsons?"

She nods.

I rub salt on the wound. "Shouldn't you have protected him . . . them?"

She seethes. "Gabriel surprised us. I wounded him. But he escaped again."

"Again?"

"Belial and I nearly ended him in 1800. And again in 1937."

"When Gabriel saved a little girl," I say.

Babalon freezes. Turns and locks her gaze on me. "How did you know?"

"I met that little girl. She's still alive and she's doing great, by the way."

The insult angers her. Animal growls rise from somewhere within her. "Sooner or later—Gabriel will return to try and free the souls I've imprisoned."

"Why do you make people jump?" I ask her.

"I don't. When a soul loses hope, it's naturally drawn to me. My prisoners made their own decisions, sealed their own fates."

A radio frequency for lost souls. Tune in to WSAD.

"I failed Belial," she admits with regret. "But I won't fail again. With you, I'll win. Together, we'll revive Crowley's magik and claim millions of souls for our own. We'll gain so much power and strength that Gabriel will crumble."

I back away.

"You'll live in wealth," she says, pointing the spear at me. "Every urge will be satisfied. And your name will never be forgotten."

"I've been to hell," I say to her, "and I don't want to go back." I turn my back on her and bound up the steps to the top of the bridge. The rain pounds down. A shadowy figure stands under a lamppost in an alcove near the center. I approach guardedly. Recognize him when I get close. It's Tall Kevin.

"What are you doing up here?" I ask him.

"The voice. She's talking to me again." He leaps up, grabs the fence, plants his big sneaker on the base of the lamppost, and throws one of his long legs over the side of the railing.

He's playing a joke on me. "Get down from there," I yell at him. "It's not funny."

Ever so vacantly, he says, "Hi, Kane." Then, "Bye, Kane."

In a split second he's up, over, and gone. Disappears in the darkness. There are no screams. Just a dull, splashy thud a few seconds later.

Holy shit.

I look over the railing. Nothing but darkness and rain.

Babalon lands behind me. "You have sympathy for that hopeless monkey." She spits over the rail.

My head spins. I'm overcome with nausea, deep in my belly. "He was someone's father," I say, staring over the ledge. "He played basketball."

"Do what I say," she growls, "or this will happen again . . . to someone else you know. You forget—a part of me is already inside you." She's in my head, rooting around. She smiles. "I hear names," she says. "Ned. Eva. Teresa."

I'm good and fucked. "Get away from me."

Slowly and forcefully, she growls again, "Do what I say."

"And what's that?" I ask, voice quavering.

"Find the box that belonged to Jack Parsons. Inside are the items necessary for the ritual to forge our union. Bring the box to me."

"Where is it?"

"It's close. I can sense its presence, but Gabriel's mark fell upon it when he defeated Belial. It's hidden. Find it. Do it now." She takes flight, disappearing into the night.

I cross the bridge in a mental fog. On the Pasadena side, I dial 911. "I just drove across the Colorado Street Bridge," I tell the operator. "I think I saw someone jump." I hang up before the voice asks me any questions.

I duck into the shadows and wait. The rain stops. I hear a siren a few minutes later. A police car arrives. The cop hikes down the ravine. Just as dawn breaks, I walk back onto the bridge and look down, playing the part of an obnoxious bystander.

The cop phones it in. Mike sits on the ground next to Tall Kevin's body, rocking in place, head in hands. Fifteen minutes later, the coroner's van arrives. No easy way to get the body out. Cop and two guys in scrubs drag the body bag all the way up the steep dirt path to the top of the ravine.

I hear "Hostile Bridge" playing in my head. New words bubble up from the bottom of the bridge and fill my head. They fit in after the long guitar-heavy instrumental bridge. I grab my iPad. Sit on a concrete bench in the alcove and type the words I hear:

> *Across this bridge walk the blessed and the cursed*
> *Here journey the best and the worst*
> *On this bridge, angels of darkness and light*
> *Souls won and lost in an unending fight*
> *Above this bridge dreams are lost and shattered*
> *Here hope and faith are bruised and battered*
> *Under this bridge, lost souls with no rest*
> *Haunted for failing life's greatest test*
> *Across this bridge, hear the lonesome cry*
> *In this place, we choose to live or die*

. . .

I drive to rehearsal in Van Nuys. I'm exhausted and rain-soaked. I curl up and crash in the corner.

Everyone rolls in around noon. I get up and move around. I'm in a megasurly mood. Drexel staggers in with a guy I know—Cameron Leflore, lead guitarist from the Pontius Pilots. They're baked. Giggly. All phony cheery. Meth? Ecstasy—maybe coke? All of the above? And unless Jack Daniels just started selling a signature fragrance, they've also been boozing. What the fuck?

"Mr. Leflore?" Bo says. "To what do we owe the honor?"

"Drexel says you're looking for a guitar."

I walk over and shake Cameron's hand. Weak shake. He's a couple years younger than me. Doughy. Could stand to lose twenty. Long, layered hair covers his eyes. He keeps his head down, won't look me in the eye when we shake. "We met at the El Rey," I say.

"This is Kane, our current hack," Drexel tells him.

Fight-or-flight response kicks in hard. I stay focused on Cameron. Block Drexel out. Pretend he's a ghost. He doesn't like it.

Ira walks over and shakes Cameron's hand. "Drexel's jumping the gun a little. We're not planning on holding auditions for a few more weeks."

"Fuck auditions," Drexel snaps at Ira. "This is our man."

The way Ira looks at Drexel—he smells drugs. This is trouble. Bo looks like he's sitting in a building that's on fire.

"Shit, I'm here," Cameron says. "How about I sit in?"

Ira looks at me. What can I do? Throwing a tantrum will send Ira packing. I know it. I'll play it cool. "Sure," I say.

I'm stunned Cameron would consider leaving such a solid band as the Pilots. Good chance they'll land a deal soon—a bigger one than ours. And Cameron's their secret sauce.

He unpacks his smoky gray Paul Reed Smith. Gorgeous guitar. "You cool playing rhythm?" I ask before he starts.

"I'll shake sleigh bells if there's a deal," he says. "What? Are you worried I can't play chords?"

He plugs into his Mesa Boogie amp and warms up by running through a slick repertoire of chord-driven songs—classic rock to modern. The Who. The Killers. Some dead-on Zeppelin. White Stripes. Then he tops it off with a long blues solo that rocks. Jesus, this guy smokes me.

We start rehearsing with Cameron playing rhythm. We've played on the same bill with the Pilots enough that we know most of each other's songs. Cameron dives right in. His timing is perfect, but his chord structure is too complex. He's stepping all over my lead. I give him a couple of friendly hand signals to rein it in, but the prick ignores me. He's playing too loud. I walk over and tell him to turn it down, but he blows me off. Turns it into a fucking duel. We're butting heads—falling way out of synch with Jay and Joanie.

Enough. I cut it off.

Drexel loves this guy. Practically laps up Cameron's sack. "You're awesome, dude." He bows to Cameron. "We're not worthy." Then he looks at Ira. "I'd say we have our man. Make it happen, record man."

I look at Ira who looks at Bo who looks at me. All I do is shake my head, just slightly, but that's enough for Drexel to go apeshit. "This guy blows you out of the water," he shouts in my face. "You know it."

Ira nods to Cameron, then the door. "Do you mind giving us a minute?"

Cameron has steam coming out of his ears. He thinks we should be kissing his ass, offering him a job on the spot. But he's smart enough to pack his guitar and bite his tongue.

"Thanks for dropping by," Ira says. "We'll be in touch."

Cameron slams his guitar case shut and disappears out the door without a good-bye.

Drexel's tweaking. He's drenched in sweat. From across the room, he yells at me, "I say we fire your ass and hire him."

I could do a lot of things. Stomp his guts out. Call him out for being wasted. Defend myself and my role in the band.

Fuck it.

I do the only thing that won't make me look like an asshole—pack up my guitar. "See you tomorrow," I say. I walk out calmly. Drive across the street to a liquor store in a strip mall. Melt down. Load up.

I wasn't an asshole. I'm proud of myself.

Another storm rolls in. I hole up in my apartment and set out to, as Troy used to say before we fired him, "get righteously fucked up" on an eighteen-pack of Bud and a half gallon of Wild Turkey.

Shot and beer.

I lay there, staring at the ceiling, and start stressing out over Babalon's threat. Find Parson's magik box or else. She mentioned Ned. Eva. Teresa. I'd blocked it out of my mind at practice, but now it's all I can think about.

Shots and beers.

I begin to research Jack Parsons' mysterious black box in the two books Ned gave me and on a bunch of websites. I don't find anything definitive. Some say it was destroyed in the explosion. Others say Parsons' wife hid it after his death. But now she's dead. And that's all I have to go on.

Jesus Christ—there's no way out of this. Gotta cut ties with everyone. Babalon will mine my thoughts and go after anyone rattling around in my brain. No one's safe. I feel caged and cornered.

Shot and beer.

My phone's been on vibrate. Over the course of the last few hours, I missed calls from Eva, Ned, Bo, and several from Teresa. For their own good, I don't listen to any of their messages.

Gotta find Ahchancha's cave painting. Gotta drink that potion. Can't do it alone. No way. Need Eva's help. But I'll be putting her at risk.

Shot and beer.

I'm nobody's slave. Gotta find a way to beat Babalon, drive her back to hell.

Shot and beer.

There's a news alert flash on my phone. Headline:

TEEN CHARGED IN FACEBOOK MURDER. LURES EX-FRIEND TO SUICIDE.

Links to the AP wire. Byline: Eva Kells. Her story went national. Check Drudge, AOL News, Yahoo, CNN.com. Story is everywhere. Media is in a feeding frenzy.

Text message from Teresa:

Reporters in my driveway. Access Hollywood is here.
Eva Kells—do u know her? Help!

I can't. I'm wigging out.

Shot and beer.

I pass out facedown.

Twenty-six

I roll over at six. Scrape myself off the floor, run to the john. Poison comes out of every orifice. Liver feels pickled. Head feels like there's an ax sticking out of it.

I gargle and down three Tylenol with a quart of water. Peel the plastic off the lid of a Pedialyte bottle and down it. Brew a pot of coffee so strong it would get Stephen Hawking on his feet. I'll live.

I check my voice messages.

Teresa: *Where are you?*

Ned: *Just checking in.*

Eva: *What happened at rehearsal?*

Bo: *Blah, blah—something about rehearsal.*

Cowboy Hank Hansen: *Bagged a rattler. Get here fast or I'll have to kill it without you.*

Hit return call. He's up. "Not too early?" I ask.

"I'm up before the sun," he says. "Just saddling the horses."

"So you got one?"

"Four o'clock yesterday. Almost stepped on it behind the barn. It's in a sack in the shed. Can you get over here now? I start the trail rides at nine."

"You bet."

Rush-hour traffic treats me kindly. No accidents. But my hangover is epic and reflexes are shot. I nearly rear-end a car. Make it to the camp by eight.

Hank is unloading bales of hay off a delivery truck. "We've gotta do this fast," he says. "My busload of kids will be here any minute."

We enter the shed. He grabs the burlap sack that's moving. "Six-footer," he says. "An old one."

He hands me a rusty machete. "Did you ever do this before?"

"No," I admit.

Hank lays down the ground rules. "When I toss it out, I'll hold its head down with the hoe. You whack it with the machete—good and hard—about a foot behind the head. Whack it till you've cut all the way through. Ready?"

"Yeah." Adrenaline races.

Hank dons work gloves. Tosses me a pair for myself. I put them on. He unfastens the sack. "On the count of three. One . . . two . . . three—" He tosses the rattler out of the sack. It winds itself up for just an instant, then slithers toward the door. Hank is all over it. The rattler sounds—loud. He slams the hoe down on its head, pins it to the floor. "Now," he yells.

Whack! I slice through the snake like a Ginsu on paper. The body slithers off behind my feet. I jump. "Grab the body and toss it in that bucket," he tells me. I grab the body. Creepiest damn feeling ever as it slithers through my palms. Toss it in the bucket. It tries to slither out, but drops back inside. "Grab the hoe," Tim commands. "Keep the head pinned down. It can still bite." He moves in behind the head and puts a death grip on it. Positions his fingers carefully and says, "Let go."

He stands with the head in his gloved hand. Squeezes the side of the jaws until the snake's mouth opens wide. Huge-ass fangs protrude. "Hand me an empty bottle," he orders, nodding to a huge trash can filled with recyclables. "Hold it from the bottom," he tells me. I hold it still. He positions the snakes fangs directly over the lid, squeezes the sides of the snake's head with all his might. Venom drips into the bottle—a teaspoon or two.

Hank tosses the head across the shed. When it hits the floor, it snaps its jaws three times, then freezes. The body in the bucket has also stopped slithering. There's an inch of blood pooled in the

bottom. Hank hands me another empty Pepsi bottle. "Fill 'er up."
I fill the bottle up halfway with blood and tighten the lid.

The bus pulls in. Kids emerge. "Do me a favor," Hank says,
handing me a shovel. "Go down by the riverbed and bury the
head. Dig at least a three-foot hole."

"What about the body?"

"I'll skin it and give the meat to my golf buddy. He makes a
hell of a stew."

I shovel up the head. Hank goes out and greets the kids
warmly and I follow. "The kids *oooh* and *ahhhh* as I pass and make
my way toward the riverbed beyond the camp, the same riverbed
where Jack Parsons conducted his rocket experiments.

There, in the shadow of the NASA campus on the hill, I dig
the hole. When I toss dirt on the snake's head, its jaws snap one
last time. I thank it. Somehow I think Ahchancha would want
me to do that.

I return to the shed, grab my bottles, and wave good bye
to Hank. He's too busy lining up kids up for their trail ride to
notice.

I make a mental checklist before I turn the key in the ignition.
I have everything I need—jimsonweed, rattlesnake venom and
blood, salt, and water. But I can't do this alone. If there really is a
cave behind a waterfall, I'll have to rappel down to it.

I need Eva. I have no other choice. I'll call her after rehearsal.
Rehearsal? Jesus. What's the fallout from yesterday? I almost forgot about all that.

I check Bo's message again and listen this time. He tells me to
bring in my guitarist of choice today. It's not a formal audition,
more of a lesson Ira wants to teach Drexel. I can't wait to see that
little prick's face when I show up with a guitarist in tow. I call Pat
Boreo. Give him the news. He tells me he can't blow off work. I
tell him this is a once-in-a-lifetime chance. Paint him a picture of
rock stardom. Finally, I convince him to call in with the flu, pack
his guitar, and head to Van Nuys pronto.

Pat and I pull into Uncle Rehearsal Studio at the same time, early. We walk in together, the first two to arrive. "Any advice?" he asks me as he sets his amp.

"Kiss the singer's ass. Compliment the rich-looking guy."

"Ira Bowersock? He'll be here?"

"Yep."

"Shit. I better not suck."

One by one, they file in. In order: Bo, Joanie, Jay, Ira, and then Drexel, who smells like he's been on another bender. He's carrying around a big bottle of Evian. I think it's filled with vodka. Five minutes after he staggers in, Eva peeks through the doorway. What the fuck?

I feel the rage bubbling up inside me.

She wants to up the ante in this game? Fine.

"She's cool," Drexel says, waving her in.

Eva comes in looking way uncomfortable. Gestures for me to step outside. I ignore her. She jots down a note. Hands it to me. We really are in grade school. *He shouldn't be driving. Followed him. Almost took out a street full of parked cars.* I write back: *Tough shit. Your problem.*

Drexel finally notices there's a stranger in his midst. "Who's this bald motherfucker?"

"He's just gonna sit in," I say to Drexel with a smirk.

I introduce Pat, who pulls out his vintage '64 chocolate sunburst Telly. He runs through some Radiohead tunes. They sound easy, but it takes finesse to get them just right. Ira understands. Pat plays and sings. He's got a good voice.

Jay likes what he hears. Picks up his bass and jams along.

Pat follows up with some U2—"Vertigo" and "All Because of You." Great guitar songs. Rolls into an impressive Beatles medley. Lights up the room. Plays John, Paul, and George's individual solos in the "The End." Nails all three.

Ira has that cool look sneaking through his poker face. I think he likes him. But who cares? This is about sticking it to Drexel.

Pat sits in for our rehearsal. Drexel's way off, but we work around him. It's about the music today, not the voice.

Pat plays perfect rhythm to my lead. No surprise there. We spent hundreds of hours lying around each other's apartments last year, playing and listening to music. We're synched. He always knows where I'm headed and covers my back when I screw up or miss a note.

The music pops. He's that minisplash of bitters that finishes off a perfect Manhattan. He knows our entire set. Surprises even me when he breezes through "Pound of Hate." Didn't think he'd have time to listen to the MP3 I emailed him, let alone learn it.

Pat fidgets with his amp and plugs in my Les Paul. Pops a slide on his finger. He plays Duane Allman to my Clapton on "Layla." Pure chemistry. When we finish I don't say a word. Don't need to. Pat's guitar said it all.

Pat packs up and shakes Ira's hand. "An honor," he says. Good move. He hugs Joanie. Shakes Jay's hand, compliments his bass playing. Says to Drexel, "You're awesome, dude."

Drexel gives him the brush.

Pat knows not to overstay his welcome. He leaves without fanfare.

While I'm packing my gear, Eva walks over, says, "We need to talk."

Before I can tell her to go fuck herself, Ira says, "He was good."

Drexel laughs hard and loud. "Shaved-head looks are old. Pasty fucker looks like a cancer patient."

Ira's loses patience fast. "So he'll wear a cap. Or a top hat. Or a fucking crown. Sober up," he yells at Drexel. "That shit was lightning in a bottle."

The room bristles with tension. I break the fucking camel's back by announcing, "I have some new lyrics for 'Hostile Bridge.' Anyone wanna hear?"

Almighty hell breaks loose. Drexel picks up the chair Ira was just sitting on and hurls it through the window looking out into the hallway. Glass flies everywhere. Drexel darts straight at me. Throws a wild punch that grazes my cheek. Jay tackles him, but Drexel springs up like a gymnast. His sunglasses fly off. His eyes are red and glazed. Bo puts a bear hug on him. He and Jay hold him back. Drexel shouts at me—full volume, "You work for me. Now you're trying to steal my band!" He's foaming at the mouth.

"Drugs making you a little paranoid?" I yell back.

Eva gets between us, stands closer to me.

Drexel points at me. "I want this fucker out," he tells Bo. Looks at me with his bloodshot eyes. "You're fired, bitch."

"Calm down," Bo tells him.

"No. I want Cameron Leflore from the Pilots."

"I want. I want!" I shout. "Give this little whiney shit a pacifier and a rattle."

"It's him or me, Mr. Boss Man," Drexel screams at Ira.

I look at Eva. "Get your boyfriend out of here, Yoko," I snap. She's not amused.

Ira storms over to Joanie's drum kit and hits the crash cymbal. "Shut the fuck up!" he shouts. "All of you!"

Silence.

"Take tomorrow off," Ira says. "Cool off. Sober up and come back here Friday ready to play or this ends here and now. I will not risk my reputation Saturday night if this is how it is. Understood?" He grabs his thousand-dollar sport coat and storms out, kicking broken glass out of his path.

We all look at each other. I'm gonna kill Drexel if I stay. Adrenaline courses through me. I feel strong enough to lift a car. I look at Eva with pure intensity. "You leave here right now with me or we're finished for good. Understand?"

She follows me out. Suck on that, Drexel. I can hear Drexel pitching another tantrum as we leave.

In the parking lot, Eva slaps me a good one. "Yoko?!"

I look at her but won't apologize.

She starts, "Drexel is—"

I cut her off. "Don't mention his name," I warn her. "And don't let your head swell. Could give a fuck less what you do. This is about business. We need to find that cave painting."

"Why now?"

"*Now*! It's life and death. We do it now—while I'm pissed off and have the nerve."

She sighs. "I still have the climbing gear in my trunk."

"Then drive."

"We only have three hours of daylight left, tops," she warns. "We have to reach those falls before it gets dark or we won't be able to reach the cave."

"Then drive fast."

Eva punches the gas. "Keep your eyes peeled for cops," she says.

"If a cop pulls us over I'll kill him with my bare hands."

Twenty-seven

We haul ass, make it to the trailhead near the top of Lake Avenue in Altadena in less than an hour. In rush-hour traffic, that's miraculous. Eva leads us on a ninety-minute hike that takes us up the Sam Merrill Trail to the top of Echo Mountain. We walk past remnants of century-old train tracks—all that's left of the old Mount Lowe Railway. Can't help but wonder if the anti-gravitational pull of Gravity Hill—the spot where the Archangel Gabriel arrived—extends far up into the San Gabriel Mountains. Might explain how, well over a hundred years ago, Thaddeus Lowe managed to build an electric incline railway system that could climb five-thousand feet high through steep and treacherous canyons.

At the top of Echo Mountain, Eva and I stop briefly to catch our breath. We don't allow ourselves to linger and block out the view of the gorgeous sunset from the 3,500-foot peak. We bolt past the ruins of the Echo Mountain House, a luxury hotel built in 1894 that, Eva tells me, burned down in 1900. From the peak, we descend down a steep, rocky trail into Rubio Canyon. It's a rugged, beautiful spot. Four waterfalls are visible from our vantage point. Not much daylight left. Eva takes out the binoculars. Studies each waterfall quickly before daylight fades. Points to the biggest—a multistage waterfall—and says, "That's Leontine Falls." Hands me the binoculars. "Have a look. Tell me what you see."

The waterfall begins with a fifteen-foot drop to a rock ledge that forms a natural pool. The water cascades down a deadly vertical drop. "The little pool is called Diana's Bath," Eva says. "Look behind it—in the outcropping of rock jutting out from the cliff wall. Does that look like it might be a cave entrance to you?"

I squint, adjusting the binoculars. "If it is, there are rocks covering it," I say. "How can we find out?"

I hand the binoculars back to Eva. She spots a water pipe about twenty feet above the top of the falls. "There," she says. "Just like the website said. It's the old pipe that carried water to the hotel. Climbers use that pipe as anchor support for descents."

I can't believe I'm gonna do this. At night.

"We only have a few minutes of daylight left," Eva points out. "We get one shot at this. If that's not the cave, then we have to come back another day. Agreed?"

"Okay."

"This is so stupid," Eva says on the way to the top of the falls. "It's gonna be hard enough hiking back down that trail in the dark. What am I thinking? What if something happens? What if you have a bad reaction to whatever it is you're gonna be dosing yourself with?"

"We're here. Let's just do it," I snap.

Halfway across the rock-strewn trail to the top of the falls, we both slip on loose footing. I don't say it out loud, but she's right. This is stupid.

Eva secures the anchor system on the pipe, secures the rope, and helps me into the climbing harness just as the last sliver of daylight fades. I double-check that I have everything before Eva zips up my backpack.

We look at each other, but don't say the obvious—that we're idiots. "Be careful," she says. "Nice and slow."

I begin the descent. Despite the spray of cold water in my face, compared to the bridge, the fifteen-foot descent is a piece of cake. I drop straight into the waist-high water of the pool on the ledge. I'm there before I can even panic. "Okay," I yell. "Made it."

"Leave the harness on," Eva yells down.

"You think I'm crazy enough to take it off?" I yell back. I steal a glance over the edge. Jesus. At least a hundred feet straight down into a pile of boulders. I open my backpack and shine the flashlight on the cliff wall. There is a crack—a tiny opening. I peek inside and confirm—Damn, it's the cave. "Found it," I yell to Eva.

"Excellent," she shouts. "Yell up to me when you're ready. I'll pull you up. But you're gonna have to help by climbing. I can't pull that much deadweight."

"Poor choice of words," I yell.

I start rolling the rocks away from the entrance. The smallest one fits in my palm. The biggest takes all my strength to budge a few inches out of the way. I clear an opening big enough to fit in and crawl inside.

It's a tiny space. More of a nook than a cave. Ten by ten, maybe smaller. I shine my flashlight on the back wall and there it is—Ahchancha's cave painting. White-and-red paint. Mostly geometric patterns. Interconnected diamond chains in vertical rows. Spirals. Figure eights. Cross-hatching. Neat rows of zigzagged horizontal lines—like pattern on the bodysuits of the souls trapped under the bridge. Primitive-looking stick figure of Babalon—wings, armor, and spear. A serpent of fire above her.

I sit on the ground. The sound of the waterfall echoing off the walls is vibrational—hypnotic. A stiff breeze outside blows in a cool mist. I open my backpack and lay out the Pepsi bottles and Ziploc bags. I take out a plastic grocery bag of sage brush and kindling I gathered on the hike up Echo Mountain and a pack of matches from the club Voyeur and start a little fire. Lots of smoke at first. The smell of sage is powerful.

Potion-mixing time. I pour a cup full of Fiji water into my

Rolling Stones coffee mug. Add a fist full of Hawaiian sea salt.
The jimsonweed is all dry and crumbly in the Ziploc bag. I grab
a handful—leaves, flowers, seeds, and stems. Crush it in my fist.
Brush it into the cup. Open the Pepsi bottles and pour the rattlesnake blood and venom into the cocktail. Add more sage and
kindling to the fire. Take off my shirt and use it to hold the mug
over the flame until the concoction is scalding hot. I blow on it a
few times and chug it down in one gulp. Tastes like ass.

I sit and stare at the pictograph.

Don't feel a thing.

Stare.

My feet itch. Boots are soaked.

Stare.

Ten minutes pass.

Fifteen.

Twenty.

Nothing.

I climb out of the cave. Yell up to Eva, "Nothing's happen—"

It kicks in.

A column of blue light shoots straight up the canyon and
turns the water in the pool sparkling white. I see shapes in the
light. Hazy figures bathed in white. I dive back into the cave.

I shine the flashlight on the painting and stare.

It's moving.

The geometric shapes dissolve into each other. Then suddenly
the wall turns blinding white. A vision appears.

I'm there. At the bridge. With Babalon. I watch it play out.
Experience it through my own eyes. See what I have to do to
send the wicked witch back to hell. I need the Indian Ahchancha's
help. There are objects I need. Items to gather. Rituals I'll need to
carry out. I need to gather sage and burn it. I can't even begin to
plan out the details when my brain's being ripped in half. I can't
order it in my mind; everything feels like a movie on fast forward.
I just try to retain the images the best I can.

A sinking feeling grips me whole. Good news: Babalon can be defeated. Bad news: I'll probably die.

It starts here and requires a whole new fucked-up plan.

I pack up and crawl out of the cave. My brain is on fire, my legs numb. I topple face-first into the pool and then finally regain my footing. "Get me out of here," I yell to Eva.

She yanks the rope. I pull myself up the rock wall and climb for my life. The rocks jutting out of the cliff wall I'm climbing have faces. They stare. Speak. Sing. Red lightning bolts strike above and below me. I scream. The rocks laugh at me.

Eva doesn't even have to break a sweat. I climb hard and fast out of sheer terror. The faces become hands that reach for me. I grab one of them. It's reptilian with green scales and black fingernails.

I'm having a full-fledged psychedelic meltdown.

I close my eyes. Eva pulls. I climb like a motherfucker. Land face-first in the water next to Eva's feet. I'm drenched. My eyes are bugging.

Made it.

Shafts of light shoot at me from all directions. "Bad trip," I tell Eva. "Talk me down."

"You can do this," Eva assures me. "Just keep moving, double-timing it—you'll sweat it out of your system."

She leads the way up the steep hill to Echo Mountain, then down the hiking trail for the long trek back to the car. She's tough. Doesn't baby me for a second, in fact she orders me to keep up.

I drop to my knees and vomit.

"Christ, you poisoned yourself," she cries. She shines the flashlight in my eyes. Sounds panicky. "I think your eyes are bleeding. Jesus! If you die I'm gonna kill you."

The hike is surreal. The hallucinations are worse than any acid trip I've taken. Trees and scrub brush speak to me. I see flashes of Indians. The moon bounces around the sky like a pinball. I feel like I'm levitating one minute and sinking in quicksand the next.

When we reach the car after what feels to me like a lifetime, Eva thanks God aloud. I pitch a shitfit and refuse to get in her car.

"Why? What's wrong?" she asks.

"Your car's a big lizard," I tell her. "It's gonna swallow me."

She's way out of patience. "Get the fuck in! Now!" she screams at me.

I obey like a scared puppy.

"Where to now?" she asks.

"San Gabriel Mission," I tell her. "But first, drive by Devil's Gate Dam."

I'm trippin' balls the whole ride to the dam. Cars are alive. Beings of light whizz by. Traffic lights are so bright they scorch my eyes. The car gets hot, then cold, then hot again. All the while, I guide her along side roads to the dam. I have to tell her to pull over when we cross the gorge. I jump out of the car and lean over the barrier. Gaze into the chasm with the devil heads. Rust-colored glow emanates from the bottom. I'm looking at molten lava bubbling from a volcano crater. Demonic figures burst from the heat like missiles being launched. They arc skyward, taking flight in all directions over the city.

Eva stands by my side. "What? What do you see?"

"The Devil's Gate," I tell her.

"Where?" She doesn't see what I see.

"It's a gateway to hell."

"I don't see a thing."

I'm weeping.

"Calm down," she says.

"Get me out of here," I plead. "Take me to the mission. Now. I need to find Ahchancha. I need the cross that Ahchancha carved."

Eva panics. "Are you going to try to steal a cross from a church?"

"I'm going to borrow it," I snap. "Just drive."

Eva hits the freeway. Races east. I'm tripping that we're speeding through the belly of a giant snake. I hear a voice behind me say, "Turn me on, dead man." For a split second, I see Aleister Crowley in the backseat. Blink and he's gone.

Fucked-Up Plan—Part One.

A cross to bear.

Eva pulls up in front of the mission. I have to find a way inside. I need that cross. It's 12:30 AM. There's still traffic on the street. This'll be risky.

"Loop around a few times," I tell Eva. "I'll be out in a couple of minutes. We'll have to haul ass out of here. Straight to the freeway. You ready?"

Eva's wigging out. "What are you gonna do?"

"Just have the getaway car ready," I tell her before jumping out and running.

I head to a locked gate next to the old mission church and meditate. Send out a call—"Ahchancha, hear me." The iron fence vibrates. Gate rattles. Hair stands up on my arms. I see a hazy white figure on the other side of the fence. "Listen to me," I say. "I've seen the painting. I know what we need to do. We have to act fast. I need two things—you and your cross. Can you get me inside?"

The figure disappears. Energy dissipates. I turn on the trap, don my earpiece. Pick up a signal. Follow it to the gift shop. Locked. Look through the window. Ahchancha materializes in the form of a white mist that envelops the security system panel against the back wall. The energy of Ahchancha's spirit creates a surge that overloads the system. It lights up like the Vegas Strip. Sparks fly. It blows.

I run back to the gate. Jump the fence. Sprint through the cemetery to the museum in the back. Break the glass on the door. Zigzag to the room with Ahchancha's cross on the wall. Christ's eyes just blinked at me. I'm still tripping, but I shake it off as best as I can. Cross is weighty—twenty pounds easy, maybe more. "We need this," I say to the air. "Are you here with me?"

I hear a loud *RAP!* on a glass case.

"I need to take you with me," I announce. "Somewhere you can't meet me on your own."

Two *Raps!*

"Stand still," I order. I take out the trap. Aim. Squeeze the trigger. The boom shatters the glass in the case. Got him.

Back in the cemetery, dead bodies crawl out of the ground. Statues move. I run past a reproduction of the *Pietà*. Mary drops Jesus off her lap and chases me.

I block it all out and focus on the front gate. I slide the cross under the fence. I'm up and over just as Eva pulls up. Dive in her car with the cross. Sweating like a pig. Heart pounding out of my chest.

"Oh, shit?" she yells. "You really did steal it."

"I just borrowed it," I say.

"I don't believe it—I'm driving a getaway car."

"You're Bonnie and I'm Clyde," I tell her.

"Now where?"

"My place."

Fucked-Up Plan—Part Two.

Powwow.

Eva helps me get wired up and monitors me as I go in. Figured it would be hard as hell to project my soul with a head full of whatever I'm tripping on, but I'm gone in record time. Note to self: *This elixir helps the journey along.*

Ahchancha looks me over, reads me like a billboard. Says it in his native tongue; I hear it in English: "You've had your vision quest."

Nod. "I've seen what I need to do. . . . and what you need to do."

"Tell me."

I do. The look of joy when I tell him Belial is already dead . . . priceless.

I ask him why I need loads of sage. He tells me it will purify the bridge, weaken Babalon. I ask him if he knows where I can find Jack Parsons' magik box. He doesn't know who or what I'm talking about. I'm on my own on that one.

"The next time I free your soul," I tell him, "you'll be in the presence of Babalon." He looks pleased. "Keep her away from me—at least for a few minutes."

He clenches both fists, lets out a war cry. "I will fight," he says, emphatically. "The sage will strengthen me. I will protect you."

I give him a nod of gratitude. "When it happens, fight her until the souls under the bridge are freed. The second they're free, forget about me. Leave with them or you'll be stuck here forever. Do you understand?"

"Yes," he says.

"Promise me you'll go—no matter what."

He makes a sign. Two arms crossed over his chest. I hear the meaning in my mind: "My word."

"I don't know how long it will take me to find the sage and the black box," I warn.

"I will wait here and prepare," he says.

"But be ready—anytime," I tell him. "Any last advice?"

He nods. "To destroy evil you must wage a war that's yours alone."

I look at him, a little confused.

"There are many religions, many cultures—each with their own rituals for banishing evil. But don't rely on anything but the power from inside yourself. Do you understand?"

"I think so." I make the same sign he made and offer my hand. He takes it and shakes hard.

"We must sing in preparation for battle," he says.

Ahchancha begins to pound out a drumbeat on the table. He chants—he's got a good voice—and invites me to sing. The drumbeat sounds familiar. I join in, expand the beat. Turn it into that unforgettable drum beat of "Sunshine of Your Love." We sing the words. They're meaningful. Ahchancha gets into it. He sings the words in his native tongue. He digs Cream.

. . .

Eva goes above and beyond by driving me back to my car, still in the parking lot of Uncle Rehearsal Studio in Van Nuys. Her cell phone keeps ringing, but she ignores it. At long last, she asks me, "Teresa Burrows—what's going on between you?"

"We're friends."

"That's all?"

I don't answer. Volley a question back. "Are you going easy on her with the story and everything?"

"Yes."

"Good," I say. "Keep the wolves away. Be respectful. Tell the story the way you do. Poor woman's been through hell. She deserves your best."

"I know," Eva says.

"I'm glad it's you she's talking to."

"Thanks."

Eva looks over. "You care about her, don't you?" I don't answer. "Don't you?" she repeats.

"Like you care about Drexel?"

Her phone rings again. I can tell by her face it's him. She doesn't answer.

We sit in silence the rest of the way. I invite her to breakfast when she drops me off. She politely declines.

"Guess this is good-bye—for now." Truthfully, it's probably forever.

"You're gonna do this thing you won't tell me about, aren't you?"

"I have to."

"Why do it alone? I'll help you. So will Ned."

"No," I say and mean it. "You'd be in danger. Both of you. Promise me you won't tell Ned."

I see reluctance all over her face.

"Promise me," I say.

"Is that really what you want?"

Nod.

"Okay, then."

"Don't contact me again. I'll call you when it's over. Or not."

We look at each other. So much to say, but not a word spoken. We broke each other's hearts.

"Bye, Eva," I say.

"Bye, Kane."

I watch her drive away.

Twenty-eight

Fucked-Up Plan—Part Three.

Black Box Project.

I'm back at my place and drowning in anxiety. The urge to drink is strong, but I push it down. Need to think clearly.

Text message from Eva that says: *Lay low.* Plus a link to a small mention in the *Times* about a burglary at the San Gabriel Mission. One item has gone missing: a cross. Byline: Eva Kells. Smart thinking.

Burning question of the day: *Where the hell am I going to find Jack Parsons' box?* I've been through the books. Searched the web. It's led nowhere. Saw one picture of it in the book *Sex and Rockets*. Other than that, nothing.

I lay on my sofa and brainstorm.

The last place the box was seen was at the site of the explosion. There's nothing left of the old mansion and backyard lab where the explosion occurred. Maybe the police confiscated it when they investigated Parsons' death. The books indicate that Parsons' wife, Marjorie Cameron, was the last person seen with the box. At the time of her death she was living in Hollywood. Yet Babalon said the box is close.

What about Aleister Crowley's Ordo Templi Orientis lodge? Parsons was a leader in the organization. He ran it out of his mansion. Maybe another occultist in the order inherited the box. Does the O.T.O. even exist anymore?

Google: *O.T.O. Los Angeles.* Leads to a generic, vague website, but I'm able to confirm that there are branches all over the country, including in L.A. It's no longer in Pasadena—but down the freeway in Glendale. Jot down the address. It's worth a look.

I click around the website some more. There's a message from the master of the lodge—Frater Lieber.

Bingo.

Anna was mixed up with him. He was on her Facebook friends list. She was a member of the lodge he operated. There were tons of text messages between them. She was having an affair with him last year. Even though Detective Alvarez cleared Frater Lieber as a suspect in Anna's death, maybe he knows where Parsons' box is. Maybe he even has it.

I race outside to my car. Dig through the trunk until I come out with the manila envelope with Anna Burrows' IM transcripts and run back inside. Find their IM thread, some photos they exchanged. He's married. Scumbag really did a number on Anna's psyche. He's a forty-something schmuck with a beer belly. Owns a heating and air-conditioning business, but portrays himself as a supernatural guru. He pushed the lodge on her hard. Twisted her brain like a pretzel. Guy needs a serious beating.

Some of the lodge activities take place at a warehouse he mentions often. I google his business. Oriflamme Heating and Air. Lame website. I scribble down the address—North Hollywood.

Back to the messages. In one thread, they plan to rendezvous at his office. He promises to initiate her into a higher level of the order by conducting a sexual ritual. Texts her again a few minutes later. His wife is suspicious. He'll be late. Tells her to get there and prepare the altar. Lets her know about a key hidden inside a light fixture on the side of the building. Gives her the code to disarm the security system—666. Douche bag.

I fall asleep thinking about where I'd stab him first.

When I wake up it's dark outside. Needed the sleep bad. More messages from Teresa. Not now. I must stay focused.

I grab a pair of leather gloves, my lucky necklace, and back-pack.

Drive to La Crescenta. The O.T.O. lodge is in a storefront in a tiny strip mall. It's locked up, dark. A big sign above the window reads: *Lam of God Church*. Name serves two purposes: to blaspheme Christianity and to honor Lam, a supernatural being Aleister Crowley claimed to communicate with. I shine my flashlight through the window. A little office is set up. Two desks. Computer and printer. Copier. No file cabinets. Bare walls. It's a mailing address, that's it.

I drive to Oriflamme on Lankershim in North Hollywood. It's a cinder-block building. Bars on the windows. Around back, there's a parking lot, a garage, and a warehouse surrounded by a wrought-iron fence topped with spirals of razor wire. I spot the light fixture on the side.

I notice a light is on in one of the windows, so I park across the street and watch. The fence rolls open and a van pulls into the lot just after nine. Two guys get out, go in for a few minutes, and then leave in their own cars. Light still on.

9:36 PM. Light goes out. A woman and a man leave through the front door. It's him. I feel like hitting the gas and plowing him right into the building.

I hit Starbucks down the street and get jacked up on espresso until closing time, give it some extra time in case he comes back, then I return to Oriflamme. Here I go. Playing with fire. If I fuck this up, I'll end up in jail for the long haul. I pop off my license plates to be safe. Drive a few blocks and park on Saticoy.

I wait until the coast is clear before I examine the light fixture, wearing gloves to be safe. I feel around and come out with a key. Open the front door. The warning alarm sounds. I quickly find the keypad and enter 666. Thank Christ, it's still the code.

Use my pocket flash light to look around but don't turn on any lights. Three offices and a little conference room. I rummage through file cabinets. Nothing about the O.T.O. All business. I spy a family photo on Frater Lieber's desk. Wife and two daughters. Shitbag.

I head out back. The warehouse and garage are padlocked. Shit.

Go back and check the boss' desk. Dig out a key ring full of lots of keys.

The ninth one I try works on the garage. Four company vans are lined up, but nothing else. I find the key to the warehouse. It's full of furnaces and air conditioners. Messy as hell. Another locked door in the back. Try the keys.

Bingo.

It's a big storage room illuminated by a single red ceiling globe. Black-and-white checkered floor. Smells like incense and stale aftersex. This is where they hold their rituals, their sex magik. This is where they conduct the Gnostic mass. Four rows of wooden pews face a purple velvet backdrop. Against the curtain, an inverted crucifix hangs above an altar draped with a black cloth. Atop the altar sits a stone tablet carved with hieroglyphics. Beneath that, on a little ledge, is a leather-bound copy of Crowley's *Liber AL vel Legis*—*The Book of the Law*. Under that, twenty-two candles in silver candlesticks are arranged precisely. A chalice surrounded by red silk roses rests in the center. A sword and a spear are leaning against the front of the altar.

Two six-foot obelisks—one white, one black—stand on opposite sides. An old church organ sits nearby. A white robe, a red cape, and a crown in the shape of a serpent hang on a coat rack in the corner. It all looks so cheesy in the light. Like the set of a grade-school play.

There are two big locked file cabinets. I find the right key on the ring.

It's a gold mine.

Lodge archives dating back to 1934. I grab handfuls of the interesting looking ones—as many as I can carry. Fill my backpack until it's busting, and then carefully lock everything up. I return the key ring to Frater Lieber's desk. Rearm the security system. Lock the front door, return the key, and double-time it to my car.

I examine the files back at my place. Minutes of meetings, membership lists, an entire folder of old photos from the 1940s. I recognize Jack Parsons and L. Ron Hubbard in many of them. Shots from a costume party in 1948. Parsons, an ornery grin on his face, is wearing a comic devil's costume—horns and pitchfork in hand. His wife—Marjorie Cameron—looks shitfaced as the evil queen from *Snow White*. Flip through some more.

I stop dead.

Drop the rest of the photos and stare at the one in my hands.

It's a couple, arm-in-arm. The woman is dressed as a lion tamer. The man is the lion. It's Millie Barrington and Stanley Tekulve.

I go back to the folder with the membership lists.

Fuck me.

She was a member from 1944 to 1950.

That old witch hooked me and reeled me in. Set me up.

It's after one, but this can't wait. I dial Ronnie Barrington on his cell. Wake him out of a dead sleep. "Who is this?"

"Kane Pryce."

"Can't this wait until the morning?"

"No. I need to see your mother—now."

"Mother's asleep."

"Wake her up."

"Out of the question," he grumbles. "I take it this is about the job?"

"Sure as hell is."

"Mother will be anxious to hear. We're in Pasadena for the opening of the Bukowski exhibition at our library. Shall we say breakfast? The Barrington Arms? Nine AM?"

"I'll be there."

Twenty=nine

I walk past a long row of Barrington family portraits hanging in the corridor of the luxury hotel, between the lobby and the terrace where breakfast is being served. This place is another jewel in Millie's treasure chest.

Millie and Ronnie Barrington sit at a table next to a three-tiered terra-cotta fountain in the center of the patio. Ronnie stands and Millie waves me over.

She's decked out in a yellow dress. Chipper. Dentures glistening. Several hundred thousand dollars worth of jewelry shimmering in the morning sun. The old coot even has diamonds in her hairpins. "Where's your colleague Mr. Ross? I do hope he's well," Millie says.

"He's fine."

"Sit, please," Ronnie says. He's wearing the same black suit he was wearing the first time I met him. Alcohol doesn't treat him well. He's so pale he looks like a ghost in the sunshine.

Millie hands me a menu. "You really must try the Eggs Benedict."

I stare daggers at her. "I'm not hungry."

A waitress appears. "Coffee?"

"Bloody Mary," I say.

"That sounds delightful," Millie says with a big, bright morning laugh. "Ronnie?"

"Why not?" her son answers.

"Three Bloody Marys, darling," Millie tells the waitress.

I open the folder I'm carrying, toss the photograph of Millie and Stanley on the table.

She doesn't miss a beat. "Now that was a party," she says with that laugh. Her skin is like wax paper, but her emerald eyes are like a child's.

"Interesting company you keep," I say.

Millie looks at her son. "Ronnie, darling," she says, "will you excuse us for a moment."

He takes offense. "But, Mother, the drinks——"

"Please, son," Millie says, firmly.

Ronnie waddles off in a funk.

"You lied to me. You set me up," I say, when he's gone. "Why? To kill me?"

"No, dear boy. To save me."

"From what? From who?"

"I'm certain you already know that."

"Babalon?"

The waitress arrives with our drinks. We stop talking until she's gone.

"When you're young," Millie continues, "you do foolish things. I, for example, dreamed of being a princess who would grow up to become queen of the land. I outgrew that dream. Then I dreamed a new dream. To be a star. That dream fizzled. I stood on top of that bridge one night when the Santa Ana winds were howling and considered jumping—just for a minute, mind you—when my fairy godmother appeared and told me I could reclaim the dream from my youth. She would help me find a prince to marry and a kingdom to rule."

"But only if you gave her something in return," I say.

Millie nods. "And now I want that something back. You see, when a queen grows old and grows weary of her throne, her treasures, her power—she realizes that the only thing she truly owns—the only thing she truly possesses—is the spirit that defines her. When that happens, she begins to appreciate the good in the world."

I just laugh. "Too late."

"It's never to late," she says. "I'm not good, but I'm not bad either. And I will not be condemned for something I did when I was too young to know better."

"You made your bed," I say. "Go lie in the flames, Millie."

She shakes her head and points a bony finger at me. "I intend to win this game—and you *will* help me," she says, like a command.

"Or what?" I sass back. "I end up dead at the bottom of the bridge like your housekeeper?"

"You don't know what you're talking about," she scolds.

"And you don't know what you're up against."

"Belial is already gone," she points out. "Babalon can be defeated, too. If she goes, I win. And I told you once, I always make it a point to win."

I fire her a look of pure hatred. "I should let you rot, you old bag."

"But you can't," she says. "You're too far down the rabbit hole. Am I right?" She grins at me, lets out a throaty chuckle.

"There's only one way to send Babalon back to hell," I tell her. "I know how to do it. But there's something that I need."

"Anything money can buy," she promises.

"Money can't buy this." I toss a photo of Millie, Jack Parsons, and L. Ron Hubbard on the table.

"Hubbard," she says, pointing to the photo. "He wasn't serious about Crowley or magik. The only thing he cared about was money—and who he could steal it from. But he was smart—very persuasive." She looks at Jack Parsons and smiles warmly. "Jackie Boy," she says, "God, was he a handsome man. A dedicated occultist. Brilliant, but mad. Slowly driven insane by the forces he unleashed." She flips through a few more photos of him. "Dark looks and a dark soul."

"Parsons had a box—a black box that he kept private things in. Occult objects. Rituals."

Millie smiles at a long-forgotten memory. "A pentagram on top. Serpents and dragons. Inscriptions in the ancient language of the angels."

"You know about it?"

She nods. "It was Jack's most prized possession."

"That's what I need. If I don't get it—and fast—you can kiss your soul good-bye."

Millie gives me a look like: *no big deal.* "The box was buried."

"Where?"

"Devil's Gate Dam," she tells me. "It was Jack's favorite place."

"Tell me everything," I order her.

"After the explosion, Jack was cremated. His ashes, along with his treasured possessions, were locked in the box. There was a ceremony, a small gathering of friends. Rituals were performed in his honor. An orgy commenced." She stops to smirk, see if I'm shocked. "When it was over, Jack's wife, Marjorie, buried the box at the base of Satan's Rock. She placed a curse on anyone who might disturb Jack's remains. Marjorie used to say the Hounds of Hell guard the spot."

"Which of the rock formations are you talking about?"

"The one at the very bottom of the dam."

"I've seen it from up top," I tell her. But how do I get down there?"

She plots out the route on the table with her drink stirrer. "There's a narrow staircase—part of the dam's construction. It goes from the top of the dam into a tunnel. At the end of the tunnel is Satan's Rock."

Ronnie returns to the terrace. He's pacing, anxious to come back and get his mitts on his drink. "Ronnie must not know of any of this," she says.

I grab my Bloody Mary and down it in a couple gulps. Grab Millie's and chug it. Spill Ronnie's all over the table. I gather up the photos and shove them back in my folder.

"I'm counting on you," she says.

"Go to hell," I tell her.

. . .

At Hahamongna Watershed Park, I hike to the top of the dam and look down at Satan's Rock. From this side, I can't see stairs. Across the bridge, I find a tunnel that leads through the dam to the top of the ravine on the other side. Looks like a straight drop down, but I follow a barbed-wire fence that surrounds it. Millie was right. There is a staircase.

I can't break in and enter city property in broad daylight. Plus, I need a shovel and a powerful bolt cutter to handle the chain locking the gate. And I'm not unearthing that box until I'm prepared to face Babalon. Opening that box might alert her, send her after me, or worse, after someone I know.

I'll finish this—stand tall on that godforsaken bridge and face her. But not yet.

Hell or high water, I'm performing at the Roxy tomorrow night. It'll probably be the last thing I ever do, but I'm gonna know what it feels like to make it for once in my miserable life. No one's taking that away from me. Not Babalon. Or anyone else.

I block it all out as I drive to rehearsal, switching gears in my life yet again.

Everyone's on their best behavior. Ira starts with a pep talk. "I hope you all got the douche baggery out of your systems," he says.

We all laugh, except for Drexel. He seems sober, but distant—quiet.

This will be appearing in the *Los Angeles Times Magazine* on Sunday morning. He passes around a proof. Our latest band photo takes up half the page. The article is titled "Ready to Rock." It includes miniprofiles of six bands. We're one of them. "Our blurb," Ira says, "is courtesy of Eva Kells. I know a few of you know her."

"Read it," Bo says. "I don't have my specs."

Ira clears his throat, says in his DJ voice, "Astral Fountain. With industry legend Ira Bowersock just signing them as the franchise act on his new label, Deep Lever Records, most L.A. insiders are betting on this band to break out. Straight in your face bare-bones rock and roll, creative musicianship, loyal fans, and Drexel, the most charismatic front man since Axl Rose haunted the Strip. The group's live performances are electrifying—loud and hard. Equal measures of fun and danger sweep through their packed venues."

"That kicks ass," Jay says.

"Nice write-up for you," Ira says to Drexel. Drexel perks up, but he's not as cocky as I'd expect after praise like that.

"Let's run through our set," Bo says.

While we set up Ira tells us, "Tomorrow night will be the last time it'll just be the four of you playing together. Everything's going to get bigger and more serious starting next week. It's important—no, it's goddamn critical—that you rise to the occasion. It's the Roxy. Holy ground. Honor that stage. Every important player in the industry will be there. Reporters from coast-to-coast will be ready to proclaim you rock gods by Sunday morning—provided you don't suck. So I want you to feel pressure, but I also want you to remember to enjoy yourselves. You're a great band. Remember that. Remember what got you here. And you," he adds pointing to Joanie. "Let Troy's fans know why you're our badass little drummer girl."

Joanie nods, makes a power fist.

"Now let's get on with this," Ira says, "and get out of here early so we can all rest."

"I want everyone there early tomorrow—by six PM," Bo orders. "Alert, sober, and rested." He looks each one of us in the eye, waits until we all give him some sign of agreement.

We run through our set. Smooth and easy. Don't push ourselves too hard. Drexel goes light on the vocals. Drinks about a gallon of iced tea.

On the way out, I nudge Drexel. Whisper, "Are we cool?" so Ira doesn't hear us.

Drexel just sighs and shakes his head.

"I'm not trying to take the band over," I assure him. "I'm just trying to make it better."

Drexel waits until we're in the parking lot to speak. "I know what you're doing," he says with his little smart-ass grin. "And I know why you're doing it. I'm fucking your girl."

My hands become fists. *Don't do it. Don't blow it. Walk away.* I compromise. Won't hit him, but won't bite my tongue either. I get right in his face. "I know you're not fucking her anymore. She told me. Told me what a raging, fucking asshole you really are. We laughed about it all day yesterday. You're a fucking child. Yeah, maybe you fucked her once or twice. But a punk-ass little bitch like you sure couldn't hang on to her." Like a dagger in his heart. "Stick with your groupies, Drexel. They're your speed."

His head drops. His confidence is drained. He dons his sunglasses and turns away. I walk to my car, gun smoking. "Don't get comfortable," he yells to me. "You'll be out of this band sooner or later."

I give him the finger and drive off.

Thirty

I drive home. My intentions for the evening are good. I'll get myself something decent to eat. Drink a lot of water. Pop a couple Ambiens. Go to bed and sleep in.

What's that quote? *The road to hell is paved with the best intentions.*

Teresa is waiting for me in the lobby of my apartment building. "Kane, I haven't heard from you. I was worried."

I can't deal. Wanna run. "Sorry. It's been a crazy couple of days."

"I really need to talk to you. I won't stay long."

I invite her up. We sit on the fire escape and share a beer. So much for the water. "The reporters won't stop hounding me," she says. "It's awful."

"What's the latest?" I ask her.

"Piper still hasn't confessed," Teresa says. "Bridget hired Mark Geragos. God knows how she's paying for that. Probably had to put up her house."

"Did you talk to any reporters?"

"I only spoke to the one you mentioned."

"Eva Kells?"

"That's her."

"She treating you fairly?"

"She's okay. At first she tried to pry information out of me. Tried to get me to say something that would become 'the quote' that says it all."

"What did you do?"

"Told her to back off. That it's private. It's my pain. Mine alone. And I don't want to share it yet. I told her when I have something to say, I'll say it to her."

"And she was okay with it?"

"Yes. She's nice. How do you know her?"

I pretend I'm looking at the police chopper overhead. "She's an old friend."

"She said a lot of nice things about you."

"Really?" The urge to dig is great.

"I said a lot of nice things about you, too."

I look through the window at my clock. "That's nice. Thanks."

"I got a call from *People* magazine. They offered me a hundred thousand dollars for an interview."

"That's a lot of money."

"I don't know what to do."

"Ask Eva," I say. "She'll give you better advice than I will."

I'm jittery and impatient. It must show.

"You want me to leave, don't you?"

"I really need some time to myself," I tell her. "I'm sorry."

She's hurt, but pretends she's not. "I'm just glad you're okay. I was worried."

"I'm sorry I didn't call you," I say. "It's just very nerve-racking right now. This gig Saturday night—there's a lot on the line. I can't screw up."

"I understand."

I walk her to the door. "There were no reporters around when I left. Hope that's still the case."

"News tends to blow over fast. Fifteen minutes and all that," I say.

Reach for the doorknob. She looks at me. "You don't want any company then."

"It's not that—"

"I can't tempt you?" She reaches down and grabs a handful through my jeans.

"Tomorrow night—when this is all over."

She's still hurt. "Okay."

"You're gonna be there, right?" I ask.

"Wouldn't miss it."

There's a knock on my door. Probably Pat Boreo wondering how he did.

It's Eva. Good God. Road to hell, all right.

Eva looks at Teresa. Awkward. "Oh, hi."

"Hi," Teresa says back.

"I'm sorry, am I interrupting?" Eva asks, all uneasy.

"I was just leaving," Teresa replies.

"Eva dates our lead singer," I say for no good reason.

"I do?" Eva asks, annoyed.

They both look at me.

"How are you?" Eva asks Teresa.

"It's a little calmer than it was."

"Well, let me know if there's anything I can do to help."

"Actually, Teresa could use some advice—about a *People* magazine interview," I say.

"Sure," Eva says. "Just call me and we'll talk."

"I'll see you tomorrow," Teresa says to me. She plants a kiss on my lips. "Good luck."

She darts out the door. Eva's smiling at me. It's not an entirely pleasant smile.

"What?" I ask.

"She's riding the Kane train. I knew it."

"Shut up," I say playfully.

"Tasty meat for a cougar."

"Now I know how Drexel feels."

"Please," she scoffs. "You can't sling that arrow until I at least turn thirty."

"Shouldn't you be rocking Drexel to sleep after his bath?"

"I told you—I cut that off."

"You broke up?"

"Excuse me, asshole. You have to be dating someone to break up. We just carried on a little. Had a couple of fun nights. No harm done."

If she only knew how much it crushed me, whatever it was.

Wait. She does. She knows everything. She's enjoying this.

Eva picks up a band flyer off my desk. "You know he has a drug problem, right?" she asks.

"What was your first clue?"

She doesn't answer. Just shakes her head, a look of worry on her face.

"He fell off the wagon," I tell her. "I was with him when it happened."

"He told me. Told me a lot of things."

"Really?"

"Told me a wonderful little story about the Triplets of Melrose."

Oh, shit.

Shoots me an inquisitive look. "Was that a metaphor or were they really siblings? Drexel was a bit fucked up and unclear."

"So what?" I snap. "No harm done."

"It's not like I care," she says. "I'm just curious. Honestly, you can stick it anywhere you want, whenever you want. It's your business."

"What do you want me to say? I told you already—I screwed up. I asked for another chance."

"And I said no."

"Sure he's got talent, but Drexel's a fucking idiot. You're not. What are you trying to prove? What is it with you?"

"I don't know," she snaps.

"I like how we're at least always honest with each other. So would you just say it?"

"Say what?" she shouts. "And what are you trying to prove? What do you have in common with a forty-year-old suburban widow. What's with your 'knight in shining armor coming to the rescue of distraught mothers' thing?"

"I don't know."

"You treat most people like garbage, but you have this soft spot for poor, distressed mothers. And they're always brunettes with big tits. What is it with you?"

Enough already. Just say it from the heart. "I fucked up when I let you go. End of story. Happy?"

She doesn't answer.

"You got your answer. So now give me mine. Why Drexel?"

"Duh!" she finally says. "It was a revenge fuck."

Takes a while for that one to land and detonate.

"I guess we're even now," she says. "But maybe not with the threesomes and all."

We're both spent.

I look at her. Make sure she's looking back. "Can we just end this and hook the fuck up?"

Say yes. Say yes. My soul for a yes.

"I don't know," she says.

"What does that mean?"

"I'm not ready for that yet."

"Well, call me when you are. In the meantime, I'm going to sleep."

"All right, I'll leave."

"Will you be at the show tomorrow night?"

"I don't think so."

"Why?"

"It's your night. Drexel's night. I'm an interloper."

"What's that mean?"

"I don't belong."

"Maybe not, but you're sorely needed."

"Go. Do your thing, Kane. And I'll do mine."

She kisses my cheek. "Break a leg."

Stop her half way down the hall. "Do me a favor?"

"What?"

"Don't go near the bridge."

"Probably not on my immediate to-do list."

"Promise me."

"Okay, I promise."

"Promise me something else."

"What?"

"You'll at least think about me and you." She stares at me. I think she wants to stay. Maybe not.

She smiles. "Kane closes his door on a brunette. Now a blonde. Is a redhead next?"

"Yeah." I look at my watch. "She's late."

When Eva's gone, I call Detective Alvarez on his cell. "I just spoke to Teresa Burrows. Wanted to get your take."

"The kid won't confess," he says. "Tried every trick in the book. Brought the mother in. Gave her a going-over."

"And?"

"The mother posted bail. The kid's out. They lawyered up. Looks like we're gonna be burning a lot of taxpayer money. But it's a landmark case. National media will be covering it. DA's balls are on the line now."

"So?"

"So we'll win. We have to. Any and all means necessary. Case is too high profile. No choice now."

"How's the mother holding up?"

"Not too well."

"Well, tell her to hang in there. I'll stay in touch."

I lack the energy to go out to get takeout. Nuke a frozen pizza instead.

I try to sleep, but my mind races. I toss and turn.

Goddamnit!

I'm thinking beyond tomorrow night. Can't stop myself.

I get up. Grab a notebook and paper. Can't leave anything to chance for my showdown with Babalon. I jot down a list of everything I'll need for my fucked-up plan to commence. Fifteen things. Some I have. Most I still need to get.

I rack my brain. Am I forgetting something? Think. Think harder. I'm wide awake, stressing.

It's gonna be a long night.

Thirty-one

Somewhere along the line I fall asleep. And stay asleep. Awaken in the morning to "Hostile Bridge" playing over and over in my mind. Hear Drexel singing it. The lyrics to the chorus just appear:

Entomb me in a shroud of gray
In this world I no longer stay
Shout from gray spires with the voice of the living
Leap from this life, into jaws unforgiving

Like before, I don't know where these or any of the words have come from. Another gift from the voice that spoke through the IVeR?

Crowley's goblet is fully charged. Should I? No. Not until tonight's gig is behind me. No distractions. Not today.

But I can't push down the urge. The temptation is too great. I place Crowley's goblet atop the device and power it up. I'll just see what comes through. Maybe just say hello to Karl.

Static charge around the coils crackles. I tune the ectometer. More radio static. Distant, echoey booms. I search the frequencies slowly, precisely. Then I hear a far-off voice. I adjust the settings. The voice grows stronger. "Karl?" I say. "Is it you?"

I brace. Wait to hear a Beatles tune.

A voice sings "Hostile Bridge." It's the same sing-songy British voice I heard the day I wrote "Pound of Hate."

"You're not Karl. Where's Karl?" I ask the voice.

The voice stops singing, says, "Dead." No shit, Sherlock. I figured that a disembodied voice that speaks through crystals, magnets, and electricity might not be among the living.

"Where is Karl?"

"Gone."

"Who are you?"

"Guess."

"Give me a hint."

"My cup runneth over." Whatever the fuck that means.

"What are you—a muse?"

A throaty chuckle. "You amuse me."

"Who are you? Tell me now."

The voice toys with me. Mumbles slowly, "I am Karl . . . I am Kral . . . I am Krawl." Then, clear and loud, full volume that rocks my apartment: "I am Crowley."

Oh, shit! *My cup runneth over.* The crystal goblet. Aleister Crowley.

A voice that's part man, part animal: "I am the Beast."

The goblet on the IVeR glows emerald green, vibrates. I fucked up royally, opened a gateway straight to Crowley when I started using the goblet to power the IVeR. I should have fucking known better. Idiot.

I'm pissed off. Not to mention scared. "What do you want?" I ask.

"Your guitar. Your voice. Your audience. Babalon be praised!" The shrill, commanding voice howls. "Babalon shall walk the earth."

"You're feeding me these songs," I say. "It's you."

"You're not the first."

My brain does flip-flops. I remember the rock-and-roll folklore. Jimmy Page lived in Crowley's estate on the shores of Loch Ness in Scotland. It's said that he channeled Led Zeppelin's sound, their songs, on that property. Images flash. Crowley on the *Sgt. Pepper's* cover. The Doors gathered in reverence around a bust of Crowley on the back of their album, *The Doors 13*. Ozzy belting out "Mr. Crowley." Marilyn Manson's lyrics with all kinds of Crowley quotes and references. Are you kidding me? It's not bullshit?

"Stay away from me," I command, but not at all convincingly.

"Too late. You are the vessel. You are the messenger."

The goblet sparks. Transmission lost. The IVeR powers down.

Nausea grips me. I may faint. I feel Babalon and Crowley somewhere deep inside me.

I go straight to my Mac. Google three words: *Bridge Aleister Crowley*.

Fuck me!

First page of entries—a poem written by Crowley in 1905—"On Garret Hostel Bridge." I hold my breath as I read the first line. Get the wind knocked right out of me. Not our lyrics verbatim, but our song lyrics, my lyrics, are full of his phrases: *white mist, gray spires, towers, vapour, sleepy river.* It's all there.

I'm not creative. I'm not brilliant. I'm a fucking channel.

Block it out.

Just block it out.

Get through tonight, then figure it out.

Grab my gear.

There's a girl outside my apartment door. Young. Skinny. Long, straight black hair and black minidress. Kabbalah tattoos on her arms and neck. She's staring at me as I lock up. "Do I know you?" I ask.

"Do me," she says. "Right here."

"Excuse me?"

"I want to get with the greatest guitar player in the world. You're gonna be a star."

"How did you find me?"

"It was easy."

Groupies. The dream realized. But all I can see when I look at her is Crowley—that shiny bald head, moon face, soulless black eyes.

"Beat it," I tell her.

I arrive at the Roxy four hours early. Stand under the famous marquee on Sunset. There it is in black and white—our name. Damn. I stop and smell the roses.

I stake out a corner of the dressing room and prep my guitars. Limber up. Try to meditate, but keep hearing Crowley's voice speaking to me in my head. End up putting in earphones and cranking tunes just to drown out the sound.

The sound check is overwhelming. Ira has a new state-of-the-art sound board and lighting rig in place. Our stage manager, Syd, is shitting bricks. But Ira's calm. He paid for a seasoned tech crew to make sure all the equipment syncs up by showtime. Brett, my volunteer guitar tech, arrives early. He adjusts the settings on my amp as I warm up. Restrings my Strat. Tunes it. A dependable guy.

I soak up the venue. Open floor. Two bars in the back. Roped-off VIP tables upstairs.

We run through a few songs just after six. Instrumentals only. Drexel hasn't shown yet.

Everything is ready and waiting—tested and retested—by seven.

No Drexel.

We try to keep the mood light backstage. Joanie cracks us up with stories about her volatile romance with a Lakers cheerleader.

Drexel's still M.I.A. Ira looks worried. Tries to call him.

Eight o'clock.

Caterer arrives. Nice spread—paninis, salad, pasta. Eat well, but don't overdo it. Gotta do those flying splits and all. There's beer and liquor in the room, but we're all pretending it's not there. Joanie and I agree to do one shot before we hit the stage. For now it's Red Bulls and Diet Cokes.

We digest our food.

No Drexel.

Bo's freaking out. "Has anyone heard from him?" We all shake our heads. "Keep trying to get him on the phone," Bo orders.

Eight thirty.

Black jeans and tee. Lucky necklace. Skull boots.

Eight forty-five.

Ira walks in. He's livid. "They're all here," he says. "*Rolling Stone. Spin. Variety. Billboard. Mojo.* We have MTV. *PopEater. Stereogum.* Perez Hilton. We've got coverage out the ass. But we don't have a fucking singer!"

"Chill, tan man, you've got a fucking singer." Drexel walks in looking like he was just revived from a coma. He's fucked up. Glazed over. Unsteady on his feet. Gravelly.

"Jesus Christ!" Ira shouts. "Sober him up! Get his ass onstage!" He grabs Drexel by the collar. "You fuck this up, you're dead."

Drexel hocks up a thick one and spits right in Ira's face.

Ira flicks the spit away, cocks his fist, and winds up. He stops just short of punching Drexel in the face, but buries the punch instead into Drexel's stomach.

All the air rushes out of Drexel. He crumbles into a ball on the floor.

"Get him on that fucking stage," Ira shouts at me as he storms out.

Bo slumps in a chair. He just saw the end of the world.

I grab Drexel off the floor and sit him down. Pour black coffee down his throat. Feed him a big spoonful of horseradish from the buffet table to clear his head. "Pull it together, dude. You can do this."

"That chick," Drexel says to me, laughing. "That crazy tall chick can fucking party." He lets out a deafening "Yeah!"

Brett walks over. "You're not going on with him like this, are you?"

Before I can answer, Syd opens the door. We hear the roar of the crowd.

"Let's go," Bo orders. Says it like we're off to our execution.

Syd lights the way. We take our places on the dark stage. Drexel falls on his back, spread-eagle. Oh no.

Bo grabs the stage mic. "Hollywood and Deep Lever Records proudly present: A merry band of Sunset badasses. Drink deeply from Astral Fountain!"

The light of God shines upon us. Drexel springs to his feet like a gymnast. We tear into "User." The band's dead-on. Drexel's a hot, steaming mess. A step behind and he can't catch up. His voice is gravelly, hoarse. Maybe the crowd will chalk it up to a bad mic. Probably not.

Of the capacity crowd of five hundred, only about a hundred fifty are paying fans. The rest are record execs, members of the media—and celebrities. I scan the crowd right away. Spot Teresa against the wall by the back bar. No sign of Eva. Look up in the ViP section. Ira works the crowd.

Focus on one of the ViP tables. Two guys. Spy a top hat and a white mane of hair. Jaw drops. Can't be. It's Slash and Jimmy Page. Two guitar legends.

And they're watching me play.

We steamroll right into "Creed." Shit. Drexel's off-key. He's spinning in circles. I walk up behind him. Give him a nudge. A look that says: *Sing it right.* Dance back to my spot. Drexel grabs the mic stand and comes barreling at me like a charging bull. Don't spot him coming until it's too late. He dives through the air, head butts me clean—right above the eye—and knocks me on my ass. I black out for a second. Blood spurts from a cut above my eyelid.

Somehow I'm on my feet fast. I got my bell rung—hard. My vision blurs but I still manage to play.

Drexel tries to climb the Marshal Stacks, but loses his balance. He takes a wicked fall and lands on his face.

I hear a few screams. Even more laughs.

Drexel rises like a zombie. He walks to center stage. Pulls down his leather pants. Shakes his dick at the crowd. Turns around, bends over, spreads his ass cheeks. Not only shows them a full moon, but its darkest crater.

The crowd goes ballistic. Beer bottles crash around us. We duck and cover. The sound is an indefinable combination of stunned silence, raucous laughter, and rage.

Drexel hikes up his pants, salutes the crows with double birds, walks offstage and straight out the back door.

I don't know what's more ludicrous. What Drexel just did or the fact that we don't stop playing?

Jay steps up. We jam. Flex our muscle. I lead us into a bluesy improvisation. Jay and Joanie are locked in on me. We're a damn good band. At least the crowd will see that.

I look over at Bo in the wings. He's chugging a bottle of Jack Daniels. I nod at him. Gives us a halfhearted wave to keep playing.

We amp up the jam, roll it into "Pound of Hate." I look at Jay. He looks at me. One of us has to sing the fucker. He nods at me.

I step up, center stage. *What the fuck am I doing here?* Tear into the vocals with everything I've got. All eyes are on me. I don't enjoy it a bit.

Ira works the ViP, but it's a lost cause. Jimmy Page stares down, an old man with a cherub's face. Gives me a look like: *Hang in there, man.* But Slash stands and walks out. Others follow.

While I'm singing my guts out, the crowd gets restless. People head for the exits. Jay rushes over, harmonizes with me. Crowd thins out fast.

I'm way out of my comfort zone.

It shows.

The song ends.

We tried. But we went down with the ship.

Bo waves us off, takes the mic, walks to center stage a beaten man. "Ladies and gents—as you could tell, out lead singer has come down with a bad case of Sunset Fever. Unfortunately, we must cancel tonight's performance. Full refunds are available for those fans who purchased tickets. Stay tuned. You'll be notified when the event is rescheduled. Thank you and drive safely."

Ira looks at me as I walk off. "You gave it the old college try. Took balls, Kane."

And that's that.

It's over.

Over before it even began. There's no way out of this hole. Start throwing dirt on our coffin.

Backstage, it's like a funeral. Hell, it is a funeral. We're all too stunned to speak. Jay throws up. Then packs up and is the first to leave.

"Wanna go get drunk and chase tail with me?" Joanie asks.

"Nah," I say.

Teresa finds me backstage. "Not tonight," I say.

"You were great, Kane," she says. "You shined up there."

"I'm a poser," I say. "I'm not a front man."

"You could be," she tells me. "You will be."

"It's over."

"Just come with me."

"I think I need to be alone," I say.

"I understand. Tomorrow?"

"Sure. Thanks for coming."

"Just come over if you change your mind."

Pick up my guitar cases. Walk out the front doors onto Sunset. A boulevard of broken dreams, all right. Look up at the marquee. Someone from the club, one hell of a critic, got up there and rearranged the letters. An hour ago it read:

Deep Lever Presents: Astral Fountain

Now it says:

Deep Latrine Ass Fountain

That about sums it up.

I walk around the corner to my car. Toss my guitar cases in the trunk. My phone rings. Ira Bowersock. "I need a drink. Want to talk to you."

"Sure. How about the Rainbow?"

"We'll get laughed out of there," Ira says.

"The Frolic Room," I suggest next.

"On Hollywood and Vine?" Ira asks.

"Yeah."

"Haven't been there in years," Ira says. "Sounds good."

Ira beats me to the bar. He's sitting there with an iPad and a big glass of scotch. Take the stool next to him. He slides the iPad over. The story's already all over the blogs. Apparently, there's been an arrest warrant issued for Drexel for indecent exposure.

Gabe the bartender comes over with a Harp and a shot of Jameson. Look over at the jukebox. "This place has the best jukebox in the world. But I sure as hell don't feel like listening to music right now."

Ira sips his scotch. "You know, in thirty years, when people are still talking about the biggest meltdown in Sunset Strip history, we can say we were not only there. We lived it."

"We're not getting a second chance are we?"

"No."

He doesn't elaborate. He could rub it in. Or tear me a new asshole. Instead, he just raises his glass and says, "Cheers."

"I'm sorry," I say.

"Not your fault. You were a pro. It's just rock and roll. And I'm getting too old."

"You would have made us great."

"Oh well," he says, "better to find out earlier than later." He shows me a check. $250K. "That was the band's advance," he says. "Split that five ways. Not a bad job." He tears the check in half. So much for not rubbing it in. "So what's next for you, Kane?"

"No idea."

"Hang in there," Ira says. "You're smart. You're a solid guitarist. You can write songs. But you're not a front man."

"You could say that."

"You'll land on your feet. Don't give up."

I get choked up.

Ira drops two twenties on the bar. "Stay in touch," he tells me. Then he's out the door.

The bartender walks over with the whiskey bottle. "Rough night?"

I don't answer. I'm fighting like hell to hide the fact that I'm crying. The reality of it hits me square. The dream is over. It was so close I had a hand on it. But it's over.

Then my heartbreak gives way to rage.

The bartender pours a stiff shot. "On the house," he says.

I let the whiskey sit.

When he realizes I'm not going to drink it, the bartender says, "Wise choice, my friend. Liquid solutions don't make things better. You can't run from your problems, Kane. They follow. Gotta face them with a clear mind."

I see red. "You're full of nothing but contradictory, bullshit advice," I hiss at him. "When I had my hands around your neck, I should have kept squeezing."

"Take it easy," he warns me.

I grab the shot off the bar and down it. Slam the glass on the bar. "Fill that glass again," I order him, "and get the fuck out of my sight."

He obeys.

I sip this shot. Savor it. My head rattles with problems. I feel Babalon stirring in me. Hear Crowley's voice in my head if I listen hard. I'm leading Teresa on. I need Eva. I'm worried about Ned. Need to fix things. Right my life.

I stand.

"Stay safe, Kane," the bartender says with a wave.

I go straight home.

It's time.

Pull out my list of fifteen things.

Plan it all in my head.

For once, I sleep soundly.

Thirty-two

I get up early. Take out my list and check off the things I already have:

9. *Matches*
13. *Crowley's goblet*
14. *Ahchancha's cross*
15. *The trap*

Begin gathering the rest.

Fucked-Up Plan—Part Four.

Lying to Ned.

I drive over the bridge on the way to Ned's place.

He still looks like shit. Exhausted. Pale. In need of a long shower. The stack of papers has grown. A second whiteboard is crammed with algorithms.

He asks about the gig. I tell him I don't want to talk about it. Enough said. "Sorry," is, thankfully, all he says.

"How are you?" I ask, worry in my voice.

"I'm making solid progress," he tells me. "A few more months, and I'll be able to spec out the design—figure out what it'll cost down to the penny."

"You need to take it easy," I warn him. "You don't look so good."

"I'm all right," he assures me. "Just racking my brain. It's actually good. Feel like shit, but also feel alive again."

Maybe this is the best medicine for him.

"I need a favor," I say.

"Shoot."

"I need to borrow the camper."

"For what?"

"For a street race," I say. "What do you think? I want to go camping."

"You? Camping? Bullshit," he says. "I know you too well, Kane. What are you up to?"

"Nothing," I bark, defensively. "I want to get away for a few days. Clear my head."

Ned stares me down. "I don't buy it."

"All right," I admit. "It's a woman."

"Oh," he says, becoming instantly less suspicious. "Eva?"

"No."

"Ah," Ned says, curious. "A new girlfriend?"

"Maybe," I say. "A few days in the wilderness and we'll find out."

"Good for you," Ned says. "Who is she?"

"Someone I met. You'll meet her soon . . . maybe."

"Where are you taking her?"

I pull an answer out of my ass. Remember seeing freeway signs somewhere up north. "Beach camping at El Capitan."

"Been there," Ned says. "It's nice."

He spends the next fifteen minutes telling me where the best camping spots in Central California are. In excruciating detail. He brings out maps. I'm ready to blow my head off. Finally, he hands me the keys.

"I'll leave my car here," I tell him. "I'll be back—whenever . . ."

"Remember to change the sheets," he says.

I look at him. Have that same feeling I had with Eva. Might be the last time I see him. It'll for sure be the last time he sees his camper. I should say something memorable. Meaningful. But my tongue's tied. "Bye, Ned," is all I manage. Anything more and I'll break down.

I walk to the camper. Make sure the metal detector is still in the storage hold. Climb behind the wheel. Check the first two things off my list:

1. *Ned's camper*
2. *Ned's metal detector*

Hit the road. Camper handles like shit. The brakes are toast. Don't know how he drives this hunk of junk.

Fucked-Up Plan—Part Five.

OSH, by gosh.

I stop at Orchard Supply Hardware in Pasadena. I'm pretty clueless when it comes to hardware stores, but a geezer floor manager walks me from aisle-to-aisle until I find everything. I whip out my MasterCard and drop two hundred and change on:

3. *Knipex mini bolt cutters*
4. *shovel*
5. *machete*
6. *work gloves*
7. *100 Hefty lawn bags*
8. *four gas cans*
10. *sharp-ass penknife*

Fucked-Up Plan—Part Six

Sage advice.

I drive to Camp Hahamongna.

I sit at a picnic table near Hank's cabin, waiting for him to return from a trail ride. Surf on my phone. Stretch out. Doze off.

Someone kicks my boots. I open my eyes. "Here for a riding lesson? Beginner's class is in forty-five minutes."

"Question for you," I say, standing up and stretching. "Is there sage growing around here?"

"Come on," he says. Walks to his Honda ATV and tells me to jump on the back. I grab on and he tears from the campground into the Arroyo. Bumpy as hell. I feel like Travolta on the mechanical bull. He laughs and whoops it up. The more I yell, "Whoa," the more reckless he drives.

Half mile up the rocky, dry streambed, within sight of the fence that marks the beginning of NASA's property, he stops. I climb off the ATV. He points to a thicket of brush. Walks over and cracks a branch off one of the bushes. "Smell it," he tells me.

It's not my favorite fragrance. To me, smells like mild BO.

I take in the view. Sagebrush lines both sides of the streambed.

"Do you care if I take some?" I ask.

"Not my property," Hank says. "City of Pasadena's. As long as sage isn't on the state's protected plants list, take as much as you want."

"Hold that thought," I tell him.

I google California's protected plant list on my iPhone. No sage, I show him.

"I'm from Missouri where courtesy goes a long way. Seeing as you were polite enough to ask me before you just came down here chopping, you can park in my lot and cross my property," he says. "Don't destroy the plants—that's my only rule. Just prune them back."

"Okay. Thanks."

"How much do you need?" he asks. "A bag full?"

"Many bags full. . . . Hundreds of bags full. . . . Hefty bags."

Looks at me, shakes his head. "A shaman's work is never done, eh?"

"Something like that."

"Do you need to borrow a machete?"

"I'm okay, thanks. Unless you want to help."

"You're on your own, shaman."

He rides me back to the camper to get my supplies. Gives me a quick lesson on how to handle the machete, cut the brush without wrecking it. Then he leaves me to work my ass off.

Three hours later, I'm exhausted. Twenty-three bags of sage and counting. I feel the burn in muscles I didn't even know I had. My hands are numb. Around dusk, Hank drives by in a beat-up pickup truck. "You still alive?" he asks, handing me a bottle of water.

My phone rings. Teresa.

"What are you up to?" she asks.

"Hard labor."

"Feeling any better?"

"Hell no."

"Come on over—I'll do something about that."

She's just up the 210 a bit. I might as well go. Put an end to this. Part on good terms. "I'll be there in thirty."

Hank helps me load the bags on the cab of his pickup and drives me back to the camper. I toss the bags inside.

It's a lot of sage. Far from the shitload I need, but it's a start.

When Teresa sees me she says, "You weren't kidding when you said hard labor."

I'm dirty, sweaty, and sunburned. "Can I take a shower?" I ask.

Before I'm even lathered up, Teresa joins me. So much for ending it. We go at it in the shower and again in the bedroom.

All that manual labor got me revved up. We blow off a lot of steam.

Teresa washes my jeans and shirt. I parade around in a towel while she makes lasagna. We drink two bottles of cabernet with dinner. Crack open a third for dessert.

We're lying on a lounge chair on her back patio. "Run away with me," she says. "I mean it. There's nothing holding you back now."

"I don't know . . ."

"We can always come back to L.A. if we miss it. Come on, Kane. I don't know much, but I know we have a good thing here. Let's see how far we can take it."

It takes energy to dump someone. And tonight, I don't have any. Hem and haw. Talk, but say absolutely nothing.

"I know," she says. "Let's watch *Thelma and Louise*. It'll inspire you."

All the exercise has conked me out. Movie sounds good. I can regroup. Think about what I'm going to say. How I'm going to say it.

Collapse on her sofa. The cabernet hits me hard.

"This is my favorite movie," Teresa says. "Just the motivation we need."

Starts out good, but slow. Fighting hard to not doze off. Thelma and Louise are going on a little getaway together—momentary escape from their not-so-great lives. They hit a roadhouse. Start pounding shots. Thelma flirts it up with a guy.

Phone vibrates. Pick it up. Text message from Eva:

What happened last night? How bad was it? Drexel is stalking me.

Where do I begin? Do I even reply?

Teresa shoots me a look. She's annoyed. Think about how to reply to Eva with an eye still on the movie.

Thelma gets shitfaced and woozy. Guy leads her into the parking lot for a breath of fresh air. Bends her over the trunk of a car and tries to rape her. Pretty intense scene. Louise shows up. *Boom.* She blows away the shitbag rapist. Thelma and Louise are on the run.

Try to be nonchalant as I respond to Eva:

Stay away from Drexel. He's fucked up.

Teresa looks at me all pissed off. "You're missing it."

Toss the phone on the coffee table. Wait for Eva to reply. She doesn't.

I keep one eye on the TV. Detectives are on the scene. They start tracking Thelma and Louise.

My mind is on Eva. What did she mean by *stalking*? Is Drexel crazy enough to hurt her . . . or worse? Christ, maybe I should call her.

Thelma and Louise cross paths with a cowboy stud hitchhiking at a gas station. They give him a ride. Brad Pitt. So young, he's raw—like a cute puppy. Overdone Southern accent worthy of the *Beverly Hillbillies.* Suspension of disbelief goes out the window. So aware that he's never seen a cow or a tractor or a horse in his life. Louise's boyfriend shows up—asks who the cowboy is. She introduces him. "This is J.D."

What? Something's wrong. I'm drunk and confused. I look at Teresa. Sorry, I got distracted. Harvey Keitel—the detective—who was he interviewing after what's his name got shot?"

Teresa gets mad that she has to pause and recap. "After Louise shot Harlan, the detective interviewed the waitress from the roadhouse."

It hits me like a baseball bat to the face. Holy mother of fuck. I can't move. I'm light-headed. I crawl off the couch.

"What's wrong?" she asks.

"Feeling a little sick," I say. "Pause it."

"Hope it wasn't my lasagna."

I hit the bathroom. Cold water on my face. Back to the living room. "I'm sorry," I say. "I have to go."

"Why?"

"The text message I got. It was fallout from last night."

"Is it about your singer?"

"Yeah."

"Is he okay?"

"That's what I need to find out."

"Of course," she says. "Go."

"Thanks for the great dinner."

"Sex wasn't bad either," she says. "Call me tomorrow?"

"Sure."

On my way to the camper, I half expect an arrow in my back.

I can't go home. Too drunk on wine. Plus, Teresa knows where I live. Psychopath might come after me. Drive down Foothill Boulevard. I'm shell-shocked. Pull into a steakhouse parking lot. Hit the wood-paneled bar. Knock down four shots of Jameson. Turn it over in my head. Am I just drunk? Paranoid? Is this my imagination running amok?

I don't know. Order a double.

Her husband keeled over at thirty-eight. He was an athlete. She lands a settlement.

Her daughter commits suicide. She's talking lawsuit.

Another double.

Always talking about starting over—escaping. Reinventing herself.

She's smart. Studies psychology. She's a writer—uses her imagination. Thinks up crazy plots.

It all adds up.

It was her. She's J. D. Harlan.

One more double. Bartender cuts me off.

What do I do now? Confront her? Call Alvarez? Turn her in?

Wine and whiskey aren't mixing well. Gonna puke.

I whip out the MasterCard. Sixty-six bucks and I didn't even eat. I puke in the parking lot. Decorate a BMW with lasagna.

Why do I do this to myself?

Do I need help?

No, I need evidence. Proof. I'll go back to Teresa's. Snoop around. Ask to use her computer.

But not tonight.

I stagger back to the camper. Meltdown. A blinding headache. Images of Teresa and Babalon meld together. Eva's in trouble. Ned's a wreck. The band is fucked. Can't take it.

I'm crying.

I wanna put a bullet in my brain. Not to kill myself—just to stop the noise in my head.

I get behind the wheel. See two steering wheels.

No fucking way.

I crawl into the back. Collapse facedown into a Hefty bag full of sage.

Down and out.

Thirty-three

I wake up in the morning alone.

Really alone.

Ferocious hangover.

I gotta get up now. Move. Sweat out this poison.

I drive to a gas station. Fill the tank and the individual gas cans. Buy a half-dozen bottles of Gatorade. MasterCard charge: $96.

I drive to Hank's. He's on a trail ride, so I hike back to Sage Central myself with my work gloves, machete, Gatorade, and Hefty bags.

I chop, bag, and think all day. Only throw up twice, which, for a hangover of this magnitude, is pretty good. I feel better by the afternoon.

I still don't know what I'm gonna do about Teresa. Now that I'm sober I rethink it. I wasn't being paranoid. It wasn't the alcohol or exhaustion. She did it.

Midafternoon a little girl riding a pony approaches wearing a camp T-shirt and cap. Eight or nine years old, I'd guess. Pretty little dark-haired, dark-skinned girl. Looks like a little Indian maiden riding up. She reaches down from her saddle and hands me a big bottle of water and a Subway sandwich bag.

She's shy. "Mr. Hansen told me to ride down and give this to you."

"You rode down here all by yourself?" I look up and see Hank standing on the crest of the hill a few hundred yards away. He waves.

"I did," she says.

"Impressive. What's your name?"

"Angela."

"What's your horse's name?"

"It's a pony."

"What's your pony's name?"

"Sparkle. She's a girl pony."

I pet the soft spot between the brown pony's eyes. "Thank you. And thank Mr. Hansen for me."

"Okay." She looks at the brush, the Hefty bags. "Whatcha chopping down those bushes for?"

"They just need trimming."

She looks over at a patch of orange poppies. "You're not gonna kill those flowers, are you?"

I didn't really even notice them until she pointed them out. Other than her, they're the only pretty things in the desolate riverbed. "No, I won't hurt the flowers."

"Orange isn't my favorite color," she says. "But I still think they're pretty. My favorite color is purple. What's yours?" she asks.

"Black—I guess."

"That's a silly color to like," she says. "Black is scary. Aren't you afraid of the dark?"

"No."

"You should be."

I smile.

"You look tired," she says.

"It's hard work trimming these bushes."

"You look sad, too."

I guess a smart kid can read you like the front page.

She's wearing a handmade necklace. It's a little wooden smiley face on a rope chain. She takes it off and hands it to me. "Here," she says. "Maybe this will cheer you up."

Sweet kid. "I don't want to take your pretty necklace."

"It's okay. We made them today at camp. I'll make another one."

"Thank you, Angela. It cheered me up already."

She rides back toward the camp. I tear into the sub. Hits the spot.

I attach the smiley-face pendant to my lucky necklace in between religious medals and talismans.

I chop and bag into the night.

Full moon.

I fill the last bag and add it to the mountain of Hefty bags.

I'll never get the smell of sage out of my nose.

I've done one hell of a job blocking it out, but it's been percolating in my mind all day. If I'm still alive after tomorrow, I'm going to see Alvarez. Turn Teresa in.

Headlights crest the hill. Hank and I fill his entire truck cab with the bags. They're stacked high. So many that he has to tie them down so they don't spill out on the bumpy ride back.

I toss the bags in the camper until it's stuffed full from floor-to-ceiling.

Hank wishes me well. He thinks I'm nuts, I can tell.

Done. Pull out the list. Check off:

12. *shitloads of sage*

9:18 PM.

Sit on the back bumper of the camper. I whip out my new penknife. My hands are numb. I can barely feel the knife. I begin whittling the bottom of Ahchancha's cross. The two-hundred-year-old wood is rock hard. Good thing the geezer at OSH sharpened it for me before I left. I whittle the base of the cross to a fine, sharp point.

It's ready. I place the cross in the passenger seat of the camper and lock it up.

• • •

9:48 PM.

Fucked-up Plan—Part Three, Continued.

On to Satan's Rock.

I attach the bolt cutters to my belt loop. Tie the metal detector and shovel on my back and walk the horse trail toward Devil's Gate Dam. A full moon shines like blue sunlight. Don't even need my flashlight. I reach the top of the dam in less than half an hour.

I scope it out. Coast is clear. Park is closed. I'm alone. Don't see any surveillance cameras. Doesn't mean they're not hidden somewhere. Gotta be fast.

I pass through the tunnel that leads to the other side of the dam. I reach the locked gate leading to the stairway down and take the bolt cutters to the chain. My hands are toast. I lean in using all my weight. Focus. Breathe. Summon strength. Struggle for over a minute, until . . .

Snap. The chain breaks and the padlock hits the ground.

I kick the gate open. Down the metal staircase. Steep, slippery stairs. Feels like I'm falling off a cliff. My footsteps clang and echo off the wall of the dam.

The stairs lead to a tunnel that descends to the bottom of the dam. I walk through and come face-to-face with Satan's Rock. It radiates energy—an aura of destruction. Destruction of the Indian culture that once lived here. Maybe even one day, the destruction of the world. I can just see Jack Parsons sitting here, notebook in hand, having his *eureka* moment in the creation of the solid rocket fuel that, today, propels not only rockets, but nuclear warheads that could end the world.

I power up Ned's metal detector and wave it a few inches above the earth. Big beep—front and center. I pinpoint the spot and drive the shovel into the ground.

Dig.

I hit metal a few feet down.

I smooth away the dirt. A pentagram. Text written in an unrecognizable language. I reach into the hole. Pry the square box loose. Heavy—at least fifteen pounds. About a foot cubed. It's rusty. A dragon on one side; serpent on the other.

Got it. Mentally check off the final item:

11. *Jack Parsons' magik box*

I'm about to open the box, when the stairs above me clang. Someone's coming. Fast.

What did Millie say—Parsons' widow put a curse on anyone who disturbed Jack's grave? The Hounds of Hell stand guard? Or maybe just a security guard from the Pasadena Department of Water and Power. Or a cop. Whoever it is, I can't go back the way I came.

I look around. I'm screwed.

Straight ahead there's nothing but dense brush and a dry streambed full of ankle-breaking rocks.

Footsteps are coming fast. The clanging gets louder, then stops. I hear the steps echo in the tunnel.

I have no choice.

I ditch the shovel and metal detector. Grab the box.

And run.

Straight into the brush. Like running through treetops. I trip all over the rocky ground. Moonlight is drowned out by the thick vegetation. I take a branch to the face. Bleeding. Someone—something—remains in hot pursuit. Really fast. It negotiates the riverbed better than me. Seems low to the ground. Gaining.

Quick flashes of light around me—high and low. Bright, then dim.

What the hell?

I keep running. Tripping.

I turn my ankle. Block the pain. Run faster.

I find a clearing. Sprint. Keep a death grip on the box. Feels like a dog is chasing me.

Moonlight again. I see a flat path just up a grassy hill. My boots slip out from under me as I try to reach the top. I toss the box up and crawl on my hands and knees the last few feet. I snatch the box like a fumbled football and sprint down the path. Can see headlights in the distance. Light around the Rose Bowl a half mile dead ahead. Can't hear the footsteps anymore.

The path leads to a golf course. I run down a fairway, across a green to a street that bisects the course. A few cars pass by. Whoever—whatever—was chasing me is gone. Put the box down on the side of the road and sit on top of it. Dial Hank.

He answers, "You know when I told you I'm up before the sun? That's because I'm asleep before it sets."

"I need a big favor," I say. "Really need your help."

He grumbles about getting out of bed, but does.

Pulls up ten minutes later. On the ride back, he looks at me. Bleeding from a cut on my forehead. Shirt torn. Drenched in sweat. Holding a box with a pentagram on my lap. He hits the brakes. "Are you some kind of devil worshiper?"

"No."

"'Cause if you are, you can get right out of this truck. I'm a God-fearing man from Missouri and I won't stand for any kind of Satanic crap."

"Listen—there's been a lot of dark shit that's gone on around here. I'm trying to end it. That's the truth. It's dangerous to tell you anything more. If you don't believe me, fuck it—I'll walk back."

"I believe you . . . I guess. I've seen a few strange things over the years. Weird lights. Shadows. Heard some odd noises coming from the dam and the Arroyo."

"Then you know."

"Always wondered about it."

"I'm trying to set things right," I say.

He drops me off at the camper. "I'm just gonna sleep here tonight if that's okay. I'll be gone in the morning—won't bother you again."

He tips his cowboy hat, shakes my hand. "Good luck, Shaman Kane. Keep fighting the good fight."

Adios, cowboy.

I sit in the driver's seat. I lock the door, but crack the window. The smell of sage is getting to me. There's no room in the back to sleep. The driver seat's not bad. I can keep a lookout in case the box attracts Babalon.

I open the box. Take out a piece of parchment. Unroll it. It's titled: *The Enochian Keys*. It's covered in occult symbols and recitations in an unrecognizable language.

I reach in and pull out a dagger. A pentagram on the eight-inch, blue-tinged blade. The handle is in the form of a horned, winged being—head bowed, wings wrapped around the body like a cloak. The being stands on two fanged serpents that form the cross guard at the base of the blade. It's pretty obvious who the being is—Lucifer. The big cheese. This is an ancient relic. Evil. It vibrates in my hands. Can't hold it long. Forces inside me are both drawn to, and repulsed, by the sight of it.

I dig out a gold coin. Heads: a pentagram; tails: the chalice and roses logo of the O.T.O..

I hold a silver bell aloft and ring it.

Pull out an urn. Open it—ashes and bone fragments. All that's left of Jack Parsons.

I flip through some photographs in an envelope: Marjorie Cameron, Parsons' second wife; Aleister Crowley wearing a tri-angle hat with occult symbols; photos from O.T.O. gatherings.

I lift out the last few items: One of Parsons' tiny test rockets. Three thirty-five-millimeter film canisters (God knows what he filmed himself doing). Statue of Pan, the wild, horned Greek god of fertility.

I put everything back inside. Slam the box shut. Bad energy floods out of it.

I have everything I need.

But I won't do it tonight.

I'll sleep. Sober up. Give my soul a wash, cleanse my sewer of a mind. Meditate. Get my head straight. Find some peace. Prepare for death in case I fail.

I'm *not* going back to hell.

I'll call Detective Alvarez before I go. Tell him about Teresa.

Then I'll go back to that steakhouse. Get a meal worthy of being my last. Have a few belts of the best whiskey in the house.

I might call Eva and Ned before I leave, but it's probably better if I just write them notes and mail them.

Gonna be a busy day tomorrow. Gonna do it all.

Then I'm gonna go and knock that bitch off the bridge.

Or die trying.

But for now—sleep.

11:09 PM.

I lean back in the driver's seat and close my eyes. The phone rings a few minutes later. Teresa.

"Can't talk right now," I say.

Through sobs she says, "You know."

"Know what?"

"I know you know."

Christ, not now. "Know what?"

"I'm a monster."

Gotta end the call. Dial Alvarez—now. "I don't know what you're talking about."

"I'm going away."

"You keep saying that."

"I'm going away—forever."

"Teresa, listen to me—"

"I'm going to join Anna."

"Don't do it, Teresa. Just stop where you are."

She weeps. "I'm in the same spot where Anna jumped."

"No!"

"Good-bye, Kane. I'm sorry."

Click.

I fumble in my pocket for the keys. Punch the gas. Kick up a mean cloud of dirt as I barrel out of the campground.

Dial Teresa. No answer. Keep trying. Nada.

11:27 PM.

I drive across the bridge slowly. No sign of her.

I'm too late.

I loop around from the other side. Double-check. She's not there.

I drive down. Tear into the condo parking lot, grab my flashlight, and sprint down South Arroyo to the trailhead leading down the ravine. I haul ass down the dirt path. Can't be more than ten minutes since she called. Maybe she's still alive. Depends on where she jumped from.

"Teresa," I scream when I reach the bottom. I run toward the concrete river channel—shine my light down. She's not there. I scour the riverbed. Cross a footbridge to the other side of the channel. Search the thick brush. No sign of her, so I turn back.

Then I see a figure. Run faster. Aim the flashlight.

It's Mike—leaning against one of the pylons.

"Mike—did you just hear anything? See anything?"

He sits there, head slumped, motionless. I nudge him. "Wake up, bro." He falls onto his side, rolls onto his back. There's a bullet hole in his bloody forehead.

I hear rustling in the brush behind me. Footsteps.

I swing around.

Teresa's pointing a revolver at me.

Strange what you think about the moment you're gonna die. I remember us on my fire escape watching an alley-cat toy with a mouse. She rooted for the cat.

I know how that mouse felt.

"You're gonna kill me?"

"No," she says, nodding at Mike. "He is . . . or he did. He shot you. Then shot himself."

"*You're* going to kill me," I repeat with finality. "Like you killed this guy. Like you killed your husband, your daughter."

"I don't have a choice, do I?"

"No one knows. I haven't told anyone. I'll never tell anyone." Try to buy time. "Let's do what you said—take off. We'll start over."

"Just like Thelma and Louise?" she asks.

"Yeah."

"I'm not stupid, Kane," she says. "You don't love me. You don't even like me. You're a terrible liar."

"And you're fucking crazy."

"At least I know who I am now," she says with certainty. "You never will. When I gave up living for *other people*, doing what *other people* told me was what I needed to do, I became a real person. And I realized there was only one way to truly ensure that the people who have held me back never hold me back again."

"How can you say *people*? You're talking about your husband, your own child, Teresa!"

"I'm talking about the mistakes I made and how I solved them."

"You murdered them," I say point-blank, hoping the words will magically snap her out of insanity.

"And I saved myself," she says, coldly. "I do what I want. Do you hear me? You could be like me, too."

I know that mantra. Hear Crowley's voice in my head: *Do what thou wilt.* "Did you ever read those fucked-up books Anna had in her bedroom?"

"No."

"Too bad. You'd love 'em."

"Look at you," she says with disdain. "You have no idea who you are from one day to the next. One minute you like someone, the next minute you hate them. You're miserable all the time. You're alone and you always will be. You can't face life without your bottle of whiskey. So you tell me—which one of us is crazy?"

"The one fucked up enough to kill her own family." Fuck this. I'm not going out begging. "The one who's going to die by lethal injection," I add.

"Good-bye, Kane," she says.

Thump. Thump. Thump. Above us. Out of nowhere.

The beating of wings? Babalon? Or something else?

A chopper zooms over us, descends rapidly, and hovers just above the bridge.

It all happens in a confusing flash. The chopper distracts Teresa for a millisecond. As her eyes dart up, the chopper blinds us with its search light and I dive for the gun.

Teresa fires the pistol. The bullet whizzes by me. I hear footsteps from behind me as I get a hand on the gun. I end up flat on my face, trying in vain to pull Teresa down.

"Freeze!" I hear from behind.

I roll over. The barrel of the gun is pointed in my face.

Bang!

Teresa drops the gun. The force of the bullet slamming into her thigh spins her around.

Bang!

Another bullet buries itself in her ass. She drops facedown, screaming in agony. The wound looks wicked with a jillion-watt bulb shining on it.

Two cops, guns in hand, emerge from the darkness. They pounce on Teresa, and grab the gun.

Detective Alvarez runs in a second later from the trail on the other side of the bridge. The chopper drowned out the sound of their approach.

Alvarez helps me up. "You okay?"

"I think so."

"You're sure you're not hit?"

"Bullet missed me—somehow."

Alvarez leads me away while the cops cuff Teresa. "Must be your lucky day," he says.

Thirty=four

3:33 AM.

After the ambulance hauls Teresa away and the coroner's van leaves with Mike's body, Alvarez grills me like a cheese sandwich. He's pissed off at me for not contacting him the second I suspected it was Teresa. I pretend I never figured it out. Tell him I'm just a dumb guitar player mixed up with the wrong lady. He doesn't buy it. He blames me for Mike's death. That's tough to hear. He's probably right.

Turns out Alvarez had both of our iPhones tapped. Teresa and I were being followed, listened in on. We were both tracked to the bridge via our phones' GPS systems.

I go apeshit when I hear that. Don't really know exactly what to bitch about, so I bitch about everything—the massive invasion of privacy in almost the same breath as the too-slow follow-up (the bullet did whizz by me, after all).

Like every other cop I've ever known, Alvarez won't go into specifics, just says it was a complex process that "set precedent" and happened fast. Didn't get bogged down in the normal bureaucracy because it was the first case of its kind. Involved the Pasadena police, the local FBI, Homeland Security, Apple, and AT&T.

He questions me for a half hour. I question him right back, ask him what tipped him off about Teresa. Three things, he tells me. First, he couldn't break Piper or Bridget May. Couldn't get a confession out of them. They blabbed on for hours about everything but the crime. Seeing as they weren't the sharpest tools in the shed, Alvarez doubted pretty quickly that they had the technical smarts to pull it off. Second, Teresa was in the May house the morning Piper discovered the iPhone in the bedroom. Teresa came with an olive branch to patch things up, but a nasty argument erupted. Right then, Alvarez says, Teresa cooked her goose, became a suspect. Third, Alvarez did a lot of sleuthing early on. He was suspicious out of the gate. Teresa collected on life insurance policies on both the husband and daughter, getting a six-figure settlement in her husband's death. Got a pending lawsuit against Facebook. He dug around. Teresa took a writing course two semesters ago. Submitted a feature treatment in which a disgruntled nurse sets up her boss, a prick of a doctor, by planting kiddie porn on his iPhone.

"That's when I knew," Alvarez says. "It was just a matter of tracking and monitoring Teresa."

"Why didn't you fucking tell me?" I shout at him.

"Had to make sure you weren't involved," he answers.

"And it took her firing a shot at me for you to finally figure that out?"

"When she called you and confessed, we nailed her and cleared you."

"Lucky for me the bullet missed."

"Hey, it's a pain in the ass to get down to the bottom of that bridge," Alvarez explains all defensively. "If she would have tried to shoot you anywhere else, I guarantee I would have stopped her from pulling the trigger."

"Thanks," I say.

Because murder by social networking (I coin the phrase social deathworking and Alvarez loves it) isn't your standard legal fare, Alvarez is not sure how the next forty-eight hours are going to play out. He talks fast. There'll probably be a preliminary hearing and arraignment, but it might actually go to a grand jury. I don't even know what a grand jury fucking is. I feel like I'm on an episode of *Law and Order.* Right before he leaves, Alvarez tells me to be available 24/7. I'll be subpoenaed as a witness for sure—the star witness. Tells me I'll be giving sworn testimony either way. Whatever it all means, it's gonna suck. It's gonna cost me time and probably money. I may have to lawyer up.

Alvarez takes off. "Can't believe I have to hike the whole way up a dirt trail in these nice shoes," he gripes.

I'm alone beneath the bridge. If you don't count the demon and the trapped souls.

Questions—under oath—start tomorrow. I've got to get my story straight in my head. I start replaying everything in my mind, but I can't concentrate. I'm exhausted. I keep staring up at the dome of the courthouse building. Babalon is up there. I feel her. I wonder what she thinks of the spectacle tonight, and how much she had to do with it. Wonder why she's keeping her distance.

I'm not ready to face her.

Not tonight.

I've gotta get out of here now, before she shows.

I start walking toward the path leading up the ravine.

"Kane," someone yells at me from on top of the bridge.

I freeze. Look up. See a person. He climbs up the rail and stands beneath an alcove lamp.

My eyes focus. It's Drexel.

He's in the same clothes he was wearing when he walked offstage Saturday night.

"What are you doing here?" I yell up. My voice bounces off the beams under the bridge. "How did you find me?"

"I need to talk to you, bro," he shouts down. "I'm sorry. I fucked up." His words echo.

"Whatever. Too late to change things now."

"Help me, Kane."

"You don't need my help. You need Betty Ford's." Feels good to zing him.

"Where are we? How did I even get here?"

I can't tell if he's royally fucked up or has just totally cracked. Fuck it. Who cares. We're finished.

His voice changes. He sounds like a scared kid. He whimpers, then he shouts down, "That chick—the one in black—she won't leave me alone, dude. She won't get out of my head."

Oh, shit. I've got to get him out of here. Get us both out of here. "Stay there," I say. "I'll be right up."

"No, I'll be right down," he shouts. Drexel raises his arms and does a swan dive exactly the way he jumps into the mosh pit.

He lands ten feet from me. Like a human grenade exploding. Spring-loaded organs. I'm in shock, covered in Drexel's blood and guts. I can't breathe. Can't scream.

And then she's there. Babalon. Smiling. She wasn't kidding. She lured someone I know here.

I want her head on a spit. "I told you I'd bring the box. You didn't give me enough time—"

"I'm not punishing you," she says, opening her arms, summoning me to embrace her. "I'm giving you a gift."

"Gift?"

"Your hatred drove him straight to me. Your will lured him here."

"You're a liar." I'm crying and don't even know it. "You killed him."

"He killed himself. Rejoice," she shouts. "He would have held us back."

"Leave me alone."

"You have Jack Parsons' box. I know. Bring it to me now. The ritual will bring us together."

"No."

"Do it now or I'll end you here."

"I said no."

"Then Ned and Eva will be the next jumpers."

Checkmate.

No choice. Time is now. Or never.

"Don't force me to destroy you," she says. "Let me protect you. Guide you. Enrich you. Help me create you."

I nod. "You win. I'll go get the box."

I march all the way up to the camper alone. I can hear Babalon's wings beating in the darkness above. She's keeping a close watch. I relive the psychedelic vision I had. And remember exactly what to do.

I open the door to the camper. Everything's ready . . . except me. But here I go.

I pull out of the parking lot. Hang a left on South Arroyo, punch the gas, and barrel straight downhill. I gain momentum. Twenty . . . thirty . . . forty miles an hour. Grip the wheel in a death clutch. Instead of following the road left where it swerves, I go straight. Full speed. Crash through the locked gate and down the narrow road to the little bridge under the big bridge. The windshield shatters. Front bumper and grill are torn away. I lose control. The camper tips onto two wheels, but rights itself. I slam the brakes. Swerve, but manage to keep the camper from flipping off the bridge into the river channel. Smoke pours from under the hood.

I'm directly under the center of the bridge. I leap out, Parsons' box under one arm, backpack on the other. Babalon glides in and lands. "Open the box," she commands. "Lay the parchment and dagger before me."

I obey.

She points down. "Take the dagger—trace a pentagram in the air."

I pick up the dagger. Trace the five-pointed star in the air. Take a few steps back. "I want to add something to the ritual."

We lock eyes. I back away slowly. No sudden moves. I reach down and into my backpack without ever turning my back or breaking eye contact and pull out Crowley's goblet. She's pleased. "Yes," she says. "Do it."

I lay the goblet down. Act reverent.

"Take the parchment," she orders next. "Repeat my words. Recite the Invocation of the Bornless One." She chants, recites in another language—the native tongue of angels and demons. Sounds like backwards speak.

I move toward my backpack again. She's angry. "Do what I say!"

"Just one more thing—a gift," I say. "For the ritual."

She raises her spear in my direction, suspicious. Shit. I move fast. In one fluid motion, I reach in the backpack, pull out the soul trap, and press the blue button. The luminous spirit of Ahchancha blasts from the barrel in the form of a white light that shoots straight at a stunned Babalon. She's stunned, reels, takes flight, and sends a forceful blast my way that sends the trap sailing out of my hands thirty feet into the dense brush on the other side of the bridge.

Ahchancha attacks, remains hot on Babalon's trail.

They battle. The light show in the night sky is spectacular, but I can't stop to watch.

Move. Now!

Speed!

A spirit versus a demon. No match. Ahchancha won't hold her off for long.

I grab the parchment and dagger and toss it back in the box with the rest of Jack Parsons' Satanic mementos. I slam the lid and place Crowley's goblet on the pentagram. Reach inside the passenger door of the camper and grab Ahchancha's cross.

I hear war cries from above. The Indian's kicking ass up there. His cries seem to awaken the souls trapped in the underside of the bridge. Energy pulsates. A blue glow shines down from the suspended cluster of souls.

I stand above Parsons' box with Ahchancha's cross in my hands. Eye up Crowley's goblet. It glistens. I can hear that fat fuck's voice in my head crying, "No!"

I raise the cross above my head. Drive its sharpened butt end through the goblet. Like it's the tip of fucking Excalibur, the cross tears through the crystal and Parsons' box like butter. When the cross, goblet, and box meet, the objects disintegrate and transform into pure energy. A colossal column of light rises and takes the form of a fiery serpent that dances in the sky and winds itself around the arches of the bridge.

What begins as a soundless reverberation becomes a violent, thundering shock wave. It's deafening. So loud I can see it.

I run to the camper and throw open the back door. I grab one of the gasoline cans and douse the nearest bags. I grab Ned's lighter. Nice big flame. The interior of the camper starts to burn. All the Hefty bags of bone-dry sage erupt. Flames head toward the gas cans.

I haul ass back over the little bridge. Ten yards . . . twenty . . . thirty.

The battle above me rages. I hear the Indian's war cries.

Kaboom!

Ned's camper explodes.

The force of the blast sends me over the side of the small bridge. I land on my back. Crunch. I roll through brush to the bottom of the bridge. The smell of burning sage rises, floods the night. Sage clouds envelop the bridge, meet the snakelike wave of luminous energy constricting the bridge's arches. The smoke thickens as it cleanses the bridge. The structure sways and buckles. I'm pretty damn sure the whole thing is about to come straight down on me.

Missiles of light fire in all directions. One of the ornate lampposts on top of the bridge explodes, setting off a chain reaction. All fifty of them blow in succession. Like sonic booms. The supernatural energy squeezing the bridge meets the electricity of hundred-year-old lights.

Ka-motherfucking-*boom!*

The blast envelopes the bridge and shakes the earth. Another explosion comes from the bridge's understructure. The trapped souls are blown free. The cluster bursts apart into individual orbs of dancing light. A heavy blanket of fog rolls in and draws in the orbs. They vanish. No doubt on the express train to the Medicantium. The battle between Babalon and Ahchancha ends abruptly when a spiraling tower of light descends from above and sucks in the Indian's spirit. Express train to heaven.

The energy swirling around the bridge dissipates as the fog lifts. The tower of light dissolves. The earthquake ends.

Then a mighty blast of cool wind—magnificently fresh air— blows down the riverbed from the San Gabriel Mountains.

Babalon's curse is broken.

It ends just like the vision.

It's over.

I won.

I breathe in the cool, fresh air and feel a wave of peace.

The feeling only lasts a second.

Babalon lands right in front of me. Her eyes burn red. So much for sending her back to hell with her tail between her legs. The souls are freed, but she's still here. And she's pissed.

This I didn't see coming.

Her wings span wide. She flies straight up. Like I'm metal and she's a magnet, I fly up alongside her. She lands on the ledge of the bridge—dead center. Suspends me in thin air, facedown. I hang there, looking down into a black abyss.

"You fool!" she growls. "Why do you resist? Look at me." My neck twists in her direction. My eyes are forced open. "We are the same."

"No, we're not."

"You're a dark spirit—a selfish, ugly, depraved, unrepentant, cruel man full of hatred."

"You're right," I say. "But I don't always want to be."

My neck wrenches facedown. I can't close my eyes. "Look down," she commands. "Feel what they felt. Die like they died."

She keeps me hanging. Savors my terror. Drinks my hopelessness.

This is it.

Game over.

I lost.

My recurring dream is about to become reality.

Don't give her the satisfaction. Don't give up. Die fighting.

I try to remember prayers of exorcism I've read. They all
jumble together. I want my last words to be my own—not
some superstitious recitation. What did Ahchancha tell me?
'To destroy evil, you must wage a war that's yours alone.' I accept
that I'm going to die. But goddamnit, if I am, this bitch is going
with me.

I yank on my lucky necklace until the chain breaks. Clutch it
in my hand. It's mine. My creation. My mojo. The only weapon
I have left.

I relive good moments. There aren't many, but there's
enough. I stare at the medals and talismans on the necklace.
Remember how and when I got each one. I smile when I see the
smiley-face pendant the little girl gave me this morning when
she brought me food and water. I think of Eva. Ned. Music.
My dad. A future that might have been had I not been such a
fuck-up about things. I think about it all and bathe it in white
light. Ignore her. Breathe in, breathe out. Energize my chakras.
My head moves. So do my arms. Turn my head and give her
the best badass look I have. Hurl my necklace right at her and
scream, "To hell with you." I wait for her to melt away like the
Wicked Witch.

Instead . . . she laughs.

I'm fucked.

And then—*Wham!* A blinding flash. Something from behind
her burns a perfect hole through her torso that I can see straight
through. She screams, drops her spear, disintegrates in flames.
Like a trapdoor opening, I fall—straight down.

Three seconds stretch into three minutes. Whoever said your entire life flashes before your eyes at the moment of your death was not talking out his ass. Somehow I see it all—a little good and a lot of bad. Hey, I tried. At least the bridge is cleared. Babalon is gone.

I'm okay with dying.

I brace for impact.

I see Eva's face.

Then someone grabs me by the collar and yanks me upward. I hear the beating of wings. See him out of the corner of my eye— white wings. I look back. A face. Hallucinating. Must already be dead. I look again. Can't be.

I hit the ground with mighty—but not lethal—force. My back explodes. I can't move. My feet twitch. Hands shake. Vision blurs. Air rushes out of my lungs. I lay there looking up. Watch the biggest fucking white bird I've ever seen fly up and over the Colorado Street Bridge, vanishing into the night.

I roll my head to the right. Drexel's dead eyes stare at me from twenty feet away. I roll my head left. Spot Babalon's sphere and my broken necklace a few feet away. I can't stand. Drag myself. Pain blinds me. Legs go numb. Reach. Reach further. Grab the necklace and the sphere. Hold them tight.

I start to die.

I sink into the ground. Life drains away.

A light. Blinding white light.

Thump. Thump. Thump.

An angel? Heaven?

The light gets brighter.

The sound gets louder.

Sirens.

No angel.

Police helicopter. Again.

Voices.

Footsteps.

Faces looking down.
Paramedics. Cops.
A brace on my neck.
Strapped to a board.
Needle in the arm.
All goes black.

Thirty-five

7:01 AM.

I dream that I'm flying. It's nighttime. I'm over the bridge. I'm chasing an owl. It has a human face.

His face.

Dawn breaks. The owl becomes a dove. I follow it toward the San Gabriel Mountains. Zoom over Gravity Hill. Higher we climb. We glide in circles over Rubio Canyon's waterfalls. The dove vanishes. I fall.

My eyes open wide. I bolt upright in a hospital emergency room. Feels like a blowtorch on my back. Spiders crawling under the brace around my neck. Immeasurable pain. I scream. A nurse rushes in, eases me onto my back. Tells me not to move. I spy her ID badge. I'm in Barrington Memorial Hospital. Two people on the other side of the curtain from me are talking about the big earthquake. "It was 4.7 on the Richter scale," I hear someone say. "Centered right under Pasadena."

Detective Cliff DuPree shows up, closes the curtain around my bed.

My first instinct is to shake his hand, but my arm is too heavy and numb to move. "What are you doing here?"

"Here to check on you," he says.

"Thanks."

"And here to help clean up another one of your messes."

"You're gonna need a big broom."

"What happened?" he wants to know. "Tell me everything."

I don't have to sugarcoat anything with DuPree. He's known me since I was seventeen. Bailed me out of a lot of jams. He's the only person besides Eva and Ned who knows what I do and believes what I say. Through shock and trauma, I wave him close and tell him everything. The whole story, beginning to end.

When I'm finished, I look at him. "I'm in big trouble, aren't I?"

"Let me see what I can find out," he says.

Two orderlies come in. They tell me I'm on my way to get tests.

No health insurance. What's this gonna cost me? Probably better off dead.

10:33 AM.

While two doctors tell me about my severely sprained neck and what they call "multilevel transverse process fractures in my second and third lumbar vertebras," Ned shows up. Doesn't interrupt the doctors. "Consider yourself lucky," the doctor tells me. "You don't appear to have any serious internal injuries."

"What now?" I ask.

The cute female doctor tells me I may need surgery, but that can only be determined by a spinal surgeon after more X-rays and MRI imaging is done once the swelling subsides. For now, it's complete bed rest. A little walking every day, if I can—ten minutes at a time, three times a day. Provided the final tests for internal injuries are negative, I'll be released by this evening.

She writes me a prescription for OxyContin. Gives me a nice fat dose before she leaves with the other doctor. Every cloud has a silver lining.

Ned looks awful. Torn. I know the look. He's relieved that I'm not dead. But angry that I lied. And guilty he wasn't there.

"Tell me you have the trap," I say.

He nods. "Had to really dig around down there, but I found it."

Major relief. I was stressing out bad. Thought it was gone. "Thank God," I say.

"No, thank me. Now what the hell happened?"

"I totaled the camper. I'm sorry, Ned."

"I don't care about that piece of shit. What were you doing back at the bridge? Tell me everything."

"I just want to enjoy the drugs. Can we talk about it later?"

"No. Now."

Fine. I fess up. Tell him everything. DuPree. Now Ned. Telling the story wipes me out. I'm relieved when I get to the end.

Ned's pissed off. Not about the camper. About me lying to him. Again.

"I swear, I don't know why I hang in there with you," he gripes.

"Me neither."

"When are you gonna quit treating me like an asshole?"

Now I'm pissed off. "I was doing you a favor."

"Go ahead—justify it to yourself," he yells. "You always do."

"Justify it?" I see red. And tell him the part of the story I glossed over. That he was on Babalon's radar. So was Eva. Their lives were in danger. I had no choice but to go it alone.

"You didn't have to lie," he says, calmer now. "We're partners. I can take care of myself."

"Not against her," I assure him.

He stares at me. He can see the ordeal in my eyes. Sees the state of my body. "If you would have told me a week ago that one of us was going to be on a hospital bed today, I would've bet the farm it was gonna be me."

"Are you snapping out of your depression yet?"

"Starting to."

"It wasn't just you. It was Babalon. I know it." I get angry. Tell Ned, "We have to be more careful. We just can't go walking into places without knowing what might be there. We go looking for one thing, we might end up stumbling upon something completely different, something we can't handle."

Ned shakes his head. "Sounds familiar. Didn't I just say that to you recently?"

"I don't think so."

"Jesus," he mutters.

He reaches over and pats my hand. Has that Dad look on his face again. "Thanks for looking out for me, buddy," he says.

2:43 PM.

I've been moved to a room with a TV to await my test results. Ned and I watch *Ghost Hunters* on SyFy. I never let myself watch it before. We bitch and moan about how they're rich and we're not.

A cute blond doctor comes in. California gurl. About my age. Probably has a Mercedes and a 401(k). Yet another reminder that I should take life more seriously. "How's the Oxy treating you?"

"Like a new best friend. What's the verdict?"

"You're going home," she says. "No major internal injuries. Some swelling in the abdomen, but no bleeding. Do want to point one thing out, though. Your liver enzymes are high. Are you a heavy drinker?"

Belch. "Don't know if I'd hay seavy."

"You should cut down. Way down."

"Okay, I'll keep that in mind." I nod at Ned. *Get me out of here*, my look says. "Did you bring my flask?" I ask him.

The doctor doesn't laugh. "I'll start the discharge process."

Cliff DuPree comes in with a serious look on his face. "We need to talk."

Shit. I know that tone. "What?"

"Been scoping out the situation over at the Pasadena Police Department." DuPree looks at Ned like: *Who's this guy?*

"He's my friend," I say.

"This is Ned?" They shake hands. "Long overdue," DuPree says.

Ned slaps my leg. "Thanks for keeping my boy here out of jail."

"Not an easy task," DuPree says.

"Just say it—what kind of trouble am I in? What am I gonna be charged with?"

A long dramatic pause from DuPree, and then, "Nothing."

"What?"

"Old lady Barrington took care of it. No charges."

"How?"

"The official report: After Teresa Burrows was taken into custody and you were questioned, your buddy came to the bridge to kill himself. Two witnesses driving across the bridge saw him leap. In a state of shock, you tried to catch your friend, break his fall." DuPree looks at Ned. "Did you know your camper was reported stolen?"

"No, it wasn't," Ned says.

"According to a police report it was. Last night it went missing from your building's parking lot. Thieves—most likely kids—took it for a joyride. Crashed it through the gate leading under the bridge. Set it on fire for kicks."

"You're kidding, right?" Ned asks.

"Then," DuPree continues, "the earthquake set off a massive power outage that started at the bridge and spread through most of Pasadena. It was a hell of a busy night under that bridge."

"The old lady can just snap her fingers and make all that happen?" I ask.

DuPree nods.

"Now that's power," Ned says.

"You dodged a bullet, Kane," DuPree tells me.

"Two of them," I say. "Remember, I got shot at."

"Don't know how you do it," DuPree says. "Somebody up there's looking out for you."

"Did you talk to Detective Alvarez?" I ask him. "They might have to wait for their sworn testimony with me in this condition."

"Teresa Burrows confessed," DuPree says. "Seven o'clock this morning. She shot the bum in the head. Set her daughter up. Overdosed her husband on ephedra and something called foxglove before he ran the L.A. Marathon. The press is going apeshit. They're camped outside the jail. Networks and all. Teresa says she'll only speak to one reporter about her confession—Eva Kells from the *L.A. Times*."

Ned looks at me. "Goddamn," he marvels. "You're lucky. She's a psycho. You really did dodge a couple of bullets."

8:18 PM.

Back home.

What an ordeal. Took me a good ten minutes to fold myself into Ned's car. Did it inch by agonizing inch. Felt every bump, every pothole, like a flaming arrow to the spine. Ned practically had to carry me up the flight of stairs to my apartment. A wonder he didn't fuck up his own back.

Gotta give him props. Ned's a champ. Helped me stretch out on the sofa. Went out, filled my prescription, bought me groceries, a fifth of Jameson, more pillows to elevate my legs.

I wash down my OxyContin with a glass of Jameson on the rocks. Ned's on the phone with Eva, filling her in. I can't tell the story again. Sounds like she just got back from interviewing Teresa in the county lockup.

Ned holds the phone down, mouths: *she wants to come over.*

"In the morning," I say. "I'm not gonna be awake much longer."

"How about in the morning?" he says to her. "Okay, then."

Ned pockets his phone. "I better go."

"And about the camper—"

"Forget about it." Ned stares down at me. "It was on its last legs."

"Thanks, Ned."

"Listen to the doctor," he warns me. "Bed rest."

"Right."

"Maybe in a week or two you can take up yoga or something. That might help."

"I can't lift my feet six inches off the floor and you want me to do yoga?"

"I said in a couple of weeks. Young bodies heal fast."

"But old souls don't."

"I'll check in on you tomorrow."

I smile at him. "Thanks, Dad."

He freezes. "What did you say?" he asks, shocked.

I let it linger. Act woozier than I am and just shrug.

"You're welcome," he says with tears in his eyes.

Ned locks the door behind him.

Got everything I need within reach: painkillers, remote control, iPod, and whiskey. Before I can grab any of it, I'm out.

Thirty-six

3:22 AM.

Somewhere between sleep and consciousness I hear him. Crowley. His sing-songey voice announces another song title—"Happy Dust." The song plays. It's incomplete, but the backbones are there. It's a gem.

I stir. Reach for my pen and notebook. Jot down the gist of it before it fades. Give the finger to the air. "You don't own me."

Which reminds me . . .

It takes all my effort to stand. I shouldn't attempt this. Not yet. But I need to.

I take baby steps to the closet. Grab a broom. Barely ever used it. Waves of pain stop me dead every few steps. I use the broom handle to push my guitar cases from the living room across the floor to my bedroom closet. I lower myself to the floor inch by god-awful inch. Use the handle to shove the guitar cases in the hiding spot behind the wall where I keep the trap. Lean in and cover the opening. Almost pass out from the pain.

May they rest in peace.

I'm done with rock and roll.

Maybe I'll learn to play the saxophone. Become a jazz man.

I stare at my bed. Looks inviting, but if I lay down, I won't be getting back up easily. I shuffle back to the couch. Takes forever.

Pop two Oxies. Couple of huge belts of whiskey.

I stand there. Relive my fall. I wasn't hallucinating. It was him.

Fuck bed rest. I'm up.

I need to find out for sure.

Takes about ten minutes for the booze and pills to numb me whole.

I use my cane to make it down the stairwell, out the front door to Yucca. Not bad for a loser with a broken back.

Everything goes numb. Feels like I'm floating.

Takes forever, but I drag myself to Hollywood and Vine. God knows the damage I'm doing to my spine.

But I need to know.

Frolic Room is locked. Neon sign is dark.

I knock.

Neon sign flickers and lights. Click. Door knob turns. Door swings open.

Walk in. Empty. Dark. As always, musty.

I take Babalon's sphere out of my pocket and knock on the bar with it. It's cold in my hand. One by one, the saucer lamps flicker on. Jukebox starts on its own. Miles Davis. Don't know him well enough yet to name the song.

"It's called "Deception," a voice says.

The doorway to the storage room at the far end of the bar glows white. Gabe emerges from the light, steps up to the bar. Dressed as he always is in white shirt, black vest, and bow tie. "Jameson?" he asks.

"Nah. Gabriel. How about a glass of truth."

He smiles, pours me a shot.

I size him up. "It was you."

He pours himself a shot. "Cheers."

"You killed Babalon. You broke my fall."

"Just barely," he says.

"You don't look like you did at the bridge."

"Those were my work clothes," he says.

"No wisecracks. Not tonight."

"You know about spirits, Kane. We're all energy. And energy

transforms." He turns his back and looks into the mirror behind the bar. I watch his reflection change from bartender Gabe to the winged, armor-clad being who saved me, to one of my old landladies, to a liquor store clerk I used to bullshit with, to the little girl who brought me a sandwich Monday, and back to Gabe the bartender.

"What are you saying? You're stalking me?"

"More like keeping an eye on you."

"Why?"

"Lots of reasons."

"For instance?"

"You're in over your head. That device you carry around—the soul trap—it's dangerous. You're interfering between worlds. Do you even know what its true purpose is?"

I look at him like I do, but I don't. He knows. Can't bluff him.

"Find out," he tells me. "Before it costs you dearly."

"Tell me," I say.

"Some lessons have to be learned alone. Remember that." He pours us another round. "The other reason I watched you is strictly self-serving."

"What's that mean?"

"I knew you'd find her. Or she'd find you. You're her type. Figured she'd drop her guard."

"So you used me?"

"No. I capitalized on a battlefield advantage."

"What battlefield?"

"I come from one world. She comes from another. But this place, this world—this is the in-between where we battle."

"Over what?"

"Souls. We want to elevate them. They want to destroy them. It's a conflict as old as time."

"They had you at a two-to-one disadvantage. But you beat Belial," I say, raising my glass. "You've beat Babalon. Took you what—over two centuries?"

"That's a blink of an eye to me."

"Now what?"

"Now I leave."

"And go where?"

"Another place and time."

"And do what?"

"I'm a messenger, Kane. I'll keep on delivering the Big Guy's message."

"Which is?"

"It's different for every person. Every place. Every time."

"So all these decades while you were healing between scrapes, preparing for your next battle, you were what? Delivering messages here?"

"Here and a few other bars around town. I get around."

"Why not a church?"

"Churches, temples, mosques—they're man-made institutions unwelcoming to the lost and hopeless. Whereas, a place like this—it was built for the lost and hopeless. It's Hollywood and Vine, baby—Boulevard of Broken Dreams. A lot of desperate souls make the decision to end their lives, but a lot of them decide to keep on living. Sometimes, they find their way to one of these barstools. And I give them whatever message I have to inspire them, help them keep fighting another day. Just like I've inspired you from time to time."

"You're fooling yourself," I say "No one really listens."

"Some do. But most are like you—in one ear and out the other. It does get to me sometimes. I guess I've been here too long."

"I feel that way about L.A. a lot," I admit.

"Try being here since 1774."

Gabe refills and raises his glass. "To victory."

"You had some help. Ahchancha for one."

"Already thanked him."

"He made it through his door?"

"And had a special place waiting for him."

"And don't forget to thank me. You did use me."

"You're lucky I was there or you'd be dead. I'd say I protected you. Dare I say—I was a guardian."

"Well, in some fucked-up way, I protected you, too."

"I'll second that. Cheers," he says. We clink shot glasses.

I sip my drink and think about all the times I sat here and drank and listened to music and been annoyed by this guy . . . or whatever he is. All these years of knowing with certainty that there's sure as hell something down below, but clueless if there's something up above. And this is how I get my answer. I'm disappointed. "You know something," I tell Gabe. "You've rubbed me the wrong way since day one."

Gabe shoots a sarcastic pout. "Oh, boy, now I'm hurt. You liked her better."

"What does that say about heaven and God?" I ask him.

"Doesn't say a thing about that. It's the message you don't like. The messenger's irrelevant."

"And there's a heaven?"

"It's a fine club to be a member of, Kane. Well worth the struggle to reach. Trust me, it's better than hellfire. Wish I could tell you more, but them's the rules."

I take Babalon's sphere out of my pocket and lay it on the bar between me and Gabe. "She was one tough lady," Gabe says. He reaches for the sphere. I yank it back. "It won't do you any good," he says. "And it can't hurt me anymore."

"Then why do you want it?"

"Souvenir. I've earned the right to carry it." He reaches in his own pocket and pulls out a different sphere. "This one was Belial's."

"Kind of like taking a scalp?"

"Never thought of it that way, but yeah," he says.

I can tell—it's more than a scalp or a souvenir. "You're lying."

He laughs. "Angels never lie."

"Then why don't you just take it from me?"

He doesn't answer. "You can't, can you?" No reply. "Why?" He just shakes his head at me. A secret, I guess.

"I propose a trade," I say.

"Propose away."

"Three things. Bring me the demon Alastor's sphere."

"Why?"

"He'll be coming after me."

"Pointless. You couldn't wield the weapon if he did."

"Then bring me the angel who can."

Gabe gives me a *maybe* look and shrug. "What else?" he asks

"A girl named Anna Burrows, the last girl who jumped off the bridge."

"What about her?" he asks.

"She might as well have been pushed off that bridge," I tell him. "I want you to get her out of that prison she's locked away in."

"The Medicantium is not a prison," Gabe assures me.

"It is to her," I say. "It wasn't her fault."

Gabe smiles and winks at me. I see a flash in the mirror at the far end of the bar. Anna Burrows stands with her father. He gives me a quick wave of thanks. Anna blows me a kiss, then gives me the finger, a big smile on her face. "It was already taken care of," Gabe says as father and daughter vanish. "The universe has a way of correcting itself."

"Good," I say.

Gabe reaches over the bar and pats me on the shoulder. "I'm impressed, Kane. Really, I am. You actually thought of someone other than yourself."

He's being sarcastic. I think. "And number three," I continue, "tell me what I need to know about the soul trap."

"I can't. You have to find it out for yourself."

"Then give me a hint."

"I did. And I'll give you one more. Start paying attention to what you hear in your skull, and your answers will come."

I finish my drink, turn my back on him, and head out the door.

I see Gabe's reflection in the mirror as I'm leaving. He's smiling. "Did you ever hear the one about the preschooler who thought he was carrying a *Ghostbusters* backpack, but it was really one of those nuclear briefcases that went missing from Russia?"

I ignore him. Regroup on Hollywood Boulevard. I'm so fucked up, I'm in another stratosphere. I feel pain, but it's miles in the distance. Take a few steps. Then a few more. Like I'm gliding. Make it a block. I stop on the corner of Hollywood Boulevard and Ivar Avenue and take a breather. Just so happens that I'm in front of the L. Ron Hubbard Life Exhibition. I look through the window into the exhibit lobby. A bust of Hubbard stands front and center. It's not my eyes playing tricks on me—Hubbard looks like he has reptilian scales.

Fuck him and his Crowley-inspired Church of Scientology. Goddamn occult-loving huckster's one of the reasons I'm standing here with a broken back.

I look around. Coast is clear. No traffic. An unexpected burst of strength, fueled by anger and self-pity, fills me. I limp over, yank the trash can on the corner out of the sidewalk, and smash the glass door. Drag myself in the lobby and topple Hubbard's bust, which shatters.

Alarms blare. Take off. No idea how, but I'm trotting—way unsteadily. Straight up Ivar. Left on Yucca. Left leg dead and dragging. Make it to the vestibule of my building. Sirens scream by.

I'm on a roll.

I head to my car. Take forever to crawl inside. Drive. Everything's a blur.

• • •

4:47 AM.

I knock on Eva's door. She opens it. Takes one look at me. "Jesus."

"No, but I drank with one of his friends tonight."

"You didn't drive like this?"

"Actually, it was more like flying."

I stagger in. "I talked to Ned. I was going to come and see you first thing in the morning," she says.

"I'm a fucking mess."

She takes mercy. Leads me to her bedroom. Helps me onto her bed. Lies next to me and curls up.

I'm gone.

Somewhere in and out of a deep sleep, I remember where I am. She stirs in the dark. Feel her thigh against my hand. She moves closer. Not sleeping, but not fully awake. My hand roams. And then she's on top of me.

And I'm healed.

Crowley's voice is silent. No more songs in my head.

At last, I rest.

7:18 AM.

I'm startled awake by a bang. Eva picks her keys off the floor. "Sorry," she says. "Didn't mean to wake you up."

She's dressed, ready for work. Putting on lip gloss in her medicine cabinet mirror, throwing things into her purse. I'm naked under the sheets. "Did something happen last night?"

She turns and smiles at me. "You don't remember?"

"Felt like a dream."

"You could say that."

I speak to her reflection. "Is this the part where you tell me it was all a big mistake?"

"No. Relax. Just because you had cobwebs doesn't mean I did."

"Was I? . . ."

"Oh, yeah," she says smiling. "If that's your broken back mode, then we're good."

"Wish I would have been there—all there."

"Next time."

"I guess I should go."

"I want you to stay here for a while."

"Really?"

"I want to keep an eye on you."

The stars align. What's this feeling? Joy? "Okay," I say. "Thanks."

And she's out the door and I'm tucked away safely inside her apartment.

It's cozy.

And all is finally right.

Thirty=seven

A gainst doctor's orders, I get up after two days to attend Drexel's funeral. Eva goes to my place and puts together a respectable black outfit for me to wear. My back feels even worse. Roaming around Hollywood Boulevard in the middle of the night was not a good move. I hit the Oxy hard in order to do this.

Because I'm as slow as a ninety-year-old with a walker, Eva and I are the last ones to arrive at the Cathedral Mausoleum at Hollywood Forever Cemetery. It's a circus outside. We have to push our way past the paparazzi.

The media ate the story up.

Within twenty-four hours of his suicide, Drexel was famous the world over. The blogs turned him into an overnight sensation. His Facebook page got over a million hits in one day. Drexel's finally a star.

Teresa, now Drexel. Eva drove two nationally prominent stories in one week.

She has arrived.

Someone sticks a microphone in my face and asks me how I feel about it. Woman from *Dateline* whispers in my ear she can guarantee me fifty grand for an interview about what happened at the bridge. I push my way past them and walk through the iron doors. An usher hands me a program. Drexel did have a real name after all: Drew Xavier Ellingford. So much for being the bastard son of a rock god. Turns out Drexel's father owns a chain of Mercedes dealerships, including the one in Beverly Hills.

The service is already underway. Pews are full. Standing room only. I wave hello to Bo, Joanie, Pat, Ira, the Triplets of Melrose. Place is old. Cold marble, top to bottom. Ten-foot statues of Christ's disciples stand guard along the walls. Seems like hundreds of boxes of Kleenex everywhere—gentle reminder that I'm surrounded by actors, both living and dead. I lean against a statue of Saint Peter for support. Surrounded by death. Tombs line the hallways to the left and right of the lobby chapel. Urns in floor-to-ceiling glass cases in the main hall. Place is crawling with ghosts. Not gonna think about that today.

There he lies in an outfit I've seen him wear a hundred times on stage. A white casket surrounded by a wall of flowers. A poster-size headshot on an easel. Microphone stand next to the coffin. From where I'm standing in the back, he looks natural, like he's sleeping on the sofa at the recording studio. Someone did a bang-up job of masking the blunt-force trauma his body endured.

Jay delivers a nice eulogy about the day he and Drexel met. He goes a little overboard at the end by comparing it to the day John Lennon met Paul McCartney at a church fair in Liverpool. But what the hell.

The priest practically canonizes Drexel before wrapping up with a final prayer.

Before the crowd disburses, Bo walks to the podium, announces that a gathering of friends and family will take place this afternoon at Drexel's parents' house in Bel Air. A procession will be leaving momentarily.

"I don't want to go," I say.

Eva says, "We should." She looks toward the coffin. "Let's go say good-bye."

We walk to the casket. Drexel's wearing his Ray-Bans. Close up, he looks waxy. Eva crosses herself, walks away. She's not comfortable around death. Look down, say to him in my mind,

"Sorry, Drexel. Wrong place, wrong time. Caught in the cross-hairs. Wasn't your fault."

Wait to hear something back. Nothing.

We file out with the rest of the mourners.

There's a motorcade through Hollywood. We wind our way up narrow streets of Bel Air. The procession stops at the gates of a mansion. Valet parking at his funeral. Drexel would have loved that.

We follow the crowd of mourners through the gates to what looks like fucking stately Wayne Manor. Stone, ivy-covered walls. Arched stained glass windows. As big as a hotel. More rooms than my apartment building. Museumlike furnishings. Two pools—indoor and out. Movie theater. Feels like I'm on a set.

Open bar. Crowd hits it hard. Turns into a weepy Irish wake. Crowd huddles poolside. Stunning view of the city. Can just imagine Drexel out here as a kid eating his Cheerios with a silver spoon while an army of servants tell him how gorgeous and brilliant he is.

Drexel's mother, Pamela—a bejeweled, striking blonde in her late forties who looks a decade younger—speaks. Talks about her only child when he was a boy. It's sweet. Eva tears up along with most of the crowd. Drexel's father looks broken and no amount of money can fix him. Praises his son for marching to his own tune despite the fact that it often drove him crazy. Those are about the only genuine sentiments shared.

A microphone gets passed around. I wanna puke. People get so sappy when they're on stage and drunk. The gist: Lots of weeping. Lots of "*if he would have only called me I could have stopped him*" sackcloth-and-ashes bullshit. A few nice, funny stories, but not many. Drexel wasn't a nice guy. Or a funny one.

Jay speaks from the heart. Through tears, he says, "He was the best friend I ever had. I can't imagine playing another note without him. Doubt I ever will."

Bo touts him as one of the greatest talents he'd ever seen.

Microphone gets handed to Eva. She doesn't know what to say. Should just pass it on, but she doesn't. "We went out for a . . ." She gets tongue-tied—a first. She rebounds with, "He was one of a kind." Eva—always crafting a line that simpletons can digest.

Eva hands me the microphone. Christ. Sick of this town full of liars. I take a sip of whiskey—drink the truth. "I knew Drexel. He was many things. One, a giant pain in the ass. Two, brutally self-absorbed," I say. A few mild laughs; a few sounds of discomfort. "Three, mesmerizing," I continue. "Call it showmanship or charisma—whatever—but if this guy was in the corner reading a magazine, you had to watch. Four, he was wickedly skilled. He had more talent than anyone I've ever played with, maybe ever saw. He commanded his audience." I let the words settle, search for the right summary. "I think if you *genuinely* possess all four of these attributes, then you're very special. Drexel was a fucking rock star. The tragedy is he never got to shine. Let's drink to him."

The crowd claps, then hits the bar with fury.

"Ready to go?" Eva asks.

"Got to hit the john first," I say. "Damn medicine."

I bid farewell to Jay and Joanie. Bo stops me on the way to the bathroom. "I'll call you next week," he says. "I think we're gonna carry on without him."

"Without us," I tell him.

"You're out?"

"I'm out."

Bo crushes his plastic cup. "Fuck."

"See ya, Bo."

"Just let it settle, Kane," Bo says. "You might feel different in a month or two."

"Good luck," I tell him.

Someone's taking an eternity in the bathroom off the kitchen. Try another one. Locked. It's an emergency.

I grab the rail and pull myself up a spiral staircase past a crystal chandelier. Must be a bathroom up here somewhere. Enter the master bedroom. Holy hell. The place is bigger than my entire apartment. Four-post bed with red velvet curtains. Persian rug. A wall of built-in bookshelves. A Miró above the fireplace. Killer balcony that overlooks pristine gardens. And the greatest shitter these eyes have ever seen.

Make it in the nick of time. Sweet relief.

I stop and scan the bookshelves on my way out. Serious collectors. Mostly old, leather-bound editions. Eyes locked on one book, newer than the dusty volumes around it. Gold-embossed unicursal hexagram on a black leather spine. Aleister Crowley's symbol.

I open the book. It's a photo album. Drexel's mother, Pamela—late teens, early twenties? Supermodel looks. Magnetic blue eyes. Perfect body. Shot after shot of her with the greats: Jimmy Page. Mick Jagger. David Bowie. Axl Rose. Bruce Dickinson. Timothy Leary. Even a photo with young, fresh Marilyn Manson, dated 1990. Fuck, that was three years before he got a record deal.

Fuck.

Pamela enters the bedroom. "We should have met much earlier," she says. "Drew spoke of you often."

"You have some interesting friends," I say, putting the photo album back on the shelf.

I feel a chill. A presence descends. Hear Crowley in my head. He's humming. Gotta get out of here.

"Drew said you were quite the songwriter. Maybe you should write a song called "You Can't Stop This.""

I feel like all my blood is draining away. "Who are you?"

"I'm the mother who sacrificed her only son. A demand from Babalon to empower the ritual meant to join you and her. A ritual you saw fit to destroy."

I'm dizzy. Feels like the walls are closing in on me.

"My son was born unto Crowley, unto Babalon and Bohemia. It was he who attracted you, the magnet that pulled you in. But you destroyed everything."

I bolt straight past her out of the room. She follows me to the top of the staircase. Her words drip venom: "I curse you for what you did." I limp down the stairs. "Crowley will never stop singing in your head," she says.

I grab Eva's arm. "What's wrong?" she asks.

Block the pain. Run. Out of the door, down the driveway, through the gates.

Thirty=eight

It's been the longest two weeks of my life.

I'm either in bed, on the sofa, or taking pathetic little walks around Eva's apartment building. I watch shitloads of TV. Catch the end of *Thelma and Louise,* which had been so rudely interrupted (can't believe they died). Finish that Charlie Huston novel. Start an eBook about Columbine.

Spend hours talking to Eva about everything and nothing. We're a good match. We argue more than I like, but it's good, spirited debate. She's fun. She's smart. She's beautiful. And I'm happy.

No nighttime extracurricular activities since the night I showed up on her doorstep. Joint decision to wait until I can give it my all. In the meantime, the tension builds. The good kind of tension that only comes once during a romance. I'm all for milking it.

Master Choi pops in every other day for a house call. He has me up and around the first week. Treatment combines energy healing with acupuncture and meditation. Slow going, but I get a little better every day. Dude knows I'll probably take forever to pay him, but he continues to show.

I feel so much better after one of Choi's sessions, that I sneak out while Eva is at work. Spend that afternoon, and the following three in a chair at High Voltage Tattoo. I describe what I want to Kat, who gets it down better than a police sketch artist. I now have Babalon inked on one shoulder, Alastor on the other. Call it my latest artistic statement.

I pop in the Frolic Room after the tattoos are done. No sign of Gabe. May never see or hear from him again. I affix Babalon's sphere to my lucky necklace for safekeeping, just in case I cross paths with Gabe again.

Bo calls me four times. Tries hard to get me back. When I declined at the funeral, I meant it. He tells me they'll be auditioning singers indefinitely until they find the right voice. I wish him a lot of luck. They won't find another Drexel. Kudos for trying.

Ned tells me he had a face-to-face meeting with Millie Barrington the day after I cleared the bridge. He talked all tough, tried to bully her into paying us more, but Millie broke his balls, ate him alive. Countered every point he raised, reminded him that she protected me, covered my tracks, kept me out of jail. No argument there. In the end, on top of the original $200K, she agreed to pay my mounting medical expenses and buy Ned a new camper. Knowing how Ned likes to push things, I expect it'll be a motorcoach for the ages.

Ned picks me up. Takes me for my MRI. I won't know if I'm going under the knife until I see a specialist next week.

We head to the bridge for a blessing ceremony I put together. Besides me and Ned, I invite Millie and Ronnie Barrington, Father Paul from San Gabriel Mission, Rabbi Harold Balk from Temple Beth Emet, Brother Tavish from the Self Realization Fellowship, Venerable Master Lin Hsuan from the Hsi Lai Temple, Imam Marwan from the Islamic Center, and Chief Red Wing from the Gabrielino-Tongva tribal council. Just like with my lucky necklace, I figure it's best to cover all bases. Each participant offers prayers to cleanse and purify the bridge and the land around it. I have to fight back a laugh when I see Millie Barrington making a sign of the cross. I half-expect a lightning bolt to strike.

All in all, it's a powerful, moving event. Proud of myself for cooking it up.

Ned and I thank the participants. We linger with Millie and Ronnie after the holy men leave. Millie seems at peace. Ronnie's stinking drunk as usual.

"Today's payday," Ned says to Millie.

"Mother didn't forget," Ronnie says. He hands Ned an envelope. Ned hands it to me. A cashier's check made out to Soul Trappers, Inc., for two hundred thousand dollars. Ned's in the process of setting up a corporation. Talked to a lawyer and an accountant. Says it's the best way to handle things taxwise. Told him fine as long as I'm chairman of the board, get business cards, and score an immediate bonus.

"I want you to do me a favor," I say to Millie as we begin our ascent up the trail.

"We're through negotiating," she says.

"This falls under the good deed clause," I say. "Have the brush cleared down here. Add some picnic tables. Maybe some playground equipment. This place needs a good dose of fun and laughter. I smell a donation—anonymous, of course."

She smiles at that. "You know," she says, "I think I read somewhere that a park was originally in the plans when the bridge was built in 1909."

"Better late than never," Ned says.

Ned and Ronnie walk ahead. I linger back with Millie. "I'm sorry, I'm getting old," she says.

I take her hand. "I'm half crippled, so we make good hiking buddies."

"I'm sorry you were injured," she says. "But you're young. When you're young, the body can heal and regenerate."

"And when you're old, your soul can," I say. "How does it feel?" I ask.

"It feels . . . victorious. You know, I make it a point to always win."

"No matter the consequences," I finish. "So does this mean you'll be turning over a new leaf?"

"No more leaves on this tree. It's the December of my soul, Kane. I've been bad," she says with a wink. "And I've been good, too. Even though I pretend I don't, I prefer the latter. Took me a good eighty-five years to figure that out. Thank you for helping me."

"Any advice for someone still in his bad phase?"

"One step at a time, my young friend. Don't be in a rush. Have a lot of fun while you're young. Then when you get older, and your responsibilities mount, and life loses some of its luster, learn to dance with the devil, not serve him. Then when you're old, like me, you can kick the devil's ass back to hell."

I laugh. "Got to say, Millie, you're full of the worst advice I've ever heard. Did you have a Bloody Mary before you got here?"

She laughs.

Up the hill we walk, arm in arm, at a snail's pace. I look up at the bridge above us. "Are you still going to have your ashes scattered here?" I ask.

"Of course." Then she adds with a wink, "But not for a very long time."

An hour later, Ned and I are atop the bridge alone, sitting in the alcove from where Tall Kevin and Drexel jumped. The place feels a million pounds lighter.

We pass the check back and forth between us.

"Two hundred thousand," Ned says. "What are you gonna do with your cut?"

"I think I'll buy a tiger," I say.

"Invest it in your music career."

"I'm done with that."

"Maybe go to college. Get a degree."

"Are you fucking kidding me?" Hand the check back to Ned. "How about you? You've got the new camper covered. Why not travel?"

"I don't know. Maybe. I'm kind of wiped out at the moment. Think I'll just hide in my office and regroup."

"Nothing wrong with that."

"I was thinking," Ned says, "maybe we should invest some of this. Maybe a lot of it."

"In what?"

"In us. Maybe we expand the business."

"Maybe."

"After this," he says, looking over the side of the bridge, "everything should be a cakewalk."

"But it never is."

"You know that thing I've been working on—the ability to trap large numbers? Well I think I've proven it's doable—at least theoretically. Here's what I'm thinking: We combine what I've been working on with what you did to clear this bridge. We do that, and we'll be able to handle a stadium full of ghosts. Bigger jobs equals bigger bucks."

He's dreaming again. But maybe not. "We'll see," is all I say.

Ned's on a roll. "Let Eva start leaking some stories about this case. We'll ask old lady Barrington to put out the word. It'll start popping up on the Internet. You watch. It's great fodder for urban legend. We'll fucking spin it like masters."

"So we keep going? Together?"

"What else are we gonna do?

I let that hang.

"Been thinking about something else, too," Ned says. "We should do something. The right thing."

I know what he's going to say. "Eva?" He nods. "Been thinking the same thing."

"We should cut her in," he says.

"She'll say no," I tell him. "Her story about Teresa and Anna Burrows exploded. So did her profile on Drexel. She's about to hit the big time."

"Still, we should offer," Ned says.

"We should. I need her." Catch myself. Eva and I haven't gone public yet. Say instead, "We need her." Can't pull anything over on Ned. He picks up on it. Smiles.

I stand and stretch my back. Still have blinding pain, tingling, and numbness down my left leg. Look over the side of the bridge, say to Ned, "It's a long way down . . ."

"As you have seen," Ned says.

I remember Karl's words. Get a chill.

"I have a gift for you," I say. I give him the postcard of the bridge, the one I swiped from the pawnshop.

He looks at it. "I was at least hoping for a new metal detector." He flips it over and points to the handwriting. "And it's used."

"Found it in a box in a pawnshop."

Ned reads it aloud:

> *August 24, 1946. Dear Mother: My bus arrived in Pasadena this afternoon. Having survived the horror of war, I'm ready to embrace this life and achieve my dreams. Here I stand on this grand bridge, hope in my heart, wondering what my future holds. Pen in hand, I begin work today on the novel that I hope earns me not only respect, but enough wealth to bring you and Dad out West someday soon. To the future! With love and appreciation. Your loving son, Charles.*

We're silent for awhile. Then Ned says, "I wonder whatever happened to him."

"Wondered the same thing, so I looked him up."

"Was his novel ever published?"

"Nope. But he had a long career as a TV writer. Rod Serling gave him his big break. Wrote about twenty-five episodes of *The Twilight Zone*."

"Hey, that's your favorite show."

"He died in 2001."

"Wonder if he ever moved his folks West from . . . Pittsburgh," he says, checking the address.

"His parents died right here in Pasadena in the '70s. Charles made good."

Ned smiles. Think he's getting a little misty. "I can really keep this?" he asks.

"It's yours." I probably have a dumb grin on my face like a kid giving his dad a bottle of aftershave on Father's Day.

"Thanks," he says, pocketing the card. "To the future."

"Let's hurry up and get a drink in our hands so we can toast to that."

"I'm hungry," he says.

We start walking. I'm in the mood for a blowout. "Let's get fucked up and eat like pigs. We'll call Eva."

"Where to?"

"Musso and Frank."

"Perfect."

"Ask Ruben the bartender about the ghost of the writer in the back corner booth. He sees him at closing time."

"No shit?"

"There are all kinds of ghosts in Musso and Frank."

"Maybe we should clear it out for them."

"No way," I say. "Some places are meant to be haunted."

Thirty=nine

I wake up with my Musso & Frank hangover, courtesy of Ruben. We tore it up. Eva ducked out early, but Ned and I went the distance. The drinking got out of hand.

I'm nervous about the call I'm about to make. I stammer all-over myself, but manage to get my request out. Twenty minutes later, I get a call back. It's approved. Double-check the address of the facility. Can't believe I'm really going to do this.

I disappear. Eva doesn't know what I'm up to. Neither does Ned. Today, I'm a man of mystery.

I drive to Echo Park. Wait in a sterile-looking lobby. A loud buzz. Two wide hallway doors swing open. A chubby red-haired woman in a bad blue pants suit shakes my hand. "I'm Debbie McVine, director of administration. We spoke this morning."

Introduce myself. Repeat my request.

"Come with me," she says.

No turning back now. I hesitate, then follow.

She leads me down a corridor past a TV lounge behind a wall of glass. A small group watches *Bewitched*.

This place is forced happiness. Linoleum floor shines bright. Walls are painted cheery yellow. A Muzak version of "Penny Lane" plays at a tame volume.

She buzzes us through a hallway door and we walk outside. An outdoor patio, surrounded by a fern garden, has been cozied up with a picnic table and lounge chairs.

"Wait here," Debbie tells me. "I'll be back with the group."

"Hang on," I say, looking for some clarification. "All of these people coming, they're . . . ?" Don't how to phrase it to make it PC.

"Yes," she says. "They're all suicide survivors." She leaves me on the patio alone.

I look around. It hits me: *This is a stupid idea.*

Debbie escorts a group of very suspicious-looking people onto the patio. I size them up, one by one, take a guess at what got them there. Young guy—late teens (sexual-identity conflict). Old guy—probably homeless (schizophrenia). Guy in his early fifties (career gone south). Teenage girl who reminds me of Anna (outsider). Middle-aged woman (meth written all over her). I'm not gonna get to know any of them well enough to find out the real reasons they're here. Debbie told me I'm not to engage any of them in individual conversation.

Debbie introduces me. "This is Kane Pryce," she tells them. "He wanted to drop by and say a few words. Please be courteous and give him a warm Gateways welcome."

All eyes are on me. No notes. Just say what comes. "You'd probably rather be watching TV than sitting here on a nice day listening to a douche bag like me, so I'll keep it short and sweet."

"Thank God," the old man says. He looks at Debbie. "Am I gonna get credit for sitting through this shit?"

"No," Debbie snaps at him. "And stop being rude to our guest."

The old prick throws me off my game. Don't know where to go with this. So I start babbling. "I once thought long and hard about ending my life. But I didn't. Someone I knew—she reminded me that life was a precious gift."

Eyeballs roll in unison. More than one big sigh. Losing my bearings.

"A friend of mine just ended his life. He didn't even really get started. It was a big mistake. It might have been because of me . . . which really makes it hard."

Sighs turn into groans. Nasty looks. Someone imitates a violin. They've heard this all before. Probably on a bad TV show. I've

F. J. LENNON

totally lost them. Gotta tell them something new, something they haven't heard yet.

"I won't go into the exact circumstances, but I recently had what's called a near-death experience. I went where you would have gone if you would have succeeded in doing what you all tried to do. You know . . ."

"Bullshit," the teenage girl says. "There's nothing out there."

"I'm not bullshitting," I say. "I was there. And it's a cold place."

"Here's where you tell us about the perils of hell," the young guy says. "I knew you were some kind of born-again Bible-thumping motherfucker."

"I'm not," I snap. "And the place I went wasn't hell . . . though I've been there, too."

Debbie looks scared, like she's about to call and get a room ready for me.

I keep rambling. "I learned something when I walked into that fog." I pause. Brace. No smart-ass remarks. Good. "I learned it's *not worth it*. You think you're escaping from your problems, but you're not. You carry all your baggage with you. You have to work out this shit one way or another. So you might as well do it here." Not bad. Need a summary. Something I read somewhere: "I learned that suicide is a permanent solution to a temporary problem."

The guy in his fifties laughs. "Come on, pal—Phil Donahue coined that phrase."

"I don't know who that is," I admit, "but he's right." I rack my brain for another crumb of inspiration. Remember something Gabe told me right before I choked him. "Another guy—well not really a guy—told me once, '*you can't have a rainbow without the rain.*'"

"Jesus!" the meth head yells. "Dolly Parton said that. What are you gonna pull out of your ass next, jagoff? Don't you have anything original to say?"

"Yeah," I snap. "Here's an original thought for all you assholes:

The people in your miserable, shitty life who you've let down time and again would still rather see you alive then dead."

Silence.

"That's it. That's all I have to say. Go away. Get back to *Bewitched*." I swat them away with a wave of my hand.

Some applause. A pat on the back. The male and female teenagers linger. Can't believe I give them my email address and cell number. What the hell am I getting into?

Debbie looks at me. "That was different."

"What can I say? I'm an asshole in progress."

Then I ask her if she can recommend some other places for me to visit.

I walk toward Echo Park.

All in all, an unmitigated friggin' disaster, but you've got to start somewhere. Baby steps are better than no steps at all (one of Dolly Parton's tits probably said that).

I'm not giving up like I usually do. Gonna do this once a week. Okay, probably more like once a month. I'm not going to tell Eva or Ned or anyone.

I reach the park. Walk around the lake to blow off steam. Stiff wind blows water from the towering fountains all over me. It's probably teeming with bacteria and the filth of a hundred transients who bathe here. But the mist feels good. Like a baptism.

What's the glass half-empty summation here?

I sucked—fell flat on my face.

How about the glass half full?

I tried.

And I'll try again. Trying feels better than sitting on my ass doing nothing.

I'm not kidding myself. There's a suicide bridge in practically every town in the world. Lost souls will always jump or suck carbon monoxide or shoot themselves. Odds are that at least one of the people I just met will end up doing it again, and succeeding. But maybe I can stop someone, someday from making the mother of all mistakes.

Did I mention I pretty much hate everyone? I think I did. Maybe it's time to get over that.

At least that's how I feel right now.

Talk to me again after I cross L.A. in rush-hour traffic.

Acknowledgments

I wish to thank:

My mother, Jean Lennon. Thank you for being an eternal bedrock of faith, optimism, encouragement, and unconditional love.

My large and very supportive family.

Peter Steinberg—friend, collaborator, and agent.

Emily Bestler for including me on her new publishing label and for guiding this project. And everyone at Atria Books who contributed to the publication of *Devil's Gate:* Judith Curr, David Brown, Ariele Fredman, Kate Cetrulo, Caroline Porter, Isolde Sauer, Dana Sloan, Alicia Brancato, Rachel Zugschwert, Jeanne Lee, and John Vairo Jr. A very special thanks to you all.

Brett Roach—for doing a stellar job researching for me.

Dave Warhol (Kane Pryce's godfather) for being my dependable and trusted sounding board. Seth Shapiro, Michael Bross, and Jeremy Ross for your unique insights into musicianship and the music biz. Pablos Holman for your brilliant technical advice. And Tim McGhee (the real Hank) for taking me on some bumpy ATV rides around Devil's Gate Dam.

My early readers—family members and close friends—for your encouragement, honest feedback, and useful suggestions: fellow author Lisa Wood Shapiro, Lee Ann Lennon-Costanzo, Bill Perry, Shirl Porter, Dr. Kimberly Eddy, Gene and Linda Mauro, Nicole and Frank Radish, Tony Battaglia, Jeff Cook, Sam Gasowski, and Cliff Kamida.

Matthew Snyder at CAA, for your ongoing support.

Seth Jarrett for your encouragement and for creating my favorite television show—*Celebrity Ghost Stories*.

Julie Sessing at Sessing Music Services for all your help.

The Red Hot Chili Peppers and Todd Mumford for allowing me to open the novel with the brilliant lyrics to "Under the Bridge." I don't know who is the bigger fan of the Chili Peppers—me or Kane Pryce. It's an honor.

Chris Tellez and Alex Hudson for creating my website.

Doris Huertes, Ivana Ezrol, Kathy Harper, and Nicole Radish for taking good care of my daughter when I was knee-deep.

Sue Shakespeare and Ellen Marro for investigating beneath the Colorado Street Bridge with me and sharing your unique insights. My father-in-law, Nick Kampo, and my sister, Lee Ann Lennon-Costanzo, for also exploring with me under the bridge.

All my friends and colleagues at Entertainment Games, Inc.

My daughter Olivia. My pal and lucky charm. The party didn't start until you arrived.

And my daughter Clara, who arrived just before this book went to print. Welcome to the party, baby girl.

And finally, extra special thanks to my wife, Laura Kampo. With love and gratitude for fighting the good fight and enduring it all. And once again, you really pulled this book together.

Author's Note

W hile I was writing this book, the line between fact and fiction blurred to a disturbing level—five people committed suicide by leaping off the Colorado Street Bridge; two of them occurred in the same week. I have a friend who is the most gifted psychic I've ever met. She contacted me shortly after these suicides and told me that she knew one of these victims and had received a message that she wanted to share with me. To say I was intrigued was an understatement. The message she said she received was this: *"I made a terrible mistake. I thought the pain and hopelessness would end when I jumped, but it didn't. I still exist and so does my pain. And now I can't leave here."*

Those words rang true. I spent a lot of time under that bridge during the period when I was writing. And every time I was there, I was overpowered by negative emotions, namely feelings of regret that seemed to echo and swirl. In my mind, the real message of the Colorado Street Bridge is this: there's no peace at the end of that 180-foot journey from top to bottom. Only more pain and sadness.

If you or someone you know feels hopeless or suicidal, please call the Suicide Prevention National Hotline: 1-800-SUICIDE (1-800-784-2433).